D1326215

EVERYMAN, I will go with thee,

and be thy guide,

In thy most need to go by thy side

ROBERT LOUIS (LEWIS) STEVENSON
Born at Edinburgh in 1850. Exchanged
engineering for the law in 1871; called to the
Bar in 1875, but never practised. Visited
America and married in 1880. Settled in
Samoa in 1889–90. Died there in 1894.

ROBERT LOUIS STEVENSON

St Ives

INTRODUCTION BY

M. R. RIDLEY, M.A.

Lecturer at Bedford College, London;
formerly Fellow of Balliol College, Oxford

611250/F

DENT: LONDON

EVERYMAN'S LIBRARY

© Introduction, J. M. Dent & Sons Ltd, 1958
All rights reserved
Made in Great Britain
at the
Aldine Press · Letchworth · Herts
for
J. M. DENT & SONS LTD
Aldine House · Bedford Street · London
First included in Everyman's Library 1934
Last reprinted 1968

NO. 904

SBN: 460 00904 4

INTRODUCTION

It was Stevenson's habit to call a halt in the course of writing his longer tales. 'I have to leave off,' he said, 'and forget the tale for a little; then I can return upon it fresh and with interest revived.' But *St Ives* was even more intermittent than most, and played a sort of triple Box and Cox with *The Ebb Tide* and *Weir of Hermiston*. When he had finished *Catriona* Stevenson started on *Weir*, roughed out the action and wrote the opening chapters in the last two or three months of 1892. The inspiration flagged and he wisely did not force himself, but turned off on to another road. He had come on the idea for the opening of *St Ives* while looking over the old records for material for *Weir*, and it was at first intended to be no more than a short story, but as he worked on it he saw in it the germ of a full-length novel, and by the end of January 1893 he had ten chapters drafted, and much of the rest of the action outlined, though, to judge by the chapter headings which he sent to Colvin, it was considerably different from what we now have. Work was interrupted by a trip to Sydney, and not, for the time being, resumed. After making an attempt at a short story which came to nothing, he went back to an unfinished piece of work which he had begun three years before in collaboration with Lloyd Osbourne; 'there was all that good work lying useless,' he says, 'and I had to finish it.' Finish it he did, but rather with determination than with enthusiasm, and he records in June 1893 that after 'thirteen days about as nearly in Hell as a man could expect to live through' he has got to the end of 'the excruciating *Ebb Tide*.' He was indeed completely worked out, and when, two months later, he took up *Weir* again, he found it beyond him, and took refuge in the less exacting *St Ives*.

He now worked at it pretty steadily, with inevitable interruptions. One needs always to remember, what it is easy to forget, that in the last few years of his life Stevenson was much more than just a writer. He wrote, and he wrote hard, to make the necessary money for the expenses which his life in Samoa entailed. But he was also a much occupied man of affairs, deeply involved in the internal politics of

Introduction

Samoa, holding a remarkable position in the confidence of the islanders, and never refusing a call to lay aside his own immediate business to give them his help in theirs.

It is here, I think, that we find the reason for the weaknesses of *St Ives*. And it is worth noticing what Stevenson, almost always a good judge of his own work, thought of it. At first he thought it would 'not be wholly bad. It is written in rather a funny style; a little stilted and left-handed; the style of St Ives; . . . *St Ives* is unintellectual, and except as an adventure novel, dull. But the adventures seem to me sound and pretty probable; and it is a love story. Speed his wings!' But later he was less pleased: 'It is a mere tissue of adventures; the central figure not very well or very sharply drawn; no philosophy, no destiny, to it; some of the happenings very good in themselves, I believe, but none of them *bildende*, none of them constructive, except in so far perhaps as they make up a kind of sham picture of the time, all in italics and all out of drawing. Here and there, I think, it is well written; and here and there it's not. Some of the episodic characters are amusing, I do believe; others not, I suppose. However, they are the best of the thing such as it is.' And still later, in September, three months before his death, he writes a few sentences which make painfully clear how jaded, even exhausted, he was. 'I have been trying hard to get along with *St Ives*. I should now lay it aside for a year and I daresay I should make something of it after all. Instead of that, I have to kick against the pricks, and break myself, and spoil the book, if there were anything to spoil, which I am far from saying. I'm as sick of the thing as ever anyone can be; it's a rudderless hulk; it's a pagoda, and you can just feel—or I can feel—that it might have been a pleasant story, if it had been blessed only at baptism.'

The job of towing this rudderless hulk into harbour was more repellent than Stevenson could face. He left her derelict, to be salvaged later by a fellow craftsman, turned, for the third time, to *Weir of Hermiston*, and worked at it for the few weeks till his death with a vitality astonishingly renewed and in a glowing ardour of creation.

Of *St Ives* there is little one can say that has not been said by Stevenson already. It is a patchy piece of work. Stevenson was always stronger on isolated scenes and characters

Introduction

than on construction, but even by his own standards *St Ives* is excessively episodic. Many of the adventures, though entertaining enough, do nothing to advance the plot, such as it is. But there are some brilliant scenes, especially perhaps that of the disinheriting of the rascally cousin by the dying count. Then, the main character, St Ives himself, is not, I think, well drawn, since Stevenson seems unable to make up his mind what kind of person he wants him to be, and so the portrait is blurred; nor is Flora more distinct, certainly not in the same class as either of her two immediate predecessors, Catriona and Barbara Grant. But in the other scale are a number of minor characters who are drawn with admirable precision and spring to life from the pages; Flora's aunt and Rowley are a perpetual delight, to mention only two among many, but there is one who is peculiarly typical of Stevenson, the old French colonel who has broken his parole to get home to his sick daughter. He is utterly irrelevant, most delicately etched, and very moving.

The style is like the characterization of St Ives, never continuing in one stay. Sometimes it is normal Stevenson, sometimes Stevenson a trifle archaized, sometimes Stevenson trying to be St Ives—and at least once there is a most inappropriate Americanism. The result is uneasily distracting.

None the less, if we are content to relish the good things that are put before us, and do not blunt our appetites by pining for a different menu, we shall find the meal palatable, some of it piquant, and at least none of it ill cooked.

The book was left with a quarter of it still to be written. The completion was carried out by 'Q,' and a better choice could not have been made. I doubt whether any reader, left to himself, would feel where the break comes. 'Q' caught both temper and style with sympathetic felicity, and the suture is as near as may be invisible.

M. R. RIDLEY.

1958.

SELECT BIBLIOGRAPHY

ESSAYS (including history and biography); FABLES. *The Pentland Rising*, 1866; *The Charity Bazaar, an Allegorical Dialogue*, 1868; *An Appeal to the Clergy of the Church of Scotland*, 1875; *Picturesque Notes on Edinburgh*, 1878; *Virginibus Puerisque*, 1881; *Familiar Studies of Men and Books*, 1882; *The Silverado Squatters*, 1883; *Memories and Portraits*, 1887; *Memoir of Fleeming Jenkin*, 1888; *Father Damien*, 1890; *Across the Plains*, 1892; *A Footnote to History*, 1892; *War in Samoa*, 1893; *Fables*, 1896; *Essays in the Art of Writing*, 1905; *Lay Morals*, 1911; *Records of a Family of Engineers*, 1912.

TRAVEL. *An Inland Voyage*, 1878; *Travels with a Donkey in the Cevennes*, 1879; *The South Seas* (privately 1890), 1900; *Essays of Travel*, 1905.

PLAYS (all in collaboration with W. E. Henley). *Deacon Brodie*, 1880; *Admiral Guinea*, 1884; *Beau Austin*, 1884; *Robert Macaire*, 1885. (All privately printed: the first three published in one volume, 1892.)

SHORT STORIES. *New Arabian Nights*, 1882; *More New Arabian Nights. The Dynamiter*, 1885; *The Merry Men*, 1887.

NOVELS (including fiction other than short stories). *Treasure Island*, 1883; *Prince Otto*, 1885; *The Strange Case of Dr Jekyll and Mr Hyde*, 1886; *Kidnapped*, 1886; *The Black Arrow*, 1888; *The Master of Ballantrae*, 1889; *The Wrong Box* (in collaboration with Lloyd Osbourne), 1889; *The Wrecker* (with Lloyd Osbourne), 1892; *Catriona*, 1893; *Island Nights' Entertainments*, 1893; *The Ebb-Tide* (with Lloyd Osbourne), 1894; *Weir of Hermiston*, 1896; *St Ives* (completed by Q), 1898.

POEMS. *A Child's Garden of Verses*, 1885; *Underwoods*, 1887; *Ballads*, 1890; *Songs of Travel*, 1896.

LETTERS. *Vailima Letters*, 1895; *Letters to his Family and Friends*, 1899.

EDITIONS. The *Edinburgh*, 1894–8, ed. S. Colvin, and in part revised by Stevenson himself; of subsequent editions the *Pentland* and the *Swanston* may be mentioned. The *Tusitala* edition of his works by Lloyd Osbourne, 1923, contains 5 vols. of letters.

BIOGRAPHY AND CRITICISM. Graham Balfour, *The Life of Robert Louis Stevenson*, 1901; J. A. Steuart, *Robert Louis Stevenson, Man and Writer*, 1924; D. Daiches, *Robert Louis Stevenson: a Revaluation*, 1946; M. Elwin, *The Strange Case of Robert Louis Stevenson*, 1950.

BIBLIOGRAPHY. Col. W. F. Prideaux, C.S.I., *A Bibliography of Robert Louis Stevenson*, 1903, revised 1917.

NOTE TO THE FIRST EDITION

The following tale was taken down from Mr. Stevenson's dictation by his stepdaughter and amanuensis, Mrs. Strong, at intervals between January 1893 and October 1894 (see "Vailima Letters," pp. 242–246, 299, 324, 334, and 350). About six weeks before his death he laid the story aside to take up "Weir of Hermiston." The thirty chapters of "St. Ives" which he had written (the last few of them apparently unrevised) brought the tale within sight of its conclusion, and the intended course of the remainder was known in outline to Mrs. Strong. For the benefit of those readers who do not like a story to be left unfinished, the delicate task of supplying the missing chapters has been entrusted to Mr. Quiller-Couch, whose work begins at Chap. XXXI.

[*Sidney Colvin*]

CONTENTS

CHAP.   PAGE

INTRODUCTION by M. R. Ridley   .   .   v

I. A TALE OF A LION RAMPANT   .   .   5

II. A TALE OF A PAIR OF SCISSORS   .   16

III. MAJOR CHEVENIX COMES INTO THE STORY, AND GOGUELAT GOES OUT .   .   21

IV. ST. IVES GETS A BUNDLE OF BANK NOTES .   30

V. ST. IVES IS SHOWN A HOUSE   .   .   36

VI. THE ESCAPE   43

VII. SWANSTON COTTAGE   .   .   .   51

VIII. THE HEN-HOUSE   57

IX. THREE IS COMPANY, AND FOUR NONE .   63

X. THE DROVERS   73

XI. THE GREAT NORTH ROAD   .   .   82

XII. I FOLLOW A COVERED CART NEARLY TO MY DESTINATION .   .   .   91

XIII. I MEET TWO OF MY COUNTRYMEN   .   101

XIV. TRAVELS OF THE COVERED CART   .   108

XV. THE ADVENTURES OF THE ATTORNEY'S CLERK   114

XVI. THE HOME-COMING OF MR. ROWLEY'S VISCOUNT   .   .   .   127

XVII. THE DESPATCH-BOX   .   .   .   134

XVIII. MR. ROMAINE CALLS ME NAMES   .   141

XIX. THE DEVIL AND ALL AT AMERSHAM PLACE 149

XX. AFTER THE STORM   .   .   .   157

XXI. I BECOME THE OWNER OF A CLARET-COLOURED CHAISE .   .   .   166

XXII. CHARACTER AND ACQUIREMENTS OF MR. ROWLEY .   .   .   174

XXIII. THE ADVENTURES OF THE RUNAWAY COUPLE .   .   .   181

XXIV. THE INN-KEEPER OF KIRKBY-LONSDALE . 191

XXV. I MEET A CHEERFUL EXTRAVAGANT   .   198

XXVI. THE COTTAGE AT NIGHT   .   .   203

XXVII. THE SABBATH DAY .   .   .   211

XXVIII. EVENTS OF MONDAY: THE LAWYER'S PARTY .   .   .   220

Contents

CHAP.		PAGE
XXIX.	EVENTS OF TUESDAY: THE TOILS CLOSING.	232
XXX.	EVENTS OF WEDNESDAY: THE UNIVERSITY OF CRAMOND	242
XXXI.	EVENTS OF THURSDAY: THE ASSEMBLY BALL	251
XXXII.	EVENTS OF FRIDAY MORNING: THE CUTTING OF THE GORDIAN KNOT . .	265
XXXIII.	THE INCOMPLETE AERONAUTS . . .	276
XXXIV.	CAPTAIN COLENSO	291
XXXV.	IN PARIS—ALAIN PLAYS HIS LAST CARD .	307
XXXVI.	I GO TO CLAIM FLORA	320

CHAPTER I

A TALE OF A LION RAMPANT

IT was in the month of May 1813 that I was so unlucky as to fall at last into the hands of the enemy. My knowledge of the English language had marked me out for a certain employment. Though I cannot conceive a soldier refusing to incur the risk, yet to be hanged for a spy is a disgusting business; and I was relieved to be held a prisoner of war. Into the Castle of Edinburgh, standing in the midst of that city on the summit of an extraordinary rock, I was cast with several hundred fellow-sufferers, all privates like myself, and the more part of them, by an accident, very ignorant, plain fellows. My English, which had brought me into that scrape, now helped me very materially to bear it. I had a thousand advantages. I was often called to play the part of an interpreter, whether of orders or complaints, and thus brought in relations, sometimes of mirth, sometimes almost of friendship, with the officers in charge. A young lieutenant singled me out to be his adversary at chess, a game in which I was extremely proficient, and would reward me for my gambits with excellent cigars. The major of the battalion took lessons of French from me while at breakfast, and was sometimes so obliging as to have me to join him at the meal. Chevenix was his name. He was stiff as a drum-major and selfish as an Englishman, but a fairly conscientious pupil and a fairly upright man. Little did I suppose that his ramrod body and frozen face would, in the end, step in between me and all my dearest wishes; that upon this precise, regular, icy soldierman my fortunes should so nearly shipwreck! I never liked, but yet I trusted him; and though it may seem but a trifle, I found his snuff-box with the bean in it come very welcome.

For it is strange how grown men and seasoned soldiers can go back in life; so that after but a little while in prison, which is after all the next thing to being in the nursery, they grow absorbed in the most pitiful, childish interests, and a sugar biscuit or a pinch of snuff become things to follow after and scheme for!

We made but a poor show of prisoners. The officers had been all offered their parole, and had taken it. They lived mostly in suburbs of the city, lodging with modest families, and enjoyed their freedom and supported the almost continual evil tidings of the Emperor as best they might. It chanced I was the only gentleman among the privates who remained. A great part were ignorant Italians, of a regiment that had suffered heavily in Catalonia. The rest were mere diggers of the soil, treaders of grapes or hewers of wood, who had been suddenly and violently preferred to the glorious state of soldiers. We had but the one interest in common; each of us who had any skill with his fingers passed the hours of his captivity in the making of little toys and *articles of Paris ;* and the prison was daily visited at certain hours by a concourse of people of the country, come to exult over our distress, or—it is more tolerant to suppose—their own vicarious triumph. Some moved among us with a decency of shame or sympathy. Others were the most offensive personages in the world, gaped at us as if we had been baboons, sought to evangelise us to their rustic, northern religion as though we had been savages, or tortured us with intelligence of disasters to the arms of France. Good, bad, and indifferent, there was one alleviation to the annoyance of these visitors; for it was the practice of almost all to purchase some specimen of our rude handiwork. This led, amongst the prisoners, to a strong spirit of competition. Some were neat of hand, and (the genius of the French being always distinguished) could place upon sale little miracles of dexterity and taste. Some had a more engaging appearance; fine features were found to do as well as fine merchandise, and an air of youth in particular (as it appealed to the sentiment of pity in our visitors) to be a source of profit. Others again enjoyed some acquaintance with the language, and were able to recommend the more agreeably to purchasers such trifles as they had to sell. To the first of these advantages I could lay no claim, for my fingers were all thumbs. Some at least of the others I possessed; and finding much entertainment in our commerce, I did not suffer my advantages to rust. I have never despised the social arts, in

A Tale of a Lion Rampant

which it is a national boast that every Frenchman should excel. For the approach of particular sorts of visitors I had a particular manner of address, and even of appearance, which I could readily assume and change on the occasion rising. I never lost an opportunity to flatter either the person of my visitor, if it should be a lady, or, if it should be a man, the greatness of his country in war. And in case my compliments should miss their aim, I was always ready to cover my retreat with some agreeable pleasantry, which would often earn me the name of an " oddity " or a " droll fellow." In this way, although I was so left-handed a toy-maker, I made out to be rather a successful merchant; and found means to procure many little delicacies and allevia-tions, such as children or prisoners desire.

I am scarcely drawing the portrait of a very melancholy man. It is not indeed my character; and I had, in a com-parison with my comrades, many reasons for content. In the first place, I had no family; I was an orphan and a bachelor; neither wife nor child awaited me in France. In the second, I had never wholly forgot the emotions with which I first found myself a prisoner; and although a military prison be not altogether a garden of delights, it is still prefer-able to a gallows. In the third, I am almost ashamed to say it, but I found a certain pleasure in our place of residence: being an obsolete and really mediæval fortress, high placed and commanding extraordinary prospects, not only over sea, mountain, and champaign, but actually over the thorough-fares of a capital city, which we could see blackened by day with the moving crowd of the inhabitants, and at night shining with lamps. And lastly, although I was not in-sensible to the restraints of prison or the scantiness of our rations, I remembered I had sometimes eaten quite as ill in Spain, and had to mount guard and march perhaps a dozen leagues into the bargain. The first of my troubles, indeed, was the costume we were obliged to wear. There is a horrible practice in England to trick out in ridiculous uniforms, and as it were to brand in mass, not only convicts but military prisoners, and even the children in charity schools. I think some malignant genius had found his masterpiece of irony in the dress which we were condemned to wear: jacket, waist-coat, and trousers of a sulphur or mustard yellow, and a shirt of blue-and-white striped cotton. It was conspicuous, it was cheap, it pointed us out to laughter—we, who were old soldiers, used to arms, and some of us showing noble scars,— like a set of lugubrious zanies at a fair. The old name of that rock on which our prison stood was (I have heard since then) the *Painted Hill*. Well, now it was all painted a bright yellow with our costumes; and the dress of the soldiers who guarded us being of course the essential British red rag, we made up together the elements of a lively picture of hell. I have again and again looked round upon my fellow-prisoners, and felt my anger rise, and choked upon tears, to behold them thus parodied. The more part, as I have said, were peasants, somewhat bettered perhaps by the drill-sergeant, but for all that ungainly, loutish fellows, with no more than a mere barrack-room smartness of address: indeed, you could have seen our army nowhere more discreditably represented than in this Castle of Edinburgh. And I used to see myself in fancy, and blush. It seemed that my more elegant carriage would but point the insult of the travesty. And I re-membered the days when I wore the coarse but honourable coat of a soldier; and remembered further back how many of the noble, the fair, and the gracious had taken a delight to tend my childhood. . . . But I must not recall these tender and sorrowful memories twice; their place is further on, and I am now upon another business. The perfidy of the Britannic Government stood nowhere more openly confessed than in one particular of our discipline: that we were shaved twice in the week. To a man who has loved all his life to be fresh shaven, can a more irritating indignity be devised? Monday and Thursday were the days. Take the Thursday, and conceive the picture I must present by Sunday evening! And Saturday, which was almost as bad, was the great day for visitors.

Those who came to our market were of all qualities, men and women, the lean and the stout, the plain and the fairly pretty. Sure, if people at all understood the power of beauty, there would be no prayers addressed except to Venus; and the mere privilege of beholding a comely woman is worth paying for. Our visitors, upon the whole, were not much to boast of; and yet, sitting in a corner and very much ashamed of myself and my absurd appearance, I have again and again tasted the finest, the rarest, and the most ethereal pleasures in a glance of an eye that I should never see again—and never

A Tale of a Lion Rampant

wanted to. The flower of the hedgerow and the star in heaven satisfy and delight us: how much more the look of that exquisite being who was created to bear and rear, to madden and rejoice, mankind!

There was one young lady in particular, about eighteen or nineteen, tall, of a gallant carriage, and with a profusion of hair in which the sun found threads of gold. As soon as she came in the courtyard (and she was a rather frequent visitor) it seemed I was aware of it. She had an air of angelic candour, yet of a high spirit; she stepped like a Diana, every movement was noble and free. One day there was a strong east wind; the banner was straining at the flagstaff; below us the smoke of the city chimneys blew hither and thither in a thousand crazy variations; and away out on the Forth we could see the ships lying down to it and scudding. I was thinking what a vile day it was, when she appeared. Her hair blew in the wind with changes of colour; her garments moulded her with the accuracy of sculpture; the ends of her shawl fluttered about her ear and were caught in again with an inimitable deftness. You have seen a pool on a gusty day, how it suddenly sparkles and flashes like a thing alive? So this lady's face had become animated and coloured; and as I saw her standing, somewhat inclined, her lips parted, a divine trouble in her eyes, I could have clapped my hands in applause, and was ready to acclaim her a genuine daughter of the winds. What put it in my head, I know not: perhaps because it was a Thursday and I was new from the razor; but I determined to engage her attention no later than that day. She was approaching that part of the court in which I sat with my merchandise, when I observed her handkerchief to escape from her hands and fall to the ground; the next moment the wind had taken it up and carried it within my reach. I was on foot at once: I had forgot my mustard-coloured clothes, I had forgot the private soldier and his salute. Bowing deeply, I offered her the slip of cambric.

" Madam," said I, " your handkerchief. The wind brought it me."

I met her eyes fully.

" I thank you, sir," said she.

" The wind brought it me," I repeated. " May I not take it for an omen? You have an English proverb, ' It's an ill wind that blows nobody good.' "

" Well," she said, with a smile, " ' One good turn deserves another.' I will see what you have."

She followed me to where my wares were spread out under lee of a piece of cannon.

" Alas, mademoiselle!" said I, "I am no very perfect craftsman. This is supposed to be a house, and you see the chimneys are awry. You may call this a box if you are very indulgent; but see where my tool slipped! Yes, I am afraid you may go from one to another, and find a flaw in everything. *Failures for Sale* should be on my signboard. I do not keep a shop; I keep a Humorous Museum." I cast a smiling glance about my display, and then at her, and instantly became grave. "Strange, is it not," I added, "that a grown man and a soldier should be engaged upon such trash, and a sad heart produce anything so funny to look at?"

An unpleasant voice summoned her at this moment by the name of Flora, and she made a hasty purchase and rejoined her party.

A few days after she came again. But I must first tell you how she came to be so frequent. Her aunt was one of those terrible British old maids, of which the world has heard much; and having nothing whatever to do, and a word or two of French, she had taken what she called an *interest in the French prisoners*. A big, bustling, bold old lady, she flounced about our market-place with insufferable airs of patronage and condescension. She bought, indeed, with liberality, but her manner of studying us through a quizzing-glass, and playing cicerone to her followers, acquitted us of any gratitude. She had a tail behind her of heavy, obse-quious old gentlemen, or dull, giggling misses, to whom she appeared to be an oracle. "This one can really carve prettily: is he not a quiz with his big whiskers?" she would say. "And this one," indicating myself with her gold eye-glass, "is, I assure you, quite an oddity." The oddity, you may be certain, ground his teeth. She had a way of stand-ing in our midst, nodding around, and addressing us in what she imagined to be French: "*Bienne, hommes! ça va bienne?*" I took the freedom to reply in the same lingo: "*Bienne, femme! ça va couci-couci tout d'même, la bour-geoise!*" And at that, when we had all laughed with a little more heartiness than was entirely civil, " I told you he was quite an oddity!" says she in triumph. Needless to say, these passages were before I had remarked the niece.

The aunt came on the day in question with a following rather more than usually large, which she manœuvred to and fro about the market and lectured to at rather more than usual length, and with rather less than her accustomed tact. I kept my eyes down, but they were ever fixed in the same direction, quite in vain. The aunt came and went, and pulled us out, and showed us off, like caged monkeys; but the niece kept herself on the outskirts of the crowd and on the opposite side of the courtyard, and departed at last as she had come, without a sign. Closely as I had watched her, I could not say her eyes had ever rested on me for an instant; and my heart was overwhelmed with bitterness and blackness. I tore out her detested image; I felt I was done with her for ever; I laughed at myself savagely, because I had thought to please; when I lay down at night sleep forsook me, and I lay, and rolled, and gloated on her charms, and cursed her insensibility, for half the night. How trivial I thought her! and how trivial her sex! A man might be an angel or an Apollo, and a mustard-coloured coat would wholly blind them to his merits. I was a prisoner, a slave, a contemned and despicable being, the butt of her sniggering countrymen. I would take the lesson: no proud daughter of my foes should have the chance to mock at me again; none in the future should have the chance to think I had looked at her with admiration. You cannot imagine any one of a more resolute and independent spirit, or whose bosom was more wholly mailed with patriotic arrogance, than I. Before I dropped asleep, I had remembered all the infamies of Britain, and debited them in an overwhelming column to Flora.

The next day, as I sat in my place, I became conscious there was some one standing near; and behold, it was herself! I kept my seat, at first in the confusion of my mind, later on from policy; and she stood, and leaned a little over me, as in pity. She was very still and timid; her voice was low. Did I suffer in my captivity? she asked me. Had I to complain of any hardship?

"Mademoiselle, I have not learned to complain," said I. "I am a soldier of Napoleon."

She sighed. "At least you must regret *La France*," said

she, and coloured a little as she pronounced the words, which she did with a pretty strangeness of accent.

"What am I to say?" I replied. "If you were carried from this country, for which you seem so wholly suited, where the very rains and winds seem to become you like ornaments, would you regret, do you think? We must surely all regret! the son to his mother, the man to his country; these are native feelings."

"You have a mother?" she asked.

"In heaven, mademoiselle," I answered. "She, and my father also, went by the same road to heaven as so many others of the fair and brave: they followed their queen upon the scaffold. So, you see, I am not so much to be pitied in my prison," I continued: "there are none to wait for me; I am alone in the world. 'Tis a different case, for instance, with yon poor fellow in the cloth cap. His bed is next to mine, and in the night I hear him sobbing to himself. He has a tender character, full of tender and pretty sentiments; and in the dark at night, and sometimes by day when he can get me apart with him, he laments a mother and a sweetheart. Do you know what made him take me for a confidant?"

She parted her lips with a look, but did not speak. The look burned all through me with a sudden vital heat.

"Because I had once seen, in marching by, the belfry of his village!" I continued. "The circumstance is quaint enough. It seems to bind up into one the whole bundle of those human instincts that make life beautiful, and people and places dear—and from which it would seem I am cut off!"

I rested my chin on my knee and looked before me on the ground. I had been talking until then to hold her; but I was now not sorry she should go: an impression is a thing so delicate to produce and so easy to overthrow! Presently she seemed to make an effort.

"I will take this toy," she said, laid a five-and-sixpenny piece in my hand, and was gone ere I could thank her.

I retired to a place apart near the ramparts and behind a gun. The beauty, the expression of her eyes, the tear that had trembled there, the compassion in her voice and a kind of wild elegance that consecrated the freedom of her movements, all combined to enslave my imagination and inflame my heart. What had she said? Nothing to signify; but her eyes had met mine, and the fire they had kindled burned inextinguishably in my veins. I loved her; and I did not fear to hope. Twice I had spoken with her; and in both interviews I had been well inspired, I had engaged her sympathies, I had found words that she must remember, that would ring in her ears at night upon her bed. What mattered if I were half shaved and my clothes a caricature? I was still a man, and I had drawn my image on her memory. I was still a man, and, as I trembled to realise, she was still a woman. Many waters cannot quench love; and love, which is the law of the world, was on my side. I closed my eyes, and she sprang up on the background of the darkness, more beautiful than in life. " Ah! " thought I, " and you too, my dear, you too must carry away with you a picture, that you are still to behold again and still to embellish. In the darkness of night, in the streets by day, still you are to have my voice and face, whispering, making love for me, encroaching on your shy heart. Shy as your heart is, *it* is lodged there—*I* am lodged there; let the hours do their office—let time continue to draw me ever in more lively, ever in more insidious colours." And then I had a vision of myself, and burst out laughing.

A likely thing, indeed, that a beggar-man, a private soldier, a prisoner in a yellow travesty, was to awake the interest of this fair girl! I would not despair; but I saw the game must be played fine and close. It must be my policy to hold myself before her, always in a pathetic or pleasing attitude; never to alarm or startle her; to keep my own secret locked in my bosom like a story of disgrace, and let hers (if she could be induced to have one) grow at its own rate; to move just so fast, and not by a hair's-breadth any faster, than the inclination of her heart. I was the man, and yet I was passive, tied by the foot in prison. I could not go to her; I must cast a spell upon her at each visit, so that she should return to me; and this was a matter of nice management. I had done it the last time—it seemed impossible she should not come again after our interview; and for the next I had speedily ripened a fresh plan. A prisoner, if he has one great disability for a lover, has yet one considerable advantage: there is nothing to distract him, and he can spend all his hours ripening his love and preparing its manifestations. I had been then some days upon a piece of carving—no less than the emblem of Scotland, the Lion Rampant. This I proceeded to finish with what skill I was possessed of; and when at last I could do no more to it (and, you may be sure, was already regretting I had done so much), added on the base the following dedication:—

À LA BELLE FLORA

LE PRISONNIER RECONNAISSANT

A. D. St. Y. D. K.

I put my heart into the carving of these letters. What was done with so much ardour, it seemed scarce possible that any should behold with indifference; and the initials would at least suggest to her my noble birth. I thought it better to suggest: I felt that mystery was my stock-in-trade; the contrast between my rank and manners, between my speech and my clothing, and the fact that she could only think of me by a combination of letters, must all tend to increase her interest and engage her heart.

This done, there was nothing left for me but to wait and to hope. And there is nothing further from my character: in love and in war, I am all for the forward movement; and these days of waiting made my purgatory. It is a fact that I loved her a great deal better at the end of them, for love comes, like bread, from a perpetual rehandling. And besides, I was fallen into a panic of fear. How, if she came no more, how was I to continue to endure my empty days? how was I to fall back and find my interest in the major's lessons, the lieutenant's chess, in a twopenny sale in the market, or a halfpenny addition to the prison fare?

Days went by, and weeks; I had not the courage to calculate, and to-day I have not the courage to remember; but at last she was there. At last I saw her approach me in the company of a boy about her own age, and whom I divined at once to be her brother.

I rose and bowed in silence.

" This is my brother, Mr. Ronald Gilchrist," said she. " I have told him of your sufferings. He is so sorry for you! "

" It is more than I have the right to ask," I replied; " but among gentlefolk these generous sentiments are natural. If your brother and I were to meet in the field, we should meet like tigers; but when he sees me here disarmed and helpless, he forgets his animosity." (At which, as I had ventured to expect, this beardless champion coloured to the ears for pleasure.) " Ah, my dear young lady," I continued, " there are many of your countrymen languishing in my country, even as I do here. I can but hope there is found some French lady to convey to each of them the priceless consolation of her sympathy. You have given me alms; and more than alms— hope; and while you were absent I was not forgetful. Suffer me to be able to tell myself that I have at least tried to make a return; and for the prisoner's sake deign to accept this trifle."

So saying, I offered her my lion, which she took, looked at in some embarrassment, and then, catching sight of the dedication, broke out with a cry—

" Why, how did you know my name? " she exclaimed.

" When names are so appropriate, they should be easily guessed," said I, bowing. " But indeed, there was no magic in the matter. A lady called you by name on the day I found your handkerchief, and I was quick to remark and cherish it."

" It is very, very beautiful," said she, " and I shall be always proud of the inscription.—Come, Ronald, we must be going." She bowed to me as a lady bows to her equal, and passed on (I could have sworn) with a heightened colour.

I was overjoyed: my innocent ruse had succeeded; she had taken my gift without a hint of payment, and she would scarce sleep in peace till she had made it up to me. No green-horn in matters of the heart, I was besides aware that I had now a resident ambassador at the court of my lady. The lion might be ill chiselled; it was mine. My hands had made and held it; my knife—or, to speak more by the mark, my rusty nail—had traced those letters; and simple as the words were, they would keep repeating to her that I was grateful and that I found her fair. The boy had looked like a gawky, and blushed at a compliment; I could see besides that he regarded me with considerable suspicion; yet he made so manly a figure of a lad, that I could not withhold from him my sympathy. And as for the impulse that had made her bring and introduce him, I could not sufficiently admire it. It seemed to me finer than wit, and more tender than a caress. It said (plain as language), " I do not and I cannot know you. Here is my brother—you can know him; this is the way to me—follow it."

St. Ives

CHAPTER II

A TALE OF A PAIR OF SCISSORS

I was still plunged in these thoughts when the bell was rung that discharged our visitors into the street. Our little market was no sooner closed than we were summoned to the distribution, and received our rations, which we were then allowed to eat according to fancy in any part of our quarters.

I have said the conduct of some of our visitors was unbearably offensive; it was possibly more so than they dreamed —as the sight-seers at a menagerie may offend in a thousand ways, and quite without meaning it, the noble and unfortunate animals behind the bars; and there is no doubt but some of my compatriots were susceptible beyond reason. Some of these old whiskerandos, originally peasants, trained since boyhood in victorious armies, and accustomed to move among subject and trembling populations, could ill brook their change of circumstance. There was one man of the name of Goguelat, a brute of the first water, who had enjoyed no touch of civilisation beyond the military discipline, and had risen by an extreme heroism of bravery to a grade for which he was otherwise unfitted—that of *maréchal des logis* in the 22nd of the line. In so far as a brute can be a good soldier he was a good soldier; the Cross was on his breast, and gallantly earned; but in all things outside his line of duty the man was no other than a brawling, bruising, ignorant pillar of low pothouses. As a gentleman by birth, and a scholar by taste and education, I was the type of all that he least understood and most detested; and the mere view of our visitors would leave him daily in a transport of annoyance, which he would make haste to wreak on the nearest victim, and too often on myself.

It was so now. Our rations were scarce served out, and I had just withdrawn into a corner of the yard, when I perceived him drawing near. He wore an air of hateful mirth, a set of young fools, among whom he passed for a wit, followed him with looks of expectation; and I saw I was about to be the object of some of his insufferable pleasantries. He took a place beside me, spread out his rations, drank to me derisively from his measure of prison beer, and began. What he said it would be impossible to print; but his admirers, who believed their wit to have surpassed himself, actually rolled among the gravel. For my part, I thought at first I should have died. I had not dreamed the wretch was so observant; but hate sharpens the ears, and he had counted our interviews and actually knew Flora by her name. Gradually my coolness returned to me, accompanied by a volume of living anger that surprised myself.

" Are you nearly done? " I asked. " Because if you are, I am about to say a word or two myself."

" Oh, fair play! " said he. " Turn about! The Marquis of Carabas to the tribune."

" Very well," said I. " I have to inform you that I am a gentleman. You do not know what that means, hey? Well, I will tell you. It is a comical sort of animal; springs from another strange set of creatures they call ancestors; and, in common with toads and other vermin, has a thing that he calls feelings. The lion is a gentleman; he will not touch carrion. I am a gentleman, and I cannot bear to soil my fingers with such a lump of dirt. Sit still, Philippe Goguelat! sit still and do not say a word, or I shall know you are a coward; the eyes of our guards are upon us. Here is your health! " said I, and pledged him in the prison beer. " You have chosen to speak in a certain way of a young child," I continued, " who might be your daughter, and who was giving alms to me and some others of us mendicants. If the Emperor "—saluting—" if my Emperor could hear you, he would pluck off the Cross from your gross body. I cannot do that; I cannot take away what his Majesty has given; but one thing I promise you—I promise you, Goguelat, you shall be dead to-night."

I had borne so much from him in the past, I believe he thought there was no end to my forbearance, and he was at first amazed. But I have the pleasure to think that some of my expressions had pierced through his thick hide; and besides, the brute was truly a hero of valour, and loved fighting for itself. Whatever the cause, at least, he had soon pulled himself together, and took the thing (to do him justice) handsomely.

" And I promise you, by the devil's horns, that you shall have the chance! " said he, and pledged me again; and again I did him scrupulous honour.

The news of this defiance spread from prisoner to prisoner

with the speed of wings; every face was seen to be illuminated like those of the spectators at a horse-race; and indeed you must first have tasted the active life of a soldier, and then mouldered for a while in the tedium of a jail, in order to understand, perhaps even to excuse, the delight of our companions. Goguelat and I slept in the same squad, which greatly simplified the business; and a committee of honour was accordingly formed of our shed-mates. They chose for president a sergeant-major in the 4th Dragoons, a greybeard of the army, an excellent military subject, and a good man. He took the most serious view of his functions, visited us both, and reported our replies to the committee. Mine was of a decent firmness. I told him the young lady of whom Goguelat had spoken had on several occasions given me alms. I reminded him that, if we were now reduced to hold out our hands and sell pill-boxes for charity, it was something very new for soldiers of the Empire. We had all seen bandits standing at a corner of a wood truckling for copper halfpence, and after their benefactors were gone spitting out injuries and curses. " But," said I, " I trust that none of us will fall so low. As a Frenchman and a soldier, I owe that young child gratitude, and am bound to protect her character, and to support that of the army. You are my elder and my superior: tell me if I am not right."

He was a quiet-mannered old fellow, and patted me with three fingers on the back. " *C'est bien, mon enfant*," says he, and returned to his committee.

Goguelat was no more accommodating than myself. " I do not like apologies nor those that make them," was his only answer. And there remained nothing but to arrange the details of the meeting. So far as regards place and time we had no choice; we must settle the dispute at night, in the dark, after a round had passed by, and in the open middle of the shed under which we slept. The question of arms was more obscure. We had a good many tools, indeed, which we employed in the manufacture of our toys; but they were none of them suited for a single combat between civilised men, and, being nondescript, it was found extremely hard to equalise the chances of the combatants. At length a pair of scissors was unscrewed; and a couple of tough wands being found in a corner of the courtyard, one blade of the scissors was lashed solidly to each with resined twine—the twine

A Tale of a Pair of Scissors

coming I know not whence, but the resin from the green pillars of the shed, which still sweated from the axe. It was a strange thing to feel in one's hand this weapon, which was no heavier than a riding-rod, and which it was difficult to suppose would prove more dangerous. A general oath was administered and taken, that no one should interfere in the duel nor (suppose it to result seriously) betray the name of the survivor. And with that, all being then ready, we composed ourselves to await the moment.

The evening fell cloudy; not a star was to be seen when the first round of the night passed through our shed and wound off along the ramparts; and as we took our places, we could still hear, over the murmurs of the surrounding city, the sentries challenging its further passage. Leclos, the sergeant-major, set us in our stations, engaged our wands, and left us. To avoid blood-stained clothing, my adversary and I had stripped to the shoes; and the chill of the night enveloped our bodies like a wet sheet. The man was better at fencing than myself; he was vastly taller than I, being of a stature almost gigantic, and proportionately strong. In the inky blackness of the shed, it was impossible to see his eyes; and from the suppleness of the wands, I did not like to trust to a parade. I made up my mind accordingly to profit, if I might, by my defect; and as soon as the signal should be given, to throw myself down and lunge at the same moment. It was to play my life upon one card: should I not mortally wound him, no defence would be left me; what was yet more appalling, I thus ran the risk of bringing my own face against his scissor with the double force of our assaults, and my face and eyes are not that part of me that I would the most readily expose.

" *Allez !* " said the sergeant-major.

Both lunged in the same moment with an equal fury, and but for my manœuvre both had certainly been spitted. As it was, he did no more than strike my shoulder, while my scissor plunged below the girdle into a mortal part; and that great bulk of a man, falling from his whole height, knocked me immediately senseless.

When I came to myself I was laid in my own sleeping-place, and could make out in the darkness the outline of perhaps a dozen heads crowded around me. I sat up, " What is it? " I exclaimed.

"Hush!" said the sergeant-major. "Blessed be God, all is well." I felt him clasp my hand, and there were tears in his voice. "'Tis but a scratch, my child; here is papa, who is taking good care of you. Your shoulder is bound up; we have dressed you in your clothes again, and it will all be well."

At this I began to remember. "And Goguelat?" I gasped.

"He cannot bear to be moved; he has his bellyful; 'tis a bad business," said the sergeant-major.

The idea of having killed a man with such an instrument as half a pair of scissors seemed to turn my stomach. I am sure I might have killed a dozen with a firelock, a sabre, a bayonet, or any accepted weapon, and been visited by no such sickness of remorse. And to this feeling every unusual circumstance of our rencounter, the darkness in which we had fought, our nakedness, even the resin on the twine, appeared to contribute. I ran to my fallen adversary, kneeled by him, and could only sob his name.

He bade me compose myself. "You have given me the key of the fields, comrade, said he. "*Sans rancune !*"

At this my horror redoubled. Here had we two expatriated Frenchmen engaged in an ill-regulated combat like the battles of beasts. Here was he, who had been all his life so great a ruffian, dying in a foreign land of this ignoble injury, and meeting death with something of the spirit of a Bayard. I insisted that the guards should be summoned and a doctor brought. "It may still be possible to save him," I cried.

The sergeant-major reminded me of our engagement. "If you had been wounded," said he, "you must have lain there till the patrol came by and found you. It happens to be Goguelat—and so must he! Come, child, time to go to by-by." And as I still resisted, "Champdivers!" he said, "this is weakness. You pain me."

"Ay, off to your beds with you!" said Goguelat, and named us in a company with one of his jovial gross epithets.

Accordingly the squad lay down in the dark and simulated, what they certainly were far from experiencing, sleep. It was not yet late. The city, from far below, and all around us, sent up a sound of wheels and feet and lively voices. Yet awhile, and the curtain of the cloud was rent across, and in the space of sky between the eaves of the shed and the irregular outline of the ramparts a multitude of stars appeared. Meantime, in the midst of us lay Goguelat, and could not always withhold himself from groaning.

We heard the round far off; heard it draw slowly nearer. Last of all, it turned the corner and moved into our field of vision: two file of men and a corporal with a lantern, which he swung to and fro, so as to cast its light in the recesses of the yards and sheds.

"Hullo!" cried the corporal, pausing as he came by Goguelat.

He stooped with his lantern. All our hearts were flying. "What devil's work is this?" he cried, and with a startling voice summoned the guard.

We were all afoot upon the instant; more lanterns and soldiers crowded in front of the shed; an officer elbowed his way in. In the midst was the big naked body, soiled with blood. Some one had covered him with his blanket; but as he lay there in agony, he had partly thrown it off.

"This is murder!" cried the officer. "You wild beasts, you will hear of this to-morrow."

As Goguelat was raised and laid upon a stretcher, he cried to us a cheerful and blasphemous farewell.

CHAPTER III

MAJOR CHEVENIX COMES INTO THE STORY, AND GOGUELAT GOES OUT

THERE was never any talk of a recovery, and no time was lost in getting the man's deposition. He gave but the one account of it: that he had committed suicide because he was sick of seeing so many Englishmen. The doctor vowed it was impossible, the nature and direction of the wound forbidding it. Goguelat replied that he was more ingenious than the other thought for, and had propped up the weapon in the ground and fallen on the point—"just like Nebuchadnezzar," he added, winking to the assistants. The doctor, who was a little, spruce, ruddy man of an impatient temper, pished and pshawed and swore over his patient. "Nothing to be made of him!" he cried. A perfect heathen. If we could only find the weapon!" But the weapon had ceased to exist. A little resined twine was perhaps blowing about in the castle gutters; some bits of broken stick may have trailed in corners; and behold, in the pleasant air of the morning, a dandy prisoner trimming his nails with a pair of scissors!

Finding the wounded man so firm, you may be sure the authorities did not leave the rest of us in peace. No stone was left unturned. We were had in again and again to be examined, now singly, now in twos and threes. We were threatened with all sorts of impossible severities and tempted with all manner of improbable rewards. I suppose I was five times interrogated, and came off from each with flying colours. I am like old Souvaroff, I cannot understand a soldier being taken aback by any question; he should answer, as he marches on the fire, with an instant briskness and gaiety. I may have been short of bread, gold or grace; I was never yet found wanting in an answer. My comrades, if they were not all so ready, were none of them less staunch; and I may say here at once that the inquiry came to nothing at the time, and the death of Goguelat remained a mystery of the prison. Such were the veterans of France! And yet I should be disingenuous if I did not own this was a case apart; in ordinary circumstances, some one might have stumbled or been intimidated into an admission; and what bound us together with a closeness beyond that of mere comrades was a secret to which we were all committed and a design in which all were equally engaged. No need to inquire as to its nature: there is only one desire, and only one kind of design, that blooms in prisons. And the fact that our tunnel was near done supported and inspired us.

I came off in public, as I have said, with flying colours; the sittings of the court of inquiry died away like a tune that no one listens to; and yet I was unmasked—I, whom my very adversary defended, as good as confessed, as good as told the nature of the quarrel, and by so doing prepared for myself in the future a most anxious, disagreeable adventure. It was the third morning after the duel, and Goguelat was still in life, when the time came round for me to give Major Chevenix a lesson. I was fond of this occupation; not that he paid me much—no more, indeed, than eighteenpence a month, the customary figure, being a miser in the grain; but because I liked his breakfasts and (to some extent)

Major Chevenix comes into Story

himself. At least, he was a man of education; and of the others with whom I had any opportunity of speech, those that would not have held a book upside down would have torn the pages out for pipelights. For I must repeat again that our body of prisoners was exceptional: there was in Edinburgh Castle none of that educational busyness that distinguished some of the other prisons, so that men entered them unable to read, and left them fit for high employments. Chevenix was handsome, and surprisingly young to be a major; six feet in his stockings, well set up, with regular features and very clear grey eyes. It was impossible to pick a fault in him, and yet the sum-total was displeasing. Perhaps he was too clean; he seemed to bear about with him the smell of soap. Cleanliness is good, but I cannot bear a man's nails to seem japanned. And certainly he was too self-possessed and cold. There was none of the fire of youth, none of the swiftness of the soldier, in this young officer. His kindness was cold, and cruel cold; his deliberation exasperating. And perhaps it was from this character, which is very much the opposite of my own, that even in these days, when he was of service to me, I approached him with suspicion and reserve.

I looked over his exercise in the usual form, and marked six faults.

" H'm. Six," says he, looking at the paper. " Very annoying! I can never get it right."

" Oh, but you make excellent progress! " I said. I would not discourage him, you understand, but he was congenitally unable to learn French. Some fire, I think, is needful, and he had quenched his fire in soapsuds.

He put the exercise down, leaned his chin upon his hand, and looked at me with clear, severe eyes.

" I think we must have a little talk," said he.

" I am entirely at your disposition," I replied; but I quaked, for I knew what subject to expect.

" You have been some time giving me these lessons," he went on, " and I am tempted to think rather well of you. I believe you are a gentleman."

" I have that honour, sir," said I.

" You have seen me for the same period. I do not know how I strike you; but perhaps you will be prepared to believe that I also am a man of honour," said he.

23

" I require no assurances; the thing is manifest," and I bowed.

" Very well, then," said he. " What about this Goguelat?"

" You heard me yesterday before the court," I began. " I was awakened only——"

" Oh yes; I ' heard you yesterday before the court,' no doubt," he interrupted, " and I remember perfectly that you were ' awakened only.' I could repeat the most of it by rote, indeed. But do you suppose that I believed you for a moment?"

" Neither would you believe me if I were to repeat it here," said I.

" I may be wrong—we shall soon see," says he; " but my impression is that you will not ' repeat it here.' My impression is that you have come into this room, and that you will tell me something before you go out."

I shrugged my shoulders.

" Let me explain," he continued. " Your evidence, of course, is nonsense. I put it by, and the court put it by."

" My compliments and thanks!" said I.

" You *must* know—that's the short and the long," he proceeded. " All of you in shed B are bound to know. And I want to ask you where is the common-sense of keeping up this farce, and maintaining this cock-and-bull story between friends. Come, come, my good fellow, own yourself beaten, and laugh at it yourself."

" Well, I hear you, go ahead," said I. " You put your heart in it."

He crossed his legs slowly. " I can very well understand," he began, " that precautions have had to be taken. I dare say an oath was administered. I can comprehend that perfectly." (He was watching me all the time with his cold, bright eyes.) " And I can comprehend that, about an affair of honour, you would be very particular to keep it."

" About an affair of honour?" I repeated, like a man quite puzzled.

" It was not an affair of honour, then?" he asked.

" What was not? I do not follow," said I.

He gave no sign of impatience; simply sat awhile silent, and began again in the same placid and good-natured voice: " The court and I were at one in setting aside your evidence. It could not deceive a child. But there was a difference

24

between myself and the other officers, because *I knew my man* and they did not. They saw in you a common soldier, and I knew you for a gentleman. To them your evidence was a leash of lies, which they yawned to hear you telling. Now, I was asking myself, how far will a gentleman go? Not surely so far as to help hush a murder up? So that— when I heard you tell how you knew nothing of the matter, and were only awakened by the corporal, and all the rest of it—I translated your statements into something else. Now, Champdivers," he cried, springing up lively and coming towards me with animation, " I am going to tell you what that was, and you are going to help me to see justice done: how, I don't know, for of course you are under oath—but somehow. Mark what I'm going to say."

At that moment he laid a heavy, hard grip upon my shoulder; and whether he said anything more or came to a full stop at once, I am sure I could not tell you to this day. For, as the devil would have it, the shoulder he laid hold of was the one Goguelat had pinked. The wound was but a scratch; it was healing with the first intention; but in the clutch of Major Chevenix it gave me agony. My head swam; the sweat poured off my face; I must have grown deadly pale.

He removed his hand as suddenly as he had laid it there.

" What is wrong with you? " said he.

" It is nothing," said I. " A qualm. It has gone by."

" Are you sure? " said he. " You are as white as a sheet."

" Oh no, I assure you! Nothing whatever. I am my own man again," I said, though I could scarce command my tongue.

" Well, shall I go on again? " says he. " Can you follow me? "

" Oh, by all means! " said I, and mopped my streaming face upon my sleeve, for you may be sure in those days I had no handkerchief.

" If you are sure you can follow me. That was a very sudden and sharp seizure," he said doubtfully. " But if you are sure, all right, and here goes. An affair of honour among you fellows would, naturally, be a little difficult to carry out, perhaps it would be impossible to have it wholly regular. And yet a duel might be very irregular in form, and, under the peculiar circumstances of the case, loyal enough in effect. Do you take me? Now, as a gentleman and a soldier."

His hand rose again at the words and hovered over me. I could bear no more, and winced away from him. " No," I cried, " not that. Do not put your hand upon my shoulder. I cannot bear it. It is rheumatism," I made haste to add. " My shoulder is inflamed and very painful."

He returned to his chair and deliberately lighted a cigar. " I am sorry about your shoulder," he said at last. " Let me send for the doctor."

" Not in the least," said I. " It is a trifle. I am quite used to it. It does not trouble me in the smallest. At any rate, I don't believe in doctors."

" All right," said he, and. sat and smoked a good while in a silence which I would have given anything to break. " Well," he began presently, " I believe there is nothing left for me to learn. I presume I may say that I know all."

" About what? " said I boldly.

" About Goguelat," said he.

" I beg your pardon. I cannot conceive," said I.

" Oh," says the major, " the man fell in a duel, and by your hand! I am not an infant."

" By no means," said I. " But you seem to me to be a good deal of a theorist."

" Shall we test it? " he asked. " The doctor is close by. If there is not an open wound on your shoulder, I am wrong. If there is——" He waved his hand. " But I advise you to think twice. There is a deuce of a nasty drawback to the experiment—that what might have remained private between us two becomes public property."

" Oh, well! " said I, with a laugh, " anything rather than a doctor! I cannot bear the breed."

His last words had a good deal relieved me, but I was still far from comfortable.

Major Chevenix smoked awhile, looking now at his cigar ash, now at me. " I'm a soldier myself," he says presently, " and I've been out in my time and hit my man. I don't want to run any one into a corner for an affair that was at all necessary or correct. At the same time, I want to know that much, and I'll take your word of honour for it. Otherwise, I shall be very sorry, but the doctor must be called in."

" I neither admit anything nor deny anything," I re-

Major Chevenix comes into Story

turned. "But if this form of words will suffice you, here is what I say: I give you my parole, as a gentleman and a soldier, there has nothing taken place amongst us prisoners that was not honourable as the day."

"All right," says he. "That was all I wanted. You can go now, Champdivers."

And as I was going out he added, with a laugh: "By-the-bye, I ought to apologise: I had no idea I was applying the torture!"

The same afternoon the doctor came into the courtyard with a piece of paper in his hand. He seemed hot and angry, and had certainly no mind to be polite.

"Here!" he cried. "Which of you fellows knows any English? Oh!"—spying me—"there you are, what's your name! *You'll* do. Tell these fellows that the other fellow's dying. He's booked; no use talking; I expect he'll go by evening. And tell them I don't envy the feelings of the fellow who spiked him. Tell them that first."

I did so.

"Then you can tell 'em," he resumed, "that the fellow, Goggle—what's his name?—wants to see some of them before he gets his marching orders. If I got it right, he wants to kiss or embrace you, or some sickening stuff. Got that? Then here's a list he's had written, and you'd better read it out to them—I can't make head or tail of your beastly names—and they can answer *present*, and fall in against that wall."

It was with a singular movement of incongruous feelings that I read the first name on the list. I had no wish to look again on my own handiwork; my flesh recoiled from the idea; and how could I be sure what reception he designed to give me? The cure was in my own hand! I could pass that first name over—the doctor would not know—and I might stay away. But to the subsequent great gladness of my heart, I did not dwell for an instant on the thought, walked over to the designated wall, faced about, read out the name Champdivers," and answered myself with the word "Present."

There were some half-dozen on the list, all told; and as soon as we were mustered, the doctor led the way to the hospital, and we followed after, like a fatigue party, in single file. At the door he paused, told us "a fellow" would see each of us alone, and, as soon as I had explained that, sent me by myself into the ward. It was a small room, white-washed; a south window stood open on a vast depth of air and a spacious and distant prospect; and from deep below, in the Grassmarket, the voices of hawkers came up clear and far away. Hard by, on a little bed, lay Goguelat. The sunburn had not yet faded from his face, and the stamp of death was already there. There was something wild and unmannish in his smile, that took me by the throat; only death and love know or have ever seen it. And when he spoke, it seemed to shame his coarse talk.

He held out his arms as if to embrace me. I drew near with incredible shrinkings, and surrendered myself to his arms with overwhelmed disgust. But he only drew my ear down to his lips.

"Trust me," he whispered. "*Je suis bon bougre, moi.* I'll take it to hell with me, and tell the devil."

Why should I go on to reproduce his grossness and triviali-ties? All that he thought, at that hour, was even noble, though he could not clothe it otherwise than in the language of a brutal farce. Presently he bade me call the doctor; and when that officer had come in, raised a little up in his bed, pointed first to himself and then to me, who stood weeping by his side, and several times repeated the expres-sion, "Frinds—frinds—dam frinds."

To my great surprise, the doctor appeared very much affected. He nodded his little bob-wigged head at us, and said repeatedly, "All right, Johnny—me comprong."

Then Goguelat shook hands with me, embraced me again, and I went out of the room sobbing like an infant.

How often have I not seen it, that the most unpardonable fellows make the happiest exits! It is a fate we may well envy them. Goguelat was detested in life; in the last three days, by his admirable staunchness and consideration, he won every heart; and when word went about the prison the same evening that he was no more, the voice of conversation became hushed as in a house of mourning.

For myself, I was like a man distracted; I cannot think what ailed me: when I awoke the following day, nothing remained of it; but that night I was filled with a gloomy fury of the nerves. I had killed him; he had done his utmost to protect me; I had seen him with that awful smile.

Major Chevenix comes into Story

And so illogical and useless is this sentiment of remorse that I was ready, at a word or a look, to quarrel with somebody else. I presume the disposition of my mind was imprinted on my face; and when a little after, I overtook, saluted, and addressed the doctor, he looked on me with commiseration and surprise.

I had asked him if it was true.

" Yes," he said, " the fellow's gone."

" Did he suffer much? " I asked.

" Devil a bit; passed away like a lamb," said he. He looked on me a little, and I saw his hand go to his fob. " Here, take that! no sense in fretting," he said, and, putting a silver two-penny bit in my hand, he left me.

I should have had that twopenny framed to hang upon the wall, for it was the man's one act of charity in all my knowledge of him. Instead of that, I stood looking at it in my hand and laughed out bitterly, as I realised his mistake; then went to the ramparts, and flung it far into the air like blood money. The night was falling; through an embrasure and across the gardened valley I saw the lamp-lighters hasting along Princes Street with ladder and lamp, and looked on moodily. As I was so standing a hand was laid upon my shoulder, and I turned about. It was Major Chevenix, dressed for the evening, and his neckcloth really admirably folded. I never denied the man could dress.

" Ah! " said he, " I thought it was you, Champdivers. So he's gone? "

I nodded.

" Come, come," said he, " you must cheer up. Of course it's very distressing, very painful and all that. But do you know, it ain't such a bad thing either for you or me? What with his death and your visit to him I am entirely reassured."

So I was to owe my life to Goguelat at every point.

" I had rather not discuss it," said I.

" Well," said he, " one word more, and I'll agree to bury the subject. What did you fight about? "

" Oh what do men ever fight about? " I cried.

" A lady ? " said he.

I shrugged my shoulders.

" Deuce you did! " said he. " I should scarce have thought it of him."

And at this my ill-humour broke fairly out in words.
" He!" I cried. " He never dared to address her—only
to look at her and vomit his vile insults! She may have
given him sixpence: if she did, it may take him to heaven
yet!"

At this I became aware of his eyes set upon me with a
considering look, and brought up sharply.

" Well, well," said he. " Good-night to you, Champdivers. Come to me at breakfast-time to-morrow, and
we'll talk of other subjects."

I fully admit the man's conduct was not bad: in writing
it down so long after the events I can even see that it was
good.

CHAPTER IV

ST. IVES GETS A BUNDLE OF BANK NOTES

I WAS surprised one morning, shortly after, to find myself
the object of marked consideration by a civilian and a
stranger. This was a man of the middle age; he had a
face of a mulberry colour, round black eyes, comical tufted
eyebrows, and a protuberant forehead, and was dressed in
clothes of a Quakerish cut. In spite of his plainness, he
had that inscrutable air of a man well-to-do in his affairs.
I conceived he had been some while observing me from a
distance, for a sparrow sat betwixt us quite unalarmed on
the breech of a piece of cannon. So soon as our eyes met,
he drew near and addressed me in the French language,
which he spoke with a good fluency but an abominable
accent.

" I have the pleasure of addressing Monsieur le Vicomte
Anne de Kéroual de Saint-Yves?" said he.

" Well," said I, " I do not call myself all that; but I have
a right to, if I chose. In the meanwhile I call myself plain
Champdivers, at your disposal. It was my mother's name,
and good to go soldiering with."

" I think not quite," said he; " for if I remember rightly,
your mother also had the particle. Her name was Flori-
monde de Champdivers."

" Right again!" said I, " and I am extremely pleased to
meet a gentleman so well informed in my quarterings. Is

monsieur Born himself?" This I said with a great air of assumption, partly to conceal the degree of curiosity with which my visitor had inspired me, and in part because it struck me as highly incongruous and comical in my prison garb and on the lips of a private soldier.

He seemed to think so too, for he laughed.

"No, sir," he returned, speaking this time in English; "I am not '*born*' as you call it, and must content myself with *dying*, of which I am equally susceptible with the best of you. My name is Mr. Romaine—Daniel Romaine—a solicitor of London City, at your service; and, what will perhaps interest you more, I am here at the request of your great-uncle, the Count."

"What!" I cried, "does M. de Kéroual de St. Yves remember the existence of such a person as myself, and will he deign to count kinship with a soldier of Napoleon?"

"You speak English well," observed my visitor.

"It has been a second language to me from a child," said I. "I had an English nurse; my father spoke English with me; and I was finished by a countryman of yours and a dear friend of mine, a Mr. Vicary."

A strong expression of interest came into the lawyer's face.

"What!" he cried, "you knew poor Vicary?"

"For more than a year," said I; "and shared his hiding-place for many months."

"And I was his clerk, and have succeeded him in business," said he. "Excellent man! It was on the affairs of M. de Kéroual that he went to that accursed country, from which he was never destined to return. Do you chance to know his end, sir?"

"I am sorry," said I, "I do. He perished miserably at the hands of a gang of banditti, such as we call *chauffeurs*. In a word, he was tortured, and died of it. See," I added—kicking off one shoe, for I had no stockings; "I was no more than a child, and see how they had begun to treat myself."

He looked at the mark of my old burn with a certain shrinking. "Beastly people!" I heard him mutter to himself.

"The English may say so with a good grace," I observed politely.

Such speeches were the coin in which I paid my way among

this credulous race. Ninety per cent. of our visitors would have accepted the remark as natural in itself and creditable to my powers of judgment, but it appeared my lawyer was more acute.

" You are not entirely a fool, I perceive," said he.

" No," said I; " not wholly."

" And yet it is well to beware of the ironical mood," he continued. " It is a dangerous instrument. Your great-uncle has, I believe, practised it very much, until it is now become a problem what he means."

" And that brings me back to what you will admit is a most natural inquiry," said I. " To what do I owe the pleasure of this visit? how did you recognise me? and how did you know I was here? "

Carefully separating his coat skirts, the lawyer took a seat beside me on the edge of the flags.

" It is rather an odd story," says he, " and, with your leave, I'll answer the second question first. It was from a certain resemblance you bear to your cousin, M. le Vicomte."

" I trust, sir, that I resemble him advantageously? " said I.

" I hasten to reassure you," was the reply: " you do. To my eyes, M. Alain de St.-Yves has scarce a pleasing exterior. And yet, when I knew you were here, and was actually look-ing for you—why, the likeness helped. As for how I came to know your whereabouts, by an odd enough chance, it is again M. Alain we have to thank. I should tell you, he has for some time made it his business to keep M. de Kéroual informed of your career; with what purpose I leave you to judge. When he first brought the news of your—that you were serving Buonaparte, it seemed it might be the death of the old gentleman, so hot was his resentment. But from one thing to another, matters have a little changed. Or I should rather say, not a little. We learned you were under orders for the Peninsula, to fight the English; then that you had been commissioned for a piece of bravery, and were again reduced to the ranks. And from one thing to another (as I say), M. de Kéroual became used to the idea that you were his kinsman and yet served with Buonaparte, and filled instead with wonder that he should have another kinsman who was so remarkably well informed of events in France. And it now became a very disagreeable question, whether the young gentleman was not a spy? In short, sir, in seeking to disserve you, he had accumulated against himself a load of suspicions."

My visitor now paused, took snuff, and looked at me with an air of benevolence.

" Good God, sir! " says I, " this is a curious story."

" You will say so before I have done," said he. " For there have two events followed. The first of these was an encounter of M. de Kéroual and M. de Mauséant."

" I know the man to my cost," said I; " it was through him I lost my commission."

" Do you tell me so? " he cried. " Why, here is news! "

" Oh, I cannot complain! " said I. " I was in the wrong. I did it with my eyes open. If a man gets a prisoner to guard and lets him go, the least he can expect is to be degraded."

" You will be paid for it," said he. " You did well for yourself and better for your king."

" If I had thought I was injuring my emperor," said I, " I would have let M. de Mauséant burn in hell ere I had helped him, and be sure of that! I saw in him only a private person in a difficulty: I let him go in private charity; not even to profit myself will I suffer it to be misunderstood."

" Well, well," said the lawyer, " no matter now. This is a foolish warmth—a very misplaced enthusiasm, believe me! The point of the story is that M. de Mauséant spoke of you with gratitude, and drew your character in such a manner as greatly to affect your uncle's views. Hard upon the back of which, in came your humble servant, and laid before him the direct proof of what we had been so long suspecting. There was no dubiety permitted. M. Alain's expensive way of life, his clothes and mistresses, his dicing and racehorses, were all explained: he was in the pay of Buonaparte, a hired spy, and a man that held the strings of what I can only call a convolution of extremely fishy enterprises. To do M. de Kéroual justice, he took it in the best way imaginable, destroyed the evidences of the one great-nephew's disgrace—and transferred his interest wholly to the other."

" What am I to understand by that? " said I.

" I will tell you," says he. " There is a remarkable inconsistency in human nature which gentlemen of my cloth have a great deal of occasion to observe. Selfish persons can live without chick or child, they can live without all mankind except perhaps the barber and the apothecary; but when it comes to dying, they seem physically unable to die without an heir. You can apply this principle for yourself. Viscount Alain, though he scarce guesses it, is no longer in the field. Remains, Viscount Anne."

" I see," said I, " you give a very unfavourable impression of my uncle, the Count."

" I had not meant it," said he. " He has led a loose life—sadly loose—but he is a man it is impossible to know and not to admire; his courtesy is exquisite."

" And so you think there is actually a chance for me? " I asked.

" Understand," said he: " in saying as much as I have done, I travel quite beyond my brief. I have been clothed with no capacity to talk of wills, or heritages, or your cousin. I was sent here to make but the one communication: that M. de Kéroual desires to meet his great-nephew."

" Well," said I, looking about me on the battlements by which we sat surrounded, " this is a case in which Mahomet must certainly come to the mountain."

" Pardon me," said Mr. Romaine; " you know already your uncle is an aged man; but I have not yet told you that he is quite broken up, and his death shortly looked for. No, no, there is no doubt about it—it is the mountain that must come to Mahomet."

" From an Englishman, the remark is certainly significant," said I; " but you are of course, and by trade, a keeper of men's secrets, and I see you keep that of Cousin Alain, which is not the mark of a truculent patriotism, to say the least."

" I am first of all the lawyer of your family! " says he.

" That being so," said I, " I can perhaps stretch a point myself. This rock is very high, and it is very steep; a man might come by a devil of a fall from almost any part of it, and yet I believe I have a pair of wings that might carry me just so far as to the bottom. Once at the bottom I am helpless."

" And perhaps it is just then that I could step in," returned the lawyer. " Suppose by some contingency, at which I make no guess, and on which I offer no opinion——"

But here I interrupted him. " One word ere you go further. I am under no parole," said I.

" I understood so much," he replied, " although some of you French gentry find their word sit lightly on them."

Gets a Bundle of Bank Notes

" Sir, I am not one of those," said I.

" To do you plain justice, I do not think you one," said he. " Suppose yourself, then, set free and at the bottom of the rock," he continued, " although I may not be able to do much, I believe I can do something to help you on your road. In the first place I would carry this, whether in an inside pocket or my shoe." And he passed me a bundle of bank notes.

" No harm in that," said I, at once concealing them.

" In the second place," he resumed, " It is a great way from here to where your uncle lives—Amersham Place, not far from Dunstable; you have a great part of Britain to get through; and for the first stages, I must leave you to your own luck and ingenuity. I have no acquaintance here in Scotland, or at least " (with a grimace) " no dishonest ones. But farther to the south, about Wakefield, I am told there is a gentleman called Burchell Fenn, who is not so particular as some others, and might be willing to give you a cast forward. In fact, sir, I believe it's the man's trade: a piece of knowledge that burns my mouth. But that is what you get by meddling with rogues; and perhaps the biggest rogue now extant, M. de Saint-Yves, is your cousin, M. Alain."

" If this be a man of my cousin's," I observed, " I am perhaps better to keep clear of him? "

" It was through some paper of your cousin's that we came across his trail," replied the lawyer. " But I am inclined to think, so far as anything is safe in such a nasty business, you might apply to the man Fenn. You might even, I think, use the Viscount's name; and the little trick of family resemblance might come in. How, for instance, if you were to call yourself his brother? "

" It might be done," said I. " But look here a moment? You propose to me a very difficult game: I have apparently a devil of an opponent in my cousin; and, being a prisoner of war, I can scarcely be said to hold good cards. For what stakes, then, am I playing? "

" They are very large," said he. " Your great-uncle is immensely rich—immensely rich. He was wise in time; he smelt the revolution long before; sold all that he could, and had all that was movable transported to England through my firm. There are considerable estates in England; Amersham Place itself is very fine; and he has much money, wisely invested. He lives, indeed, like a prince. And of what use is it to him? He has lost all that was worth living for—his family, his country; he has seen his king and queen murdered; he has seen all these miseries and infamies," pursued the lawyer, with a rising inflection and a heightening colour; and then broke suddenly off,—" In short, sir, he has seen all the advantages of that government for which his nephew carries arms, and he has the misfortune not to like them."

" You speak with a bitterness that I suppose I must excuse," said I; " yet which of us has the more reason to be bitter? This man, my uncle, M. de Kéroual, fled. My parents, who were less wise perhaps, remained. In the beginning, they were even republicans; to the end they could not be persuaded to despair of the people. It was a glorious folly for which, as a son, I reverence them. First one and then the other perished. If I have any mark of a gentleman, all who taught me died upon the scaffold, and my last school of manners was the prison of the Abbaye. Do you think you can teach bitterness to a man with a history like mine? "

" I have no wish to try," said he. " And yet there is one point I cannot understand: I cannot understand that one of your blood and experience should serve the Corsican. I cannot understand it: it seems as though everything generous in you must rise against that—domination."

" And perhaps," I retorted, " had your childhood passed among wolves, you would have been overjoyed yourself to see the Corsican Shepherd."

" Well, well," replied Mr. Romaine, " it may be. There are things that do not bear discussion."

And with a wave of his hand he disappeared abruptly down a flight of steps and under the shadow of a ponderous arch.

CHAPTER V

ST. IVES IS SHOWN A HOUSE

THE lawyer was scarce gone before I remembered many omissions; and chief among these, that I had neglected to get Mr. Burchell Fenn's address. Here was an essential point neglected; and I ran to the head of the stairs to find myself already too late. The lawyer was beyond my view; in the archway that led downward to the castle gate, only the red coat and the bright arms of a sentry glittered in the shadow; and I could but return to my place upon the ramparts.

I am not very sure that I was properly entitled to this corner. But I was a high favourite; not an officer, and scarce a private, in the castle would have turned me back, except upon a thing of moment; and whenever I desired to be solitary, I was suffered to sit here behind my piece of cannon unmolested. The cliff went down before me almost sheer, but mantled with a thicket of climbing trees; from farther down, an outwork raised its turret; and across the valley I had a view of that long terrace of Princes Street which serves as a promenade to the fashionable inhabitants of Edinburgh. A singularity in a military prison, that it should command a view on the chief thoroughfare!

It is not necessary that I should trouble you with the train of my reflections, which turned upon the interview I had just concluded and the hopes that were now opening before me. What is more essential, my eye (even while I thought) kept following the movement of the passengers on Princes Street, as they passed briskly to and fro—met, greeted, and bowed to each other—or entered and left the shops, which are in that quarter, and, for a town of the Britannic provinces, particularly fine. My mind being busy upon other things, the course of my eye was the more random; and it chanced that I followed, for some time, the advance of a young gentleman with a red head and a white greatcoat, for whom I cared nothing at the moment, and of whom it is probable I shall be gathered to my fathers without learning more. He seemed to have a large acquaintance: his hat was for ever in his hand; and I dare say I had already observed him exchanging compliments with half-a-dozen, when he drew up at last before a young man and a young lady whose tall persons and gallant carriage I thought I recognised.

It was impossible at such a distance that I could be sure, but the thought was sufficient, and I craned out of the embrasure to follow them as long as possible. To think that such emotions, that such a concussion of the blood, may have been inspired by a chance resemblance, and that I may have stood and thrilled there for a total stranger! This distant view, at least, whether of Flora or of some one else, changed in a moment the course of my reflections. It was

all very well, and it was highly needful I should see my
uncle; but an uncle, a great-uncle at that, and one whom
I had never seen, leaves the imagination cold; and if I were
to leave the castle, I might never again have the opportunity
of finding Flora. The little impression I had made, even
supposing I had made any, how soon it would die out! how
soon I should sink to be a phantom memory, with which
(in after days) she might amuse a husband and children!
No, the impression must be clenched, the wax impressed
with the seal, ere I left Edinburgh. And at this the two
interests that were now contending in my bosom came
together and became one. I wished to see Flora again; and
I wanted some one to further me in my flight and to get me
new clothes. The conclusion was apparent. Except for
persons in the garrison itself, with whom it was a point of
honour and military duty to retain me captive, I knew, in
the whole country of Scotland, these two alone. If it were
to be done at all, they must be my helpers. To tell them
of my designed escape while I was still in bonds, would be
to lay before them a most difficult choice. What they might
do in such a case, I could not in the least be sure of, for (the
same case arising) I was far from sure what I should do
myself. It was plain I must escape first. When the harm
was done, when I was no more than a poor wayside fugitive,
I might apply to them with less offence and more security.
To this end it became necessary that I should find out where
they lived and how to reach it; and feeling a strong confidence that they would soon return to visit me, I prepared a
series of baits with which to angle for my information. It
will be seen the first was good enough.

Perhaps two days after, Master Ronald put in an appearance by himself. I had no hold upon the boy, and preter-
mitted my design till I should have laid court to him and
engaged his interest. He was prodigiously embarrassed,
not having previously addressed me otherwise than by a
bow and blushes; and he advanced to me with an air of one
stubbornly performing a duty, like a raw soldier under fire.
I laid down my carving; greeted him with a good deal of
formality, such as I thought he would enjoy; and finding
him to remain silent, branched off into narratives of my
campaigns such as Goguelat himself might have scrupled
to endorse. He visibly thawed and brightened; drew more

Is Shown a House

near to where I sat; forgot his timidity so far as to put many questions; and at last, with another blush, informed me he was himself expecting a commission.

" Well," said I, " they are fine troops, your British troops in the Peninsula. A young gentleman of spirit may well be proud to be engaged at the head of such soldiers."

" I know that," he said; " I think of nothing else. I think shame to be dangling here at home and going through with this foolery of education, while others, no older than myself, are in the field."

" I cannot blame you," said I. " I have felt the same myself."

" There are—there are no troops, are there, quite so good as ours? " he asked.

" Well," said I, " there is a point about them: they have a defect,—they are not to be trusted in a retreat. I have seen them behave very ill in a retreat."

" I believe that is our national character," he said—God forgive him!—with an air of pride.

" I have seen your national character running away at least, and had the honour to run after it! " rose to my lips, but I was not so ill-advised as to give it utterance. Every one should be flattered, but boys and women without stint; and I put in the rest of the afternoon narrating to him tales of British heroism, for which I should not like to engage that they were all true.

" I am quite surprised," he said at last. " People tell you the French are insincere. Now, I think your sincerity is beautiful. I think you have a noble character. I admire you very much. I am very grateful for your kindness to—to one so young," and he offered me his hand.

" I shall see you again soon? " said I.

" Oh, now! Yes, very soon," said he. " I—I wish to tell you. I would not let Flora—Miss Gilchrist, I mean—come to-day. I wished to see more of you myself. I trust you are not offended; you know, one should be careful about strangers."

I approved his caution, and he took himself away: leaving me in a mixture of contrarious feelings, part ashamed to have played on one so gullible, part raging that I should have burned so much incense before the vanity of England; yet, in the bottom of my soul, delighted to think I had made a friend—-or, at least, begun to make a friend—of Flora's brother.

As I had half expected, both made their appearance the next day. I struck so fine a shade betwixt the pride that is allowed to soldiers and the sorrowful humility that befits a captive, that I declare, as I went to meet them, I might have afforded a subject for a painter. So much was high comedy, I must confess; but so soon as my eyes lighted full on her dark face and eloquent eyes, the blood leaped into my cheeks—and that was nature! I thanked them, but not the least with exultation; it was my cue to be mournful, and to take the pair of them as one.

"I have been thinking," I said, "you have been so good to me, both of you, stranger and prisoner as I am, that I have been thinking how I could testify to my gratitude. It may seem a strange subject for a confidence, but there is actually no one here, even of my comrades, that knows me by my name and title. By these I am called plain Champdivers, a name to which I have a right, but not the name which I should bear, and which (but a little while ago) I must hide like a crime. Miss Flora, suffer me to present to you the Vicomte Anne de Kéroual de Saint-Yves, a private soldier."

"I knew it!" cried the boy; "I knew he was a noble!"

And I thought the eyes of Miss Flora said the same, but more persuasively. All through this interview she kept them on the ground, or only gave them to me for a moment at a time, and with a serious sweetness.

"You may conceive, my friends, that this is rather a painful confession," I continued. "To stand here before you vanquished, a prisoner in a fortress, and take my own name upon my lips, is painful to the proud. And yet I wished that you should know me. Long after this, we may yet hear of one another—perhaps Mr. Gilchrist and myself in the field and from opposing camps—and it would be a pity if we heard and did not recognise."

They were both moved; and began at once to press upon me offers of service, such as to lend me books, get me tobacco if I used it, and the like. This would have been all mighty welcome, before the tunnel was ready. Now it signified no more to me than to offer the transition I required.

"My dear friends," I said—" for you must allow me to

call you that, who have no others within so many hundred
leagues—perhaps you will think me fanciful and sentimental; and perhaps indeed I am; but there is one service that
I would beg of you before all others. You see me set here
on the top of this rock in the midst of your city. Even with
what liberty I have, I have the opportunity to see a myriad
roofs, and I dare to say, thirty leagues of sea and land. All
this hostile! Under all these roofs my enemies dwell;
wherever I see the smoke of a house rising, I must tell myself
that some one sits before the chimney and reads with joy
of our reverses. Pardon me, dear friends, I know that you
must do the same, and I do not grudge at it! With you,
it is all different. Show me your house then, were it only
the chimney, or, if that be not visible, the quarter of the
town in which it lies! So, when I look all about me, I shall
be able to say: ' *There is one house in which I am not quite
unkindly thought of.*' "

Flora stood a moment.

" It is a pretty thought," said she, " and, as far as regards
Ronald and myself, a true one. Come, I believe I can
show you the very smoke out of our chimney."

So saying, she carried me round the battlements towards
the opposite or southern side of the fortress, and indeed to
a bastion almost immediately overlooking the place of our
projected flight. Thence we had a view of some foreshortened
suburbs at our feet, and beyond of a green, open, and irregular
country rising towards the Pentland Hills. The face of one
of these summits (say two leagues from where we stood)
is marked with a procession of white scars. And to this she
directed my attention.

" You see these marks? " she said. " We call them the
Seven Sisters. Follow a little lower with your eye, and
you will see a fold of the hill, the tops of some trees, and a
tail of smoke out of the midst of them. That is Swanston
Cottage, where my brother and I are living with my aunt.
If it gives you pleasure to see it, I am glad. We, too, can
see the castle from a corner in the garden, and we go there in
the morning often—do we not, Ronald?—and we think of
you, M. de Saint-Yves; but I am afraid it does not altogether
make us glad."

" Mademoiselle! " said I, and indeed my voice was scarce
under command, " if you knew how your generous words

—how even the sight of you—relieved the horrors of this place, I believe, I hope, I know, you would be glad. I will come here daily and look at that dear chimney and these green hills, and bless you from the heart, and dedicate to you the prayers of this poor sinner. Ah! I do not say they can avail!"

"Who can say that, M. de Saint-Yves?" she said softly. "But I think it is time we should be going."

"High time," said Ronald, whom (to say the truth) I had a little forgotten.

On the way back, as I was laying myself out to recover lost ground with the youth, and to obliterate, if possible, the memory of my last and somewhat too fervent speech, who should come past us but the major? I had to stand aside and salute as he went by, but his eyes appeared entirely occupied with Flora.

"Who is that man?" she asked.

"He is a friend of mine," said I. "I give him lessons in French, and he has been very kind to me."

"He stared," she said,—" I do not say, rudely; but why should he stare?"

"If you do not wish to be stared at, mademoiselle, suffer me to recommend a veil," said I.

She looked at me with what seemed anger. "I tell you the man stared," she said.

And Ronald added: "Oh, I don't think he meant any harm. I suppose he was just surprised to see us walking about with a pr—with M. Saint-Yves."

But the next morning, when I went to Chevenix's rooms, and after I had dutifully corrected his exercise—" I compliment you on your taste," said he to me.

"I beg your pardon?" said I.

"Oh, no, I beg yours," said he. "You understand me perfectly, just as I do you."

I murmured something about enigmas.

"Well, shall I give you the key to the enigma?" said he leaning back. "That was the young lady whom Goguelat insulted and whom you avenged. I do not blame you. She is a heavenly creature."

"With all my heart, to the last of it!" said I. "And to the first also, if it amuses you! You are become so very acute of late that I suppose you must have your own way."

The Escape

" What is her name? " he asked.

" Now, really! " said I. " Do you think it likely she has told me? "

" I think it certain," said he.

I could not restrain my laughter. " Well, then, do you think it likely I would tell you? " I cried.

" Not a bit," said he. " But come, to our lesson! "

CHAPTER VI

THE ESCAPE

THE time for our escape drew near, and the nearer it came the less we seemed to enjoy the prospect. There is but one side on which this castle can be left either with dignity or safety; but as there is the main gate and guard, and the chief street of the upper city, it is not to be thought of by escaping prisoners. In all other directions an abominable precipice surrounds it, down the face of which (if anywhere at all) we must regain our liberty. By our concurrent labours in many a dark night, working with the most anxious precautions against noise, we had made out to pierce below the curtain about the south-west corner, in a place they call the *Devil's Elbow*. I have never met that celebrity; nor (if the rest of him at all comes up to what they call his elbow) have I the least desire of his acquaintance. From the heel of the masonry, the rascally, breakneck precipice descended sheer among waste lands, scattered suburbs of the city, and houses in the building. I had never the heart to look for any length of time—the thought that I must make the descent in person some dark night robbing me of breath; and, indeed, on anybody not a seaman or a steeple-jack, the mere sight of the *Devil's Elbow* wrought like an emetic.

I don't know where the rope was got, and doubt if I much cared. It was not that which gravelled me, but whether, now that we had it, it would serve our turn. Its length, indeed, we made a shift to fathom out; but who was to tell us how that length compared with the way we had to go? Day after day, there would be always some of us stolen out to the *Devil's Elbow* and making estimates of the descent, whether by a bare guess or the dropping of stones. A private of pioneers remembered the formula for that—or else remembered part of it and obligingly invented the remainder. I had never any real confidence in that formula; and even had we got it from a book, there were difficulties in the way of the application that might have daunted Archimedes. We durst not drop any considerable pebble lest the sentinels should hear, and those that we dropped we could not hear ourselves. We had never a watch—or none that had a second-hand; and though every one of us could guess a second to a nicety, all somehow guessed it differently. In short, if any two set forth upon this enterprise, they invariably returned with two opinions, and often with a black eye in the bargain. I looked on upon these proceedings, although not without laughter, yet with impatience and disgust. I am one that cannot bear to see things botched or gone upon with ignorance; and the thought that some poor devil was to hazard his bones upon such premises, revolted me. Had I guessed the name of that unhappy first adventurer, my sentiments might have been livelier still.

The designation of this personage was indeed all that remained for us to do; and even in that we had advanced so far that the lot had fallen on Shed B. It had been determined to mingle the bitter and the sweet; and whoever went down first, the whole of his shed-mates were to follow next in order. This caused a good deal of joy in Shed B, and would have caused more if it had not still remained to choose our pioneer. In view of the ambiguity in which we lay as to the length of the rope and the height of the precipice—and that this gentleman was to climb down from fifty to seventy fathoms on a pitchy night, on a rope entirely free and with not so much as an infant child to steady it at the bottom, a little backwardness was perhaps excusable. But it was, in our case, more than a little. The truth is, we were all womanish fellows about a height; and I have myself been put, more than once, *hors de combat* by a less affair than the rock of Edinburgh Castle.

We discussed it in the dark and between the passage of the rounds; and it was impossible for any body of men to show a less adventurous spirit. I am sure some of us, and myself first among the number, regretted Goguelat. Some were persuaded it was safe, and could prove the same by argument; but if they had good reasons why some one else

The Escape

should make the trial, they had better still why it should not be themselves. Others, again, condemned the whole idea as insane; among these, as ill-luck would have it, a seaman of the fleet; who was the most dispiriting of all. The height, he reminded us, was greater than the tallest ship's mast, the rope entirely free; and he as good as defied the boldest and strongest to succeed. We were relieved from this deadlock by our sergeant-major of dragoons.

" Comrades," said he, " I believe I rank you all; and for that reason, if you really wish it, I will be the first myself. At the same time, you are to consider what the chances are that I may prove to be the last, as well. I am no longer young—I was sixty near a month ago. Since I have been a prisoner, I have made for myself a little *bedaine*. My arms are all gone to fat. And you must promise not to blame me, if I fall and play the devil with the whole thing."

" We cannot hear of such a thing! " said I. " M. Laclas is the oldest man here; and, as such, he should be the very last to offer. It is plain, we must draw lots."

" No," said M. Laclas; " you put something else in my head! There is one here who owes a pretty candle to the others, for they have kept his secret. Besides, the rest of us are only rabble; and he is another affair altogether. Let Champdivers—let the noble go the first."

I confess there was a notable pause before the noble in question got his voice. But there was no room for choice. I had been so ill-advised, when I first joined the regiment, as to take ground on my nobility. I had been often rallied on the matter in the ranks, and had passed under the by-names of *Monseigneur* and *the Marquis*. It was now needful I should justify myself and take a fair revenge.

Any little hesitation I may have felt passed entirely unnoticed, from the lucky incident of a round happening at that moment to go by. And during the interval of silence there occurred something that sent my blood to the boil. There was a private in our shed called Clausel, a man of a very ugly disposition. He had made one of the followers of Goguelat; but, whereas Goguelat had always a kind of monstrous gaiety about him, Clausel was no less morose than he was evil-minded. He was sometimes called *the General*, and sometimes by a name too ill-mannered for repetition. As we all sat listening, this man's hand was

laid on my shoulder, and his voice whispered in my ear:
" If you don't go, I'll have you hanged, Marquis! "

As soon as the round was past—" Certainly, gentlemen!"
said I. " I will give you a lead, with all the pleasure in the
world. But, first of all there is a hound here to be punished.
M. Clausel has just insulted me, and dishonoured the French
army; and I demand that he run the gauntlet of this shed."

There was but one voice asking what he had done, and,
as soon as I had told them, but one voice agreeing to the
punishment. The General was, in consequence, extremely
roughly handled, and the next day was congratulated by all
who saw him on his *new decorations*. It was lucky for us
that he was one of the prime movers and believers in our
projects of escape, or he had certainly revenged himself
by a denunciation. As for his feelings towards myself,
they appeared, by his looks, to surpass humanity; and I
made up my mind to give him a wide berth in the future.

Had I been to go down that instant, I believe I could
have carried it well. But it was already too late—the day
was at hand. The rest had still to be summoned. Nor
was this the extent of my misfortune; for the next night,
and the night after, were adorned with a perfect galaxy
of stars, and showed every cat that stirred in a quarter of a
mile. During this interval, I have to direct your sympathies
on the Vicomte de Saint-Yves! All addressed me softly,
like folk round a sick-bed. Our Italian corporal, who had
got a dozen of oysters from a fishwife, laid them at my feet,
as though I were a Pagan idol; and I have never since been
wholly at my ease in the society of shellfish. He who was
the best of our carvers brought me a snuffbox, which he
had just completed, and which, while it was yet in hand,
he had often declared he would not part with under fifteen
dollars. I believe the piece was worth the money too!
And yet the voice stuck in my throat with which I must
thank him. I found myself, in a word, to be fed up like a
prisoner in a camp of anthropophagi, and honoured like the
sacrificial bull. And what with these annoyances, and the
risky venture immediately ahead, I found my part a trying
one to play.

It was a good deal of a relief when the third evening closed
about the castle with volumes of sea-fog. The lights of
Princes Street sometimes disappeared, sometimes blinked

The Escape

across at us no brighter than the eyes of cats; and five steps from one of the lanterns on the ramparts it was already groping dark. We made haste to lie down. Had our jailors been upon the watch, they must have observed our conversation to die out unusually soon. Yet I doubt if any of us slept. Each lay in his place, tortured at once with the hope of liberty and the fear of a hateful death. The guard call sounded; the hum of the town declined by little and little. On all sides of us, in their different quarters, we could hear the watchmen cry the hours along the street. Often enough, during my stay in England, have I listened to these gruff or broken voices; or perhaps gone to my window when I lay sleepless, and watched the old gentleman hobble by upon the causeway with his cape and his cap, his hanger and his rattle. It was ever a thought with me how differently that cry would re-echo in the chamber of lovers, beside the bed of death, or in the condemned cell. I might be said to hear it that night myself in the condemned cell! At length a fellow with a voice like a bull's began to roar out in the opposite thoroughfare:

" Past yin o'cloak, and a dark, harry moarnin'."

At which we were all silently afoot.

As I stole about the battlements towards the—gallows, I was about to write—the sergeant-major, perhaps doubtful of my resolution, kept close by me, and occasionally proffered the most indigestible reassurances in my ear. At last I could bear them no longer.

" Be so obliging as to let me be! " said I. " I am neither a coward nor a fool. What do *you* know of whether the rope be long enough? But I shall know it in ten minutes! "

The good old fellow laughed in his moustache, and patted me.

It was all very well to show the disposition of my temper before a friend alone; before my assembled comrades the thing had to go handsomely. It was then my time to come on the stage; and I hope I took it handsomely.

" Now, gentlemen," said I, " if the rope is ready, here is the criminal! "

The tunnel was cleared, the stake driven, the rope extended. As I moved forward to the place, many of my comrades caught me by the hand and wrung it, an attention I could well have done without.

St. Ives

"Keep an eye on Clausel!" I whispered to Laclas; and with that, got down on my elbows and knees, took the rope in both hands, and worked myself, feet foremost, through the tunnel. When the earth failed under my feet, I thought my heart would have stopped; and a moment after I was demeaning myself in mid-air like a drunken jumping-jack. I have never been a model of piety, but at this juncture prayers and a cold sweat burst from me simultaneously.

The line was knotted at intervals of eighteen inches, and to the inexpert it may seem as if it should have been even easy to descend. The trouble was, this devil of a piece of rope appeared to be inspired, not with life alone, but with a personal malignity against myself. It turned to the one side, paused for a moment, and then spun me like a toasting-jack to the other; slipped like an eel from the clasp of my feet; kept me all the time in the most outrageous fury of exertion; and dashed me at intervals against the face of the rock. I had no eyes to see with; and I doubt if there was anything to see but darkness. I must occasionally have caught a gasp of breath, but it was quite unconscious. And the whole forces of my mind were so consumed with losing hold and getting it again, that I could scarce have told whether I was going up or coming down.

Of a sudden I knocked against the cliff with such a thump as almost bereft me of my sense; and, as reason twinkled back, I was amazed to find that I was in a state of rest, that the face of the precipice here inclined outwards at an angle which relieved me almost wholly of the burthen of my own weight, and that one of my feet was safely planted on a ledge. I drew one of the sweetest breaths in my experience, hugged myself against the rope, and closed my eyes in a kind of ecstasy of relief. It occurred to me next to see how far I was advanced on my unlucky journey, a point on which I had not a shadow of a guess. I looked up: there was nothing above me but the blackness of the night and the fog. I craned timidly forward and looked down. There, upon a floor of darkness, I beheld a certain pattern of hazy lights, some of them aligned as in thorough-fares, others standing apart as in solitary houses; and before I could well realise it, or had in the least estimated my distance, a wave of nausea and vertigo warned me to lie back and close my eyes. In this situation I had really

The Escape

but the one wish, and that was: something else to think of!
Strange to say, I got it: a veil was torn from my mind,
and I saw what a fool I was—what fools we had all been—
and that I had no business to be thus dangling between
earth and heaven by my arms. The only thing to have
done was to have attached me to a rope and lowered me,
and I had never the wit to see it till that moment!

I filled my lungs, got a good hold on my rope, and once
more launched myself on the descent. As it chanced, the
worst of the danger was at an end, and I was so fortunate
as to be never again exposed to any violent concussion.
Soon after I must have passed within a little distance of a
bush of wallflower, for the scent of it came over me with
that impression of reality which characterises scents in
darkness. This made me a second landmark, the ledge
being my first. I began accordingly to compute intervals
of time: so much to the ledge, so much again to the wallflower, so much more below. If I were not at the bottom
of the rock, I calculated I must be near indeed to the end
of the rope, and there was no doubt that I was not far from
the end of my resources. I began to be lightheaded and to
be tempted to let go,—now arguing that I was certainly
arrived within a few feet of the level and could safely risk
a fall, anon persuaded I was still close at the top and it was
idle to continue longer on the rock. In the midst of which
I came to a bearing on plain ground, and had nearly wept
aloud. My hands were as good as flayed, my courage
entirely exhausted, and, what with the long strain and the
sudden relief, my limbs shook under me with more than the
violence of ague, and I was glad to cling to the rope.

But this was no time to give way. I had (by God's single
mercy) got myself alive out of that fortress; and now I had
to try to get the others, my comrades. There was about
a fathom of rope to spare; I got it by the end, and searched
the whole ground thoroughly for anything to make it fast to.
In vain: the ground was broken and stony, but there grew
not there so much as a bush of furze.

"Now then," thought I to myself, "here begins a new
lesson, and I believe it will prove richer than the first. I
am not strong enough to keep this rope extended. If I do
not keep it extended the next man will be dashed against
a precipice. There is no reason why he should have my

extravagant good luck. I see no reason why he should not fall—nor any place for him to fall on but my head."

From where I was now standing there was occasionally visible, as the fog lightened, a lamp in one of the barrack windows, which gave me a measure of the height he had to fall and the horrid force that he must strike me with. What was yet worse, we had agreed to do without signals: every so many minutes by Laclas' watch another man was to be started from the battlements. Now, I had seemed to myself to be about half-an-hour in my descent, and it seemed near as long again that I waited, straining on the rope for my next comrade to begin. I began to be afraid that our conspiracy was out, that my friends were all secured, and that I should pass the remainder of the night, and be discovered in the morning, vainly clinging to the rope's end like a hooked fish upon an angle. I could not refrain, at this ridiculous image, from a chuckle of laughter. And the next moment I knew, by the jerking of the rope, that my friend had crawled out of the tunnel and was fairly launched on his descent. It appears it was the sailor who had insisted on succeeding me: as soon as my continued silence had assured him the rope was long enough, Gautier, for that was his name, had forgot his former arguments, and shown himself so extremely forward, that Laclas had given way. It was like the fellow, who had no harm in him beyond an instinctive selfishness. But he was like to have paid pretty dearly for the privilege. Do as I would, I could not keep the rope as I could have wished it; and he ended at last by falling on me from a height of several yards, so that we both rolled together on the ground. As soon as he could breathe he cursed me beyond belief, wept over his finger, which he had broken, and cursed me again. I bade him be still and think shame of himself to be so great a cry-baby. Did he not hear the round going by above? I asked; and who could tell but what the noise of his fall was already remarked, and the sentinels at the very moment leaning upon the battlements to listen?

The round, however, went by, and nothing was discovered; the third man came to the ground quite easily; the fourth was, of course, child's play; and before there were ten of us collected, it seemed to me that, without the least injustice to my comrades, I might proceed to take care of myself.

Swanston Cottage

I knew their plan: they had a map and an almanack, and designed for Grangemouth, where they were to steal a ship. Suppose them to do so, I had no idea they were qualified to manage it after it was stolen. Their whole escape, indeed, was the most haphazard thing imaginable; only the impatience of captives and the ignorance of private soldiers would have entertained so misbegotten a device; and though I played the good comrade and worked with them upon the tunnel, but for the lawyer's message I should have let them go without me. Well, now they were beyond my help, as they had always been beyond my counselling; and, without word said or leave taken, I stole out of the little crowd. It is true I would rather have waited to shake hands with Laclas, but in the last man who had descended I thought I recognised Clausel, and since the scene in the shed my distrust of Clausel was perfect. I believed the man to be capable of any infamy, and events have since shown that I was right.

CHAPTER VII

SWANSTON COTTAGE

I HAD two views. The first, was, naturally, to get clear of Edinburgh Castle and the town, to say nothing of my fellow-prisoners; the second to work to the southward so long as it was night, and be near Swanston Cottage by morning. What I should do there and then, I had no guess, and did not greatly care, being a devotee of a couple of divinities called Chance and Circumstance. Prepare, if possible; where it is impossible, work straight forward, and keep your eyes open and your tongue oiled. Wit and a good exterior— there is all life in a nutshell.

I had at first a rather chequered journey: got involved in gardens, butted into houses, and had even once the misfortune to awake a sleeping family, the father of which, as I suppose, menaced me from the window with a blunderbuss. Altogether, though I had been some time gone from my companions, I was still at no great distance, when a miserable accident put a period to the escape. Of a sudden the night was divided by a scream. This was followed by the sound of something falling, and that again by the report of a musket from the Castle battlements. It was strange to hear the alarm spread through the city. In the fortress drums were beat and a bell rung backward. On all hands the watchmen sprang their rattles. Even in that limbo or no-man's-land where I was wandering, lights were made in the houses; sashes were flung up; I could hear neighbouring families converse from window to window, and at length I was challenged myself.

" Wha's that? " cried a big voice.

I could see it proceeded from a big man in a big nightcap, leaning from a one-pair window; and as I was not yet abreast of his house, I judged it was more wise to answer. This was not the first time I had had to stake my fortunes on the goodness of my accent in a foreign tongue; and I have always found the moment inspiriting, as a gambler should. Pulling around me a sort of greatcoat I had made of my blanket, to cover my sulphur-coloured livery,—" A friend! " said I.

" What like's all this collieshangie? " said he.

I had never heard of a collieshangie in my days, but with the racket all about us in the city, I could have no doubt as to the man's meaning.

" I do not know, sir, really," said I; " but I suppose some of the prisoners will have escaped."

" Bedamned! " says he.

" Oh, sir, they will be soon taken," I replied: " it has been found in time. Good morning, sir! "

" Ye walk late, sir? " he added.

" Oh, surely not," said I, with a laugh. " Earlyish, if you like! " which brought me finally beyond him, highly pleased with my success.

I was now come forth on a good thoroughfare, which led (as well as I could judge) in my direction. It brought me almost immediately through a piece of street, whence I could hear close by the springing of a watchman's rattle, and where I suppose a sixth part of the windows would be open, and the people, in all sorts of night gear, talking with a kind of tragic gusto from one to another. Here, again, I must run the gauntlet of a half-dozen questions, the rattle all the while sounding nearer; but as I was not walking inordinately quick, as I spoke like a gentleman, and the lamps were too dim to show my dress, I carried it off once more. One person, indeed, inquired where I was off to at that hour.

Swanston Cottage

I replied vaguely and cheerfully, and as I escaped at one end of this dangerous pass I could see the watchman's lantern entering by the other. I was now safe on a dark country highway, out of sight of lights and out of the fear of watchmen. And yet I had not gone above a hundred yards before a fellow made an ugly rush at me from the roadside. I avoided him with a leap, and stood on guard, cursing my empty hands, wondering whether I had to do with an officer or a mere footpad, and scarce knowing which to wish. My assailant stood a little; in the thick darkness I could see him bob and sidle as though he were feinting at me for an advantageous onfall. Then he spoke.

" My goo' frien'," says he, and at the first word I pricked my ears, " my goo' frien', will you oblishe me with lil neshary infamation? Whish roa' t' Cramond? "

I laughed out clear and loud, stepped up to the convivialist, took him by the shoulders and faced him about. " My good friend," said I, " I believe I know what is best for you much better than yourself, and may God forgive you the fright you have given me! There, get you gone to Edinburgh! " And I gave a shove, which he obeyed with the passive agility of a ball, and disappeared incontinently in the darkness down the road by which I had myself come.

Once clear of this foolish fellow, I went on again up a gradual hill, descended on the other side through the houses of a country village, and came at last to the bottom of the main ascent leading to the Pentlands and my destination. I was some way up when the fog began to lighten; a little farther, and I stepped by degrees into a clear starry night, and saw in front of me, and quite distinct, the summits of the Pentlands, and behind, the valley of the Forth and the city of my late captivity buried under a lake of vapour. I had but one encounter—that of a farm-cart, which I heard, from a great way ahead of me, creaking nearer in the night, and which passed me about the point of dawn like a thing seen in a dream, with two silent figures in the inside nodding to the horse's steps. I presume they were asleep; by the shawl, one of them should be a woman. Soon, by concurrent steps, the day began to break and the fog to subside and roll away. The east grew luminous and was barred with chilly colours, and the Castle on its rock, and the spires and chimneys of the upper town, took gradual shape, and arose, like islands, out of the receding cloud. All about me was still and sylvan; the road mounting and winding, with nowhere a sign of any passenger, the birds chirping, I suppose for warmth, the boughs of the trees knocking together, and the red leaves falling in the wind.

It was broad day, but still bitter cold and the sun not up, when I came in view of my destination. A single gable and chimney of the cottage peeped over the shoulder of the hill; not far off, and a trifle higher on the mountain, a tall old white-washed farmhouse stood among the trees, beside a falling brook; beyond were rough hills of pasture. I bethought me that shepherd folk were early risers, and if I were once seen skulking in that neighbourhood it might prove the ruin of my prospects; took advantage of a line of hedge, and worked myself up in its shadow till I was come under the garden wall of my friends' house. The cottage was a little quaint place of many rough-cast gables and grey roofs. It had something the air of a rambling infinitesimal cathedral, the body of it rising in the midst two storeys high, with a steep-pitched roof, and sending out upon all hands (as it were chapter-houses, chapels, and transepts) one-storeyed and dwarfish projections. To add to this appearance, it was grotesquely decorated with crockets and gargoyles, ravished from some mediæval church. The place seemed hidden away, being not only concealed in the trees of the garden, but, on the side on which I approached it, buried as high as the eaves by the rising of the ground. About the walls of the garden there went a line of well-grown elms and beeches, the first entirely bare, the last still pretty well covered with red leaves, and the centre was occupied with a thicket of laurel and holly, in which I could see arches cut and paths winding.

I was now within hail of my friends, and not much the better. The house appeared asleep; yet if I attempted to wake any one I had no guarantee it might not prove either the aunt with the gold eyeglasses (whom I could only remember with trembling), or some ass of a servant-maid who should burst out screaming at sight of me. Higher up I could hear and see a shepherd shouting to his dogs and striding on the rough sides of the mountain, and it was clear I must get to cover without loss of time. No doubt the holly thickets would have proved a very suitable retreat, but there was mounted on the wall a sort of signboard not uncommon in the country of Great Britain, and very damping to the adventurous: SPRING GUNS AND MANTRAPS was the legend that it bore. I have learned since that these advertisements, three times out of four, were in the nature of Quaker guns on a disarmed battery, but I had not learned it then, and even so, the odds would not have been good enough. For a choice, I would a hundred times sooner be returned to Edinburgh Castle and my corner in the bastion, than to leave my foot in a steel trap or have to digest the contents of an automatic blunderbuss. There was but one chance left —that Ronald or Flora might be the first to come abroad; and in order to profit by this chance if it occurred, I got me on the cope of the wall in a place were it was screened by the thick branches of a beech, and sat there waiting.

As the day wore on, the sun came very pleasantly out. I had been awake all night, I had undergone the most violent agitations of mind and body, and it is not so much to be wondered at, as it was exceedingly unwise and foolhardy, that I should have dropped into a doze. From this I awakened to the characteristic sound of digging, looked down, and saw immediately below me the back view of a gardener in a stable waistcoat. Now he would appear steadily immersed in his business; anon, to my more immediate terror, he would straighten his back, stretch his arms, gaze about the otherwise deserted garden, and relish a deep pinch of snuff. It was my first thought to drop from the wall upon the other side. A glance sufficed to show me that even the way by which I had come was now cut off, and the field behind me already occupied by a couple of shepherds' assistants and a score or two of sheep. I have named the talismans on which I habitually depend, but here was a conjuncture in which both were wholly useless. The copestone of a wall arrayed with broken bottles is no favourable rostrum; and I might be as eloquent as Pitt, and as fascinating as Richelieu, and neither the gardener nor the shepherd lads would care a halfpenny. In short, there was no escape possible from my absurd position: there I must continue to sit until one or other of my neighbours should raise his eyes and give the signal for my capture.

The part of the wall on which (for my sins) I was posted could be scarce less than twelve feet high on the inside; the leaves of the beech which made a fashion of sheltering me were already partly fallen; and I was thus not only perilously exposed myself, but enabled to command some part of the garden walks and (under an evergreen arch) the front lawn and windows of the cottage. For long nothing stirred except my friend with the spade; then I heard the opening of a sash; and presently after saw Miss Flora appear in a morning wrapper and come strolling hitherward between the borders, pausing and visiting her flowers—herself as fair. *There* was a friend; *here*, immediately beneath me, an unknown quantity—the gardener: how to communicate with the one and not attract the notice of the other? To make a noise was out of the question; I dared scarce to breathe. I held myself ready to make a gesture as soon as she should look, and she looked in every possible direction but the one. She was interested in the vilest tuft of chickweed, she gazed at the summit of the mountain, she came even immediately below me and conversed on the most fastidious topics with the gardener; but to the top of that wall she would not dedicate a glance! At last she began to retrace her steps in the direction of the cottage; whereupon, becoming quite desperate, I broke off a piece of plaster, took a happy aim, and hit her with it in the nape of the neck. She clapped her hand to the place, turned about, looked on all sides for an explanation, and spying me (as indeed I was parting the branches to make it the more easy), half uttered and half swallowed down again a cry of surprise.

The infernal gardener was erect upon the instant." What's your wull, miss? " said he.

Her readiness amazed me. She had already turned and was gazing in the opposite direction. " There's a child among the artichokes," she said.

" The Plagues of Egyp'! *I'll* see to them! " cried the gardener truculently, and with a hurried waddle disappeared among the evergreens.

That moment she turned, she came running towards me, her arms stretched out, her face incarnadined for the one moment with heavenly blushes, the next pale as death. " Monsieur de Saint-Yves! " she said.

" My dear young lady," I said, " this is the damnedest liberty—I know it! But what else was I to do? "

" You have escaped? " said she.

The Hen-House

" If you call this escape," I replied.

" But you cannot possibly stop there! " she cried.

" I know it," said I.   " And where am I to go? "

She struck her hands together. " I have it! " she exclaimed. " Come down by the beech trunk—you must leave no footprint in the border—quickly, before Robie can get back! I am the hen-wife here: I keep the key; you must go into the hen-house—for the moment."

I was by her side at once. Both cast a hasty glance at the blank windows of the cottage and so much as was visible of the garden alleys; it seemed there was none to observe us. She caught me by the sleeve and ran. It was no time for compliments; hurry breathed upon our necks; and I ran along with her to the next corner of the garden, where a wired court and a board hovel standing in a grove of trees advertised my place of refuge. She thrust me in without a word; the bulk of the fowls were at the same time emitted; and I found myself the next moment locked in alone with half-a-dozen sitting hens. In the twilight of the place all fixed their eyes on me severely, and seemed to upbraid me with some crying impropriety. Doubtless the hen has always a puritanic appearance, although (in its own behaviour) I could never observe it to be more particular than its neighbours. But conceive a British hen!

CHAPTER VIII

THE HEN-HOUSE

I WAS half-an-hour at least in the society of these distressing bipeds, and alone with my own reflections and necessities. I was in great pain of my flayed hands, and had nothing to treat them with; I was hungry and thirsty, and had nothing to eat or to drink; I was thoroughly tired, and there was no place for me to sit. To be sure there was the floor, but nothing could be imagined less inviting.

At the sound of approaching footsteps, my good-humour was restored. The key rattled in the lock, and Master Ronald entered, closed the door behind him, and leaned his back to it.

" I say, you know! " he said, and shook a sullen young head.

St. Ives

" I know it's a liberty," said I.

" It's infernally awkward: my position is infernally embarrassing," said he.

" Well," said I, " and what do you think of mine? "

This seemed to pose him entirely, and he remained gazing upon me with a convincing air of youth and innocence. I could have laughed, but I was not so inhumane.

" I am in your hands," said I, with a little gesture. " You must do with me what you think right."

" Ah, yes! " he cried: " if I knew! "

" You see," said I, " it would be different if you had received your commission. Properly speaking, you are not yet a combatant; I have ceased to be one; and I think it arguable that we are just in the position of one ordinary gentleman to another, where friendship usually comes before the law. Observe, I only say *arguable*. For God's sake, don't think I wish to dictate an opinion. These are the sort of nasty little businesses, inseparable from war, which every gentleman must decide for himself. If I were in your place——"

" Ay, what would you do, then? " says he.

" Upon my word, I do not know," said I. " Hesitate, as you are doing, I believe."

" I will tell you," he said. " I have a kinsman, and it is what *he* would think, that I am thinking. It is General Graham of Lynedoch—Sir Thomas Graham. I scarcely know him, but I believe I admire him more than I do God."

" I admire him a good deal, myself," said I, " and have good reason too. I have fought with him, been beaten, and run away. *Veni, victus sum, evasi.*"

" What! " he cried. " You were at Barossa? "

" There and back, which many could not say," said I. " It was a pretty affair and a hot one, and the Spaniards behaved abominably, as they usually did in a pitched field; the Marshall Duke of Belluno made a fool of himself, and not for the first time; and your friend Sir Thomas had the best of it, so far as there was any best. He is a brave and ready officer."

" Now, then, you will understand! " said the boy. " I wish to please Sir Thomas: what would he do? "

" Well, I can tell you a story," said I, " a true one too, and about this very combat of Chiclana, or Barossa as you

58

The Hen-House

call it. I was in the Eighth of the Line; we lost the eagle of the First Battalion, more betoken, but it cost you dear. Well, we had repulsed more charges than I care to count, when your 87th Regiment came on at a foot's pace, very slow but very steady; in front of them a mounted officer, his hat in his hand, white-haired, and talking very quietly to the battalions. Our Major, Vigo-Roussillon, set spurs to his horse and galloped out to sabre him, but seeing him an old man, very handsome, and as composed as if he were in a coffee house, lost heart and galloped back again. Only, you see, they had been very close together for the moment, and looked each other in the eyes. Soon after the Major was wounded, taken prisoner, and carried into Cadiz. One fine day they announced to him the visit of the General, Sir Thomas Graham. 'Well, sir,' said the General, taking him by the hand, ' I think we were face to face upon the field.' It was the white-haired officer!"

" Ah! " cried the boy—his eyes were burning.

" Well, and here is the point," I continued. " Sir Thomas fed the Major from his own table from that day, and served him with six covers."

" Yes, it is a beautiful—a beautiful story," said Ronald. " And yet somehow it is not the same—is it? "

" I admit it freely," said I.

The boy stood awhile brooding. " Well, I take my risk of it," he cried. " I believe it's treason to my sovereign—I believe there is an infamous punishment for such a crime —and yet I'm hanged if I can give you up."

I was as much moved as he. " I could almost beg you to do otherwise," I said. " I was a brute to come to you, a brute and a coward. You are a noble enemy; you will make a noble soldier." And with rather a happy idea of a compliment for this warlike youth, I stood up straight and gave him the salute.

He was for a moment confused; his face flushed. " Well, well, I must be getting you something to eat, but it will not be for six," he added, with a smile: " only what we can get smuggled out. There is my aunt in the road, you see," and he locked me in again with the indignant hens.

I always smile when I recall that young fellow; and yet, if the reader were to smile also, I should feel ashamed. If my son shall be only like him when he comes to that age, it

59

will be a brave day for me and not a bad one for his country.

At the same time I cannot pretend that I was sorry when his sister succeeded in his place. She brought me a few crusts of bread and a jug of milk, which she had handsomely laced with whisky after the Scottish manner.

" I am so sorry," she said: " I dared not bring you anything more. We are so small a family, and my aunt keeps such an eye upon the servants. I have put some whisky in the milk—it is more wholesome so—and with eggs you will be able to make something of a meal. How many eggs will you be wanting to that milk? for I must be taking the others to my aunt—that is my excuse for being here. I should think three or four. Do you know how to beat them in? or shall I do it? "

Willing to detain her a while longer in the hen-house, I displayed my bleeding palms; at which she cried out aloud.

" My dear Miss Flora, you cannot make an omelette without breaking eggs," said I; " and it is no bagatelle to escape from Edinburgh Castle. One of us, I think, was even killed."

" And you are as white as a rag, too," she exclaimed, " and can hardly stand! Here is my shawl, sit down upon it here in the corner, and I will beat your eggs. See, I have brought a fork too; I should have been a good person to take care of Jacobites or Covenanters in old days! You shall have more to eat this evening; Ronald is to bring it you from town. We have money enough, although no food that we can call our own. Ah, if Ronald and I kept house, you should not be lying in this shed! He admires you so much."

" My dear friend," said I, " for God's sake do not embarrass me with more alms. I loved to receive them from that hand, so long as they were needed; but they are so no more, and whatever else I may lack—and I lack everything—it is not money." I pulled out my sheaf of notes and detached the top one: it was written for ten pounds, and signed by that very famous individual, Abraham Newlands. " Oblige me, as you would like me to oblige your brother if the parts were reversed, and take this note for the expenses. I shall need not only food, but clothes."

" Lay it on the ground," said she. " I must not stop my beating."

The Hen-House

" You are not offended? " I exclaimed.

She answered me by a look that was a reward in itself, and seemed to imply the most heavenly offers for the future. There was in it a shadow of reproach, and such warmth of communicative cordiality as left me speechless. I watched her instead till her hens' milk was ready.

" Now," said she, " taste that."

I did so, and swore it was nectar. She collected her eggs and crouched in front of me to watch me eat. There was about this tall young lady at the moment an air of motherliness delicious to behold. I am like the English general, and to this day I still wonder at my moderation.

" What sort of clothes will you be wanting? " said she.

" The clothes of a gentleman," said I. " Right or wrong, I think it is the part I am best qualified to play. Mr. St. Ives (for that's to be my name upon the journey) I conceive as rather a theatrical figure, and his make-up should be to match."

" And yet there is a difficulty," said she. " If you got coarse clothes the fit would hardly matter. But the clothes of a fine gentleman—oh, it is absolutely necessary that these should fit! And above all, with your "—she paused a moment —" to our ideas somewhat noticeable manners."

" Alas for my poor manners! " said I. " But, my dear friend Flora, these little noticeabilities are just what mankind has to suffer under. Yourself, you see, you're very noticeable even when you come in a crowd to visit poor prisoners in the castle."

I was afraid I should frighten my good angel visitant away, and without the smallest breath of pause went on to add a few directions as to stuffs and colours.

She opened big eyes upon me. " Oh, Mr. St. Ives! " she cried—" if that is to be your name—I do not say they would not be becoming; but for a journey, do you think they would be wise? I am afraid "—she gave a pretty break of laughter—" I am afraid they would be daft-like! "

" Well, and am I not daft? " I asked her.

" I do begin to think you are," said she.

" There it is, then! " said I. " I have been long enough a figure of fun. Can you not feel with me that perhaps the bitterest thing in this captivity has been the clothes? Make me a captive—bind me with chains if you like—but let me be still myself. You do not know what it is to be a walking travesty—among foes," I added bitterly.

"Oh, but you are too unjust!" she cried. "You speak as though any one ever dreamed of laughing at you. But no one did. We were all pained to the heart. Even my aunt—though sometimes I do think she was not quite in good taste—you should have seen her and heard her at home! She took so much interest. Every patch in your clothes made us sorry; it should have been a sister's work."

"That is what I never had—a sister," said I. "But since you say that I did not make you laugh——"

"Oh, Mr. St. Ives! never!" she exclaimed. "Not for one moment. It was all too sad. To see a gentleman——"

"In the clothes of a harlequin, and begging?" I suggested.

"To see a gentleman in distress, and nobly supporting it," she said.

"And do you not understand, my fair foe," said I, "that even if all were as you say—even if you had thought my travesty were becoming—I should be only the more anxious, for my sake, for my country's sake, and for the sake of your kindness, that you should see him whom you have helped as God meant him to be seen? that you should have something to remember him by at least more characteristic than a misfitting sulphur-yellow suit, and half a week's beard?"

"You think a great deal too much of clothes," she said. "I am not that kind of girl."

"And I am afraid I am that kind of a man," said I. "But do not think of me too harshly for that. I talked just now of something to remember by. I have many of them myself, of these beautiful reminders, of these keepsakes, that I cannot be parted from until I lose memory and life. Many of them are great things, many of them are high virtues—charity, mercy, faith. But some of them are trivial enough. Miss Flora, do you remember the day that I first saw you, the day of the strong east wind? Miss Flora, shall I tell you what you wore?"

We had both risen to our feet, and she had her hand already, on the door to go. Perhaps this attitude emboldened me to profit by the last seconds of our interview; and it certainly rendered her escape the more easy.

"Oh, you are too romantic!" she said, laughing; and

with that my sun was blown out, my enchantress had fled away, and I was again left alone in the twilight with the lady hens.

CHAPTER IX

THREE IS COMPANY, AND FOUR NONE

THE rest of the day I slept in the corner of the hen-house upon Flora's shawl. Nor did I awake until a light shone suddenly in my eyes, and starting up with a gasp (for, indeed, at the moment I dreamed I was still swinging from the Castle battlements) I found Ronald bending over me with a lantern. It appeared it was past midnight, that I had slept about sixteen hours, and that Flora had returned her poultry to the shed and I had heard her not. I could not but wonder if she had stooped to look at me as I slept. The puritan hens now slept irremediably; and being cheered with the promise of supper I wished them an ironical good-night, and was lighted across the garden and noiselessly admitted to a bedroom on the ground floor of the cottage. There I found soap, water, razors—offered me diffidently by my beardless host—and an outfit of new clothes. To be shaved again without depending on the barber of the gaol was a source of a delicious, if a childish joy. My hair was sadly too long, but I was none so unwise as to make an attempt on it myself. And, indeed, I thought it did not wholly misbecome me as it was, being by nature curly. The clothes were about as good as I expected. The waistcoat was of toilenet, a pretty piece, the trousers of fine kerseymere, and the coat sat extraordinarily well. Altogether, when I beheld this changeling in the glass, I kissed my hand to him.

"My dear fellow," said I, "have you no scent?"

"Good God, no!" cried Ronald. "What do you want with scent?"

"Capital thing on a campaign," said I. "But I can do without."

I was now led, with the same precautions against noise, into the little bow-windowed dining-room of the cottage. The shutters were up, the lamp guiltily turned low; the beautiful Flora greeted me in a whisper; and when I was set down to table, the pair proceeded to help me with precautions that might have seemed excessive in the Ear of Dionysius.

"She sleeps up there," observed the boy, pointing to the ceiling; and the knowledge that I was so imminently near to the resting-place of that gold eyeglass touched even myself with some uneasiness.

Our excellent youth had imported from the city a meat pie, and I was glad to find it flanked with a decanter of really admirable wine of Oporto. While I ate, Ronald entertained me with the news of the city, which had naturally rung all day with our escape: troops and mounted messengers had followed each other forth at all hours and in all directions; but according to the last intelligence no recapture had been made. Opinion in town was very favourable to us; our courage was applauded, and many professed regret that our ultimate chance of escape should be so small. The man who had fallen was one Sombref, a peasant; he was one who slept in a different part of the Castle; and I was thus assured that the whole of my former companions had attained their liberty, and Shed A was untenanted.

From this we wandered insensibly into other topics. It is impossible to exaggerate the pleasure I took to be thus sitting at the same table with Flora, in the clothes of a gentleman, at liberty and in the full possession of my spirits and resources; of all of which I had need, because it was necessary that I should support at the same time two opposite characters, and at once play the cavalier and lively soldier for the eyes of Ronald, and to the ears of Flora maintain the same profound and sentimental note that I had already sounded. Certainly there are days when all goes well with a man; when his wit, his digestion, his mistress are in a conspiracy to spoil him, and even the weather smiles upon his wishes. I will only say of myself upon that evening that I surpassed my expectations, and was privileged to delight my hosts. Little by little they forgot their terrors and I my caution; until at last we were brought back to earth by a catastrophe that might very easily have been foreseen, but was not the less astonishing to us when it occurred.

I had filled all the glasses. "I have a toast to propose," I whispered, "or rather three, but all so inextricably interwoven that they will not bear dividing. I wish first to drink

Three is Company, Four None

to the health of a brave and therefore a generous enemy. He found me disarmed, a fugitive and helpless. Like the lion, he disdained so poor a triumph; and when he might have vindicated an easy valour, he preferred to make a friend. I wish that we should next drink to a fairer and a more tender foe. She found me in prison; she cheered me with a priceless sympathy; what she has done since, I know she has done in mercy, and I only pray—I dare scarce hope—her mercy may prove to have been merciful. And I wish to conjoin with these, for the first, and perhaps the last time, the health—and I fear I may already say the memory—of one who has fought, not always without success, against the soldiers of your nation; but who came here, vanquished already, only to be vanquished again by the loyal hand of the one, by the unforgettable eyes of the other."

It is to be feared I may have lent at times a certain resonancy to my voice; it is to be feared that Ronald, who was none the better for his own hospitality, may have set down his glass with something of a clang. Whatever may have been the cause, at least, I had scarce finished my compliment before we were aware of a thump upon the ceiling overhead. It was to be thought some very solid body had descended to the floor from the level (possibly) of a bed. I have never seen consternation painted in more lively colours than on the faces of my hosts. It was proposed to smuggle me forth into the garden, or to conceal my form under a horsehair sofa which stood against the wall. For the first expedient, as was now plain by the approaching footsteps, there was no longer time; from the second I recoiled with indignation.

"My dear creatures," said I, "let us die, but do not let us be ridiculous."

The words were still upon my lips when the door opened and my friend of the gold eyeglass appeared, a memorable figure, on the threshold. In one hand she bore a bedroom candlestick; in the other, with the steadiness of a dragoon, a horse-pistol. She was wound about in shawls, which did not wholly conceal the candid fabric of her nightdress, and surmounted by a nightcap of portentous architecture. Thus accoutred, she made her entrance; laid down the candle and pistol, as no longer called for; looked about the room with a silence more eloquent than oaths; and then, in a thrilling voice—" To whom have I the pleasure? " she said, addressing me with a ghost of a bow.

" Madam, I am charmed, I am sure," said I. " The story is a little long; and our meeting, however welcome, was for the moment entirely unexpected by myself. I am sure——" but here I found I was quite sure of nothing, and tried again. " I have the honour," I began, and found I had the honour to be only exceedingly confused. With that, I threw myself outright upon her mercy. " Madam, I must be more frank with you," I resumed. " You have already proved your charity and compassion for the French prisoners—I am one of these; and if my appearance be not too much changed, you may even yet recognise in me that *Oddity* who had the good fortune more than once to make you smile."

Still gazing upon me through her glass, she uttered an uncompromising grunt; and then, turning to her niece— " Flora," said she, " how comes he here? "

The culprits poured out for a while an antiphony of explanations, which died out at last in a miserable silence.

" I think at least you might have told your aunt," she snorted.

" Madam," I interposed, " they were about to do so. It is my fault if it be not done already. But I made it my prayer that your slumbers might be respected, and this necessary formula of my presentation should be delayed until to-morrow in the morning."

The old lady regarded me with undissembled incredulity, to which I was able to find no better repartee than a profound and I trust graceful reverence.

" French prisoners are very well in their place," she said, " but I cannot see that their place is in my private dining-room."

" Madam," said I, " I hope it may be said without offence, but (except the Castle of Edinburgh) I cannot think upon the spot from which I would so readily be absent."

At this, to my relief, I thought I could perceive a vestige of a smile to steal upon that iron countenance and to be bitten immediately in.

"And if it is a fair question, what do they call ye?" she asked.

" At your service, the Vicomte Anne de St.-Yves," said I.

" Mosha the Viscount," said she, " I am afraid you do us plain people a great deal too much honour."

Three is Company, Four None

"My dear lady," said I, "let us be serious for a moment. What was I to do? Where was I to go? And how can you be angry with these benevolent children who took pity on one so unfortunate as myself? Your humble servant is no such terrific adventurer that you should come out against him with horse-pistol and "—smiling—"bedroom candlesticks. It is but a young gentleman in extreme distress, hunted upon every side, and asking no more than to escape from his pursuers. I know your character, I read it in your face "—the heart trembled in my body as I said these daring words. "There are unhappy English prisoners in France at this day, perhaps at this hour. Perhaps at this hour they kneel as I do; they take the hand of her who might conceal and assist them; they press it to their lips as I do——"

"Here, here!" cried the old lady, breaking from my solicitations. "Behave yourself before folk! Saw ever any one the match of that? And on earth, my dears, what are we to do with him?"

"Pack him off, my dear lady," said I: "pack off the impudent fellow double-quick! And if it may be, and if your good heart allows it, help him a little on the way he has to go."

"What's this pie?" she cried stridently. "Where is this pie from, Flora?"

No answer was vouchsafed by my unfortunate and (I may say) extinct accomplices.

"Is that my port?" she pursued. "Hough! Will somebody give me a glass of my port wine?"

I made haste to serve her.

She looked at me over the rim with an extraordinary expression. "I hope ye liked it?" said she.

"It is even a magnificent wine," said I.

"Aweel, it was my father laid it down," said she. "There were few knew more about port wine than my father, God rest him!" She settled herself in a chair with an alarming air of resolution. "And so there is some particular direction that you wish to go in?" said she.

"Oh," said I, following her example, "I am by no means such a vagrant as you suppose. I have good friends, if I could get to them, for which all I want is to be once clear of Scotland; and I have money for the road." And I produced my bundle.

"English bank-notes?" she said. "That's not very handy

for Scotland. It's been some fool of an Englishman that's given you these, I'm thinking. How much is it?"

"I declare to heaven I never thought to count!" I exclaimed. "But that is soon remedied."

And I counted out ten notes of ten pound each, all in the name of Abraham Newlands, and five bills of country bankers for as many guineas.

"One hundred and twenty-six pound five," cried the old lady. "And you carry such a sum about you, and have not so much as counted it! If you are not a thief, you must allow you are very thief-like."

"And yet, madam, the money is legitimately mine," said I.

She took one of the bills and held it up. "Is there any probability, now, that this could be traced?" she asked.

"None, I should suppose; and if it were, it would be no matter," said I. "With your usual penetration, you guessed right. An Englishman brought it me. It reached me, through the hands of his English solicitor, from my great-uncle, the Comte de Kéroual de Saint-Yves, I believe the richest *émigré* in London."

"I can do no more than take your word for it," said she.

"And I trust, madam, not less," said I.

"Well," said she, "at this rate the matter may be feasible. I will cash one of these five-guinea bills, less the exchange, and give you silver and Scots notes to bear you as far as the border. Beyond that, Mosha the Viscount, you will have to depend upon yourself."

I could not but express a civil hesitation as to whether the amount would suffice, in my case, for so long a journey.

"Ay," said she, "but you havenae heard me out. For if you are not too fine a gentleman to travel with a pair of drovers, I believe I have found the very thing, and the Lord forgive me for a treasonable old wife! There are a couple stopping up by with the shepherd-man at the farm; to-morrow they will take the road for England, probably by skreigh of day—and in my opinion you had best be travelling with the stots," said she.

"For Heaven's sake do not suppose me to be so effeminate a character!" I cried. "An old soldier of Napoleon is certainly beyond suspicion. But, dear lady, to what end? and how is the society of these excellent gentlemen supposed to help me?"

Three is Company, Four None

" My dear sir," said she, " you do not at all understand your own predicament, and must just leave your matters in the hands of those who do. I dare say you have never even heard tell of the drove-roads or the drovers; and I am certainly not going to sit up all night to explain it to you. Suffice it, that it is me who is arranging this affair—the more shame to me!—and that is the way ye have to go. Ronald," she continued, " away up-by to the shepherds; rowst them out of their beds, and make it perfectly distinct that Sim is not to leave till he has seen *me*."

Ronald was nothing loath to escape from his aunt's neighbourhood, and left the room and the cottage with a silent expedition that was more like flight than mere obedience. Meanwhile the old lady turned to her niece.

" And I would like to know what we are to do with him the night! " she cried.

" Ronald and I meant to put him in the hen-house," said the encrimsoned Flora.

" And I can tell you he is to go to no such place," replied the aunt. " Hen-house, indeed! If a guest he is to be, he shall sleep in no mortal hen-house. Your room is the most fit, I think, if he will consent to occupy it on so great a suddenty. And as for you, Flora, you shall sleep with me."

I could not help admiring the prudence and tact of this old dowager, and of course it was not for me to make objections. Ere I well knew how, I was alone with a flat candlestick, which is not the most sympathetic of companions, and stood studying the snuff in a frame of mind between triumph and chagrin. All had gone well with my flight: the masterful lady who had arrogated to herself the arrangement of the details gave me every confidence; and I saw myself already arriving at my uncle's door. But, alas! it was another story with my love affair. I had seen and spoken with her alone; I had ventured boldly; I had been not ill received; I had seen her change colour, had enjoyed the undissembled kindness of her eyes; and now, in a moment, down comes upon the scene that apocalyptic figure with the nightcap and the horse-pistol, and with the very wind of her coming behold me separated from my love! Gratitude and admiration contended in my breast with the extreme of natural rancour. My appearance in her house at past midnight had an air (I could not disguise it from myself) that was insolent and underhand, and could not but minister to the worst suspicions. And the old lady had taken it well. Her generosity was no more to be called in question than her courage, and I was afraid that her intelligence would be found to match. Certainly, Miss Flora had to support some shrewd looks, and certainly she had been troubled. I could see but the one way before me: to profit by an excellent bed, to try to sleep soon, to be stirring early, and to hope for some renewed occasion in the morning. To have said so much and yet to say no more, to go out into the world upon so half-hearted a parting, was more than I could accept.

It is my belief that the benevolent fiend sat up all night to baulk me. She was at my bedside with a candle long ere day, roused me, laid out for me a damnable misfit of clothes, and bade me pack my own (which were wholly unsuited to the journey) in a bundle. Sore grudging, I arrayed myself in a suit of some country fabric, as delicate as sackcloth and about as becoming as a shroud; and, on coming forth, found the dragon had prepared for me a hearty breakfast. She took the head of the table, poured out the tea, and entertained me as I ate with a great deal of good sense and a conspicuous lack of charm. How often did I not regret the change—how often compare her, and condemn her in the comparison, with her charming niece! But if my entertainer was not beautiful, she had certainly been busy in my interest. Already she was in communication with my destined fellow-travellers; and the device on which she had struck appeared entirely suitable. I was a young Englishman who had outrun the constable; warrants were out against me in Scotland, and it had become needful I should pass the border without loss of time, and privately.

"I have given a very good account of you," said she, "which I hope you may justify. I told them there was nothing against you beyond the fact that you were put to the haw (if that is the right word) for debt."

"I pray God you have the expression incorrectly, ma'am," said I. "I do not give myself out for a person easily alarmed; but you must admit there is something barbarous and mediæval in the sound well qualified to startle a poor foreigner."

"It is the name of a process in Scots Law, and need alarm no honest man," said she. "But you are a very idle-minded

Three is Company, Four None

young gentleman; you must still have your joke, I see: I only hope you will have no cause to regret it."

"I pray you not to suppose, because I speak lightly, that I do not feel deeply," said I. "Your kindness has quite conquered me; I lay myself at your disposition, I beg you to believe, with real tenderness; I pray you to consider me from henceforth as the most devoted of your friends."

"Well, well," she said, "here comes your devoted friend the drover. I'm thinking he will be eager for the road; and I will not be easy myself till I see you well off the premises, and the dishes washed, before my servant-woman wakes. Praise God, we have gotten one that is a treasure at the sleeping!"

The morning was already beginning to be blue in the trees of the garden, and to put to shame the candle by which I had breakfasted. The lady rose from table, and I had no choice but to follow her example. All the time I was beating my brains for any means by which I should be able to get a word apart with Flora, or find the time to write her a billet. The windows had been open while I breakfasted, I suppose to ventilate the room from any traces of my passage there; and, Master Ronald appearing on the front lawn, my ogre leaned forth to address him.

"Ronald," she said, "wasn't that Sim that went by the wall?"

I snatched my advantage. Right at her back there was pen, ink, and paper laid out. I wrote: "I love you"; and before I had time to write more, or so much as to blot what I had written, I was again under the guns of the gold eyeglasses.

"It's time," she began; and then, as she observed my occupation, "Umph!" she broke off. "Ye have something to write?" she demanded.

"Some notes, madam," said I, bowing with alacrity.

"Notes," she said; "or a note?"

"There is doubtless some *finesse* of the English language that I do not comprehend," said I.

"I'll contrive, however, to make my meaning very plain to ye, Mosha le Viscount," she continued. "I suppose you desire to be considered a gentleman?"

"Can you doubt it, madam?" said I.

"I doubt it very much, at least, whether you go to the

right way about it," she said. " You have come here to me, I cannot very well say how; I think you will admit you owe me some thanks, if it was only for the breakfast I made ye. But what are you to me? A waif young man, not so far to seek for looks and manners, with some English notes in your pocket and a price upon your head. I am a lady; I have been your hostess, with however little will; and I desire that this random acquaintance of yours with my family will cease and determine."

I believe I must have coloured. " Madam," said I, " the notes are of no importance; and your least pleasure ought certainly to be my law. You have felt, and you have been pleased to express, a doubt of me. I tear them up." Which you may be sure I did thoroughly.

" There's a good lad! " said the dragon, and immediately led the way to the front lawn.

The brother and sister were both waiting us here, and, as well as I could make out in the imperfect light, bore every appearance of having passed through a rather cruel experience. Ronald seemed ashamed to so much as catch my eye in the presence of his aunt, and was the picture of embarrassment. As for Flora, she had scarce the time to cast me one look before the dragon took her by the arm, and began to march across the garden in the extreme first glimmer of the dawn without exchanging speech. Ronald and I followed in equal silence.

There was a door in that same high wall on the top of which I had sat perched no longer gone than yesterday morning. This the old lady set open with a key; and on the other side we were aware of a rough-looking, thick-set man, leaning with his arms (through which was passed a formidable staff) on a dry-stone dyke. Him the old lady immediately addressed.

" Sim," said she, " this is the young gentleman."

Sim replied with an inarticulate grumble of sound, and a movement of one arm and his head, which did duty for a salutation.

" Now, Mr. St. Ives," said the old lady, " it's high time for you to be taking the road. But first of all let me give the change of your five-guinea bill. Here are four pounds of it in British Linen notes, and the balance in small silver, less sixpence. Some charge a shilling, I believe, but I have given you the benefit of the doubt. See and guide it with all the sense that you possess."

The Drovers

"And here, Mr. St. Ives," said Flora, speaking for the first time, "is a plaid which you will find quite necessary on so rough a journey. I hope you will take it from the hands of a Scotch friend," she added, and her voice trembled.

"Genuine holly: I cut it myself," said Ronald, and gave me as good a cudgel as a man could wish for in a row.

The formality of these gifts, and the waiting figure of the drover, told me loudly that I must be gone. I dropped on one knee and bade farewell to the aunt, kissing her hand. I did the like—but with how different a passion!—to her niece; as for the boy, I took him to my arms and embraced him with a cordiality that seemed to strike him speechless. "Farewell!" and "Farewell!" I said. "I shall never forget my friends. Keep me sometimes in memory. Farewell!" With that I turned my back and began to walk away; and had scarce done so, when I heard the door in the high wall close behind me. Of course this was the aunt's doing; and of course, if I know anything of human character, she would not let me go without some tart expressions. I declare, even if I had heard them, I should not have minded in the least, for I was quite persuaded that, whatever admirers I might be leaving behind me in Swanston Cottage, the aunt was not the least sincere.

CHAPTER X

THE DROVERS

It took me a little effort to come abreast of my new companion; for though he walked with an ugly roll and no great appearance of speed, he could cover the ground at a good rate when he wanted to. Each looked at the other: I with natural curiosity, he with a great appearance of distaste. I have heard since that his heart was entirely set against me; he had seen me kneel to the ladies, and diagnosed me for a "gesterin' eediot."

"So, ye're for England, are ye?" said he.

I told him yes.

"Weel, there's waur places, I believe," was his reply; and he relapsed into a silence which was not broken during a quarter of an hour of steady walking.

This interval brought us to the foot of a bare green valley,

which wound upwards and backwards among the hills. A
little stream came down the midst and made a succession of
clear pools; near by the lowest of which I was aware of a
drove of shaggy cattle, and a man who seemed the very
counterpart of Mr. Sim making a breakfast upon bread and
cheese. This second drover (whose name proved to be
Candlish) rose on our approach.

" Here's a mannie that's to gang through with us," said
Sim. " It was the auld wife, Gilchrist, wanted it."

" Aweel, aweel," said the other; and presently, remembering his manners, and looking on me with a solemn grin,
" A fine day! " says he.

I agreed with him, and asked him how he did.

" Brawly," was the reply; and without further civilities,
the pair proceeded to get the cattle under way. This, as
well as almost all the herding, was the work of a pair of
comely and intelligent dogs, directed by Sim or Candlish in
little more than monosyllables. Presently we were ascending
the side of the mountain by a rude green track, whose presence
I had not hitherto observed. A continual sound of munching
and the crying of a great quantity of moor birds accompanied
our progress, which the deliberate pace and perennial appetite
of the cattle rendered wearisomely slow. In the midst my
two conductors marched in a contented silence that I could
not but admire. The more I looked at them, the more I was
impressed by their absurd resemblance to each other. They
were dressed in the same coarse homespun, carried similar
sticks, were equally begrimed about the nose with snuff, and
each wound in an identical plaid of what is called the shepherd's tartan. In a back view they might be described as
indistinguishable; and even from the front they were much
alike. An incredible coincidence of humours augmented the
impression. Thrice and four times I attempted to pave the
way for some exchange of thought, sentiment, or—at the least of
it—human words. An *Ay* or an *Nhm* was the sole return, and
the topic died on the hill-side without echo. I can never deny
that I was chagrined; and when, after a little more walking,
Sim turned towards me and offered me a ram's horn of snuff,
with the question " Do ye use it? " I answered, with some
animation, " Faith, sir, I would use pepper to introduce a
little cordiality." But even this sally failed to reach, or at
least failed to soften, my companions.

The Drovers

At this rate we came to the summit of a ridge, and saw the track descend in front of us abruptly into a desert vale, about a league in length, and closed at the farther end by no less barren hill-tops. Upon this point of vantage Sim came to a halt, took off his hat, and mopped his brow.

" Weel," he said, " here we're at the top o' Howden."

" The top o' Howden, sure eneuch," said Candlish.

" Mr. St. Ivey, are ye dry? " said the first.

" Now, really," said I, " is not this Satan reproving sin? "

" What ails ye, man? " said he. " I'm offerin' ye a dram."

" Oh, if it be anything to drink," said I, " I am as dry as my neighbour."

Whereupon Sim produced from the corner of his plaid a black bottle, and we all drank and pledged each other. I found these gentlemen followed upon such occasions an invariable etiquette, which you may be certain I made haste to imitate. Each wiped his mouth with the back of his left hand, held up the bottle in his right, remarked with emphasis, " Here's to ye! " and swallowed as much of the spirit as his fancy prompted. This little ceremony, which was the nearest thing to manners I could perceive in either of my companions, was repeated at becoming intervals, generally after an ascent. Occasionally we shared a mouthful of ewe-milk cheese and an inglorious form of bread, which I understood (but am far from engaging my honour on the point) to be called " shearer's bannock." And that may be said to have concluded our whole active intercourse for the first day.

I had the more occasion to remark the extraordinarily desolate nature of that country, through which the drove-road continued, hour after hour and even day after day, to wind. A continual succession of insignificant shaggy hills, divided by the course of ten thousand brooks, through which we had to wade, or by the side of which we encamped at night; infinite perspectives of heather, infinite quantities of moor-fowl; here and there, by a stream side, small and pretty clumps of willows or the silver birch; here and there, the ruins of ancient and inconsiderable fortresses—made the unchanging characters of the scene. Occasionally, but only in the distance, we could perceive the smoke of a small town or of an isolated farmhouse or cottage on the moors; more often, a flock of sheep and its attendant shepherd, or a rude field of agriculture perhaps not yet harvested. With these alleviations, we might almost be said to pass through an unbroken desert—sure, one of the most impoverished in Europe; and when I recalled to mind that we were yet but a few leagues from the chief city (where the law courts sat every day with a press of business, soldiers garrisoned the castle, and men of admitted parts were carrying on the practice of letters and the investigations of science), it gave me a singular view of that poor, barren, and yet illustrious country through which I travelled. Still more, perhaps, did it commend the wisdom of Miss Gilchrist in sending me with these uncouth companions and by this unfrequented path.

My itinerary is by no means clear to me; the names and distances I never clearly knew, and have now wholly forgotten; and this is the more to be regretted as there is no doubt that, in the course of those days, I must have passed and camped among sites which have been rendered illustrious by the pen of Walter Scott. Nay, more, I am of opinion that I was still more favoured by fortune, and have actually met and spoken with that inimitable author. Our encounter was of a tall, stoutish, elderly gentleman, a little grizzled, and of a rugged but cheerful and engaging countenance. He sat on a hill pony, wrapped in a plaid over his green coat, and was accompanied by a horse-woman, his daughter, a young lady of the most charming appearance. They overtook us on a stretch of heath, reined up as they came alongside, and accompanied us for perhaps a quarter of an hour before they galloped off again across the hillsides to our left. Great was my amazement to find the unconquerable Mr. Sim thaw immediately on the accost of this strange gentleman, who hailed him with a ready familiarity, proceeded at once to discuss with him the trade of droving and the prices of cattle, and did not disdain to take a pinch from the inevitable ram's horn. Presently I was aware that the stranger's eye was directed on myself; and there ensued a conversation, some of which I could not help overhearing at the time, and the rest have pieced together more or less plausibly from the report of Sim.

"Surely that must be an *amateur drover* ye have gotten there?" the gentleman seems to have asked.

Sim replied, I was a young gentleman that had a reason of his own to travel privately.

"Well, well, ye must tell me nothing of that. I am in the

The Drovers

law, you know, and *tace* is the Latin for a candle," answered
the gentleman. "But I hope it's nothing bad."

Sim told him it was no more than debt.

"O Lord, if that be all!" cried the gentleman; and turning
to myself, "Well, sir," he added, "I understand you are
taking a tramp through our forest here for the pleasure of the
thing?"

"Why, yes, sir," said I; "and I must say I am very well
entertained."

"I envy you," said he. "I have jogged many miles of it
myself when I was younger. My youth lies buried about
here under every heather-bush, like the soul of the licentiate
Lucius. But you should have a guide. The pleasure of
this country is much in the legends, which grow as plentiful
as blackberries." And directing my attention to a little
fragment of a broken wall no greater than a tombstone, he
told me for an example a story of its earlier inhabitants.
Years after it chanced that I was one day diverting myself
with a Waverley Novel, when what should I come upon but
the identical narrative of my green-coated gentleman upon
the moors! In a moment the scene, the tones of his voice,
his northern accent, and the very aspect of the earth and sky
and temperature of the weather, flashed back into my mind
with the reality of dreams. The unknown in the green coat
had been the Great Unknown! I had met Scott; I had
heard a story from his lips; I should have been able to write,
to claim acquaintance, to tell him that his legend still tingled
in my ears. But the discovery came too late, and the great
man had already succumbed under the load of his honours
and misfortunes.

Presently, after giving us a cigar apiece, Scott bade us
farewell and disappeared with his daughter over the hills.
And when I applied to Sim for information, his answer of
"The Shirra, man! A'body kens the Shirra!" told me,
unfortunately, nothing.

A more considerable adventure falls to be related. We
were now near the border. We had travelled for long upon
the track beaten and browsed by a million herds, our predecessors, and had seen no vestige of that traffic which had
created it. It was early in the morning when we at last perceived, drawing near to the drove-road, but still at a distance
of about half a league, a second caravan, similar to but larger

than our own. The liveliest excitement was at once exhibited
by both my comrades. They climbed hillocks, they studied
the approaching drove from under their hand, they consulted
each other with an appearance of alarm that seemed to me
extraordinary. I had learned by this time that their stand-
off manners implied, at least, no active enmity; and I made
bold to ask them what was wrong.

" Bad yins," was Sim's emphatic answer.

All day the dogs were kept unsparingly on the alert, and
the drove pushed forward at a very unusual and seemingly
unwelcome speed. All day Sim and Candlish, with a more
than ordinary expenditure both of snuff and of words, continued to debate the position. It seems that they had
recognised two of our neighbours on the road—one Faa, and
another by the name of Gillies. Whether there was an old
feud between them still unsettled I could never learn; but
Sim and Candlish were prepared for every degree of fraud or
violence at their hands. Candlish repeatedly congratulated
himself on having left " the watch at home with the mistress ";
and Sim perpetually brandished his cudgel, and cursed his ill-
fortune that it should be sprung.

" I willna care a damn to gie the daashed scoon'rel a fair
clout wi' it," he said. " The daashed thing micht come
sindry in ma hand."

" Well, gentlemen," said I, " suppose they do come on,
I think we can give a very good account of them." And I
made my piece of holly, Ronald's gift, the value of which I
now appreciated, sing about my head.

" Ay, man? Are ye stench? " inquired Sim, with a gleam
of approval in his wooden countenance.

The same evening, somewhat wearied with our day-long
expedition, we encamped on a little verdant mound, from
the midst of which there welled a spring of clear water scarce
great enough to wash the hands in. We had made our meal
and lain down, but were not yet asleep, when a growl from
one of the collies set us on the alert. All three sat up, and on
a second impulse all lay down again, but now with our cudgels
ready. A man must be an alien and an outlaw, an old soldier
and a young man in the bargain, to take adventure easily.
With no idea as to the rights of the quarrel or the probable
consequences of the encounter, I was as ready to take part with
my two drovers, as ever to fall in line on the morning of a

The Drovers

battle. Presently there leaped three men out of the heather; we had scarce time to get to our feet before we were assailed; and in a moment each one of us was engaged with an adversary whom the deepening twilight scarce permitted him to see. How the battle sped in other quarters I am in no position to describe. The rogue that fell to my share was exceedingly agile and expert with his weapon; had and held me at a disadvantage from the first assault; forced me to give ground continually, and at last, in mere self-defence, to let him have the point. It struck him in the throat, and he went down like a ninepin and moved no more.

It seemed this was the signal for the engagement to be discontinued. The other combatants separated at once; our foes were suffered, without molestation, to lift up and bear away their fallen comrade; so that I perceived this sort of war to be not wholly without laws of chivalry, and perhaps rather to partake of the character of a tournament than of a battle *à outrance*. There was no doubt, at least, that I was supposed to have pushed the affair too seriously. Our friends the enemy removed their wounded companion with undisguised consternation; and they were no sooner over the top of the brae than Sim and Candlish roused up their wearied drove and set forth on a night march.

" I'm thinking Faa's unco bad," said the one.

" Ay," said the other, " he lookit dooms gash."

" He did that," said the first.

And their weary silence fell upon them again.

Presently Sim turned to me. " Ye're unco ready with the stick," said he.

" Too ready, I'm afraid," said I. " I am afraid Mr. Faa (if that be his name) has got his gruel."

" Weel, I wouldnae wonder," replied Sim.

" And what is likely to happen? " I inquired.

" Aweel," said Sim, snuffing profoundly, " if I were to offer an opeenion, it would not be conscientious. For the plain fac' is, Mr. St. Ivy, that I div not ken. We have had crackit heids—and rowth of them—ere now; and we have had a broken leg or maybe twa; and the like of that we drover bodies make a kind of a practice like to keep among oursel's. But a corp we have none of us ever had to deal with, and I could set nae leemit to what Gillies micht consider proper in the affair. Forbye that, he would be in

St. Ives

raither a hobble himsel', if he was to gang hame wantin' Faa. Folk are awfu' throng with their questions, and parteecularly when they're no wantit."

" That's a fac," said Candlish.

I considered this prospect ruefully; and then making the best of it, " Upon all which accounts," said I, " the best will be to get across the border and there separate. If you are troubled, you can very truly put the blame upon your late companion; and if I am pursued, I must just try to keep out of the way."

" Mr. St. Ivy," said Sim, with something resembling enthusiasm, " no' a word mair! I have met in wi' mony kinds o' gentry ere now; I hae seen o' them that was the tae thing, and I hae seen o' them that was the tither; but the wale of a gentleman like you I have no sae very frequently seen the bate of."

Our night march was accordingly pursued with unremitting diligence. The stars paled, the east whitened, and we were still, both dogs and men, toiling after the wearied cattle. Again and again Sim and Candlish lamented the necessity: it was " fair ruin on the bestial," they declared; but the thought of a judge and a scaffold hunted them ever forward. I myself was not so much to be pitied. All that night, and during the whole of the little that remained before us of our conjunct journey, I enjoyed a new pleasure, the reward of my prowess, in the now loosened tongue of Mr. Sim. Candlish was still obdurately taciturn: it was the man's nature; but Sim, having finally appraised and approved me, displayed without reticence a rather garrulous habit of mind and a pretty talent for narration. The pair were old and close companions, co-existing in these endless moors in a brotherhood of silence such as I have heard attributed to the trappers of the west. It seems absurd to mention love in connection with so ugly and snuffy a couple; at least, their trust was absolute; and they entertained a surprising admiration for each other's qualities; Candlish exclaiming that Sim was " grand company ! " and Sim frequently assuring me in an aside that for " a rale, auld, stench bitch, there was nae the bate of Candlish in braid Scotland." The two dogs appeared to be entirely included in this family compact, and I remarked that their exploits and traits of character were constantly and minutely observed by the two masters. Dog stories particularly abounded with them; and not only the dogs of the present but those of the past contributed their quota. " But that was naething," Sim would begin: " there was a herd in Manar, they ca'd him Tweedie—ye'll mind Tweedie, Can'lish?" " Fine, that!" said Candlish. " Aweel, Tweedie had a dog——" The story I have forgotten; I dare say it was dull, and I suspect it was not true; but indeed, my travels with the drovers had rendered me indulgent, and perhaps even credulous, in the matter of dog stories. Beautiful, indefatigable beings! as I saw them at the end of a long day's journey frisking, barking, bounding, striking attitudes, slanting a bushy tail, manifestly playing to the spectator's eye, manifestly rejoicing in their grace and beauty—and turned to observe Sim and Candlish unornamentally plodding in the rear with the plaids about their bowed shoulders and the drop at their snuffy nose—I thought I would rather claim kinship with the dogs than with the men! My sympathy was unreturned; in their eyes I was a creature light as air; and they would scarce spare me the time for a perfunctory caress or perhaps a hasty lap of the wet tongue, ere they went back again in sedulous attendance on those dingy deities, their masters—and their masters, as like as not, damning their stupidity.

Altogether the last hours of our tramp were infinitely the most agreeable to me, and I believe to all of us; and by the time we came to separate, there had grown up a certain familiarity and mutual esteem that made the parting harder. It took place about four of the afternoon on a bare hill-side from which I could see the ribbon of the great north road, henceforth to be my conductor. I asked what was to pay.

" Naething," replied Sim.

" What in the name of folly is this?" I exclaimed. " You have led me, you have fed me, you have filled me full of whisky, and now you will take nothing!"

" Ye see we indentit for that," replied Sim.

" Indented?" I repeated; " what does the man mean?"

" Mr. St. Ivy," said Sim, " this is a matter entirely between Candlish and me and the auld wife, Gilchrist. You had naething to say to it; weel, ye can have naething to do with it, then."

" My good man," said I, " I can allow myself to be placed

in no such ridiculous position. Mrs. Gilchrist is nothing to me, and I refuse to be her debtor."

" I dinna exactly see what way ye're gaun to help it," observed my drover.

" By paying you here and now," said I.

" There's aye twa to a bargain, Mr. St. Ives," said he.

" You mean that you will not take it? " said I.

" There or thereabout," said he. " Forbye, that it would set ye a heap better to keep your siller for them you awe it to. Ye're young, Mr. St. Ivy, and thoughtless; but its my belief that, wi' care and circumspection, ye may yet do credit to yoursel'. But just you bear this in mind: that him that *awes* siller should never *gie* siller."

Well, what was there to say? I accepted his rebuke, and bidding the pair farewell, set off alone upon my southward way.

" Mr. St. Ivy," was the last word of Sim, " I was never muckle ta'en up in Englishry; but I think that I really ought to say that ye seem to me to have the makings of quite a decent lad."

CHAPTER XI

THE GREAT NORTH ROAD

It chanced that as I went down the hill these last words of my friend the drover echoed not unfruitfully in my head. I had never told these men the least particulars as to my race or fortune, as it was a part, and the best part, of their civility to ask no questions; yet they had dubbed me without hesitation English. Some strangeness in the accent they had doubtless thus explained. And it occurred to me, that if I could pass in Scotland for an Englishman, I might be able to reverse the process and pass in England for a Scot. I thought, if I was pushed to it, I could make a struggle to imitate the brogue; after my experience with Candlish and Sim, I had a rich provision of outlandish words at my command; and I felt I could tell the tale of Tweedie's dog so as to deceive a native. At the same time, I was afraid my name of St. Ives was scarcely suitable; till I remembered there was a town so called in the province of Cornwall, thought I might yet be glad to claim it for my place of origin, and decided for a Cornish family and a Scots education.

The Great North Road

For a trade, as I was equally ignorant of all, and as the most innocent might at any moment be the means of my exposure, it was best to pretend to none. And I dubbed myself a young gentleman of a sufficient fortune and an idle, curious habit of mind, rambling the country at my own charges, in quest of health, information, and merry adventures.

At Newcastle, which was the first town I reached, I completed my preparations for the part, before going to the inn, by the purchase of a knapsack and a pair of leathern gaiters. My plaid I continued to wear from sentiment. It was warm, useful to sleep in if I were again benighted, and I had discovered it to be not unbecoming for a man of gallant carriage. Thus equipped, I supported my character of the light-hearted pedestrian not amiss. Surprise was indeed expressed that I should have selected such a season of the year; but I pleaded some delays of business, and smilingly claimed to be an eccentric. The devil was in it, I would say, if any season of the year was not good enough for me; I was not made of sugar, I was no mollycoddle to be afraid of an ill-aired bed or a sprinkle of snow; and I would knock upon the table with my fist and call for t'other bottle, like the noisy and free-hearted young gentleman I was. It was my policy (if I may so express myself) to talk much and say little. At the inn tables, the country, the state of the roads, the business interest of those who sat down with me, and the course of public events, afforded me a considerable field in which I might discourse at large and still communicate no information about myself. There was no one with less air of reticence; I plunged into my company up to the neck; and I had a long cock-and-bull story of an aunt of mine which must have convinced the most suspicious of my innocence. "What!" they would have said, "that young ass to be concealing anything! Why, he has deafened me with an aunt of his until my head aches. He only wants you should give him a line, and he would tell you his whole descent from Adam downward, and his whole private fortune to the last shilling." A responsible solid fellow was even so much moved by pity for my inexperience as to give me a word or two of good advice: that I was but a young man after all—I had at this time a deceptive air of youth that made me easily pass for one-and-twenty, and was, in the circumstances, worth a fortune—that the company at inns was very mingled, that I should do well to be more care-

ful, and the like; to all which I made answer that I meant
no harm myself and expected none from others, or the devil
was in it. " You are one of those d——d prudent fellows
that I could never abide with," said I. " You are the kind
of man that has a long head. That's all the world, my dear
sir: the long-heads and the short-horns! Now, I am a short-
horn." " I doubt," says he, " that you will not go very far
without getting sheared." I offered to bet with him on that,
and he made off, shaking his head.

But my particular delight was to enlarge on politics and
the war. None damned the French like me; none was more
bitter against the Americans. And when the north-bound
mail arrived, crowned with holly, and the coachman and
guard hoarse with shouting victory, I went even so far as to
entertain the company to a bowl of punch, which I com-
pounded myself with no illiberal hand, and doled out to such
sentiments as the following:—

" Our glorious victory on the Nivelle! " " Lord Wellington, God bless him! and may victory ever attend upon his
arms! " and, " Soult, poor devil! and may he catch it again
to the same tune! "

Never was oratory more applauded to the echo—never
any one was more of the popular man than I. I promise
you, we made a night of it. Some of the company supported each other, with the assistance of boots, to their re-
spective bed-chambers, while the rest slept on the field of
glory where we had left them; and at the breakfast table the
next morning there was an extraordinary assemblage of red
eyes and shaking fists. I observed patriotism to burn much
lower by daylight. Let no one blame me for insensibility to
the reverses of France! God knows how my heart raged.
How I longed to fall on that herd of swine and knock their
heads together in the moment of their revelry! But you are
to consider my own situation and its necessities; also a certain lightheartedness, eminently Gallic, which forms a leading
trait in my character, and leads me to throw myself into new
circumstances with the spirit of a schoolboy. It is possible
that I sometimes allowed this impish humour to carry me
further than good taste approves: and I was certainly
punished for it once.

This was in the episcopal city of Durham. We sat down,
a considerable company, to dinner, most of us fine old vatted

The Great North Road

English tories of that class which is often so enthusiastic as to be inarticulate. I took and held the lead from the beginning; and the talk having turned on the French in the Peninsula, I gave them authentic details (on the authority of a cousin of mine, an ensign) of certain cannibal orgies in Galicia, in which no less a person than General Caffarelli had taken a part. I always disliked that commander, who once ordered me under arrest for insubordination; and it is possible that a spice of vengeance added to the rigour of my picture. I have forgotten the details; no doubt they were high-coloured. No doubt I rejoiced to fool these jolter-heads; and no doubt the sense of security that I drunk from their dull, gasping faces encouraged me to proceed extremely far. And for my sins, there was one silent little man at table who took my story at the true value. It was from no sense of humour, to which he was quite dead. It was from no particular intelligence, for he had not any. The bond of sympathy, of all things in the world, had rendered him clairvoyant.

Dinner was no sooner done than I strolled forth into the streets with some design of viewing the cathedral; and the little man was silently at my heels. A few doors from the inn, in a dark place of the street, I was aware of a touch on my arm, turned suddenly, and found him looking up at me with eyes pathetically bright.

" I beg your pardon, sir; but that story of yours was particularly rich. He—he! Particularly racy," said he. " I tell you, sir, I took you wholly! I *smoked* you! I believe you and I, sir, if we had a chance to talk, would find we had a good many opinions in common. Here is the ' Blue Bell,' a very comfortable place. They draw good ale, sir. Would you be so condescending as to share a pot with me? "

There was something so ambiguous and secret in the little man's perpetual signalling, that I confess my curiosity was much aroused. Blaming myself, even as I did so, for the indiscretion, I embraced his proposal, and we were soon face to face over a tankard of mulled ale. He lowered his voice to the least attenuation of a whisper.

" Here, sir," said he, " is to the Great Man. I think you take me? No? " He leaned forward till our noses touched. " Here is to the Emperor! " said he.

I was extremely embarrassed, and, in spite of the creature's innocent appearance, more than half alarmed. I thought him too ingenious, and, indeed, too daring for a spy. Yet if he were honest he must be a man of extraordinary indiscretion, and therefore very unfit to be encouraged by an escaped prisoner. I took a half course, accordingly—accepted his toast in silence, and drank it without enthusiasm.

He proceeded to abound in the praises of Napoleon, such as I had never heard in France, or at least only on the lips of officials paid to offer them.

" And this Caffarelli, now," he pursued; " he is a splendid fellow, too, is he not? I have not heard vastly much of him myself. No details, sir—no details! We labour under huge difficulties here as to unbiassed information."

" I believe I have heard the same complaint in other countries," I could not help remarking. " But as to Caffarelli, he is neither lame nor blind, he has two legs and a nose in the middle of his face. And I care as much about him as you care for the dead body of Mr. Perceval! "

He studied me with glowing eyes.

" You cannot deceive me! " he cried. " You have served under him. You are a Frenchman! I hold by the hand, at last, one of that noble race, the pioneers of the glorious principles of liberty and brotherhood. Hush! No, it is all right. I thought there had been somebody at the door. In this wretched, enslaved country we dare not even call our souls our own. The spy and the hangman, sir—the spy and the hangman! And yet there is a candle burning, too. The good leaven is working, sir—working underneath. Even in this town there are a few brave spirits, who meet every Wednesday. You must stay over a day or so, and join us. We do not use this house. Another, and a quieter. They draw fine ale, however—fair, mild ale. You will find yourself among friends, among brothers. You will hear some very daring sentiments expressed! " he cried, expanding his small chest. " Monarchy, Christianity—all the trappings of a bloated past — the Free Confraternity of Durham and Tyneside deride."

Here was a devil of a prospect for a gentleman whose whole design was to avoid observation! The Free Confraternity had no charms for me; daring sentiments were no part of my baggage; and I tried, instead, a little cold water.

" You seem to forget, sir, that my Emperor has re-established Christianity," I observed.

The Great North Road

" Ah, sir, but that was policy! " he exclaimed. " You do not understand Napoleon. I have followed his whole career. I can explain his policy from first to last. Now for instance in the Peninsula, on which you were so very amusing, if you will come to a friend's house who has a map of Spain, I can make the whole course of the war quite clear to you, I venture to say, in half-an-hour."

This was intolerable. Of the two extremes, I found I preferred the British tory; and, making an appointment for the morrow, I pleaded sudden headache, escaped to the inn, packed my knapsack, and fled, about nine at night, from this accursed neighbourhood. It was cold, starry, and clear, and the road dry, with a touch of frost. For all that, I had not the smallest intention to make a long stage of it; and about ten o'clock, spying on the right-hand side of the way the lighted windows of an alehouse, I determined to bait there for the night.

It was against my principle, which was to frequent only the dearest inns; and the misadventure that befell me was sufficient to make me more particular in the future. A large company was assembled in the parlour, which was heavy with clouds of tobacco smoke, and brightly lighted up by a roaring fire of coal. Hard by the chimney stood a vacant chair in what I thought an enviable situation, whether for warmth or the pleasure of society; and I was about to take it, when the nearest of the company stopped me with his hand.

" Beg thy pardon, sir," said he; " but that there chair belongs to a British soldier."

A chorus of voices enforced and explained. It was one of Lord Wellington's heroes. He had been wounded under Rowland Hill. He was Colbourne's right-hand man. In short, this favoured individual appeared to have served in every separate corps, and under every individual general in the Peninsula. Of course I apologised. I had not known. The devil was in it if a soldier had not a right to the best in England. And with that sentiment, which was loudly applauded, I found a corner of a bench, and awaited, with some hopes of entertainment, the return of the hero. He proved, of course, to be a private soldier. I say of course, because no officer could possibly enjoy such heights of popularity. He had been wounded before San Sebastian, and still wore his arm in a sling. What was a great deal worse for him, every

87

member of the company had been plying him with drink. His honest yokel's countenance blazed as if with fever, his eyes were glazed and looked the two ways, and his feet stumbled as, amidst a murmur of applause, he returned to the midst of his admirers.

Two minutes afterwards I was again posting in the dark along the highway; to explain which sudden movement of retreat I must trouble the reader with a reminiscence of my services.

I lay one night with the out-pickets in Castile. We were in close touch with the enemy; the usual orders had been issued against smoking, fires, and talk, and both armies lay as quiet as mice, when I saw the English sentinel opposite making a signal by holding up his musket. I repeated it, and we both crept together in the dry bed of a stream, which made the demarcation of the armies. It was wine he wanted, of which we had a good provision, and the English had quite run out. He gave me the money, and I, as was the custom, left him my firelock in pledge, and set off for the canteen. When I returned with a skin of wine, behold, it had pleased some uneasy devil of an English officer to withdraw the outposts! Here was a situation with a vengeance, and I looked for nothing but ridicule in the present and punishment in the future. Doubtless our officers winked pretty hard at this interchange of courtesies, but doubtless it would be impossible to wink at so gross a fault, or rather so pitiable a misadventure as mine; and you are to conceive me wandering in the plains of Castile, benighted, charged with a wine-skin for which I had no use, and with no knowledge whatever of the whereabouts of my musket, beyond that it was somewhere in my Lord Wellington's army. But my Englishman was either a very honest fellow, or else extremely thirsty, and at last contrived to advertise me of his new position. Now, the English sentry in Castile, and the wounded hero in the Durham public-house, were one and the same person; and if he had been a little less drunk, or myself less lively in getting away, the travels of M. St. Ives might have come to an untimely end.

I suppose this woke me up; it stirred in me besides a spirit of opposition, and in spite of cold, darkness, the highwaymen and the footpads, I determined to walk right on till breakfast-time: a happy resolution, which enabled me to

The Great North Road

observe one of those traits of manners which at once depict a country and condemn it. It was near midnight when I saw, a great way ahead of me, the light of many torches; presently after, the sound of wheels reached me, and the slow tread of feet, and soon I had joined myself to the rear of a sordid, silent, and lugubrious procession, such as we see in dreams. Close on a hundred persons marched by torchlight in unbroken silence; in their midst a cart, and in the cart on an inclined platform, the dead body of a man—the centre-piece of this solemnity, the hero whose obsequies we were come forth at this unusual hour to celebrate. It was but a plain, dingy old fellow of fifty or sixty, his throat cut, his shirt turned over as though to show the wound. Blue trousers and brown socks completed his attire, if we can talk so of the dead. He had a horrid look of a waxwork. In the tossing of the lights he seemed to make faces and mouths at us, to frown, and to be at times upon the point of speech. The cart, with this shabby and tragic freight, and surrounded by its silent escort and bright torches, continued for some distance to creak along the high-road, and I to follow it in amazement, which was soon exchanged for horror. At the corner of a lane the procession stopped, and, as the torches ranged themselves along the hedgerow-side, I became aware of a grave dug in the midst of the thoroughfare, and a provision of quicklime piled in the ditch. The cart was backed to the margin, the body slung off the platform and dumped into the grave with an irreverent roughness. A sharpened stake had hitherto served it for a pillow. It was now withdrawn, held in its place by several volunteers, and a fellow with a heavy mallet (the sound of which still haunts me at night) drove it home through the bosom of the corpse. The hole was filled with quicklime, and the bystanders, as if relieved of some oppression, broke at once into a sound of whispered speech.

My shirt stuck to me, my heart had almost ceased beating, and I found my tongue with difficulty.

" I beg your pardon," I gasped to a neighbour, " what is this? what has he done? is it allowed? "

" Why, where do you come from? " replied the man.

" I am a traveller, sir," said I, " and a total stranger in this part of the country. I had lost my way when I saw your torches, and came by chance on this—this incredible scene. Who was the man? "

"A suicide," said he. "Ay, he was a bad one, was Johnnie Green."

It appeared this was a wretch who had committed many barbarous murders, and being at last upon the point of discovery fell of his own hand. And the nightmare at the crossroads was the regular punishment, according to the laws of England, for an act which the Romans honoured as a virtue! Whenever an Englishman begins to prate of civilisation (as, indeed, it's a defect they are rather prone to), I hear the measured blows of a mallet, see the bystanders crowd with torches about the grave, smile a little to myself in conscious superiority—and take a thimbleful of brandy for the stomach's sake.

I believe it must have been at my next stage, for I remember going to bed extremely early, that I came to the model of a good old-fashioned English inn, and was attended on by the picture of a pretty chambermaid. We had a good many pleasant passages as she waited table or warmed my bed for me with a devil of a brass warming-pan, fully larger than herself; and as she was no less pert than she was pretty, she may be said to have given rather better than she took. I cannot tell why (unless it were for the sake of her saucy eyes), but I made her my confidante, told her I was attached to a young lady in Scotland, and received the encouragement of her sympathy, mingled and connected with a fair amount of rustic wit. While I slept the down-mail stopped for supper; it chanced that one of the passengers left behind a copy of the *Edinburgh Courant*, and the next morning my pretty chambermaid set the paper before me at breakfast, with the remark that there was some news from my lady-love. I took it eagerly, hoping to find some further word of our escape, in which I was disappointed; and I was about to lay it down, when my eye fell on a paragraph immediately concerning me. Faa was in hospital, grievously sick, and warrants were out for the arrest of Sim and Candlish. These two men had shown themselves very loyal to me. This trouble emerging, the least I could do was to be guided by a similar loyalty to them. Suppose my visit to my uncle crowned with some success, and my finances re-established, I determined I should immediately return to Edinburgh, put their case in the hands of a good lawyer, and await events. So my mind was very lightly made up to what proved a mighty serious matter.

I Follow a Covered Cart

Candlish and Sim were all very well in their way, and I do sincerely trust I should have been at some pains to help them, had there been nothing else. But in truth my heart and my eyes were set on quite another matter, and I received the news of their tribulation almost with joy. That is never a bad wind that blows where we want to go, and you may be sure there was nothing unwelcome in a circumstance that carried me back to Edinburgh and Flora. From that hour I began to indulge myself with the making of imaginary scenes and interviews, in which I confounded the aunt, flattered Ronald, and now in the witty, now in the sentimental manner, declared my love and received the assurance of its return. By means of this exercise my resolution daily grew stronger, until at last I had piled together such a mass of obstinacy as it would have taken a cataclysm of nature to subvert.

"Yes," said I to the chambermaid, "here is news of my lady-love indeed, and very good news too."

All that day, in the teeth of a keen winter wind, I hugged myself in my plaid, and it was as though her arms were flung around me.

CHAPTER XII

I FOLLOW A COVERED CART NEARLY TO MY DESTINATION

AT last I began to draw near, by reasonable stages, to the neighbourhood of Wakefield; and the name of Mr. Burchell Fenn came to the top in my memory. This was the gentleman (the reader may remember) who made a trade of forwarding the escape of French prisoners. How he did so: whether he had a signboard, *Escapes forwarded, apply within;* what he charged for his services, or whether they were gratuitous and charitable, were all matters of which I was at once ignorant and extremely curious. Thanks to my proficiency in English, and Mr. Romaine's bank-notes, I was getting on swimmingly without him; but the trouble was that I could not be easy till I had come to the bottom of these mysteries, and it was my difficulty that I knew nothing of him beyond the name. I knew not his trade beyond that of Forwarder of Escapes—whether he lived in town or country, whether he were rich or poor, nor by what kind of address I was to gain his confidence. It would have a very bad appearance to go along the highwayside asking after a man of whom I could give so scanty an account; and I should look like a fool, indeed, if I were to present myself at his door and find the police in occupation! The interest of the conundrum, however, tempted me, and I turned aside from my direct road to pass by Wakefield; kept my ears pricked, as I went, for any mention of his name, and relied for the rest on my good fortune. If Luck (who must certainly be feminine) favoured me as far as to throw me in the man's way, I should owe the lady a candle; if not, I could very readily console myself. In this experimental humour, and with so little to help me, it was a miracle that I should have brought my enterprise to a good end; and there are several saints in the calendar who might be happy to exchange with St. Ives!

I had slept that night in a good inn at Wakefield, made my breakfast by candle-light with the passengers of an up coach, and set off in a very ill temper with myself and my surroundings. It was still early; the air raw and cold; the sun low, and soon to disappear under a vast canopy of rain-clouds that had begun to assemble in the north-west, and from that quarter invaded the whole width of the heaven. Already the rain fell in crystal rods; already the whole face of the country sounded with the discharge of drains and ditches; and I looked forward to a day of downpour and the hell of wet clothes, in which particular I am as dainty as a cat. At a corner of the road, and by the last glint of the drowning sun, I spied a covered cart, of a kind that I thought I had never seen before, preceding me at the foot's pace of jaded horses. Anything is interesting to a pedestrian that can help him to forget the miseries of a day of rain; and I bettered my pace and gradually overtook the vehicle.

The nearer I came, the more it puzzled me. It was much such a cart as I am told the calico printers use, mounted on two wheels, and furnished with a seat in front for the driver. The interior closed with a door, and was of a bigness to contain a good load of calico, or (at a pinch and if it were necessary) four or five persons. But, indeed, if human beings were meant to travel there, they had my pity! They must travel in the dark, for there was no sign of a window; and they would be shaken all the way like a phial of doctor's stuff, for the cart was not only ungainly to look at—it was besides

I Follow a Covered Cart

very imperfectly balanced on the one pair of wheels, and pitched unconscionably. Altogether, if I had any glancing idea that the cart was really a carriage, I had soon dismissed it, but I was still inquisitive as to what it should contain and where it had come from. Wheels and horses were splashed with many different colours of mud, as though they had come far and across a considerable diversity of country. The driver continually and vainly plied his whip. It seemed to follow they had made a long, perhaps an all-night, stage; and that the driver, at that early hour of a little after eight in the morning, already felt himself belated. I looked for the name of the proprietor on the shaft, and started outright. Fortune had favoured the careless: it was Burchell Fenn!

"A wet morning, my man," said I.

The driver, a loutish fellow, shock-headed and turnip-faced, returned not a word to my salutation, but savagely flogged his horses. The tired animals, who could scarce put the one foot before the other, paid no attention to his cruelty; and I continued without effort to maintain my position alongside, smiling to myself at the futility of his attempts, and at the same time pricked with curiosity as to why he made them. I made no such formidable a figure as that a man should flee when I accosted him; and my conscience not being entirely clear, I was more accustomed to be uneasy myself than to see others timid. Presently he desisted, and put back his whip in the holster with the air of a man vanquished.

"So you would run away from me?" said I. "Come, come, that's not English."

"Beg pardon, master: no offence meant," he said, touching his hat.

"And none taken!" cried I. "All I desire is a little gaiety by the way."

I understood him to say he didn't "take with gaiety."

"Then I will try you with something else," said I. "Oh, I can be all things to all men, like the apostle! I dare to say I have travelled with heavier fellows than you in my time, and done famously well with them. Are you going home?"

"Yes, I'm a goin' home, I am," he said.

"A very fortunate circumstance for me!" said I. "At this rate we shall see a good deal of each other, going the same way; and, now I come to think of it, why should you not give me a cast? There is room beside you on the bench."

With a sudden snatch, he carried the cart two yards into the roadway. The horses plunged and came to a stop. " No, you don't!" he said, menacing me with the whip. " None o' that with me."

" None of what? " said I. " I asked you for a lift, but I have no idea of taking one by force."

" Well, I've got to take care of the cart and 'orses, I have," says he. " I don't take up with no runagate vagabones, you see, else."

" I ought to thank you for your touching confidence," said I, approaching carelessly nearer as I spoke. " But I admit the road is solitary hereabouts, and no doubt an accident soon happens. Little fear of anything of the kind with you! I like you for it, like your prudence, like that pastoral shyness of disposition. But why not put it out of my power to hurt? Why not open the door and bestow me here in the box, or whatever you please to call it? " And I laid my hand demonstratively on the body of the cart.

He had been timorous before; but at this, he seemed to lose the power of speech a moment, and stared at me in a perfect enthusiasm of fear.

" Why not? " I continued. " The idea is good. I should be safe in there if I were the monster Williams himself. The great thing is to have me under lock and key. For it does lock; it is locked now," said I, trying the door. " *A propos*, what have you for a cargo? It must be precious."

He found not a word to answer.

Rat-tat-tat, I went upon the door like a well-drilled footman. " Any one at home! " I said, and stopped to listen.

There came out of the interior a stifled sneeze, the first of an uncontrollable paroxysm; another followed immediately on the heels of it; and then the driver turned with an oath, laid the lash upon the horses with so much energy that they found their heels again, and the whole equipage fled down the road at a gallop.

At the first sound of the sneeze, I had started back like a man shot. The next moment, a great light broke on my mind, and I understood. Here was the secret of Fenn's trade; this was how he forwarded the escape of prisoners, hawking them by night about the country in his covered cart.

I Follow a Covered Cart

There had been Frenchmen close to me; he who had just sneezed was my countryman, my comrade, perhaps already my friend! I took to my heels in pursuit. " Hold hard! " I shouted. " Stop! It's all right! Stop! " But the driver only turned a white face on me for a moment, and redoubled his efforts, bending forward, plying his whip and crying to his horses; these lay themselves down to the gallop and beat the highway with flying hoofs; and the cart bounded after them among the ruts and fled in a halo of rain and spattering mud. But a minute since, and it had been trundling along like a lame cow; and now it was off as though drawn by Apollo's coursers. There is no telling what a man can do, until you frighten him!

It was as much as I could do myself, though I ran valiantly, to maintain my distance; and that (since I knew my countrymen so near) was become a chief point with me. A hundred yards farther on the cart whipped out of the high-road into a lane embowered with leafless trees, and became lost to view. When I saw it next, the driver had increased his advantage considerably, but all danger was at an end, and the horses had again declined into a hobbling walk. Persuaded that they could not escape me, I took my time, and recovered my breath as I followed them.

Presently the lane twisted at right angles, and showed me a gate and the beginning of a gravel sweep; and a little after, as I continued to advance, a red brick house about seventy years old, in a fine style of architecture, and presenting a front of many windows to a lawn and garden. Behind, I could see outhouses and the peaked roofs of stacks; and I judged that a manor-house had in some way declined to be the residence of a tenant-farmer, careless alike of appearances and substantial comfort. The marks of neglect were visible on every side, in flower-bushes straggling beyond the borders, in the ill-kept turf, and in the broken windows that were incongruously patched with paper or stuffed with rags. A thicket of trees, mostly evergreen, fenced the place round and secluded it from the eyes of prying neighbours. As I came in view of it, on that melancholy winter's morning, in the deluge of the falling rain, and with the wind that now rose in occasional gusts and hooted over the old chimneys, the cart had already drawn up at the front-door steps, and the driver was already in earnest discourse with Mr. Burchell

Fenn. He was standing with his hands behind his back—a man of a gross, misbegotten face and body, dewlapped like a bull and red as a harvest moon; and in his jockey cap, blue coat and top boots, he had much the air of a good, solid tenant-farmer.

The pair continued to speak as I came up the approach, but received me at last in a sort of goggling silence. I had my hat in my hand.

" I have the pleasure of addressing Mr. Burchell Fenn? " said I.

" The same, sir," replied Mr. Fenn, taking off his jockey cap in answer to my civility, but with the distant look and the tardy movements of one who continues to think of something else. " And who may you be? " he asked.

" I shall tell you afterwards," said I. " Suffice it, in the meantime, that I come on business."

He seemed to digest my answer laboriously, his mouth gaping, his little eyes never straying from my face.

" Suffer me to point out to you, sir," I resumed, " that this is a devil of a wet morning; and that the chimney corner, and possibly a glass of something hot, are clearly indicated."

Indeed, the rain was now grown to be a deluge; the gutters of the house roared, the air was filled with the continuous, strident crash. The stolidity of his face, on which the rain streamed, was far from reassuring me. On the contrary, I was aware of a distinct qualm of apprehension, which was not at all lessened by a view of the driver, craning from his perch to observe us with the expression of a fascinated bird. So we stood silent, when the prisoner again began to sneeze from the body of the cart, and at the sound, prompt as a transformation, the driver had whipped up his horses and was shambling off round the corner of the house, and Mr. Fenn, recovering his wits with a gulp, had turned to the door behind him.

" Come in, come in, sir," he said. " I beg your pardon, sir; the lock goes a trifle hard."

Indeed, it took him a surprising time to open the door, which was not only locked on the outside, but the lock seemed rebellious from disuse; and when at last he stood back and motioned me to enter before him, I was greeted on the threshold by that peculiar and convincing sound of the rain echoing over empty chambers. The entrance-hall, in which I now

I Follow a Covered Cart

found myself was of a good size and good proportions; potted plants occupied the corners; the paved floor was soiled with muddy footprints and encumbered with straw; on a mahogany hall-table, which was the only furniture, a candle had been stuck and suffered to burn down—plainly a long while ago, for the gutterings were green with mould. My mind, under these new impressions, worked with unusual vivacity. I was here shut off with Fenn and his hireling in a deserted house, a neglected garden, and a wood of evergreens: the most eligible theatre for a deed of darkness. There came to me a vision of two flagstones raised in the hall-floor, and the driver putting in the rainy afternoon over my grave, and the prospect displeased me extremely. I felt I had carried my pleasantry as far as was safe; I must lose no time in declaring my true character, and I was even choosing the words in which I was to begin, when the hall-door was slammed-to behind me with a bang, and I turned, dropping my stick as I did so, in time—and not any more than time—to save my life.

The surprise of the onslaught and the huge weight of my assailant gave him the advantage. He had a pistol in his right hand of a portentous size, which it took me all my strength to keep deflected. With his left arm he strained me to his bosom, so that I thought I must be crushed, or stifled. His mouth was open, his face crimson, and he panted aloud with hard animal sounds. The affair was as brief as it was hot and sudden. The potations which had swelled and bloated his carcase had already weakened the springs of energy. One more huge effort, that came near to overpower me, and in which the pistol happily exploded, and I felt his grasp slacken and weakness come on his joints; his legs succumbed under his weight, and he grovelled on his knees on the stone floor. " Spare me! " he gasped.

I had not only been abominably frightened; I was shocked besides: my delicacy was in arms, like a lady to whom violence should have been offered by a similar monster. I plucked myself from his horrid contact, I snatched the pistol—even discharged, it was a formidable weapon—and menaced him with the butt. " Spare you! " I cried, " you beast! "

His voice died in his fat inwards, but his lips still vehemently framed the same words of supplication. My anger began to pass off, but not all my repugnance; the picture he made revolted me, and I was impatient to be spared the further view of it.

"Here," said I, "stop this performance: it sickens me. I am not going to kill you, do you hear? I have need of you."

A look of relief, that I could almost have called beautiful, dawned on his countenance. "Anything—anything you wish," said he.

Anything is a big word, and his use of it brought me for a moment to a stand. "Why, what do you mean?" I asked. "Do you mean that you will blow the gaff on the whole business?"

He answered me Yes with eager asseverations.

"I know Monsieur de Saint-Yves is in it; it was through his papers we traced you," I said. "Do you consent to make a clean breast of the others?"

"I do—I will!" he cried. "The 'ole crew of 'em; there's good names among 'em. I'll be king's evidence."

"So that all shall hang except yourself? You damned villain!" I broke out. "Understand at once that I am no spy or thief-taker. I am a kinsman of Monsieur de St. Yves—here in his interest. Upon my word, you have put your foot in it prettily, Mr. Burchell Fenn! Come, stand up; don't grovel there. Stand up, you lump of iniquity!"

He scrambled to his feet. He was utterly unmanned, or it might have gone hard with me yet; and I considered him hesitating, as, indeed, there was cause. The man was a double-dyed traitor; he had tried to murder me, and I had first baffled his endeavours and then exposed and insulted him. Was it wise to place myself any longer at his mercy? With his help I should doubtless travel more quickly; doubtless also far less agreeably; and there was everything to show that it would be at a greater risk. In short, I should have washed my hands of him on the spot, but for the temptation of the French officers, whom I knew to be so near, and for whose safety I felt so great and natural an impatience. If I was to see anything of my countrymen, it was clear I had first of all to make my peace with Mr. Fenn; and that was no easy matter. To make friends with any one implies concessions on both sides; and what could I concede? What could I say of him, but that he had proved himself a villain and a fool, and the worse man?

"Well," said I, "here has been rather a poor piece of

I Follow a Covered Cart

business, which I dare say you can have no pleasure in calling to mind; and, to say truth, I would as readily forget it myself. Suppose we try. Take back your pistol, which smells very ill; put it in your pocket or wherever you had it concealed. There! Now let us meet for the first time. Give you good morning, Mr. Fenn! I hope you do very well. I come on the recommendation of my kinsman, the Vicomte de St. Yves."

"Do you mean it?" he cried. "Do you mean you will pass over our little scrimmage?"

"Why, certainly!" said I. "It shows you are a bold fellow, who may be trusted to forget the business when it comes to the point. There is nothing against you in the little scrimmage, unless that your courage is greater than your strength. You are not so young as you once were, that is all."

"And I beg of you, sir, don't betray me to the Vis-count," he pleaded. "I'll not deny but what my 'eart failed me a trifle; but it was only a word, sir, what anybody might have said in the 'eat of the moment, and over with it."

"Certainly," said I. "That is quite my own opinion."

"The way I came to be anxious about the Vis-count," he continued, "is that I believe he might be induced to form a 'asty judgment. And the business, in a pecuniary point of view, is all that I could ask; only trying, sir—very trying. It's making an old man of me before my time. You might have observed yourself, sir, that I 'aven't got the knees I once 'ad. The knees and the breathing, there's where it takes me. But I'm very sure, sir, I address a gentleman as would be the last to make trouble between friends."

"I am sure you do me no more than justice," said I; "and I shall think it quite unnecessary to dwell on any of these passing circumstances in my report to the Vicomte."

"Which you do favour him (if you'll excuse me being so bold as to mention it) exac'ly!" said he. "I should have known you anywheres. May I offer you a pot of 'ome-brewed ale, sir? By your leave! This way, if you please. I am 'eartily grateful—'eartily pleased to be of any service to a gentleman like you, sir, which is related to the Vis-count, and really a fambly of which you might well be proud! Take care of the step, sir. You have good news of 'is 'ealth, I trust? as well as that of Monseer the Count?"

St. Ives

God forgive me! the horrible fellow was still puffing and panting with the fury of his assault, and already he had fallen into an obsequious, wheedling familiarity like that of an old servant,—already he was flattering me on my family connections!

I followed him through the house into the stable-yard, where I observed the driver washing the cart in a shed. He must have heard the explosion of the pistol. He could not choose but hear it: the thing was shaped like a little blunderbuss, charged to the mouth, and made a report like a piece of field artillery. He had heard, he had paid no attention; and now, as we came forth by the back-door, he raised for a moment a pale and tell-tale face that was as direct as a confession. The rascal had expected to see Fenn come forth alone; he was waiting to be called on for that part of sexton, which I had already allotted to him in fancy.

I need not detain the reader very long with any description of my visit to the back-kitchen; of how we mulled our ale there, and mulled it very well; nor of how we sat talking, Fenn like an old, faithful affectionate dependant, and I— well! I myself fallen into a mere admiration of so much impudence, that transcended words, and had very soon conquered animosity. I took a fancy to the man, he was so vast a humbug. I began to see a kind of beauty in him, his *aplomb* was so majestic. I never knew a rogue to cut so fat; his villainy was ample, like his belly, and I could scarce find it in my heart to hold him responsible for either. He was good enough to drop into the autobiographical; telling me how the farm, in spite of the war and the high prices, had proved a disappointment; how there was " a sight of cold, wet land as you come along the 'igh-road "; how the winds and rains and the seasons had been misdirected, it seemed "o' purpose"; how Mrs. Fenn had died—" I lost her coming two year agone; a remarkable fine woman, my old girl, sir! if you'll excuse me," he added, with a burst of humility. In short, he gave me an opportunity of studying John Bull, as I may say, stuffed naked—his greed, his usuriousness, his hypocrisy, his perfidy of the back-stairs, all swelled to the superlative —such as was well worth the little disarray and fluster of our passage in the hall.

I Meet Two of My Countrymen

CHAPTER XIII

I MEET TWO OF MY COUNTRYMEN

As soon as I judged it safe, and that was not before Burchell Fenn had talked himself back into his breath and a complete good humour, I proposed he should introduce me to the French officers, henceforth to become my fellow-passengers. There were two of them, it appeared, and my heart beat as I approached the door. The specimen of Perfidious Albion whom I had just been studying gave me the stronger zest for my fellow-countrymen. I could have embraced them; I could have wept on their necks. And all the time I was going to a disappointment.

It was in a spacious and low room, with an outlook on the court, that I found them bestowed. In the good days of that house the apartment had probably served as a library, for there were traces of shelves along the wainscot. Four or five mattresses lay on the floor in a corner, with a frowsy heap of bedding; near by was a basin and a cube of soap; a rude kitchen table and some deal chairs stood together at the far end; and the room was illuminated by no less than four windows, and warmed by a little, crazy, sidelong grate, propped up with bricks in the vent of a hospitable chimney, in which a pile of coals smoked prodigiously and gave out a few starveling flames. An old, frail, white-haired officer sat in one of the chairs, which he had drawn close to this apology for a fire. He was wrapped in a camlet cloak, of which the collar was turned up, his knees touched the bars, his hands were spread in the very smoke, and yet he shivered for cold. The second—a big, florid, fine animal of a man, whose every gesture labelled him the cock of the walk and the admiration of the ladies—had apparently despaired of the fire, and now strode up and down, sneezing hard, bitterly blowing his nose, and proffering a continual stream of bluster, complaint, and barrack-room oaths.

Fenn showed me in with the brief form of introduction: "Gentlemen all, this here's another fare!" and was gone again at once. The old man gave me but the one glance out of lack-lustre eyes; and even as he looked a shiver took him as sharp as a hiccough. But the other, who represented to admiration the picture of a Beau in a Catarrh, stared at me arrogantly.

" And who are you, sir? " he asked.

I made the military salute to my superiors.

" Champdivers, private, Eighth of the Line," said I.

" Pretty business!" said he. " And you are going on with us? Three in a cart, and a great trolloping private at that! And who is to pay for you, my fine fellow? " he inquired.

" If monsieur comes to that," I answered civilly, " who paid for him? "

" Oh, if you choose to play the wit! " said he,—and began to rail at large upon his destiny, the weather, the cold, the danger and the expense of the escape, and, above all, the cooking of the accursed English. It seemed to annoy him particularly that I should have joined their party. " If you knew what you were doing, thirty thousand millions of pigs! you would keep yourself to yourself! The horses can't drag the cart; the roads are all ruts and swamps. No longer ago than last night the Colonel and I had to march half the way— thunder of God!—half the way to the knees in mud—and I with this infernal cold—and the danger of detection! Happily we met no one: a desert—a real desert—like the whole abominable country! Nothing to eat—no, sir, there is nothing to eat but raw cow and greens boiled in water—nor to drink but Worcestershire sauce! Now I, with my catarrh, I have no appetite; is it not so? Well, if I were in France, I should have a good soup with a crust in it, an omelette, a fowl in rice, a partridge in cabbages—things to tempt me, thunder of God! But here—day of God—what a country! And cold, too! They talk about Russia—this is all the cold I want! And the people—look at them! What a race! Never any handsome men; never any fine officers! "—and he looked down complacently for a moment at his waist—" And the women—what faggots! No, that is one point clear, I cannot stomach the English! "

There was something in this man so antipathetic to me, as sent the mustard into my nose. I can never bear your bucks and dandies, even when they are decent-looking and well dressed; and the Major—for that was his rank—was the image of a flunkey in good luck. Even to be in agreement with him, or to seem to be so, was more than I could make out to endure.

I Meet Two of My Countrymen

" You could scarce be expected to stomach them," said I civilly, " after having just digested your parole."

He whipped round on his heel and turned on me a countenance which I dare say he imagined to be awful; but another fit of sneezing cut him off ere he could come the length of speech.

" I have not tried the dish myself," I took the opportunity to add. " It is said to be unpalatable. Did monsieur find it so? "

With surprising vivacity the Colonel woke from his lethargy. He was between us ere another word could pass.

" Shame, gentlemen! " he said. " Is this a time for Frenchmen and fellow-soldiers to fall out? We are in the midst of our enemies; a quarrel, a loud word, may suffice to plunge us back into irretrievable distress. *Monsieur le Commandant,* you have been gravely offended. I make it my request, I make it my prayer—if need be, I give you my orders—that the matter shall stand by until we come safe to France. Then, if you please, I will serve you in any capacity. And for you, young man, you have shown all the cruelty and carelessness of youth. This gentleman is your superior; he is no longer young "—at which word you are to conceive the major's face. " It is admitted he has broken his parole. I know not his reason, and no more do you. It might be patriotism in this hour of our country's adversity, it might be humanity, necessity; you know not what in the least, and you permit yourself to reflect on his honour. To break parole may be a subject for pity and not derision. I have broken mine—I, a colonel of the Empire. And why? I have been years negotiating my exchange, and it cannot be managed; those who have influence at the Ministry of War continually rush in before me, and I have to wait, and my daughter at home is in a decline. I am going to see my daughter at last, and it is my only concern lest I should have delayed too long. She is ill, and very ill,—at death's door. Nothing is left me but my daughter, my Emperor, and my honour; and I give my honour, blame me for it who dare! "

At this my heart smote me.

" For God's sake," I cried, " think no more of what I have said! A parole? what is a parole against life and death and love? I ask your pardon; this gentleman's also. As long as I shall be with you, you shall not have cause to complain of me again. I pray God you will find your daughter alive and restored."

" That is past praying for," said the Colonel; and immediately the brief fire died out of him, and, returning to the hearth, he relapsed into his former abstraction.

But I was not so easy to compose. The knowledge of the poor gentleman's trouble, and the sight of his face, had filled me with the bitterness of remorse; and I insisted upon shaking hands with the Major (which he did with a very ill grace), and abounded in palinodes and apologies.

" After all," said I, " who am I to talk? I am in the luck to be a private soldier; I have no parole to give or to keep; once I am over the rampart, I am as free as air. I beg you to believe that I regret from my soul the use of these ungenerous expressions. Allow me . . . Is there no way in this damned house to attract attention? Where is this fellow Fenn?"

I ran to one of the windows and threw it open. Fenn, who was at the moment passing below in the court, cast up his arms like one in despair, called to me to keep back, plunged into the house, and appeared next moment in the doorway of the chamber.

" Oh, sir!" says he, " keep away from those there windows. A body might see you from the back lane."

" It is registered," said I. " Henceforward I will be a mouse for precaution and a ghost for invisibility. But in the meantime, for God's sake, fetch us a bottle of brandy! Your room is as damp as the bottom of a well, and these gentlemen are perishing of cold."

So soon as I had paid him (for everything, I found, must be paid in advance), I turned my attention to the fire, and whether because I threw greater energy into the business, or because the coals were now warmed and the time ripe, I soon started a blaze that made the chimney roar again. The shine of it, in that dark, rainy day, seemed to reanimate the Colonel like a blink of sun. With the outburst of the flames, besides, a draught was established, which immediately delivered us from the plague of smoke; and by the time Fenn returned, carrying a bottle under his arm and a single tumbler in his hand, there was already an air of gaiety in the room that did the heart good.

I poured out some of the brandy.

I Meet Two of My Countrymen

" Colonel," said I, " I am a young man and a private soldier. I have not been long in this room, and already I have shown the petulance that belongs to the one character and the ill manners that you may look for in the other. Have the humanity to pass these slips over, and honour me so far as to accept this glass."

" My lad," says he, waking up and blinking at me with an air of suspicion, " are you sure you can afford it? "

I assured him I could.

" I thank you, then: I am very cold." He took the glass out, and a little colour came in his face. " I thank you again," said he. " It goes to the heart."

The Major, when I motioned him to help himself, did so with a good deal of liberality; continued to do so for the rest of the morning, now with some sort of apology, now with none at all; and the bottle began to look foolish before dinner was served. It was such a meal as he had himself predicted: beef, greens, potatoes, mustard in a teacup, and beer in a brown jug that was all over hounds, horses, and hunters, with a fox at the far end and a gigantic John Bull—for all the world like Fenn — sitting in the midst in a bob-wig and smoking tobacco. The beer was a good brew, but not good enough for the Major; he laced it with brandy—for his cold, he said; and in this curative design the remainder of the bottle ebbed away. He called my attention repeatedly to the circumstance; helped me pointedly to the dregs, threw the bottle in the air and played tricks with it; and, at last, having exhausted his ingenuity, and seeing me remain quite blind to every hint, he ordered and paid for another himself.

As for the Colonel, he ate nothing, sat sunk in a muse, and only awoke occasionally to a sense of where he was, and what he was supposed to be doing. On each of these occasions he showed a gratitude and kind courtesy that endeared him to me beyond expression. " Champdivers, my lad, your health! " he would say. " The Major and I had a very arduous march last night, and I positively thought I should have eaten nothing, but your fortunate idea of the brandy has made quite a new man of me—quite a new man." And he would fall to with a great air of heartiness, cut himself a mouthful, and, before he had swallowed it, would have forgotten his dinner, his company, the place where he then was, and the escape he was engaged on, and become absorbed in the vision of a sick-room and a dying girl in France. The pathos of this continual preoccupation, in a man so old, sick, and over-weary, and whom I looked upon as a mere bundle of dying bones and death-pains, put me wholly from my victuals: it seemed there was an element of sin, a kind of rude bravado of youth, in the mere relishing of food at the same table with this tragic father; and though I was well enough used to the coarse, plain diet of the English, I ate scarce more than himself. Dinner was hardly over before he succumbed to a lethargic sleep; lying on one of the mattresses with his limbs relaxed, and his breath seemingly suspended—the very image of dissolution.

This left the Major and myself alone at the table. You must not suppose our *tête-à-tête* was long, but it was a lively period while it lasted. He drank like a fish or an Englishman; shouted, beat the table, roared out songs, quarrelled, made it up again, and at last tried to throw the dinner-plates through the window, a feat of which he was at that time quite incapable. For a party of fugitives, condemned to the most rigorous discretion, there was never seen so noisy a carnival; and through it all the Colonel continued to sleep like a child. Seeing the Major so well advanced, and no retreat possible, I made a fair wind of a foul one, keeping his glass full, pushing him with toasts; and sooner than I could have dared to hope, he became drowsy and incoherent. With the wrong-headedness of all such sots, he would not be persuaded to lie down upon one of the mattresses until I had stretched myself upon another. But the comedy was soon over; soon he slept the sleep of the just, and snored like a military music; and I might get up again and face (as best I could) the excessive tedium of the afternoon.

I had passed the night before in a good bed; I was denied the resource of slumber; and there was nothing open for me but to pace the apartment, maintain the fire, and brood on my position. I compared yesterday and to-day—the safety, comfort, jollity, open-air exercise and pleasant roadside inns of the one, with the tedium, anxiety, and discomfort of the other. I remembered that I was in the hands of Fenn, who could not be more false—though he might be more vindictive —than I fancied him. I looked forward to nights of pitching in the covered cart, and days of monotony in I knew not what hiding-places; and my heart failed me, and I was in two minds whether to slink off ere it was too late, and return to my former solitary way of travel. But the Colonel stood in the path. I had not seen much of him; but already I judged him a man of a childlike nature—with that sort of innocence and courtesy that, I think, is only to be found in old soldiers or old priests—and broken with years and sorrow. I could not turn my back on his distress; could not leave him alone with the selfish trooper who snored on the next mattress. "Champdivers, my lad, your health!" said a voice in my ear, and stopped me—and there are few things I am more glad of in the retrospect than that it did.

It must have been about four in the afternoon—at least the rain had taken off, and the sun was setting with some wintry pomp—when the current of my reflections was effectually changed by the arrival of two visitors in a gig. They were farmers of the neighbourhood, I suppose—big, burly fellows in greatcoats and top-boots, mightily flushed with liquor when they arrived, and, before they left, inimitably drunk. They stayed long in the kitchen with Burchell, drinking, shouting, singing, and keeping it up; and the sound of their merry minstrelsy kept me a kind of company. The night fell, and the shine of the fire brightened and blinked on the panelled wall. Our illuminated windows must have been visible not only from the back lane of which Fenn had spoken, but from the court where the farmers' gig awaited them. In the far end of the firelit room lay my companions, the one silent, the other clamorously noisy, the images of death and drunkenness. Little wonder if I were tempted to join in the choruses below, and sometimes could hardly refrain from laughter, and sometimes, I believe, from tears—so unmitigated was the tedium, so cruel the suspense, of this period.

At last, about six at night, I should fancy, the noisy minstrels appeared in the court, headed by Fenn with a lantern, and knocking together as they came. The visitors clambered noisily into the gig, one of them shook the reins, and they were snatched out of sight and hearing with a suddenness that partook of the nature of prodigy. I am well aware there is a Providence for drunken men, that holds the reins for them and presides over their troubles; doubtless he had his work cut out for him with this particular gigful! Fenn rescued his toes with an ejaculation from under the departing wheels, and turned at once with uncertain steps and devious lantern to the far end of the court. There, through the open doors of a coach-house, the shock-headed lad was already to be seen drawing forth the covered cart. If I wished any private talk with our host, it must be now or never.

Accordingly I groped my way downstairs, and came to him as he looked on at and lighted the harnessing of the horses.

"The hour approaches when we have to part," said I; "and I shall be obliged if you will tell your servant to drop me at the nearest point for Dunstable. I am determined to go so far with our friends, Colonel X and Major Y, but my business is peremptory, and it takes me to the neighbourhood of Dunstable."

Orders were given to my satisfaction, with an obsequiousness that seemed only inflamed by his potations.

CHAPTER XIV

TRAVELS OF THE COVERED CART

My companions were aroused with difficulty: the Colonel, poor old gentleman, to a sort of permanent dream, in which you could say of him only that he was very deaf and anxiously polite; the Major still maudlin drunk. We had a dish of tea by the fireside, and then issued like criminals into the scathing cold of the night. For the weather had in the meantime changed. Upon the cessation of the rain, a strict frost had succeeded. The moon, being young, was already near the zenith when we started, glittered everywhere on sheets of ice, and sparkled in ten thousand icicles. A more unpromising night for a journey it was hard to conceive. But in the course of the afternoon the horses had been well roughed; and King (for such was the name of the shock-headed lad) was very positive that he could drive us without misadventure. He was as good as his word; indeed, despite a gawky air, he was simply invaluable in his present employment, showing marked sagacity in all that concerned the care of horses, and guiding us by one short cut after another for days, and without a fault.

The interior of that engine of torture, the covered cart,

was fitted with a bench, on which we took our places; the
door was shut; in a moment, the night closed upon us solid
and stifling; and we felt that we were being driven carefully
out of the courtyard. Careful was the word all night, and it
was an alleviation of our miseries that we did not often enjoy.
In general, as we were driven the better part of the night and
day, often at a pretty quick pace and always through a
labyrinth of the most infamous country lanes and by-roads,
we were so bruised upon the bench, so dashed against the
top and sides of the cart, that we reached the end of a stage
in a truly pitiable case, sometimes flung ourselves down
without the formality of eating, made but one sleep of it until
the hour of departure returned, and were only properly
awakened by the first jolt of the renewed journey. There
were interruptions at times, that we hailed as alleviations.
At times the cart was bogged, once it was upset, and we must
alight and lend the driver the assistance of our arms; at
times, too (as on the occasion when I had first encountered it),
the horses gave out, and we had to trail alongside in mud or
frost until the first peep of daylight, or the approach to a
hamlet or a high-road, bade us disappear like ghosts into
our prison.

The main roads of England are incomparable for excel-
lence, of a beautiful smoothness, very ingeniously laid down,
and so well kept that in most weathers you could take your
dinner off any part of them without distaste. On them,
to the note of the bugle, the mail did its sixty miles a day;
innumerable chaises whisked after the bobbing post-boys;
or some young blood would flit by in a curricle and
tandem, to the vast delight and danger of the lieges. On
them, the slow-pacing waggons made a music of bells, and
all day long the travellers on horseback and the travellers on
foot (like happy Mr. St. Ives so little a while before!) kept
coming and going, and baiting and gaping at each other,
as though a fair were due, and they were gathering to it from
all England. No, nowhere in the world is travel so great a
pleasure as in that country. But unhappily our one need
was to be secret; and all this rapid and animated picture of
the road swept quite apart from us, as we lumbered up hill
and down dale, under hedge and over stone, among circuitous
by-ways. Only twice did I receive, as it were, a whiff of the
highway. The first reached my ears alone. I might have

been anywhere. I only knew I was walking in the dark night and among ruts, when I heard very far off, over the silent country that surrounded us, the guard's horn wailing its signal to the next post-house for a change of horses. It was like the voice of the day heard in darkness, a voice of the world heard in prison, the note of a cock crowing in the mid-seas—in short, I cannot tell you what it was like, you will have to fancy for yourself—but I could have wept to hear it. Once we were belated: the cattle could hardly crawl, the day was at hand, it was a nipping rigorous morning, King was lashing his horses, I was giving an arm to the old Colonel, and the Major was coughing in our rear. I must suppose that King was a thought careless, being nearly in desperation about his team, and, in spite of the cold morning, breathing hot with his exertions. We came, at last, a little before sunrise, to the summit of a hill, and saw the high-road passing at right angles through an open country of meadows and hedge-row pollards; and not only the York mail, speeding smoothly at a gallop of the four horses, but a post-chaise besides, with the post-boy titupping briskly, and the traveller himself putting his head out of the window, but whether to breathe the dawn, or the better to observe the passage of the mail, I do not know. So that we enjoyed for an instant a picture of free life on the road, in its most luxurious forms of despatch and comfort. And thereafter, with a poignant feeling of contrast in our hearts, we must mount again into our wheeled dungeon.

We came to our stages at all sorts of odd hours, and they were in all kinds of odd places. I may say at once that my first experience was my best. Nowhere again were we so well entertained as at Burchell Fenn's. And this, I suppose, was natural, and indeed inevitable, in so long and secret a journey. The first stop, we lay six hours in a barn standing by itself in a poor, marshy orchard, and packed with hay; to make it more attractive, we were told it had been the scene of an abominable murder, and was now haunted. But the day was beginning to break, and our fatigue was too extreme for visionary terrors. The second or third, we alighted on a barren heath about midnight, built a fire to warm us under the shelter of some thorns, supped like beggars on bread and a piece of cold bacon, and slept like gipsies with our feet to the fire. In the meanwhile,

Travels of the Covered Cart

King was gone with the cart, I know not where, to get a change of horses, and it was late in the dark morning when he returned and we were able to resume our journey. In the middle of another night we came to a stop by an ancient, whitewashed cottage of two stories; a privet hedge surrounded it; the frosty moon shone blankly on the upper windows; but through those of the kitchen the firelight was seen glinting on the roof and reflected from the dishes on the wall. Here, after much hammering on the door, King managed to arouse an old crone from the chimney-corner chair, where she had been dozing in the watch; and we were had in, and entertained with a dish of hot tea. This old lady was an aunt of Burchell Fenn's—and an unwilling partner in his dangerous trade. Though the house stood solitary, and the hour was an unlikely one for any passenger upon the road, King and she conversed in whispers only. There was something dismal, something of the sick-room, in this perpetual, guarded sibilation. The apprehensions of our hostess insensibly communicated themselves to every one present. We ate like mice in a cat's ear; if one of us jingled a teaspoon, all would start; and when the hour came to take the road again, we drew a long breath of relief, and climbed to our places in the covered cart with a positive sense of escape. The most of our meals, however, were taken boldly at hedgerow alehouses, usually at untimely hours of the day, when the clients were in the field or the farmyard at labour. I shall have to tell presently of our last experience of the sort, and how unfortunately it miscarried; but as that was the signal for my separation from my fellow-travellers, I must first finish with them.

I had never any occasion to waver in my first judgment of the Colonel. The old gentleman seemed to me, and still seems in the retrospect, the salt of the earth. I had occasion to see him in the extremes of hardship, hunger, and cold; he was dying, and he looked it; and yet I cannot remember any hasty, harsh, or impatient word to have fallen from his lips. On the contrary, he ever showed himself careful to please; and even if he rambled in his talk, rambled always gently,—like a humane, half-witted old hero, true to his colours to the last. I would not dare to say how often he awoke suddenly from a lethargy, and told us again, as though we had never heard it, the story of how he had earned the cross, how it had been given him by the hand of the Emperor, and of the innocent—and, indeed, foolish—sayings of his daughter when he returned with it on his bosom. He had another anecdote which he was very apt to give, by way of a rebuke, when the Major wearied us beyond endurance with dispraises of the English. This was an account of the *braves gens* with whom he had been boarding. True enough, he was a man so simple and grateful by nature, that the most common civilities were able to touch him to the heart, and would remain written in his memory; but from a thousand inconsiderable but conclusive indications, I gathered that this family had really loved him, and loaded him with kindness. They made a fire in his bedroom, which the sons and daughters tended with their own hands; letters from France were looked for with scarce more eagerness by himself than by these alien sympathisers; when they came, he would read them aloud in the parlour to the assembled family, translating as he went. The Colonel's English was elementary; his daughter not in the least likely to be an amusing correspondent, and, as I conceived these scenes in the parlour, I felt sure the interest centred in the Colonel himself, and I thought I could feel in my own heart that mixture of the ridiculous and the pathetic, the contest of tears and laughter, which must have shaken the bosoms of the family. Their kindness had continued till the end. It appears they were privy to his flight, the camlet cloak had been lined expressly for him, and he was the bearer of a letter from the daughter of the house to his own daughter in Paris. The last evening, when the time came to say good-night, it was tacitly known to all that they were to look upon his face no more. He rose, pleading fatigue, and turned to the daughter, who had been his chief ally: " You will permit me, my dear—to an old and very unhappy soldier—and may God bless you for your goodness! " The girl threw her arms about his neck and sobbed upon his bosom; the lady of the house burst into tears; " *et je vous le jure, le père se mouchait !* " quoth the Colonel, twisting his moustaches with a cavalry air, and at the same time blinking the water from his eyes at the mere recollection.

It was a good thought to me that he had found these friends in captivity; that he had started on this fatal journey from so cordial a farewell. He had broken his parole for his

Travels of the Covered Cart

daughter; that he should ever live to reach her sick-bed, that he could continue to endure to an end the hardships, the crushing fatigue, the savage cold, of our pilgrimage, I had early ceased to hope. I did for him what I was able,— nursed him, kept him covered, watched over his slumbers, sometimes held him in my arms at the rough places of the road. "Champdivers," he once said, "you are like a son to me—like a son." It is good to remember, though at the time it put me on the rack. All was to no purpose. Fast as we were travelling towards France, he was travelling faster still to another destination. Daily he grew weaker and more indifferent. An old rustic accent of Lower Normandy reappeared in his speech, from which it had long been banished, and grew stronger; old words of the *patois*, too: *Ouistreham, matrassé*, and others, the sense of which we were sometimes unable to guess. On the very last day he began again his eternal story of the cross and the Emperor. The Major, who was particularly ill, or at least particularly cross, uttered some angry words of protest. "*Pardonnez-moi, monsieur le commandant, mais c'est pour monsieur,*" said the Colonel: "Monsieur has not yet heard the circumstance, and is good enough to feel an interest." Presently after, however, he began to lose the thread of his narrative; and at last: "*Qué que j'ai ? Je m'embrouille!*" says he, "*Suffit: s'm'a la donné, et Berthe en était bien contente.*" It struck me as the falling of the curtain or the closing of the sepulchre doors.

Sure enough, in but a little while after, he fell into a sleep as gentle as an infant's, which insensibly changed into the sleep of death. I had my arm about his body at the time and remarked nothing, unless it were that he once stretched himself a little, so kindly the end came to that disastrous life. It was only at our evening halt that the Major and I discovered we were travelling alone with the poor clay. That night we stole a spade from a field—I think, near Market Bosworth—and a little farther on, in a wood of young oak trees and by the light of King's lantern, we buried the old soldier of the Empire with both prayers and tears.

We had needs invent Heaven if it had not been revealed to us; there are some things that fall so bitterly ill on this side Time! As for the Major, I have long since forgiven him. He broke the news to the poor Colonel's daughter; I am told he did it kindly; and sure, nobody could have done it without tears! His share of purgatory will be brief; and in this world, as I could not very well praise him, I have suppressed his name. The Colonel's also, for the sake of his parole. *Requiescat.*

CHAPTER XV

THE ADVENTURE OF THE ATTORNEY'S CLERK

I HAVE mentioned our usual course, which was to eat in inconsiderable wayside hostelries, known to King. It was a dangerous business; we went daily under fire to satisfy our appetite, and put our head in the lion's mouth for a piece of bread. Sometimes, to minimise the risk, we would all dismount before we came in view of the house, straggle in severally, and give what orders we pleased, like disconnected strangers. In like manner we departed, to find the cart at an appointed place, some half a mile beyond. The Colonel and the Major had each a word or two of English—God help their pronunciation! But they did well enough to order a rasher and a pot or call a reckoning; and, to say truth, these country folks did not give themselves the pains, and had scarce the knowledge, to be critical.

About nine or ten at night the pains of hunger and cold drove us to an alehouse in the flats of Bedfordshire, not far from Bedford itself. In the inn kitchen was a long, lean, characteristic-looking fellow of perhaps forty, dressed in black. He sat on a settle by the fireside, smoking a long pipe, such as they call a yard of clay. His hat and wig were hanged upon a knob behind him, his head as bald as a bladder of lard, and his expression very shrewd, cantankerous, and inquisitive. He seemed to value himself above his company, to give himself the airs of a man of the world among that rustic herd; which was often no more than his due; being, as I afterwards discovered, an attorney's clerk. I took upon myself the more ungrateful part of arriving last; and by the time I entered on the scene the Major was already served at a side table. Some general conversation must have passed, and I smelled danger in the air. The Major looked flustered, the attorney's clerk triumphant, and three or four peasants in smock-frocks (who sat about the fire to play chorus) had let their pipes go out.

Adventure of Attorney's Clerk

"Give you good-evening, sir!" said the attorney's clerk to me.

"The same to you, sir," said I.

"I think this one will do," quoth the clerk to the yokels with a wink; and then, as soon as I had given my order, "Pray, sir, whither are you bound?" he added.

"Sir," said I, "I am not one of those who speak either of their business or their destination in houses of public entertainment."

"A good answer," said he, "and an excellent principle. Sir, do you speak French?"

"Why, no, sir," said I. "A little Spanish, at your service."

"But you know the French accent, perhaps?" said the clerk.

"Well do I do that!" said I. "The French accent? Why, I believe I can tell a Frenchman in ten words."

"Here is a puzzle for you, then!" he said. "I have no material doubt myself, but some of these gentlemen are more backward. The lack of education, you know. I make bold to say that a man cannot walk, cannot hear, and cannot see, without the blessings of education."

He turned to the Major, whose food plainly stuck in his throat.

"Now, sir," pursued the clerk, "let me have the pleasure to hear your voice again. Where are you going, did you say?"

"Sare, I am go—ing to Lon—don," said the Major.

I could have flung my plate at him to be such an ass, and to have so little a gift of languages where that was the essential.

"What think ye of that?" said the clerk. "Is that French enough?"

"Good God!" cried I, leaping up like one who should suddenly perceive an acquaintance, "is this you, Mr. Dubois? Why, who would have dreamed of encountering you so far from home?" As I spoke, I shook hands with the Major heartily; and turning to our tormentor, "Oh, sir, you may be perfectly reassured! This is a very honest fellow, and a late neighbour of mine in the City of Carlisle."

I thought the attorney looked put out; I little knew the man!

"But he is French," said he, "for all that?"

" Ay, to be sure! " said I.   " A Frenchman of the emigra-
tion! None of your Buonaparté lot. I will warrant his
views of politics to be as sound as your own."

" What is a little strange," said the clerk quietly, " is that
Mr. Dubois should deny it."

I got it fair in the face and took it smiling; but the shock
was rude, and in the course of the next words I contrived to
do what I have rarely done, and make a slip in my English.
I kept my liberty and life by my proficiency all these months,
and for once that I failed, it is not to be supposed that I
would make a public exhibition of the details.   Enough, that
it was a very little error, and one that might have passed
ninety-nine times in a hundred.   But my limb of the law was
as swift to pick it up as though he had been by trade a master
of languages.

" Aha! " cries he; " and you are French, too! Your
tongue betrays you. Two Frenchmen coming into an alehouse, severally and accidentally, not knowing each other,
at ten of the clock at night, in the middle of Bedfordshire?
No, sir, that shall not pass! You are all prisoners escaping,
if you are nothing worse. Consider yourselves under arrest.
I have to trouble you for your papers."

" Where is your warrant, if you come to that? " said I.
" My papers! A likely thing that I would show my papers
on the *ipse dixit* of an unknown fellow in a hedge alehouse! "

" Would you resist the law? " says he.

" Not the law, sir! " said I. " I hope I am too good a
subject for that. But for a nameless fellow with a bald head
and a pair of gingham small-clothes, why certainly! 'Tis
my birthright as an Englishman. Where's *Magna Charta*
else? "

" We will see about that," says he; and then, addressing
the assistants, " where does the constable live? "

" Lord love you, sir! " cried the landlord, " what are you
thinking of? The constable at past ten at night! Why,
he's abed and sleep, and good and drunk two hours agone! "

" Ah that a' be! " came in chorus from the yokels.

The attorney's clerk was put to a stand. He could not
think of force; there was little sign of martial ardour about
the landlord, and the peasants were indifferent—they only
listened, and gaped, and now scratched a head, and now
would get a light to their pipes from the embers on the hearth.

Adventure of Attorney's Clerk

On the other hand, the Major and I put a bold front on the business and defied him, not without some ground of law. In this state of matters he proposed I should go along with him to one Squire Merton, a great man of the neighbourhood, who was in the commission of the peace, the end of his avenue but three lanes away. I told him I would not stir a foot for him if it were to save his soul. Next he proposed I should stay all night where I was, and the constable could see to my affair in the morning, when he was sober. I replied I should go when and where I pleased; that we were lawful travellers in the fear of God and the king, and I for one would suffer myself to be stayed by nobody. At the same time, I was thinking the matter had lasted altogether too long, and I determined to bring it to an end at once.

" See here," said I, getting up, for till now I had remained carelessly seated, " there's only one way to decide a thing like this—only one way that's right *English*—and that's man to man. Take off your coat, sir, and these gentlemen shall see fair play."

At this there came a look in his eye that I could not mistake. His education had been neglected in one essential and eminently British particular: he could not box. No more could I, you may say; but then I had the more impudence—and I had made the proposal.

" He says I'm no Englishman, but the proof of the pudding is the eating of it," I continued. And here I stripped my coat and fell into the proper attitude, which was just about all I knew of this barbarian art. " Why, sir, you seem to me to hang back a little," said I. " Come, I'll meet you; I'll give you an appetiser—though hang me if I can understand the man that wants any enticement to hold up his hands." I drew a banknote out of my fob and tossed it to the landlord. " There are the stakes," said I. " I'll fight you for first blood, since you seem to make so much work about it. If you tap my claret first, there are five guineas for you, and I'll go with you to any squire you choose to mention. If I tap yours, you'll perhaps let on that I'm the better man, and allow me to go about my lawful business at my own time and convenience, by God; is that fair, my lads? " says I, appealing to the company.

" Ay, ay," said the chorus of chawbacons; " he can't say no fairer nor that, he can't. Take off thy coat, master! "

The limb of the law was now on the wrong side of public opinion, and, what heartened me to go on, the position was rapidly changing in our favour. Already the Major was paying his shot to the very indifferent landlord, and I could see the white face of King at the back-door, making signals of haste.

"Oho!" quoth my enemy, "you are as full of doubles as a fox, are you not? But I see through you; I see through and through you. You would change the venue, would you?"

"I may be transparent, sir," says I, "but if you'll do me the favour to stand up, you'll find I can hit dam hard."

"Which is a point, if you will observe, that I had never called in question," said he. "Why, you ignorant clowns," he proceeded, addressing the company, "can't you see the fellow's gulling you before your eyes? Can't you see that he has changed the point upon me? I say he's a French prisoner, and he answers that he can box! What has that to do with it? I would not wonder but what he can dance, too—they're all dancing masters over there. I say, and I stick to it, that he's a Frenchy. He says he isn't. Well then, let him out with his papers, if he has them! If he had, would he not show them? If he had, would he not jump at the idea of going to Squire Merton, a man you all know? Now, you are all plain, straightforward Bedfordshire men, and I wouldn't ask a better lot to appeal to. You're not the kind to be talked over with any French gammon, and he's plenty of that. But let me tell him, he can take his pigs to another market; they'll never do here; they'll never go down in Bedfordshire. Why! look at the man! Look at his feet! Has anybody got a foot in the room like that? See how he stands! do any of you fellows stand like that? Does the landlord, there? Why, he has Frenchman wrote all over him, as big as a signpost!"

This was all very well; and in a different scene I might even have been gratified by his remarks; but I saw clearly, if I were to allow him to talk, he might turn the tables on me altogether. He might not be much of a hand at boxing; but I was much mistaken, or he had studied forensic eloquence in a good school. In this predicament I could think of nothing more ingenious than to burst out of the house, under the pretext of an ungovernable rage. It was certainly not very ingenious—it was elementary, but I had no choice.

Adventure of Attorney's Clerk

" You white-livered dog! " I broke out. " Do you dare to tell me you're an Englishman, and won't fight? But I'll stand no more of this! I leave this place, where I've been insulted! Here! what's to pay? Pay yourself! " I went on, offering the landlord a handful of silver, " and give me back my banknote! "

The landlord, following his usual policy of obliging everybody, offered no opposition to my design. The position of my adversary was now thoroughly bad. He had lost my two companions. He was on the point of losing me also. There was plainly no hope of arousing the company to help; and watching him with a corner of my eye, I saw him hesitate for a moment. The next, he had taken down his hat and his wig, which was of black horse hair; and I saw him draw from behind the settle a vast hooded greatcoat and a small valise. " The devil! " thought I: " is the rascal going to follow me? "

I was scarce clear of the inn before the limb of the law was at my heels. I saw his face plain in the moonlight; and the most resolute purpose showed in it, along with an unmoved composure. A chill went over me. " This is no common adventure," thinks I to myself. " You have got hold of a man of character, St. Ives! A bite-hard, a bull-dog, a weasel is on your trail; and how are you to throw him off? " Who was he? By some of his expressions I judged he was a hanger-on of courts. But in what character had he followed the assizes? As a simple spectator, as a lawyer's clerk, as a criminal himself, or—last and worst supposition—as a Bow-street " runner "?

The cart would wait for me, perhaps, half a mile down our onward road, which I was already following. And I told myself that in a few minutes' walking, Bow-street runner or not, I should have him at my mercy. And then reflection came to me in time. Of all things, one was out of the question. Upon no account must this obtrusive fellow see the cart. Until I had killed or shook him off, I was quite divorced from my companions—alone, in the midst of England, on a frosty by-way leading whither I knew not, with a sleuth-hound at my heels, and never a friend but the holly-stick.

We came at the same time to a crossing of lanes. The branch to the left was overhung with trees, deeply sunken and dark. Not a ray of moonlight penetrated its recesses;

and I took it at a venture. The wretch followed my example in silence; and for some time we crunched together over frozen pools without a word. Then he found his voice with a chuckle.

" This is not the way to Mr. Merton's," said he.

" No? " said I. " It is mine, however."

" And therefore mine," said he.

Again we fell silent; and we may thus have covered half a mile before the lane, taking a sudden turn, brought us forth again into the moonshine. With his hooded greatcoat on his back, his valise in his hand, his black wig adjusted, and footing it on the ice with a sort of sober doggedness of manner, my enemy was changed almost beyond recognition: changed in everything but a certain dry, polemical, pedantic air, that spoke of a sedentary occupation and high stools. I observed, too, that his valise was heavy; and putting this and that together, hit upon a plan.

" A seasonable night, sir," said I. " What do you say to a bit of running? The frost has me by the toes."

" With all the pleasure in life," says he.

His voice seemed well assured, which pleased me little. However, there was nothing else to try, except violence, for which it would always be too soon. I took to my heels accordingly, he after me; and for some time the slapping of our feet on the hard road might have been heard a mile away. He had started a pace behind me, and he finished in the same position. For all his extra years and the weight of his valise he had not lost a hair's breadth. The devil might race him for me—I had enough of it!

And, besides, to run so fast was contrary to my interests. We could not run long without arriving somewhere. At any moment we might turn a corner and find ourselves at the lodge gate of some Squire Merton, in the midst of a village whose constable was sober, or in the hands of a patrol. There was no help for it—I must finish with him on the spot, as long as it was possible. I looked about me, and the place seemed suitable; never a light, never a house—nothing but stubble-fields, fallows, and a few stunted trees. I stopped and eyed him in the moonlight with an angry stare.

" Enough of this foolery! " said I.

He had turned, and now faced me full, very pale, but with no sign of shrinking.

Adventure of Attorney's Clerk

"I am quite of your opinion," said he. "You have tried me at the running, you can try me next at the high jump. It will be all the same. It must end the one way."

I made my holly whistle about my head.

"I believe you know what way!" said I. "We are alone, it is night, and I am wholly resolved. Are you not frightened?"

"No," he said, "not in the smallest. I do not box, sir; but I am not a coward, as you may have supposed. Perhaps it will simplify our relations if I tell you at the outset that I walk armed."

Quick as lightning I made a feint at his head; as quickly he gave ground, and at the same time I saw a pistol glitter in his hand.

"No more of that, Mr. French-Prisoner!" he said. "It will do me no good to have your death at my door."

"Faith, nor me either!" said I: and I lowered my stick and considered the man, not without a twinkle of admiration. "You see," I said, "there is one consideration that you appear to overlook: there are a great many chances that your pistol may miss fire."

"I have a pair," he returned. "Never travel without a brace of barkers."

"I make you my compliment," said I. "You are able to take care of yourself, and that is a good trait. But, my good man! let us look at this matter dispassionately. You are not a coward, and no more am I; we are both men of excellent sense; I have good reason, whatever it may be, to keep my concerns to myself and to walk alone. Now I put it to you pointedly, am I likely to stand it? Am I likely to put up with your continued and—excuse me—highly impudent *ingérence* into my private affairs?"

"Another French word," says he composedly.

"Oh! damn your French words!" cried I. "You seem to be a Frenchman yourself!"

"I have had many opportunities by which I have profited," he explained. "Few men are better acquainted with the similarities and differences, whether of idiom or accent, of the two languages."

"You are a pompous fellow, too," said I.

"Oh, I can make distinctions, sir," says he. "I can talk with Bedfordshire peasants; and I can express myself becomingly, I hope, in the company of a gentleman of education like yourself."

"If you set up to be a gentleman——" I began.

"Pardon me," he interrupted: "I make no such claim. I only see the nobility and gentry in the way of business. I am quite a plain person."

"For the Lord's sake," I exclaimed, "set my mind at rest upon one point. In the name of mystery who and what are you?"

"I have no cause to be ashamed of my name, sir," said he, "nor yet my trade. I am Thomas Dudgeon, at your service, clerk to Mr. Daniel Romaine, solicitor of London; High Holborn is our address, sir."

It was only by the ecstasy of the relief that I knew how horribly I had been frightened. I flung my stick on the road.

"Romaine?" I cried. "Daniel Romaine? An old hunks with a red face and a big head, and got up like a Quaker? My dear friend, to my arms!"

"Keep back, I say!" said Dudgeon weakly.

I would not listen to him. With the end of my own alarm, I felt as if I must infallibly be at the end of all dangers likewise; as if the pistol that he held in one hand were no more to be feared than the valise that he carried with the other, and now put up like a barrier against my advance.

"Keep back, or I declare I will fire," he was crying. "Have a care, for God's sake! My pistol——"

He might scream as he pleased. Willy nilly, I folded him to my breast, I pressed him there, I kissed his ugly mug as it had never been kissed before and would never be kissed again; and in the doing so knocked his wig awry and his hat off. He bleated in my embrace; so bleats the sheep in the arms of the butcher. The whole thing, on looking back, appears incomparably reckless and absurd; I no better than a madman for offering to advance on Dudgeon, and he no better than a fool for not shooting me while I was about it. But all's well that ends well; or as the people in these days kept singing and whistling on the streets:—

> "There's a sweet little cherub that sits up aloft
> And looks out for the life of poor Jack."

"There!" said I, releasing him a little, but still keeping my hands on his shoulders, "*je vous ai bel et bien embrassé*—and, as you would say, there is another French word." With

his wig over one eye, he looked incredibly rueful and put out.
"Cheer up, Dudgeon; the ordeal is over, you shall be embraced no more. But do, first of all, for God's sake, put away
your pistol; you handle it as if you were a cockatrice; some
time or other, depend upon it, it will certainly go off. Here is
your hat. No, let me put it on square, and the wig before it.
Never suffer any stress of circumstances to come between you
and the duty you owe to yourself. If you have nobody else
to dress for, dress for God!

> " Put your wig straight
> On your bald pate,
> Keep your chin scraped,
> And your figure draped.

Can you match me that? The whole duty of man in a
quatrain! And remark, I do not set up to be a professional
bard; these are the outpourings of a *dilettante*."

"But, my dear sir!" he exclaimed.

"But my dear sir!" I echoed, "I will allow no man to
interrupt the flow of my ideas. Give me your opinion on
my quatrain, or I vow we shall have a quarrel of it."

"Certainly you are quite an original," he said.

"Quite," said I; "and I believe I have my counterpart
before me."

"Well, for a choice," says he, smiling, "and whether for
sense or poetry, give me

> ' Worth makes the man, and want of it the fellow:
> The rest is all but leather and prunello.' "

"Oh, but that's not fair—that's Pope! It's not original,
Dudgeon. Understand me," said I, wringing his breast-
button, "the first duty of all poetry is to be mine, sir—mine.
Inspiration now swells in my bosom, because—to tell you the
plain truth, and descend a little in style—I am devilish
relieved at the turn things have taken. So, I dare say, are
you yourself, Dudgeon, if you would only allow it. And *à
propos*, let me ask you a home question. Between friends,
have you ever fired that pistol?"

"Why, yes, sir," he replied. "Twice—at hedge-sparrows."

"And you would have fired at me, you bloody-minded
man?" I cried.

"If you go to that, you seemed mighty reckless with your
stick," said Dudgeon.

"Did I indeed? Well, well, 'tis all past history; ancient

as King Pharamond—which is another French word, if you cared to accumulate more evidence," says I. "But happily we are now the best of friends, and have all our interests in common."

"You go a little too fast, if you'll excuse me, Mr.——: I do not know your name, that I am aware," said Dudgeon.

"No, to be sure!" said I. "Never heard of it!"

"A word of explanation——" he began.

"No, Dudgeon!" I interrupted. "Be practical; I know what you want, and the name of it is supper. *Rien ne creuse comme l'émotion.* I am hungry myself, and yet I am more accustomed to warlike palpitations than you, who are but a hunter of hedge-sparrows. Let me look at your face critically: your bill of fare is three slices of cold rare roast beef, a Welsh rabbit, a pot of stout, and a glass or two of sound tawny port, old in bottle—the right milk of Englishmen." Methought there seemed a brightening in his eye and a melting about his mouth at this enumeration.

"The night is young," I continued; "not much past eleven, for a wager. Where can we find a good inn? And remark that I say *good*, for the port must be up to the occasion —not a headache in a pipe of it."

"Really, sir," he said, smiling a little, "you have a way of carrying things——"

"Will nothing make you stick to the subject?" I cried; "you have the most irrelevant mind! How do you expect to rise in your profession? The inn?"

"Well, I will say you are a facetious gentleman!" said he. "You must have your way, I see. We are not three miles from Bedford by this very road."

"Done!" cried I. "Bedford be it!"

I tucked his arm under mine, possessed myself of the valise, and walked him off unresisting. Presently we came to an open piece of country lying a thought downhill. The road was smooth and free of ice, the moonshine thin and bright over the meadows and the leafless trees. I was now honestly done with the purgatory of the covered cart; I was close to my great-uncle's; I had no more fear of Mr. Dudgeon; which were all grounds enough for jollity. And I was aware, besides, of us two as of a pair of tiny and solitary dolls under the vast frosty cupola of the midnight; the rooms decked, the moon burnished, the least of the stars lighted, the floor swept and waxed, and nothing wanting but for the band to strike up and the dancing to begin. In the exhilaration of my heart I took the music on myself—

> " Merrily danced the Quaker's wife,
> And merrily danced the Quaker."

I broke into that animated and appropriate air, clapped my arm about Dudgeon's waist, and away down the hill at a dancing step! He hung back a little at the start, but the impulse of the tune, the night, and my example, were not to be resisted. A man made of putty must have danced, and even Dudgeon showed himself to be a human being. Higher and higher were the capers that we cut; the moon repeated in shadow our antic footsteps and gestures; and it came over my mind of a sudden—really like a balm—what appearance of man I was dancing with, what a long bilious countenance he had shown under his shaven pate, and what a world of trouble the rascal had given me in the immediate past.

Presently we began to see the lights of Bedford. My Puritanic companion stopped and disengaged himself.

" This is a trifle *infra dig.*, sir, is it not? " said he. " A party might suppose we had been drinking."

" And so you shall be, Dudgeon," said I. " You shall not only be drinking, you old hypocrite, but you shall be drunk—dead drunk, sir—and the boots shall put you to bed! We'll warn him when we go in. Never neglect a precaution; never put off till to-morrow what you can do to-day! "

But he had no more frivolity to complain of. We finished our stage and came to the inn-door with decorum, to find the house still alight and in a bustle with many late arrivals; to give our orders with a prompt severity which ensured obedience, and to be served soon after at a side-table, close to the fire and in a blaze of candle-light, with such a meal as I had been dreaming of for days past. For days, you are to remember, I had been skulking in the covered cart, a prey to cold, hunger, and an accumulation of discomforts that might have daunted the most brave; and the white table napery, the bright crystal, the reverberation of the fire, the red curtains, the Turkey carpet, the portraits on the coffee-room wall, the placid faces of the two or three late guests who were silently prolonging the pleasures of digestion, and (last, but not by any means least) a glass of an excellent light dry port, put me in a humour only to be described as heavenly. The thought of the Colonel, of how he would have enjoyed this snug room and roaring fire, and of his cold grave in the wood by Market Bosworth, lingered on my palate, *amari aliquid*, like an after-taste, but was not able—I say it with shame—entirely to dispel my self-complacency. After all, in this world every dog hangs by its own tail. I was a free adventurer, who had just brought to a successful end—or, at least, within view of it—an adventure very difficult and alarming; and I looked across at Mr. Dudgeon, as the port rose to his cheeks, and a smile, that was semi-confidential and a trifle foolish, began to play upon his leathery features, not only with composure, but with a suspicion of kindness. The rascal had been brave, a quality for which I would value the devil; and if he had been pertinacious in the beginning, he had more than made up for it before the end.

"And now, Dudgeon, to explain," I began. "I know your master, he knows me, and he knows and approves of my errand. So much I may tell you, that I am on my way to Amersham Place."

"Oho!" quoth Dudgeon, "I begin to see."

"I am heartily glad of it," said I, passing the bottle, "because that is about all I can tell you. You must take my word for the remainder. Either believe me or don't. If you don't, let's take a chaise; you can carry me to-morrow to High Holborn, and confront me with Mr. Romaine; the result of which will be to set your mind at rest—and to make the holiest disorder in your master's plans. If I judge you aright (for I find you a shrewd fellow), this will not be at all to your mind. You know what a subordinate gets by officiousness; if I can trust my memory, old Romaine has not at all the face that I should care to see in anger; and I venture to predict surprising results upon your weekly salary—if you are paid by the week, that is. In short, let me go free, and 'tis an end of the matter; take me to London, and 'tis only a beginning—and, by my opinion, a beginning of troubles. You can take your choice."

"And that is soon taken," said he. "Go to Amersham to-morrow, or go to the devil if you prefer—I wash my hands of you and the whole transaction. No, you don't find me putting my head in between Romaine and a client! A good man of business, sir, but hard as millstone grit. I might get the sack, and I shouldn't wonder! But, it's a pity, too," he added, and sighed, shook his head, and took his glass off sadly.

"That reminds me," said I. "I have a great curiosity, and you can satisfy it. Why were you so forward to meddle with poor Mr. Dubois? Why did you transfer your attentions to me? And generally, what induced you to make yourself such a nuisance?"

He blushed deeply.

"Why, sir," says he, "there *is* such a thing as patriotism, I hope."

CHAPTER XVI

THE HOME-COMING OF MR. ROWLEY'S VISCOUNT

By eight the next morning Dudgeon and I had made our parting. By that time we had grown to be extremely familiar; and I would very willingly have kept him by me, and even carried him to Amersham Place. But it appeared he was due at the public-house where we had met, on some affairs of my great-uncle the Count, who had an outlying estate in that part of the shire. If Dudgeon had had his way the night before, I should have been arrested on my uncle's land and by my uncle's agent, a culmination of ill-luck.

A little after noon I started, in a hired chaise, by way of Dunstable. The mere mention of the name Amersham Place made every one supple and smiling. It was plainly a great house, and my uncle lived there in style. The fame of it rose as we approached, like a chain of mountains; at Bedford they touched their caps, but in Dunstable they crawled upon their bellies. I thought the landlady would have kissed me; such a flutter of cordiality, such smiles, such affectionate attentions were called forth, and the good lady bustled on my service in such a pother of ringlets and with such a jingling of keys. "You're probably expected, sir, at the Place? I do trust you may 'ave better accounts of his lordship's 'elth, sir. We understood that his lordship, Mosha de Carwell, was main bad. Ha, sir, we shall all feel his loss, poor, dear, noble gentleman; and I'm sure nobody more polite! They do say, sir, his wealth is enormous, and before the Revolution, quite a prince in his own country! But I beg your pardon, sir; 'ow I do run on, to be sure; and doubtless all beknown to you already! For you do resemble the family, sir. I should have known you anywheres by the likeness to the dear viscount. Ha, poor gentleman, he must 'ave a 'eavy 'eart these days."

In the same place I saw out of the inn-windows a man-servant passing in the livery of my house, which you are to think I had never before seen worn, or not that I could remember. I had often enough, indeed, pictured myself advanced to be a Marshall, a Duke of the Empire, a Grand Cross of the Legion of Honour, and some other kickshaws of the kind, with a perfect rout of flunkeys correctly dressed in my own colours. But it is one thing to imagine, and another to see; it would be one thing to have these liveries in a house of my own in Paris—it was quite another to find them flaunting in the heart of hostile England; and I fear I should have made a fool of myself, if the man had not been on the other side of the street, and I at a one-pane window. There was something illusory in this transplantation of the wealth and honour of a family, a thing by its nature so deeply rooted in the soil; something ghostly in this sense of home-coming so far from home.

From Dunstable I rolled away into a crescendo of similar impressions. There are certainly few things to be compared with these castles, or rather country seats, of the English nobility and gentry; nor anything at all to equal the servility of the population that dwells in their neighbourhood. Though I was but driving in a hired chaise, word of my destination seemed to have gone abroad, and the women curtseyed and the men louted to me by the wayside. As I came near, I began to appreciate the roots of this widespread respect. The look of my uncle's park wall, even from the outside, had something of a princely character; and when I came in view of the house itself, a sort of madness of vicarious vainglory struck me dumb and kept me staring. It was about the size of the Tuileries. It faced due north; and the last rays of the sun, that was setting like a red-hot shot amidst the tumultuous gathering of snow clouds, were reflected on the endless rows of windows. A portico of Doric columns adorned the front, and would have done honour to a temple. The servant who received me at the door was civil to a fault—I had almost said, to offence; and the hall to which he admitted me through a pair of glass doors was warmed and already partly

Home-Coming of Rowley's Viscount

lighted by a liberal chimney heaped with the roots of beeches.

"Vicomte Anne de St. Yves," said I, in answer to the man's question; whereupon he bowed before me lower still, and stepping upon one side introduced me to the truly awful presence of the major-domo. I have seen many dignitaries in my time, but none who quite equalled this eminent being; who was good enough to answer to the unassuming name of Dawson. From him I learned that my uncle was extremely low, a doctor in close attendance, Mr. Romaine expected at any moment, and that my cousin, the Vicomte de St. Yves, had been sent for the same morning.

"It was a sudden seizure, then?" I asked.

Well, he would scarcely go as far as that. It was a decline, a fading away, sir; but he was certainly took bad the day before, had sent for Mr. Romaine, and the major-domo had taken it on himself a little later to send word to the Viscount. "It seemed to me, my lord," said he, "as if this was a time when all the fambly should be called together."

I approved him with my lips, but not in my heart. Dawson was plainly in the interests of my cousin.

"And when can I expect to see my great-uncle, the Count?" said I.

In the evening, I was told; in the meantime he would show me to my room, which had been long prepared for me, and I should be expected to dine in about an hour with the doctor if my lordship had no objections.

My lordship had not the faintest.

"At the same time," I said, "I have had an accident: I have unhappily lost my baggage, and am here in what I stand in. I don't know if the doctor be a formalist, but it is quite impossible I should appear at table as I ought."

He begged me to be under no anxiety. "We have been long expecting you," said he. "All is ready."

Such I found to be the truth. A great room had been prepared for me; through the mullioned windows the last flicker of the winter sunset interchanged with the reverberation of a royal fire; the bed was open, a suit of evening clothes was airing before the blaze, and from the far corner a boy came forward with deprecatory smiles. The dream in which I had been moving seemed to have reached its pitch. I might have quitted this house and room only the night before; it was my own place that I had come to; and for the first time in my life I understood the force of the words home and welcome.

"This will be all as you would want, sir?" said Mr. Dawson. "This 'ere boy, Rowley, we place entirely at your disposition. 'E's not exactly a trained vallet, but Mossho Powl, the Viscount's gentleman, 'ave give him the benefick of a few lessons, and it is 'oped that he may give sitisfection. Hanything that you may require, if you will be so good as to mention the same to Rowley, I will make it my business myself, sir, to see you sitisfied."

So saying this eminent and already detested Mr. Dawson took his departure, and I was left alone with Rowley. A man who may be said to have wakened to consciousness in the prison of the Abbaye, among those ever graceful and ever tragic figures of the brave and fair, awaiting the hour of the guillotine and denuded of every comfort, I had never known the luxuries or the amenities of my rank in life. To be attended on by servants I had only been accustomed to in inns. My toilet had long been military, to a moment, at the note of a bugle, too often at a ditch-side. And it need not be wondered at if I looked on my new valet with a certain diffidence. But I remembered that if he was my first experience of a valet, I was his first trial as a master. Cheered by which consideration, I demanded my bath in a style of good assurance. There was a bathroom contiguous; in an incredibly short space of time the hot water was ready; and soon after, arrayed in a shawl dressing-gown, and in a luxury of contentment and comfort, I was reclined in an easy-chair before the mirror, while Rowley, with a mixture of pride and anxiety which I could well understand, laid out his razors.

"Hey, Rowley?" I asked, not quite resigned to go under fire with such an inexperienced commander. "It's all right, is it? You feel pretty sure of your weapons?"

"Yes, my lord," he replied. "It's all right, I assure your lordship."

"I beg your pardon, Mr. Rowley, but for the sake of shortness, would you mind not belording me in private?" said I. "It will do very well if you call me Mr. Anne. It is the way of my country, as I dare say you know."

Mr. Rowley looked blank.

"But you're just as much a Viscount as Mr. Powl's, are you not?" he said.

Home-Coming of Rowley's Viscount

" As Mr. Powl's Viscount? " said I, laughing. " Oh, keep
your mind easy, Mr. Rowley's is every bit as good   Only, you
see, as I am of the younger line, I bear my Christian name
along with the title.   Alain is the *Viscount ;* I am the *Viscount Anne.* And in giving me the name of Mr. Anne, I
assure you you will be quite regular."

" Yes, Mr. Anne," said the docile youth. " But about the
shaving, sir, you need be under no alarm. Mr. Powl says
I 'ave excellent dispositions."

" Mr. Powl? " said I. " That doesn't seem to me very
like a French name."

" No, sir, indeed, my lord," said he, with a burst of confidence. " No, indeed, Mr. Anne, and it do not surely. I
should say now, it was more like Mr. Pole."

" And Mr. Powl is the Viscount's man? "

" Yes, Mr. Anne," said he.   " He 'ave a hard billet, he do.
The Viscount is a very particular gentleman. I don't think
as you'll be, Mr. Anne? " he added, with a confidential smile
in the mirror.

He was about sixteen, well set up, with a pleasant, merry,
freckled face, and a pair of dancing eyes. There was an air
at once deprecatory and insinuating about the rascal that I
thought I recognised. There came to me from my own boyhood memories of certain passionate admirations long passed
away, and the objects of them long ago discredited or dead.
I remembered how anxious I had been to serve those fleeting
heroes, how readily I told myself I would have died for *them,*
how much greater and handsomer than life they had appeared.
And looking in the mirror, it seemed to me that I read the
face of Rowley, like an echo or a ghost, by the light of my
own youth. I have always contended (somewhat against
the opinion of my friends) that I am first of all an economist;
and the last thing that I would care to throw away is that
very valuable piece of property—a boy's hero-worship.

" Why," said I, " you shave like an angel, Mr. Rowley! "

" Thank you, my lord," says he. " Mr. Powl had no
fear of me. You may be sure, sir, I should never 'ave had
this berth if I 'adn't 'ave been up to Dick. We been expecting of you this month back. My eye! I never see such
preparations. Every day the fires has been kep' up, the
bed made, and all! As soon as it was known you were coming,
sir, I got the appointment; and I've been up and down since

then like a Jack-in-the-box. A wheel couldn't sound in the avenue but what I was at the window! I've had a many disappointments; but to-night, as soon as you stepped out of the shay, I knew it was my—was you. Oh, you had been expected! Why, when I go down to supper, I'll be the 'ero of the servants' 'all: the 'ole of the staff is that curious!"

"Well," said I, "I hope you may be able to give a fair account of me—sober, steady, industrious, good-tempered, and with a first-rate character from my last place?"

He laughed an embarrassed laugh. "Your hair curls beautiful," he said, by way of changing the subject. "The Viscount's the boy for curls, though; and the richness of it is, Mr. Powl tells me his don't curl no more than that much twine—by nature. Gettin' old, the Viscount is. He 'ave gone the pace, 'aven't 'e, sir?"

"The fact is," said I, "that I know very little about him. Our family has been much divided, and I have been a soldier from a child."

"A soldier, Mr. Anne, sir?" cried Rowley, with a sudden feverish animation. "Was you ever wounded?"

It is contrary to my principles to discourage admiration for myself; and, slipping back the shoulder of the dressing-gown, I silently exhibited the scar which I had received in Edinburgh Castle. He looked at it with awe.

"Ah, well!" he continued, "there's where the difference comes in! It's in the training. The other Viscount have been horse-racing, and dicing, and carrying on all his life. All right enough, no doubt; but what I do say is, that it don't lead to nothink. Whereas——"

"Whereas Mr. Rowley's?" I put in.

"My Viscount?" said he. "Well, sir, I *did* say it; and now that I've seen you, I say it again!"

I could not refrain from smiling at this outburst, and the rascal caught me in the mirror and smiled to me again.

"I'd say it again, Mr. Hanne," he said. "I know which side my bread's buttered. I know when a gen'leman's a gen'leman. Mr. Powl can go to Putney with his one! Beg your pardon, Mr. Anne, for being so familiar," said he, blushing suddenly scarlet. "I was especially warned against it by Mr. Powl."

"Discipline before all," said I. "Follow your front-rank man."

Home-Coming of Rowley's Viscount

With that, we began to turn our attention to the clothes. I was amazed to find them fit so well: not *à la diable*, in the haphazard manner of a soldier's uniform or a ready-made suit; but with nicety, as a trained artist might rejoice to make them for a favourite subject.

" 'Tis extraordinary," cried I: "these things fit me perfectly."

" Indeed, Mr. Anne, you two be very much of a shape," said Rowley.

" Who? What two? " said I.

" The Viscount," he said.

" Damnation! Have I the man's clothes on me, too? " cried I.

But Rowley hastened to reassure me. On the first word of my coming, the Count had put the matter of my wardrobe in the hands of his own and my cousin's tailors: and on the rumour of our resemblance, my clothes had been made to Alain's measure.

" But they were all made for you express, Mr. Anne. You may be certain the Count would never do nothing by 'alf: fires kep' burning; the finest of clothes ordered, I'm sure, and a body-servant being trained a-purpose."

" Well," said I, " it's a good fire, and a good set-out of clothes; and what a valet, Mr. Rowley! And there's one thing to be said for my cousin—I mean for Mr. Powl's Viscount he has a very fair figure."

" Oh, don't you be took in, Mr. Anne," quoth the faithless Rowley: " he has to be hyked into a pair of stays to get them things on! "

" Come, come, Mr. Rowley," said I, " this is telling tales out of school! Do not you be deceived. The greatest men of antiquity, including Cæsar and Hannibal and Pope Joan, may have been very glad, at my time of life or Alain's, to follow his example. 'Tis a misfortune common to all; and really," said I, bowing to myself before the mirror like one who should dance the minuet, " when the result is so successful as this, who would do anything but applaud? "

My toilet concluded, I marched on to fresh surprises. My chamber, my new valet, and my new clothes had been beyond hope: the dinner, the soup, the whole bill of fare was a revelation of the powers there are in man. I had not supposed it lay in the genius of any cook to create, out of common beef and mutton, things so different and dainty. The wine was of a piece, the doctor a most agreeable companion; nor could I help reflecting on the prospect that all this wealth, comfort, and handsome profusion might still very possibly become mine. Here were a change indeed, from the common soldier and the camp kettle, the prisoner and his prison rations, the fugitive and the horrors of the covered cart!

CHAPTER XVII

THE DESPATCH-BOX

THE doctor had scarce finished his meal before he hastened with an apology to attend upon his patient; and almost immediately after I was myself summoned and ushered up the great staircase and along interminable corridors to the bedside of my great-uncle the Count. You are to think that up to the present moment I had not set eyes on this formidable personage, only on the evidences of his wealth and kindness. You are to think besides that I had heard him miscalled and abused from my earliest childhood up. The first of the *émigrés* could never expect a good word in the society in which my father moved. Even yet the reports I received were of a doubtful nature; even Romaine himself had drawn of him no very amiable portrait; and as I was ushered into the room it was a critical eye that I cast on my great-uncle. He lay propped on pillows in a little cot no greater than a camp-bed, not visibly breathing. He was about eighty years of age, and looked it; not that his face was much lined, but all the blood and colour seemed to have faded from his body, and even his eyes, which last he kept usually closed as though the light distressed him. There was an unspeakable degree of slyness in his expression, which kept me ill at ease; he seemed to lie there with his arms folded, like a spider waiting for prey. His speech was very deliberate and courteous, but scarce louder than a sigh.

" I bid you welcome, *Monsieur le Vicomte Anne*," said he, looking at me hard with his pale eyes, but not moving on his pillows. "I have sent for you, and I thank you for the obliging expedition you have shown. It is my misfortune that I cannot rise to receive you. I trust you have been reasonably well entertained? "

The Despatch-Box

" *Monsieur mon oncle*," I said, bowing very low, " I am come at the summons of the head of my family."

" It is well," he said. " Be seated. I should be glad to hear some news—if that can be called news that is already twenty years old—of how I have the pleasure to see you here."

By the coldness of his address, not more than by the nature of the times that he bade me recall, I was plunged in melancholy. I felt myself surrounded as with deserts of friendlessness, and the delight of my welcome was turned to ashes in my mouth.

" That is soon told, *monseigneur*," said I. " I understand that I need tell you nothing of the end of my unhappy parents? It is only the story of the lost dog."

" You are right. I am sufficiently informed of that deplorable affair; it is painful to me. My nephew, your father, was a man who would not be advised," said he. " Tell me, if you please, simply of yourself."

" I am afraid I must run the risk of harrowing your sensibility in the beginning," said I, with a bitter smile, " because my story begins at the foot of the guillotine. When the list came out that night, and her name was there, I was already old enough, not in years but in sad experience, to understand the extent of my misfortune. She——" I paused. " Enough that she arranged with a friend, Madame de Chasseradès, that she should take charge of me, and by the favour of our jailers I was suffered to remain in the shelter of the *Abbaye*. That was my only refuge; there was no corner of France that I could rest the sole of my foot upon except the prison. Monsieur le Comte, you are as well aware as I can be what kind of a life that was, and how swiftly death smote in that society. I did not wait long before the name of Madame de Chasseradès succeeded to that of my mother on the list. She passed me on to Madame de Noytot; she, in her turn, to Mademoiselle de Braye; and there were others. I was the one thing permanent; they were all transient as clouds; a day or two of their care, and then came the last farewell and—somewhere far off in that roaring Paris that surrounded us—the bloody scene. I was the cherished one, the last comfort, of these dying women. I have been in pitched fights, my lord, and I never knew such courage. It was all done smiling, in the tone of good society; *belle maman* was the name I was taught to give to each; and for a day or two the new ' pretty mamma' would make much of me, show me off, teach me the minuet, and to say my prayers; and then, with a tender embrace, would go the way of her predecessors, smiling. There were some that wept too. There was a childhood! All the time Monsieur de Culemberg kept his eye on me, and would have had me out of the *Abbaye* and in his own protection, but my 'pretty mammas' one after another resisted the idea. Where could I be safer? they argued; and what was to become of them without the darling of the prison? Well, it was soon shown how safe I was! The dreadful day of the massacre came; the prison was overrun; none paid attention to me, not even the last of my 'pretty mammas,' for she had met another fate. I was wandering distracted, when I was found by some one in the interests of Monsieur de Culemberg. I understand he was sent on purpose; I believe, in order to reach the interior of the prison, he had set his hand to nameless barbarities; such was the price paid for my worthless, whimpering little life! He gave me his hand; it was wet, and mine was reddened; he led me unresisting. I remember but the one circumstance of my flight—it was my last view of my last pretty mamma. Shall I describe it to you?" I asked the Count, with a sudden fierceness.

"Avoid unpleasant details," observed my great-uncle gently.

At these words a sudden peace fell upon me. I had been angry with the man before; I had not sought to spare him; and now, in a moment, I saw that there was nothing to spare. Whether from natural heartlessness or extreme old age, the soul was not at home; and my benefactor, who had kept the fire lit in my room for a month past—my only relative except Alain, whom I knew already to be a hired spy—had trodden out the last sparks of hope and interest.

"Certainly," said I; "and, indeed, the day for them is nearly over. I was taken to Monsieur de Culemberg's—I presume, sir, that you know the Abbé de Culemberg?"

He indicated assent without opening his eyes.

"He was a very brave and a very learned man——"

"And a very holy one," said my uncle civilly.

"And a very holy one, as you observe," I continued. "He did an infinity of good, and through all the Terror kept himself from the guillotine. He brought me up, and gave me such education as I have. It was in his house in the country at

The Despatch-Box

Dammarie, near Melun, that I made the acquaintance of your agent, Mr. Vicary, who lay there in hiding, only to fall a victim at the last to a gang of *chauffeurs*."

" That poor Mr. Vicary! " observed my uncle. " He had been many times in my interests to France, and this was his first failure. *Quel charmant homme, n'est-ce pas ?* "

" Infinitely so," said I. " But I would not willingly detain you any further with a story, the details of which it must naturally be more or less unpleasant for you to hear. Suffice it that, by M. de Culemberg's own advice, I said farewell at eighteen to that kind preceptor and his books, and entered the service of France; and have since then carried arms in such a manner as not to disgrace my family."

" You narrate well; *vous avez la voix chaude*," said my uncle, turning on his pillows as if to study me. " I have a very good account of you by Monsieur de Mauséant, whom you helped in Spain. And you had some education from the Abbé de Culemberg, a man of a good house? Yes, you will do very well. You have a good manner and a handsome person, which hurts nothing. We are all handsome in the family; even I myself, I have had my successes, the memories of which still charm me. It is my intention, my nephew, to make of you my heir. I am not very well content with my other nephew, Monsieur le Vicomte; he has not been respectful, which is the flattery due to age. And there are other matters."

I was half tempted to throw back in his face that inheritance so coldly offered. At the same time I had to consider that he was an old man, and, after all, my relation; and that I was a poor one, in considerable straits, with a hope at heart which that inheritance might yet enable me to realise. Nor could I forget that, however icy his manners, he had behaved to me from the first with the extreme of liberality and—I was about to write, kindness, but the word, in that connection, would not come. I really owed the man some measure of gratitude, which it would be an ill manner to repay if I were to insult him on his deathbed.

" Your will, monsieur, must ever be my rule," said I, bowing.

" You have wit, *monsieur mon neveu*," said he, " the best wit—the wit of silence. Many might have deafened me with their gratitude. Gratitude! " he repeated, with a peculiar

intonation, and lay and smiled to himself. " But to approach
what is more important. As a prisoner of war, will it be
possible for you to be served heir to English estates? I have
no idea: long as I have dwelt in England, I have never studied
what they call their laws. On the other hand, how if Romaine should come too late? I have two pieces of business
to be transacted—to die, and to make my will; and, however
desirous I may be to serve you, I cannot postpone the first in
favour of the second beyond a very few hours."

" Well, sir, I must then contrive to be doing as I did before,"
said I.

" Not so," said the Count. " I have an alternative. I
have just drawn my balance at my banker's, a considerable
sum, and I am now to place it in your hands. It will be so
much for you and so much less——" he paused, and smiled
with an air of malignity that surprised me. " But it is
necessary it should be done before witnesses. *Monsieur le
Vicomte* is of a particular disposition, and an unwitnessed
donation may very easily be twisted into a theft."

He touched a bell, which was answered by a man having
the appearance of a confidential valet. To him he gave a
key.

" Bring me the despatch-box that came yesterday, La
Ferrière," said he. " You will at the same time present my
compliments to Dr. Hunter and M. l'Abbé, and request them
to step for a few moments to my room."

The despatch-box proved to be rather a bulky piece of
baggage, covered with Russia leather. Before the doctor
and an excellent old smiling priest it was passed over into my
hands with a very clear statement of the disposer's wishes;
immediately after which, though the witnesses remained
behind to draw up and sign a joint note of the transaction,
Monsieur de Kéroual dismissed me to my own room, La
Ferrière following with the invaluable box.

At my chamber door I took it from him with thanks, and
entered alone. Everything had been already disposed for the
night, the curtains drawn and the fire trimmed; and Rowley
was still busy with my bedclothes. He turned round as I
entered with a look of welcome that did my heart good.
Indeed, I had never a much greater need of human sympathy,
however trivial, than at that moment when I held a fortune in
my arms. In my uncle's room I had breathed the very

atmosphere of disenchantment. He had gorged my pockets; he had starved every dignified or affectionate sentiment of a man. I had received so chilling an impression of age and experience that the mere look of youth drew me to confide in Rowley: he was only a boy, his heart must beat yet, he must still retain some innocence and natural feelings, he could blurt out follies with his mouth, he was not a machine to utter perfect speech! At the same time, I was beginning to outgrow the painful impressions of my interview; my spirits were beginning to revive; and at the jolly, empty looks of Mr. Rowley, as he ran forward to relieve me of the box, St. Ives became himself again.

"Now, Rowley, don't be in a hurry," said I. "This is a momentous juncture. Man and boy, you have been in my service about three hours. You must already have observed that I am a gentleman of a somewhat morose disposition, and there is nothing that I more dislike than the smallest appearance of familiarity. Mr. Pole or Mr. Powl, probably in the spirit of prophecy, warned you against this danger."

"Yes, Mr. Anne," said Rowley blankly.

"Now there has just arisen one of those rare cases, in which I am willing to depart from my principles. My uncle has given me a box—what you would call a Christmas box. I don't know what's in it, and no more do you; perhaps I am an April fool, or perhaps I am already enormously wealthy; there might be five hundred pounds in this apparently harmless receptacle!"

"Lord, Mr. Anne!" cried Rowley.

"Now, Rowley, hold up your right hand and repeat the words of the oath after me," said I, laying the despatch-box on the table. "Strike me blue if I ever disclose to Mr. Powl, or Mr. Powl's Viscount, or anything that is Mr. Powl's, not to mention Mr. Dawson and the doctor, the treasures of the following despatch-box; and strike me sky-blue scarlet if I do not continually maintain, uphold, love, honour and obey, serve and follow to the four corners of the earth and the waters that are under the earth, the hereinafter beforementioned (only that I find I have neglected to mention him) Viscount Anne de Kéroual de St.-Yves, commonly known as Mr. Rowley's Viscount. So be it. Amen."

He took the oath with the same exaggerated seriousness as I gave it to him.

St. Ives

"Now," said I. "Here is the key for you; I will hold the lid with both hands in the meanwhile." He turned the key. "Bring up all the candles in the room, and range them alongside. What is it to be? A live gorgon, a Jack-in-the-box, or a spring that fires a pistol? On your knees, sir, before the prodigy!"

So saying, I turned the despatch-box upside down upon the table. At sight of the heap of bank paper and gold that lay in front of us between the candles, or rolled upon the floor alongside, I stood astonished.

"O Lord!" cried Mr. Rowley; "O Lordy, Lordy, Lord!" and he scrambled after the fallen guineas. "O my, Mr. Anne! what a sight o' money! Why, it's like a blessed story-book. It's like the Forty Thieves."

"Now, Rowley, let's be cool, let's be business-like," said I. "Riches are deceitful, particularly when you haven't counted them; and the first thing we have to do is to arrive at the amount of my—let me say, modest competency. If I'm not mistaken, I have enough here to keep you in gold buttons all the rest of your life. You collect the gold, and I'll take the paper."

Accordingly, down we sat together on the hearthrug, and for some time there was no sound but the creasing of bills and he jingling of guineas, broken occasionally by the exulting exclamations of Rowley. The arithmetical operation on which we were embarked took long, and it might have been tedious to others; not to me nor to my helper.

"Ten thousand pounds!" I announced at last.

"Ten thousand!" echoed Mr. Rowley.

And we gazed upon each other.

The greatness of this fortune took my breath away. With that sum in my hands, I need fear no enemies. People are arrested, in nine cases out of ten, not because the police are astute, but because they themselves run short of money; and I had here before me in the despatch-box a succession of devices and disguises that insured my liberty. Not only so; but, as I felt with a sudden and overpowering thrill, with ten thousand pounds in my hands I was become an eligible suitor. What advances I had made in the past, as a private soldier in a military prison, or a fugitive by the wayside, could only be qualified or, indeed, excused as acts of desperation. And now I might come in by the front door; I might approach the

Mr. Romaine Calls Me Names

dragon with a lawyer at my elbow, and rich settlements to offer. The poor French prisoner, Champdivers, might be in a perpetual danger of arrest; but the rich travelling Englishman, St.-Ives, in his postchaise, with his despatch-box by his side, could smile at fate and laugh at locksmiths. I repeated the proverb, exulting, *Love laughs at locksmiths!* In a moment, by the mere coming of this money, my love had become possible—it had come near, it was under my hand— and it may be by one of the curiosities of human nature, but it burned that instant brighter.

"Rowley," said I, "your Viscount is a made man."

"Why, we both are, sir," said Rowley.

"Yes, both," said I; "and you shall dance at the wedding"; and I flung at his head a bundle of bank notes, and had just followed it up with a handful of guineas, when the door opened, and Mr. Romaine appeared upon the threshold.

CHAPTER XVIII

MR. ROMAINE CALLS ME NAMES

FEELING very much of a fool to be thus taken by surprise, I scrambled to my feet and hastened to make my visitor welcome. He did not refuse me his hand; but he gave it with a coldness and distance for which I was quite unprepared, and his countenance, as he looked on me, was marked in a strong degree with concern and severity.

"So, sir, I find you here?" said he, in tones of little encouragement. "Is that you, George? You can run away; I have business with your master."

He showed Rowley out, and locked the door behind him. Then he sat down in an armchair on one side of the fire, and looked at me with uncompromising sternness.

"I am hesitating how to begin," said he. "In this singular labyrinth of blunders and difficulties that you have prepared for us, I am positively hesitating where to begin. It will perhaps be best that you should read, first of all, this paragraph." And he handed over to me a newspaper.

The paragraph in question was brief. It announced the recapture of one of the prisoners recently escaped from Edinburgh Castle; gave his name, Clausel, and added that he had entered into the particulars of the recent revolting murder in the Castle, and denounced the murderer:—

"It is a common soldier called Champdivers, who had himself escaped, and is in all probability involved in the common fate of his comrades. In spite of the activity along all the Forth and the East Coast, nothing has yet been seen of the sloop which these desperadoes seized at Grangemouth, and it is now almost certain that they have found a watery grave."

At the reading of this paragraph, my heart turned over. In a moment I saw my castle in the air ruined; myself changed from a mere military fugitive into a hunted murderer, fleeing from the gallows; my love, which had a moment since appeared so near to me, blotted from the field of possibility. Despair, which was my first sentiment, did not, however, endure for more than a moment. I saw that my companions had indeed succeeded in their unlikely design; and that I was supposed to have accompanied and perished along with them by shipwreck—a most probable ending to their enterprise. If they thought me at the bottom of the North Sea, I need not fear much vigilance on the streets of Edinburgh. Champdivers was wanted: what was to connect him with St. Ives? Major Chevenix would recognise me if he met me; that was beyond bargaining: he had seen me so often, his interest had been kindled to so high a point, that I could hope to deceive him by no stratagem of disguise. Well, even so; he would have a competition of testimony before him: he knew Clausel, he knew me, and I was sure he would decide for honour. At the same time, the image of Flora shot up in my mind's eye with such a radiancy as fairly overwhelmed all other considerations; the blood sprang to every corner of my body, and I vowed I would see and win her, if it cost my neck.

"Very annoying, no doubt," said I, as I returned the paper to Mr. Romaine.

"Is annoying your word for it?" said he.

"Exasperating, if you like," I admitted.

"And true?" he inquired.

"Well, true in a sense," said I. "But perhaps I had better answer that question by putting you in possession of the facts?"

Mr. Romaine Calls Me Names

"I think so, indeed," said he.

I narrated to him as much as seemed necessary of the quarrel, the duel, the death of Goguelat, and the character of Clausel. He heard me through in a forbidding silence, nor did he at all betray the nature of his sentiments, except that, at the episode of the scissors, I could observe his mulberry face to turn three shades paler.

"I suppose I may believe you?" said he, when I had done.

"Or else conclude this interview," said I.

"Can you not understand that we are here discussing matters of the gravest import? Can you not understand that I feel myself weighed with a load of responsibility on your account—that you should take this occasion to air your fire-eating manners against your own attorney? There are serious hours in life, Mr. Anne," he said severely. "A capital charge and that of a very brutal character and with singularly unpleasant details; the presence of the man Clausel, who (according to your account of it) is actuated by sentiments of real malignity and prepared to swear black white; all the other witnesses scattered and perhaps drowned at sea; the natural prejudice against a Frenchman and a runaway prisoner: this makes a serious total for your lawyer to consider, and is by no means lessened by the incurable folly and levity of your own disposition."

"I beg your pardon!" said I.

"Oh, my expressions have been selected with scrupulous accuracy," he replied. "How did I find you, sir, when I came to announce this catastrophe? You were sitting on the hearthrug playing, like a silly baby, with a servant, were you not, and the floor all scattered with gold and bank paper? There was a tableau for you! It was I who came, and you were lucky in that. It might have been any one—your cousin as well as another."

"You have me there, sir," I admitted. "I had neglected all precautions, and you do right to be angry. *Apropos*, Mr. Romaine, how did you come yourself, and how long have you been in the house?" I added, surprised, on the retrospect, not to have heard him arrive.

"I drove up in a chaise and pair," he returned. "Any one might have heard me. But you were not listening, I suppose? being so extremely at your ease in the very house of your enemy, and under a capital charge! And I have been long enough here to do your business for you. Ah, yes, I did it, God forgive me!—did it before I so much as asked you the explanation of the paragraph. For some time back the will has been prepared; now it is signed; and your uncle has heard nothing of your recent piece of activity. Why? Well, I had no fancy to bother him on his deathbed; you might be innocent; and at bottom I preferred the murderer to the spy."

No doubt of it but the man played a friendly part: no doubt also that, in his ill-temper and anxiety, he expressed himself unpalatably.

" You will perhaps find me over-delicate," said I. " There is a word you employed——"

" I employ the words of my brief, sir," he cried, striking with his hand on the newspaper. " It is there in six letters. And do not be so certain—you have not stood your trial yet. It is an ugly affair, a fishy business. It is highly disagreeable. I would give my hand off—I mean I would give a hundred pound down—to have nothing to do with it. And, situated as we are, we must at once take action. There is here no choice. You must at once quit this country, and get to France, or Holland, or, indeed, to Madagascar."

" There may be two words to that," said I.

" Not so much as one syllable! " he retorted. " Here is no room for argument. The case is nakedly plain. In the disgusting position in which you have found means to place yourself, all that is to be hoped for is delay. A time may come when we shall be able to do better. It cannot be now: now it would be the gibbet."

" You labour under a false impression, Mr. Romaine," said I. " I have no impatience to figure in the dock. I am even as anxious as yourself to postpone my first appearance there. On the other hand, I have not the slightest intention of leaving this country, where I please myself extremely. I have a good address, a ready tongue, an English accent that passes, and, thanks to the generosity of my uncle, as much money as I want. It would be hard indeed if, with all these advantages, Mr. St. Ives should not be able to live quietly in a private lodging, while the authorities amuse themselves by looking for Champdivers. You forget, there is no connection between these two personages."

" And you forget your cousin," retorted Romaine. " There is the link. There is the tongue of the buckle. He knows

Mr. Romaine Calls Me Names

you are Champdivers." He put up his hand as if to listen. " And, for a wager, here he is himself! " he exclaimed.

As when a tailor takes a piece of goods upon his counter, and rends it across, there came to our ears from the avenue the long tearing sound of a chaise and four approaching at the top speed of the horses. And, looking out between the curtain, we beheld the lamps skimming on the smooth ascent.

" Ay," said Romaine, wiping the window-pane that he might see more clearly. " Ay, that is he by the driving! So he squanders money along the king's highway, the triple idiot! gorging every man he meets with gold for the pleasure of arriving—where? Ah, yes, where but a debtor's jail, if not a criminal prison! "

" Is he that kind of a man? " I said, staring on these lamps as though I could decipher in them the secret of my cousin's character.

" You will find him a dangerous kind," answered the lawyer. " For you, these are the lights on a lee shore! I find I fall in a muse when I consider of him; what a formidable being he once was, and what a personable! and how near he draws to the moment that must break him utterly! we none of us like him here; we hate him, rather; and yet I have a sense—I don't think at my time of life it can be pity—but a reluctance rather, to break anything so big and figurative, as though he were a big porcelain pot or a big picture of high price. Ay, there is what I was waiting for! " he cried, as the lights of a second chaise swam in sight. " It is he beyond a doubt. The first was the signature and the next the flourish. Two chaises, the second following with the baggage, which is always copious and ponderous, and one of his valets: he cannot go a step without a valet."

" I hear you repeat the word big," said I. " But it cannot be that he is anything out of the way in stature."

" No," said the attorney. " About your height, as I guessed for the tailors, and I see nothing wrong with the result. But, somehow, he commands an atmosphere: he has a spacious manner; and he has kept up, all through life, such a volume of racket about his personality, with his chaises and his racers and his dicings, and I know not what—that somehow he imposes! It seems, when the farce is done, and he locked in Fleet prison—and nobody left but Buonaparté and Lord Wellington and the Hetman Platoff to make a work about—the world will be in a comparison quite tranquil. But this is beside the mark," he added, with an effort, turning again from the window. "We are now under fire, Mr. Anne, as you soldiers would say, and it is high time we should prepare to go into action. He must not see you; that would be fatal. All that he knows at present is that you resemble him, and that is much more than enough. If it were possible, it would be well he should not know you were in the house."

"Quite impossible, depend upon it," said I. "Some of the servants are directly in his interests, perhaps in his pay: Dawson, for an example."

"My own idea!" cried Romaine. "And at least," he added, as the first of the chaises drew up with a dash in front of the portico, "it is now too late. Here he is."

We stood listening, with a strange anxiety, to the various noises that awoke in the silent house: the sound of doors opening and closing, the sound of feet near at hand and farther off. It was plain the arrival of my cousin was a matter of moment, almost of parade, to the household And suddenly, out of this confused and distant bustle, a rapid and light tread became distinguishable. We heard it come upstairs, draw near along the corridor, pause at the door, and a stealthy and hasty rapping succeeded.

"Mr. Anne—Mr. Anne, sir! Let me in!" said the voice of Rowley.

We admitted the lad, and locked the door again behind him.

"It's *him*, sir," he panted. "He've come."

"You mean the Viscount?" said I. "So we supposed. But come, Rowley—out with the rest of it! You have more to tell us, or your face belies you!"

"Mr. Anne, I do," he said. "Mr. Romaine, sir, you're a friend of his, ain't you?"

"Yes, George, I am a friend of his," said Romaine, and to my great surprise, laid his hand upon my shoulder.

"Well, it's this way," said Rowley; "Mr. Powl have been at me! It's to play the spy! I thought he was at it from the first! From the first I see what he was after—coming round and round, and hinting things! But to-night he outs with it plump! I'm to let him hear all what you're to do beforehand, he says; and he gave me this for an arnest'—holding up half a guinea; "and I took it, so I did! Strike me sky-

Mr. Romaine Calls Me Names

blue scarlet!" says he, adducing the words of the mock oath; and he looked askance at me as he did so.

I saw that he had forgotten himself, and that he knew it. The expression of his eye changed almost in the passing of the glance from the significant to the appealing—from the look of an accomplice to that of a culprit; and from that moment he became the model of a well-drilled valet.

"Sky-blue scarlet?" repeated the lawyer. "Is the fool delirious?"

"No," said I; "he is only reminding me of something."

"Well—and I believe the fellow will be faithful," said Romaine. "So you are a friend of Mr. Anne's too?" he added to Rowley.

"If you please, sir," said Rowley.

"'Tis something sudden," observed Romaine; "but it may be genuine enough. I believe him to be honest. He comes of honest people. Well, George Rowley, you might embrace some early opportunity to earn that half-guinea, by telling Mr. Powl that your master will not leave here till noon to-morrow, if he go even then. Tell him there are a hundred things to be done here, and a hundred more that can only be done properly at my office in Holborn. Come to think of it —we had better see to that first of all," he went on, unlocking the door. "Get hold of Powl, and see. And be quick back, and clear me up this mess."

Mr. Rowley was no sooner gone than the lawyer took a pinch of snuff, and regarded me with somewhat of a more genial expression.

"Sir," said he, "it is very fortunate for you that your face is so strong a letter of recommendation. Here am I, a tough old practitioner, mixing myself up with your very distressing business; and here is this farmer's lad, who has the wit to take a bribe and the loyalty to come and tell you of it—all, I take it, on the strength of your appearance. I wish I could imagine how it would impress a jury!" says he.

"And how it would affect the hangman, sir?" I asked.

"*Absit omen!*" said Mr. Romaine devoutly.

We were just so far in our talk, when I heard a sound that brought my heart into my mouth: the sound of some one slyly trying the handle of the door. It had been preceded by no audible footstep. Since the departure of Rowley our wing of the house had been entirely silent. And we had every right to suppose ourselves alone, and to conclude that the new-comer, whoever he might be, was come on a clandestine, if not a hostile, errand.

" Who is there? " asked Romaine.

" It's only me, sir," said the soft voice of Dawson. " It's the Viscount, sir. He is very desirous to speak with you on business."

" Tell him I shall come shortly, Dawson," said the lawyer. " I am at present engaged."

" Thank you, sir! " said Dawson.

And we heard his feet draw off slowly along the corridor.

" Yes," said Mr. Romaine, speaking low, and maintaining the attitude of one intently listening, " there is another foot. I cannot be deceived!"

" I think there was indeed! " said I. " And what troubles me—I am not sure that the other has gone entirely away. By the time it got the length of the head of the stair the tread was plainly single."

" Ahem—blockaded? " asked the lawyer.

" A siege *en règle !* " I exclaimed.

" Let us come farther from the door," said Romaine, " and reconsider this damnable position. Without doubt, Alain was this moment at the door. He hoped to enter and get a view of you, as if by accident. Baffled in this, has he stayed himself, or has he planted Dawson here by way of sentinel? "

" Himself, beyond a doubt," said I. " And yet to what end? He cannot think to pass the night there! "

" If it were only possible to pay no heed! " said Mr. Romaine. " But this is the accursed drawback of your position. We can do nothing openly. I must smuggle you out of this room and out of this house like seizable goods; and how am I to set about it with a sentinel planted at your very door? "

" There is no good in being agitated," said I.

" None at all," he acquiesced. " And, come to think of it, it is droll enough that I should have been that very moment commenting on your personal appearance when your cousin came upon this mission. I was saying, if you remember, that your face was as good or better than a letter of recommendation. I wonder if M. Alain would be like the rest of us —I wonder what he would think of it? "

Mr. Romaine was sitting in a chair by the fire with his back to the windows, and I was myself kneeling on the hearthrug and beginning mechanically to pick up the scattered bills, when a honeyed voice joined suddenly in our conversation.

"He thinks well of it, Mr. Romaine. He begs to join himself to that circle of admirers which you indicate to exist already."

CHAPTER XIX

THE DEVIL AND ALL AT AMERSHAM PLACE

NEVER did two human creatures get to their feet with more alacrity than the lawyer and myself. We had locked and barred the main gates of the citadel; but unhappily we had left open the bath-room sally-port; and here we found the voice of the hostile trumpets sounding from within, and all our defences taken in reverse. I took but the time to whisper Mr. Romaine in the ear: "Here is another tableau for you!" at which he looked at me a moment with a kind of pathos, as who should say, "Don't hit a man when he's down." Then I transferred my eyes to my enemy.

He had his hat on, a little on one side; it was a very tall hat, raked extremely, and had a narrow curling brim. His hair was all curled out in masses like an Italian mountebank— a most unpardonable fashion. He sported a huge tippeted overcoat of frieze, such as watchmen wear, only the inside was lined with costly furs, and he kept it half open to display the exquisite linen, the many-coloured waistcoat, and the profuse jewellery of watch-chains and brooches underneath. The leg and the ankle were turned to a miracle. It is out of the question that I should deny the resemblance altogether, since it has been remarked by so many different persons whom I cannot reasonably accuse of a conspiracy. As a matter of fact, I saw little of it and confessed to nothing. Certainly he was what some might call handsome, of a pictorial, exuberant style of beauty, all attitude, profile, and impudence: a man whom I could see in fancy parade on the grand stand at a race-meeting, or swagger in Piccadilly, staring down the women, and stared at himself with admiration by the coal-porters. Of his frame of mind at that moment his face offered a lively if an unconscious picture. He was lividly pale, and his lip was caught up in a smile that could almost be called a snarl, of a sheer, arid malignity that appalled me and yet put me on my mettle for the encounter. He looked me up and down, then bowed and took off his hat to me.

" My cousin, I presume? " he said.

" I understand I have that honour," I replied.

" The honour is mine," said he, and his voice shook as he said it.

" I should make you welcome, I believe," said I.

" Why? " he inquired. " This poor house has been my home for longer than I care to claim. That you should already take upon yourself the duties of host here is to be at unnecessary pains. Believe me, that part would be more becomingly mine. And, by the way, I must not fail to offer you my little compliment. It is a gratifying surprise to meet you in the dress of a gentleman, and to see "—with a circular look upon the scattered bills—" that your necessities have already been so liberally relieved."

I bowed with a smile that was perhaps no less hateful than his own.

" There are so many necessities in this world," said I. " Charity has to choose. One gets relieved, and some other, no less indigent, perhaps indebted, must go wanting."

" Malice is an engaging trait," said he.

" And envy, I think? " was my reply.

He must have felt that he was not getting wholly the better of this passage at arms; perhaps even feared that he should lose command of his temper, which he reined in throughout the interview as with a red-hot curb, for he flung away from me at the word, and addressed the lawyer with insulting arrogance.

" Mr. Romaine," he said, " since when have you presumed to give orders in this house? "

" I am not prepared to admit that I have given any," replied Romaine; " certainly none that did not fall in the sphere of my responsibilities."

" By whose orders, then, am I denied entrance to my uncle's room? " said my cousin.

" By the doctor's, sir," replied Romaine; " and I think even you will admit his faculty to give them."

" Have a care, sir," cried Alain. " Do not be puffed up with your position. It is none so secure, Master Attorney. I should not wonder in the least if you were struck off the

Devil and All at Amersham Place

rolls for this night's work, and the next I should see of you were when I flung you alms at a pothouse door to mend your ragged elbows. The doctor's orders? But I believe I am not mistaken! You have to-night transacted business with the Count; and this needy young gentleman has enjoyed the privilege of still another interview, in which (as I am pleased to see) his dignity has not prevented his doing very well for himself. I wonder that you should care to prevaricate with me so idly."

"I will confess so much," said Mr. Romaine, "if you call it prevarication. The order in question emanated from the Count himself. He does not wish to see you."

"For which I must take the word of Mr. Daniel Romaine?" asked Alain.

"In default of any better," said Romaine.

There was an instantaneous convulsion in my cousin's face, and I distinctly heard him gnash his teeth at this reply; but, to my surprise, he resumed in tones of almost good humour:

"Come, Mr. Romaine, do not let us be petty!" He drew in a chair and sat down. "Understand you have stolen a march upon me. You have introduced your soldier of Napoleon, and (how, I cannot conceive) he has been apparently accepted with favour. I ask no better proof than the funds with which I find him literally surrounded—I presume in consequence of some extravagance of joy at the first sight of so much money. The odds are so far in your favour, but the match is not yet won. Questions will arise of undue influence, of sequestration, and the like: I have my witnesses ready. I tell it you cynically, for you cannot profit by the knowledge; and, if the worst come to the worst, I have good hopes of recovering my own and of ruining you."

"You do what you please," answered Romaine; "but I give it you for a piece of good advice, you had best do nothing in the matter. You will only make yourself ridiculous; you will only squander money, of which you have none too much, and reap public mortification."

"Ah, but there you make the common mistake, Mr. Romaine!" returned Alain. "You despise your adversary. Consider, if you please, how very disagreeable I could make myself, if I chose. Consider the position of your *protégé*—an escaped prisoner! But I play a great game. I condemn such petty opportunities."

151

At this Romaine and I exchanged a glance of triumph. It seemed manifest that Alain had as yet received no word of Clausel's recapture and denunciation. At the same moment the lawyer, thus relieved of the instancy of his fear, changed his tactics. With a great air of unconcern, he secured the newspaper, which still lay open before him on the table.

"I think, Monsieur Alain, that you labour under some illusion," said he. "Believe me, this is all beside the mark. You seem to be pointing to some compromise. Nothing is further from my views. You suspect me of an inclination to trifle with you, to conceal how things are going. I cannot, on the other hand, be too early or too explicit in giving you information which concerns you (I must say) capitally. Your great-uncle has to-night cancelled his will, and made a new one in favour of your cousin Anne. Nay, and you shall hear it from his own lips, if you choose! I will take so much upon me," said the lawyer, rising. "Follow me, if you please, gentlemen."

Mr. Romaine led the way out of the room so briskly, and was so briskly followed by Alain, that I had hard ado to get the remainder of the money replaced and the despatch-box locked, and to overtake them, even by running, ere they should be lost in that maze of corridors, my uncle's house. As it was, I went with a heart divided; and the thought of my treasure left unprotected, save by a paltry lid and lock that any one might break or pick open, put me in a perspiration whenever I had the time to remember it. The lawyer brought us to a room, begged us to be seated while he should hold a consultation with the doctor, and slipping out of another door, left Alain and myself closeted together.

Truly he had done nothing to ingratiate himself; his every word had been steeped in unfriendliness, envy, and that contempt which (as it is born of anger) it is possible to support without humiliation. On my part, I had been little more conciliating; and yet I began to be sorry for this man, hired spy as I knew him to be. It seemed to me less than decent that he should have been brought up in the expectation of this great inheritance, and now, at the eleventh hour, be tumbled forth out of the house door and left to himself, his poverty and his debts—those debts of which I had so ungallantly reminded him so short a time before. And we were scarce left alone ere I made haste to hang out a flag of truce.

Devil and All at Amersham Place

"My cousin," said I, "trust me, you will not find me inclined to be your enemy."

He paused in front of me—for he had not accepted the lawyer's invitation to be seated, but walked to and fro in the apartment—took a pinch of snuff, and looked at me while he was taking it with an air of much curiosity.

"Is it even so?" said he. "Am I so far favoured by fortune as to have your pity? Infinitely obliged, my cousin Anne! But these sentiments are not always reciprocal, and I warn you that the day when I set my foot on your neck, the spine shall break. Are you acquainted with the properties of the spine?" he asked with an insolence beyond qualification.

It was too much. "I am acquainted also with the properties of a pair of pistols," said I, toising him.

"No, no, no!" says he, holding up his finger. "I will take my revenge how and when I please. We are enough of the same family to understand each other, perhaps; and the reason why I have not had you arrested on your arrival, why I had not a picket of soldiers in the first clump of evergreens, to await and prevent your coming—I, who knew all, before whom that pettifogger, Romaine, has been conspiring in broad daylight to supplant me—is simply this: that I had not made up my mind how I was to take my revenge."

At that moment he was interrupted by the tolling of a bell. As we stood surprised and listening, it was succeeded by the sound of many feet trooping up the stairs and shuffling by the door of our room. Both, I believe, had a great curiosity to set it open, which each, owing to the presence of the other, resisted; and we waited instead in silence, and without moving, until Romaine returned and bade us to my uncle's presence.

He led the way by a little crooked passage, which brought us out in the sick-room, and behind the bed. I believe I have forgotten to remark that the Count's chamber was of considerable dimensions. We beheld it now crowded with the servants and dependants of the house, from the doctor and the priest to Mr. Dawson and the housekeeper, from Dawson down to Rowley and the last footman in white calves, the last plump chambermaid in her clean gown and cap, and the last ostler in a stable waistcoat. This large congregation of persons (and I was surprised to see how large it was) had the appearance, for the most part, of being ill at ease and heartily bewildered, standing on one foot, gaping like zanies, and those who were in the corners nudging each other and grinning aside. My uncle, on the other hand, who was raised higher than I had yet seen him on his pillows, wore an air of really imposing gravity. No sooner had we appeared behind him, than he lifted his voice to a good loudness, and addressed the assemblage.

"I take you all to witness—can you hear me?—I take you all to witness that I recognise as my heir and representative this gentleman, whom most of you see for the first time, the Viscount Anne de St.-Yves, my nephew of the younger line. And I take you to witness at the same time that, for very good reasons known to myself, I have discarded and disinherited this other gentleman whom you all know, the Viscount de St.-Yves. I have also to explain the unusual trouble to which I have put you all—and, since your supper was not over, I fear I may even say annoyance. It has pleased M. Alain to make some threats of disputing my will, and to pretend that there are among your number certain estimable persons who may be trusted to swear as he shall direct them. It pleases me thus to put it out of his power and to stop the mouths of his false witnesses. I am infinitely obliged by your politeness, and I have the honour to wish you all a very good evening."

As the servants, still greatly mystified, crowded out of the sick-room door, curtseying, pulling the forelock, scraping with the foot, and so on, according to their degree, I turned and stole a look at my cousin. He had borne this crushing public rebuke without change of countenance. He stood, now, very upright, with folded arms, and looking inscrutably at the roof of the apartment. I could not refuse him at that moment the tribute of my admiration. Still more so when, the last of the domestics having filed through the doorway and left us alone with my great-uncle and the lawyer, he took one step forward towards the bed, made a dignified reverence, and addressed the man who had just condemned him to ruin.

"My lord," said he, "you are pleased to treat me in a manner which my gratitude, and your state, equally forbid me to call in question. It will be only necessary for me to call your attention to the length of time in which I have been taught to regard myself as your heir. In that position, I

Devil and All at Amersham Place

judged it only loyal to permit myself a certain scale of expenditure. If I am now to be cut off with a shilling as the reward of twenty years of service, I shall be left not only a beggar, but a bankrupt."

Whether from the fatigue of his recent exertion, or by a well-inspired ingenuity of hate, my uncle had once more closed his eyes; nor did he open them now. "Not with a shilling," he contented himself with replying; and there stole, as he said it, a sort of smile over his face, that flickered there conspicuously for the least moment of time, and then faded and left behind the old impenetrable mask of years, cunning, and fatigue. There could be no mistake: my uncle enjoyed the situation as he had enjoyed few things in the last quarter of a century. The fires of life scarce survived in that frail body; but hatred, like some immortal quality, was still erect and unabated.

Nevertheless my cousin persevered.

"I speak at a disadvantage," he resumed. "My supplanter, with perhaps more wisdom than delicacy, remains in the room," and he cast a glance at me that might have withered an oak tree.

I was only too willing to withdraw, and Romaine showed as much alacrity to make way for my departure. But my uncle was not to be moved. In the same breath of a voice, and still without opening his eyes, he bade me remain.

"It is well," said Alain. "I cannot then go on to remind you of the twenty years that have passed over our heads in England, and the services I may have rendered you in that time. It would be a position too odious. Your lordship knows me too well to suppose I could stoop to such ignominy. I must leave out all my defence—your lordship wills it so! I do not know what are my faults; I know only my punishment, and it is greater than I have the courage to face. My uncle, I implore your pity: pardon me so far; do not send me for life into a debtors' jail—a pauper debtor."

"*Chat et vieux, pardonnez ?*" said my uncle, quoting from La Fontaine; and then, opening a pale-blue eye full on Alain, he delivered with some emphasis:

> "La jeunesse se flatte et croit tout obtenir;
> La vieillesse est impitoyable."

The blood leaped darkly into Alain's face. He turned to Romaine and me, and his eyes flashed.

"It is your turn now," he said. "At least it shall be prison for prison with the two viscounts."

"Not so, Mr. Alain, by your leave," said Romaine. "There are a few formalities to be considered first."

But Alain was already striding towards the door.

"Stop a moment, stop a moment!" cried Romaine. "Remember your own counsel not to despise an adversary."

Alain turned.

"If I do not despise I hate you!" he cried, giving a loose to his passion. "Be warned of that, both of you."

"I understand you to threaten Monsieur le Vicomte Anne," said the lawyer. "Do you know, I would not do that. I am afraid, I am very much afraid, if you were to do as you propose, you might drive me into extremes."

"You have made me a beggar and a bankrupt," said Alain. "What extreme is left?"

"I scarce like to put a name upon it in this company," replied Romaine. "But there are worse things than even bankruptcy, and worse places than a debtors' jail."

The words were so significantly said that there went a visible thrill through Alain; sudden as a sword-stroke, he fell pale again.

"I do not understand you," said he.

"Oh yes, you do," returned Romaine. "I believe you understand me very well. You must not suppose that all this time, while you were so very busy, others were entirely idle. You must not fancy, because I am an Englishman, that I have not the intelligence to pursue an inquiry. Great as is my regard for the honour of your house, M. Alain de St.-Yves, if I hear of you moving directly or indirectly in this matter, I shall do my duty, let it cost what it will: that is, I shall communicate the real name of the Buonapartist spy who signs his letters *Rue Grégoire de Tours*."

I confess my heart was already almost altogether on the side of my insulted and unhappy cousin; and if it had not been before, it must have been so now, so horrid was the shock with which he heard his infamy exposed. Speech was denied him; he carried his hand to his neck-cloth; he staggered; I thought he must have fallen. I ran to help him, and at that he revived, recoiled before me, and stood there with arms stretched forth as if to preserve himself from the outrage of my touch.

After the Storm

"Hands off!" he somehow managed to articulate.

"You will now, I hope," pursued the lawyer, without any change of voice, "understand the position in which you are placed, and how delicately it behoves you to conduct yourself. Your arrest hangs, if I may so express myself, by a hair; and as you will be under the perpetual vigilance of myself and my agents, you must look to it narrowly that you walk straight. Upon the least dubiety, I will take action." He snuffed, looking critically at the tortured man. "And now let me remind you that your chaise is at the door. This interview is agitating to his lordship—it cannot be agreeable for you—and I suggest that it need not be further drawn out. It does not enter into the views of your uncle, the Count, that you should again sleep under this roof."

As Alain turned and passed without a word or a sign from the apartment, I instantly followed: I suppose I must be at bottom possessed of some humanity; at least, this accumulated torture, this slow butchery of a man as by quarters of rock, had wholly changed my sympathies. At that moment I loathed both my uncle and the lawyer for their cold-blooded cruelty.

Leaning over the banisters, I was but in time to hear his hasty footsteps in that hall that had been crowded with servants to honour his coming, and was now left empty against his friendless departure. A moment later, and the echoes rang, and the air whistled in my ears, as he slammed the door on his departing footsteps. The fury of the concussion gave me (had one been still wanted) a measure of the turmoil of his passions. In a sense, I felt with him; I felt how he would have gloried to slam that door on my uncle, the lawyer, myself, and the whole crowd of those who had been witnesses to his humiliation.

CHAPTER XX

AFTER THE STORM

No sooner was the house clear of my cousin than I began to reckon up, ruefully enough, the probable results of what had passed. Here were a number of pots broken, and it looked to me as if I should have to pay for all! Here had been this proud, mad beast goaded and baited both publicly and privately, till he could neither hear nor see nor reason; where-upon the gate had been set open and he had been left free to go and contrive whatever vengeance he might find possible. I could not help thinking it was a pity that, whenever I myself was inclined to be upon my good behaviour, some friends of mine should always determine to play a piece of heroics and cast me for the hero—or the victim—which is very much the same. The first duty of heroics is to be of your own choosing. When they are not that, they are nothing. And I assure you, as I walked back to my own room, I was in no very complaisant humour: thought my uncle and Mr. Romaine to have played knuckle-bones with my life and prospects; cursed them for it roundly; had no wish more urgent than to avoid the pair of them; and was quite knocked out of time, as they say in the ring, to find myself confronted with the lawyer.

He stood on my hearthrug, leaning on the chimney-piece, with a gloomy, thoughtful brow, as I was pleased to see, and not in the least as though he were vain of the late proceedings.

" Well? " said I. " You have done it now! "

" Is he gone? " he asked.

" He is gone," said I. " We shall have the devil to pay with him when he comes back."

" You are right," said the lawyer, " and very little to pay him with but flams and fabrications, like to-night's."

" To-night's? " I repeated.

" Ay, to-night's! " said he.

" To-night's *what* ? " I cried.

" To-night's flams and fabrications."

" God be good to me, sir," said I, " have I something more to admire in your conduct than ever *I* had suspected? You cannot think how you interest me! That it was severe, I knew; I had already chuckled over that. But that it should be false also! In what sense, dear sir? "

I believe I was extremely offensive as I put the question, but the lawyer paid no heed.

" False in all senses of the word," he replied seriously. " False in the sense that they were not true, and false in the sense that they were not real; false in the sense that I boasted, and in the sense that I lied. How can I arrest him? Your uncle burned the papers! I told you so—but doubtless you have forgotten—the day I first saw you in Edinburgh Castle.

After the Storm

It was an act of generosity; I have seen many of these acts, and always regretted—always regretted! 'That shall be his inheritance,' he said, as the papers burned; he did not mean that it should have proved so rich a one. How rich, time will tell."

"I beg your pardon a hundred thousand times, my dear sir, but it strikes me you have the impudence—in the circumstances, I may call it the indecency—to appear cast down?"

"It is true," said he: "I am. I am cast down. I am literally cast down. I feel myself quite helpless against your cousin."

"Now, really!" I asked. "Is this serious? And is it perhaps the reason why you have gorged the poor devil with every species of insult? and why you took such surprising pains to supply me with what I had so little need of—another enemy? That you were helpless against him? 'Here is my last missile,' say you; 'my ammunition is quite exhausted; just wait till I get the last in—it will irritate, it cannot hurt him. There—you see!—he is furious now, and I am quite helpless. One more prod, another kick: now he is a mere lunatic! Stand behind me; I am quite helpless!' Mr. Romaine, I am asking myself as to the background or motive of this singular jest, and whether the name of it should not be called treachery?"

"I can scarce wonder," said he. "In truth it has been a singular business, and we are very fortunate to be out of it so well. Yet it was not treachery: no, no, Mr. Anne, it was not treachery; and if you will do me the favour to listen to me for the inside of a minute, I shall demonstrate the same to you beyond cavil." He seemed to wake up to his ordinary briskness. "You see the point?" he began. "He had not yet read the newspaper, but who could tell when he might? He might have had that damned journal in his pocket, and how should we know? We were—I may say, we are—at the mercy of the merest twopenny accident."

"Why, true," said I: "I had not thought of that."

"I warrant you," cried Romaine, "you had supposed it was nothing to be the hero of an interesting notice in the journals! You had supposed, as like as not, it was a form of secrecy! But not so in the least. A part of England is already buzzing with the name of Champdivers; a day or two more and the mail will have carried it everywhere: so

wonderful a machine is this of ours for disseminating intelligence! Think of it! When my father was born——
but that is another story. To return: we had here the elements of such a combustion as I dread to think of—your
cousin and the journal. Let him but glance an eye upon that
column of print, and where were we? It is easy to ask; not
so easy to answer, my young friend. And let me tell you, this
sheet is the Viscount's usual reading. It is my conviction
he had it in his pocket."

"I beg your pardon, sir," said I. "I have been unjust.
I did not appreciate my danger."

"I think you never do," said he.

"But yet surely that public scene——" I began.

"It was madness. I quite agree with you," Mr. Romaine
interrupted. "But it was your uncle's orders, Mr. Anne,
and what could I do? Tell him you were the murderer of
Goguelat? I think not."

"No, sure!" said I. "That would but have been to
make the trouble thicker. We were certainly in a very ill
posture."

"You do not yet appreciate how grave it was," he replied.
"It was necessary for you that your cousin should go, and go
at once. You yourself had to leave to-night under cover of
darkness, and how could you have done that with the Viscount
in the next room? He must go, then; he must leave without
delay. And that was the difficulty."

"Pardon me, Mr. Romaine, but could not my uncle have
bidden him go?" I asked.

"Why, I see I must tell you that this is not so simple as it
sounds," he replied. "You say this is your uncle's house, and
so it is. But to all effects and purposes it is your cousin's
also. He has rooms here; has had them coming on for thirty
years now, and they are filled with a prodigious accumulation
of trash—stays, I dare say, and powder-puffs, and such effeminate idiocy—to which none could dispute his title, even
suppose any one wanted to. We had a perfect right to bid
him go, and he had a perfect right to reply, ' Yes, I will go,
but not without my stays and cravats. I must first get
together the nine-hundred-and-ninety-nine chestsfull of insufferable rubbish, that I have spent the last thirty years
collecting—and may very well spend the next thirty hours
a-packing of.' And what should we have said to that?"

After the Storm

" By way of repartee? " I asked.   " Two tall footmen and a pair of crabtree cudgels, I suggest."

" The Lord deliver me from the wisdom of laymen! " cried Romaine.   " Put myself in the wrong at the beginning of a law-suit? No, indeed!   There was but one thing to do, and I did it, and burned my last cartridge in the doing of it.   I stunned him.   And it gave us three hours, by which we should make haste to profit; for if there is one thing sure, it is that he will be up to time again to-morrow in the morning."

" Well," said I, " I own myself an idiot.   Well do they say, *an old soldier, an old innocent !* For I guessed nothing of all this."

" And, guessing it, have you the same objections to leave England? " he inquired.

" The same," said I.

" It is indispensable," he objected.

" And it cannot be," I replied.   " Reason has nothing to say in the matter; and I must not let you squander any of yours.   It will be enough to tell you this is an affair of the heart."

" Is it even so? " quoth Romaine, nodding his head.   " And I might have been sure of it.   Place them in a hospital, put them in a jail in yellow overalls, do what you will, young Jessamy finds young Jenny.   Oh, have it your own way; I am too old a hand to argue with young gentlemen who choose to fancy themselves in love; I have too much experience, thank you.   Only, be sure that you appreciate what you risk: the prison, the dock, the gallows, and the halter—terribly vulgar circumstances, my young friend; grim, sordid, earnest; no poetry in that! "

" And there I am warned," I returned gaily.   " No man could be warned more finely or with a greater eloquence. And I am of the same opinion still.   Until I have again seen that lady, nothing shall induce me to quit Great Britain.   I have besides——"

And here I came to a full stop.   It was upon my tongue to have told him the story of the drovers, but at the first word of it my voice died in my throat.   There might be a limit to the lawyer's toleration, I reflected.   I had not been so long in Britain altogether; for the most part of that time I had been by the heels in limbo in Edinburgh Castle; and already I had confessed to killing one man with a pair of scissors; and now I was to go on and plead guilty to having settled another with a holly stick! A wave of discretion went over me as cold and as deep as the sea.

"In short, sir, this is a matter of feeling," I concluded, "and nothing will prevent my going to Edinburgh."

If I had fired a pistol in his ear he could not have been more startled.

"To Edinburgh?" he repeated. "Edinburgh? where the very paving-stones know you!"

"Then is the murder out!" said I. "But, Mr. Romaine, is there not sometimes safety in boldness? Is it not a commonplace of strategy to get where the enemy least expects you? And where would he expect me less?"

"Faith, there is something in that, too!" cried the lawyer. "Ay, certainly, a great deal in that. All the witnesses drowned but one, and he safe in prison; you yourself changed beyond recognition—let us hope—and walking the streets of the very town you have illustrated by your—well, your eccentricity! It is not badly combined indeed!"

"You approve it, then?" said I.

"Oh, approve!" said he; "there is no question of approval. There is only one course which I could approve, and that were to escape to France instanter."

"You do not wholly disapprove, at least?" I substituted.

"Not wholly; and it would not matter if I did," he replied. "Go your own way; you are beyond argument. And I am not sure that you will run more danger by that course than by any other. Give the servants time to get to bed and fall asleep, then take a country cross-road and walk, as the rhyme has it, like blazes all night. In the morning take a chaise or take the mail at pleasure, and continue your journey with all the decorum and reserve of which you shall be found capable."

"I am taking the picture in," I said. "Give me time. 'Tis the *tout ensemble* I must see: the whole as opposed to the details."

"Mountebank!" he murmured.

"Yes, I have it now; and I see myself with a servant, and that servant is Rowley," said I.

"So as to have one more link with your uncle?" suggested the lawyer. "Very judicious!"

"And, pardon me, but that is what it is," I exclaimed. "Judicious is the word. I am not making a deception fit to last for thirty years; I do not found a palace in the living granite for the night. This is a shelter tent—a flying picture —seen, admired, and gone again in the wink of an eye. What is wanted, in short, is a *trompe-l'œil* that shall be good enough for twelve hours at an inn: is it not so? "

" It is, and the objection holds. Rowley is but another danger," said Romaine.

" Rowley," said I, " will pass as a servant from a distance— as a creature seen poised on the dicky of a bowling chaise. He will pass at hand as a smart, civil fellow one meets in the inn corridor, and looks back at, and asks, and is told, ' Gentleman's servant in Number 4.' He will pass, in fact, all round except with his personal friends! My dear sir, pray what do you expect? Of course, if we meet my cousin, or if we meet anybody who took part in the judicious exhibition of this evening, we are lost; and who's denying it? To every disguise, however good and safe, there is always the weak point; you must always take (let us say— and to take a simile from your own waistcoat pocket) a snuffbox-full of risk. You'll get it just as small with Rowley as with anybody else. And the long and short of it is, the lad's honest, he likes me, I trust him; he is my servant, or nobody."

" He might not accept," said Romaine.

" I bet you a thousand pounds he does! " cried I. " But no matter; all you have to do is to send him out to-night on this cross-country business, and leave the thing to me. I tell you, he will be my servant, and I tell you, he will do well."

I had crossed the room, and was already overhauling my wardrobe as I spoke.

" Well," concluded the lawyer, with a shrug, " one risk with another: *à la guerre comme à la guerre*, as you would say. Let the brat come and be useful, at least." And he was about to ring the bell, when his eye was caught by my researches in the wardrobe. " Do not fall in love with these coats, waistcoats, cravats, and other panoply and accoutrements by which you are now surrounded. You must not run the post as a dandy. It is not the fashion, even."

" You are pleased to be facetious, sir," said I; " and not according to knowledge. These clothes are my life, they are my disguise; and since I can take but few of them, I were a fool indeed if I selected hastily! Will you understand, once and for all, what I am seeking? To be invisible, is the first point; the second, to be invisible in a post-chaise and with a servant. Can you not perceive the delicacy of the quest? Nothing must be too coarse, nothing too fine; *rien de voyant, rien qui détonne;* so that I may leave everywhere the inconspicuous image of a handsome young man of a good fortune travelling in proper style, whom the landlord will forget in twelve hours—and the chambermaid perhaps remember, God bless her! with a sigh. This is the very fine art of dress."

" I have practised it with success for fifty years," said Romaine, with a chuckle. " A black suit and a clean shirt is my infallible recipe."

" You surprise me; I did not think you would be shallow! " said I, lingering between two coats. " Pray, Mr. Romaine, have I your head? or did you travel post and with a smartish servant? "

" Neither, I admit," said he.

" Which change the whole problem," I continued. " I have to dress for a smartish servant and a Russia leather despatch-box." That brought me to a stand. I came over and looked at the box with a moment's hesitation. " Yes," I resumed. " Yes, and for the despatch-box! It looks moneyed and landed; it means I have a lawyer. It is an invaluable property. But I could have wished it to hold less money. The responsibility is crushing. Should I not do more wisely to take five hundred pounds, and intrust the remainder with you, Mr. Romaine? "

" If you are sure you will not want it," answered Romaine.

" I am far from sure of that," cried I. " In the first place, as a philosopher. This is the first time I have been at the head of a large sum, and it is conceivable—who knows himself —that I may make it fly. In the second place, as a fugitive. Who knows what I may need? The whole of it may be inadequate. But I can always write for more."

" You do not understand," he replied. " I break off all communication with you here and now. You must give me a power of attorney ere you start to-night, and then be done with me trenchantly until better days."

I believe I offered some objection.

" Think a little for once of me! " said Romaine. " I must not have seen you before to-night. To-night we are to have had our only interview, and you are to have given me the power; and to-night I am to have lost sight of you again—I know not whither, you were upon business, it was none of my affairs to question you! And this, you are to remark, in the interests of your own safety much more than mine."

" I am not even to write to you ? " I said, a little bewildered.

" I believe I am cutting the last strand that connects you with common-sense," he replied. " But that is the plain English of it. You are not even to write; and if you did, I would not answer."

" A letter, however——" I began.

" Listen to me," interrupted Romaine. " So soon as your cousin reads the paragraph, what will he do ? Put the police upon looking into my correspondence ! So soon as you write to me, in short, you write to Bow Street; and if you will take my advice, you will date that letter from France."

" The devil ! " said I, for I began suddenly to see that this might put me out of the way of my business.

" What is it now ? " says he.

" There will be more to be done, then, before we can part," I answered.

" I give you the whole night," said he. " So long as you are off ere daybreak, I am content."

" In short, Mr. Romaine," said I, " I have had so much benefit of your advice and services that I am loth to sever the connection, and would even ask a substitute. I would be obliged for a letter of introduction to one of your own cloth in Edinburgh—an old man for choice, very experienced, very respectable, and very secret. Could you favour me with such a letter ? "

" Why, no," said he. " Certainly not. I will do no such thing, indeed."

" It would be a great favour, sir," I pleaded.

" It would be an unpardonable blunder," he replied. " What ? Give you a letter of introduction ? and when the police come, I suppose, I must forget the circumstance ? No, indeed. Talk of it no more."

" You seem to be always in the right," said I. " The letter would be out of the question, I quite see that. But the lawyer's name might very well have dropped from you in the way of conversation; having heard him mentioned, I might profit by the circumstance to introduce myself; and in this way my business would be the better done, and you not in the least compromised."

"What is this business?" said Romaine.

"I have not said that I had any," I replied. "It might arise. This is only a possibility that I must keep in view."

"Well," said he, with a gesture of the hands, "I mention Mr. Robbie; and let that be an end of it!—Or wait!" he added, "I have it. Here is something that will serve you for an introduction, and cannot compromise me." And he wrote his name and the Edinburgh lawyer's address on a piece of card and tossed it to me.

CHAPTER XXI

I BECOME THE OWNER OF A CLARET-COLOURED CHAISE

What with packing, signing papers, and partaking of an excellent cold supper in the lawyer's room, it was past two in the morning before we were ready for the road. Romaine himself let us out of a window in a part of the house known to Rowley: it appears it served as a kind of postern to the servants' hall, by which (when they were in the mind for a clandestine evening) they would come regularly in and out; and I remember very well the vinegar aspect of the lawyer on the receipt of this piece of information—how he pursed his lips, jutted his eyebrows, and kept repeating, "This must be seen to, indeed! this shall be barred to-morrow in the morning!" In this pre-occupation, I believe he took leave of me without observing it; our things were handed out; we heard the window shut behind us; and became instantly lost in a horrid intricacy of blackness and the shadow of woods.

A little wet snow kept sleepily falling, pausing, and falling again; it seemed perpetually beginning to snow and perpetually leaving off; and the darkness was intense. Time and again we walked into trees; time and again found ourselves adrift among garden borders or stuck like a ram in the thicket. Rowley had possessed himself of the matches, and he was neither to be terrified nor softened. "No, I will not, Mr. Anne, sir," he would reply. "You know he tell me to wait till we were over the 'ill. It's only a little way now. Why, and I thought you was a soldier, too!" I was at least a very glad soldier when my valet consented at last to kindle a thieves' match. From this, we easily lit the lantern: and

A Claret-Coloured Chaise

thenceforward, through a labyrinth of woodland paths, were conducted by its uneasy glimmer. Both booted and great-coated, with tall hats much of a shape, and laden with booty in the form of a despatch-box, a case of pistols, and two plump valises, I thought we had very much the look of a pair of brothers returning from the sack of Amersham Place.

We issued at last upon a country by-road where we might walk abreast and without precaution. It was nine miles to Aylesbury, our immediate destination; by a watch, which formed part of my new outfit, it should be about half-past three in the morning; and as we did not choose to arrive before daylight, time could not be said to press. I gave the order to march at ease.

"Now, Rowley," said I, " so far so good. You have come, in the most obliging manner in the world, to carry these valises. The question is, what next? What are we to do at Aylesbury? or, more particularly, what are you? Thence, I go on a journey. Are you to accompany me?"

He gave a little chuckle. "That's all settled already, Mr. Anne, sir," he replied. "Why, I've got my things here in the valise—a half-a-dozen shirts and what not; I'm all ready, sir: just you lead on: *you'll* see."

"The devil you have!" said I. "You made pretty sure of your welcome."

"If you please, sir," said Rowley.

He looked up at me, in the light of the lantern, with a boyish shyness and triumph that awoke my conscience. I could never let this innocent involve himself in the perils and difficulties that beset my course, without some hint of warning, which it was a matter of extreme delicacy to make plain enough and not too plain.

"No, no," said I; "you may think you have made a choice, but it was blindfold, and you must make it over again. The Count's service is a good one; what are you leaving it for? Are you not throwing away the substance for the shadow? No, do not answer me yet. You imagine that I am a pros-perous nobleman, just declared my uncle's heir, on the thres-hold of the best of good fortune, and, from the point of view of a judicious servant, a jewel of a master to serve and stick to? Well, my boy, I am nothing of the kind, nothing of the kind."

As I said the words, I came to a full stop and held up the

lantern to his face. He stood before me, brilliantly illuminated on the background of impenetrable night and falling snow, stricken to stone between his double burden like an ass between two panniers, and gaping at me like a blunderbuss. I had never seen a face so predestined to be astonished, or so susceptible of rendering the emotion of surprise; and it tempted me as an open piano tempts the musician.

"Nothing of the sort, Rowley," I continued, in a churchyard voice. "These are appearances, petty appearances. I am in peril, homeless, hunted. I count scarce any one in England who is not my enemy. From this hour I drop my name, my title; I become nameless; my name is proscribed. My liberty, my life, hang by a hair. The destiny which you will accept, if you go forth with me, is to be tracked by spies, to hide yourself under a false name, to follow the desperate pretences and perhaps share the fate of a murderer with a price upon his head."

His face had been hitherto beyond expectation, passing from one depth to another of tragic astonishment, and really worth paying to see; but at this it suddenly cleared. "Oh, I ain't afraid!" he said; and then, choking into laughter, "why, I see it from the first!"

I could have beaten him. But I had so grossly overshot the mark that I suppose it took me two good miles of road and half-an-hour of elocution to persuade him I had been in earnest. In the course of which I became so interested in demonstrating my present danger that I forgot all about my future safety, and not only told him the story of Goguelat, but threw in the business of the drovers as well, and ended by blurting out that I was a soldier of Napoleon's and a prisoner of war.

This was far from my views when I began; and it is a common complaint of me that I have a long tongue. I believe it is a fault beloved by fortune. Which of you considerate fellows would have done a thing at once so foolhardy and so wise as to make a confidant of a boy in his teens, and positively smelling of the nursery? And when had I cause to repent it? There is none so apt as a boy to be the adviser of any man in difficulties such as mine. To the beginnings of virile common-sense he adds the last lights of the child's imagination; and he can fling himself into business with that superior earnestness that properly belongs to play. And

A Claret-Coloured Chaise

Rowley was a boy made to my hand. He had a high sense of romance, and a secret cultus for all soldiers and criminals. His travelling library consisted of a chap-book life of Wallace and some sixpenny parts of the " Old Bailey Sessions Papers " by Gurney the shorthand writer; and the choice depicts his character to a hair. You can imagine how his new prospects brightened on a boy of this disposition. To be the servant and companion of a fugitive, a soldier, and a murderer, rolled in one—to live by stratagems, disguises, and false names, in an atmosphere of midnight and mystery so thick that you could cut it with a knife—was really, I believe, more dear to him than his meals, though he was a great trencherman, and something of a glutton besides. For myself, as the peg by which all this romantic business hung, I was simply idolised from that moment; and he would rather have sacrificed his hand than surrendered the privilege of serving me.

We arranged the terms of our campaign, trudging amicably in the snow, which now, with the approach of morning, began to fall to purpose. I chose the name of Ramornie, I imagine from its likeness to Romaine; Rowley, from an irresistible conversion of ideas, I dubbed Gammon. His distress was laughable to witness: his own choice of an unassuming nickname had been Claude Duval! We settled our procedure at the various inns where we should alight, rehearsed our little manners like a piece of drill until it seemed impossible we should ever be taken unprepared; and in all these dispositions, you may be sure the despatch-box was not forgotten. Who was to pick it up, who was to set it down, who was to remain beside it, who was to sleep with it—there was no contingency omitted, all was gone into with the thoroughness of a drill-sergeant on the one hand and a child with a new plaything on the other.

" I say, wouldn't it look queer if you and me was to come to the post-house with all this luggage ? " said Rowley.

" I dare say," I replied. " But what else is to be done? "

" Well, now, sir—you hear me," says Rowley. " I think it would look more natural-like if you was to come to the post-house alone, and with nothing in your 'ands—more like a gentleman, you know. And you might say that your servant and baggage was a-waiting for you up the road. I think I could manage, somehow, to make a shift with all them dratted things—leastways if you was to give me a 'and up with them at the start."

" And I would see you far enough before I allowed you to try, Mr. Rowley!" I cried. " Why, you would be quite defenceless! A footpad that was an infant child could rob you. And I should probably come driving by to find you in a ditch with your throat cut. But there is something in your idea, for all that; and I propose we put it in execution no farther forward than the next corner of a lane."

Accordingly, instead of continuing to aim for Aylesbury, we headed by cross-roads for some point to the northward of it, whither I might assist Rowley with the baggage, and where I might leave him to await my return in the post-chaise.

It was snowing to purpose, the country all white, and ourselves walking snowdrifts, when the first glimmer of the morning showed us an inn upon the highwayside. Some distance off, under the shelter of a corner of the road and a clump of trees, I loaded Rowley with the whole of our possessions, and watched him till he staggered in safety into the doors of the *Green Dragon*, which was the sign of the house. Thence I walked briskly into Aylesbury, rejoicing in my freedom and the causeless good spirits that belong to a snowy morning; though, to be sure, long before I had arrived the snow had again ceased to fall and the eaves of Aylesbury were smoking in the level sun. There was an accumulation of gigs and chaises in the yard, and a great bustle going forward in the coffee-room and about the doors of the inn. At these evidences of so much travel on the road I was seized with a misgiving lest it should be impossible to get horses, and I should be detained in the precarious neighbourhood of my cousin. Hungry as I was, I made my way first of all to the postmaster, where he stood—a big, athletic, horsey-looking man, blowing into a key in the corner of the yard.

On my making my modest request, he awoke from his indifference into what seemed passion.

" A po'-shay and 'osses!" he cried. " Do I look as if I 'ad a po'-shay and 'osses? Damn me, if I 'ave such a thing on the premises. I don't *make* 'osses and chaises—I *'ire* 'em. You might be God Almighty!" said he; and instantly, as if he had observed me for the first time, he broke off, and lowered his voice into the confidential. " Why, now that I see you are a gentleman," said he, " I'll tell you what! If you like

A Claret-Coloured Chaise

to *buy*, I have the article to fit you. Second-'and shay by Lycett, of London. Latest style; good as new. Superior fittin's, net on the roof, baggage platform, pistol 'olsters—the most com-plete and the most gen-teel turn-out I ever see! The 'ole for seventy-five pound! It's as good as givin' her away!"

"Do you propose I should trundle it myself, like a hawker's barrow?" said I. "Why, my good man, if I had to stop here, anyway, I should prefer to buy a house and garden!"

"Come and look at her!" he cried; and, with the word, links his arm in mine and carries me to the outhouse where the chaise was on view.

It was just the sort of chaise that I had dreamed of for my purpose: eminently rich, inconspicuous, and genteel; for, though I thought the postmaster no great authority, I was bound to agree with him so far. The body was painted a dark claret, and the wheels an invisible green. The lamp and glasses were bright as silver; and the whole equipage had an air of privacy and reserve that seemed to repel inquiry and disarm suspicion. With a servant like Rowley, and a chaise like this, I felt that I could go from the Land's End to John o' Groat's House amid a population of bowing ostlers. And I suppose I betrayed in my manner the degree in which the bargain tempted me.

"Come," cried the postmaster—"I'll make it seventy, to oblige a friend!"

"The point is: the horses," said I.

"Well," said he, consulting his watch, "it's now gone the 'alf after eight. What time do you want her at the door?"

"Horses and all?" said I.

"'Osses and all!" says he. "One good turn deserves another. You give me seventy pound for the shay, and I'll 'oss it for you. I told you I didn't *make* 'osses; but I *can* make 'em, to oblige a friend."

What would you have? It was not the wisest thing in the world to buy a chaise within a dozen miles of my uncle's house; but in this way I got my horses for the next stage. And by any other it appeared that I should have to wait. Accordingly I paid the money down—perhaps twenty pounds too much, though it was certainly a well-made and well-appointed vehicle—ordered it round in half-an-hour, and proceeded to refresh myself with breakfast.

St. Ives

The table to which I sat down occupied the recess of a bay-window, and commanded a view of the front of the inn, where I continued to be amused by the successive departures of travellers—the fussy and the offhand, the niggardly and the lavish—all exhibiting their different characters in that diagnostic moment of the farewell: some escorted to the stirrup or the chaise door by the chamberlain, the chamber-maids and the waiters almost in a body, others moving off under a cloud, without human countenance. In the course of this I became interested in one for whom this ovation began to assume the proportions of a triumph; not only the under-servants, but the barmaid, the landlady, and my friend the postmaster himself, crowding about the steps to speed his departure. I was aware, at the same time, of a good deal of merriment, as though the traveller were a man of a ready wit, and not too dignified to air it in that society. I leaned forward with a lively curiosity; and the next moment I had blotted myself behind the teapot. The popular traveller had turned to wave a farewell; and behold! he was no other than my cousin Alain. It was a change of the sharpest from the angry, pallid man I had seen at Amersham Place. Ruddy to a fault, illuminated with vintages, crowned with his curls like Bacchus, he now stood before me for an instant, the per-fect master of himself, smiling with airs of conscious popu-larity and insufferable condescension. He reminded me at once of a royal duke, or an actor turned a little elderly, and of a blatant bagman who should have been the illegitimate son of a gentleman. A moment after he was gliding noise-lessly on the road to London.

I breathed again. I recognised, with heartfelt gratitude, how lucky I had been to go in by the stable-yard instead of the hostelry door, and what a fine occasion of meeting my cousin I had lost by the purchase of the claret-coloured chaise! The next moment I remembered that there was a waiter present. No doubt but he must have observed me when I crouched behind the breakfast equipage; no doubt but he must have commented on this unusual and undignified behaviour; and it was essential that I should do something to remove the impression.

" Waiter! " said I, " that was the nephew of Count Carwell that just drove off, wasn't it? "

" Yes, sir: Viscount Carwell we calls him," he replied.

A Claret-Coloured Chaise

"Ah, I thought as much," said I. "Well, well, damn all these Frenchmen, says I!"

"You may say so indeed, sir," said the waiter. "They ain't not to say in the same field with our 'ome-raised gentry."

"Nasty tempers?" I suggested.

"Beas'ly temper, sir, the Viscount 'ave," said the waiter with feeling. "Why, no longer agone than this morning, he was sitting breakfasting and reading in his paper. I suppose, sir, he come on some pilitical information, or it might be about 'orses, but he raps his 'and upon the table sudden and calls for curaçoa. It gave me quite a turn, it did; he did it that sudden and 'ard. Now, sir, that may be manners in France, but hall I can say is, that I'm not used to it."

"Reading the paper, was he?" said I. "What paper, eh?"

"Here it is, sir," exclaimed the waiter. "Seems like as if he'd dropped it."

And picking it off the floor he presented it to me.

I may say that I was quite prepared, that I already knew what to expect; but at sight of the cold print my heart stopped beating. There it was: the fulfilment of Romaine's apprehension was before me; the paper was laid open at the capture of Clausel. I felt as if I could take a little curaçoa myself, but on second thoughts called for brandy. It was badly wanted; and suddenly I observed the waiter's eye to sparkle, as it were, with some recognition; made certain he had remarked the resemblance between me and Alain; and became aware—as by a revelation—of the fool's part I had been playing. For I had now managed to put my identification beyond a doubt, if Alain should choose to make his inquiries at Aylesbury; and, as if that were not enough, I had added, at an expense of seventy pounds, a clue by which he might follow me through the length and breadth of England in the shape of the claret-coloured chaise! That elegant equipage (which I began to regard as little better than a claret-coloured ante-room to the hangman's cart) coming presently to the door, I left my breakfast in the middle and departed; posting to the north as diligently as my cousin Alain was posting to the south, and putting my trust (such as it was) in an opposite direction and equal speed.

St. Ives

CHAPTER XXII

CHARACTER AND ACQUIREMENTS OF MR. ROWLEY

I AM not certain that I had ever really appreciated before that hour the extreme peril of the adventure on which I was embarked. The sight of my cousin, the look of his face—so handsome, so jovial at the first sight, and branded with so much malignity as you saw it on the second—with his hyperbolical curls in order, with his neckcloth tied as if for the conquests of love, setting forth (as I had no doubt in the world he was doing) to clap the Bow Street runners on my trail, and cover England with handbills, each dangerous as a loaded musket, convinced me for the first time that the affair was no less serious than death. I believe it came to a near touch whether I should not turn the horses' heads at the next stage and make directly for the coast. But I was now in the position of a man who should have thrown his gage into the den of lions; or, better still, like one who should have quarrelled overnight under the influence of wine, and now at daylight, in a cold winter's morning, and humbly sober, must make good his words. It is not that I thought any the less, or any the less warmly, of Flora. But, as I smoked a grim segar that morning in a corner of the chaise, no doubt I considered, in the first place, that the letter-post had been invented, and admitted privately to myself, in the second, that it would have been highly possible to write her on a piece of paper, seal it, and send it skimming by the mail, instead of going personally into these egregious dangers, and through a country that I beheld crowded with gibbets and Bow Street officers. As for Sim and Candlish, I doubt if they crossed my mind.

At the Green Dragon Rowley was waiting on the doorsteps with the luggage, and really was bursting with unpalatable conversation.

" Who do you think we've 'ad 'ere, sir? " he began breathlessly, as the chaise drove off. " Red Breasts "; and he nodded his head portentously.

" Red Breasts? " I repeated, for I stupidly did not understand at the moment an expression I had often heard.

" Ah! " said he. " Red weskits. Runners. Bow Street runners. Two on 'em, and one was Lavender himself! I

Character of Mr. Rowley

hear the other say quite plain, ' Now, Mr. Lavender, *if* you're ready.' They was breakfasting as nigh me as I am to that postboy. They're all right; they ain't after us. It's a forger; and I didn't send them off on a false scent—Oh no! I thought there was no use in having them over our way; so I give them ' very valuable information,' Mr. Lavender said, and tipped me a tizzy for myself; and they're off to Luton. They showed me the 'andcuffs, too—the other one did—and he clicked the dratted things on my wrist; and I tell you, I believe I nearly went off in a swound! There's something so beastly in the feel of them! Begging your pardon, Mr. Anne," he added, with one of his delicious changes from the character of the confidential schoolboy into that of the trained, respectful servant.

Well, I must not be proud! I cannot say I found the subject of handcuffs to my fancy; and it was with more asperity than was needful that I reproved him for the slip about the name.

" Yes, Mr. Ramornie," says he, touching his hat. " Begging your pardon, Mr. Ramornie. But I've been very piticular, sir, up to now; and you may trust me to be very piticular in the future. It were only a slip, sir."

" My good boy," says I, with the most imposing severity, " there must be no slips. Be so good as to remember that my life is at stake."

I did not embrace the occasion of telling him how many I had made myself. It is my principle that an officer must never be wrong. I have seen two divisions beating their brains out for a fortnight against a worthless and quite impregnable castle in a pass I knew we were only doing it for discipline, because the General had said so at first, and had not yet found any way out of his own words; and I highly admired his force of character, and throughout these operations thought my life exposed in a very good cause. With fools and children, which included Rowley, the necessity was even greater. I proposed to myself to be infallible; and even when he expressed some wonder at the purchase of the claret-coloured chaise, I put him promptly in his place. In our situation, I told him, everything had to be sacrificed to appearances; doubtless, in a hired chaise, we should have had more freedom, but look at the dignity! I was so positive, that I had sometimes almost convinced myself. Not for long, you may be certain! This detestable conveyance always appeared to me to be laden with Bow Street officers, and to have a placard upon the back of it publishing my name and crimes. If I had paid seventy pounds to get the thing, I should not have stuck at seven hundred to be safely rid of it.

And if the chaise was a danger, what an anxiety was the despatch-box and its golden cargo! I had never had a care but to draw my pay and spend it; I had lived happily in the regiment, as in my father's house, fed by the great Emperor's commissariat as by ubiquitous doves of Elijah—or, my faith! if anything went wrong with the commissariat, helping myself with the best grace in the world from the next peasant! And now I began to feel at the same time the burthen of riches and the fear of destitution. There were ten thousand pounds in the despatch-box, but I reckoned in French money, and had two hundred and fifty thousand agonies; I kept it under my hand all day, I dreamed of it at night. In the inns, I was afraid to go to dinner and afraid to go to sleep. When I walked up a hill I durst not leave the doors of the claret-coloured chaise. Sometimes I would change the disposition of the funds: there were days when I carried as much as five or six thousand pounds on my own person, and only the residue continued to voyage in the treasure-chest—days when I bulked all over like my cousin, crackled to a touch with bank paper, and had my pockets weighed to bursting-point with sovereigns. And there were other days when I wearied of the thing—or grew ashamed of it—and put all the money back where it had come from: there let it take its chance like better people! In short, I set Rowley a poor example of consistency, and in philosophy, none at all.

Little he cared! All was one to him so long as he was amused, and I never knew any one amused more easily. He was thrillingly interested in life, travel, and his own melo-dramatic position. All day he would be looking from the chaise windows with ebullitions of gratified curiosity, that were sometimes justified and sometimes not, and that (taken altogether) it occasionally wearied me to be obliged to share. I can look at horses, and I can look at trees too, although not fond of it. But why should I look at a lame horse, or a tree that was like the letter Y? What exhilaration could I feel in viewing a cottage that was the same colour as " the second from the miller's " in some place where I had never been, and of which I had not previously heard? I am ashamed to complain, but there were moments when my juvenile and confidential friend weighed heavy on my hands. His cackle was indeed almost continuous, but it was never unamiable. He showed an amiable curiosity when he was asking questions; an amiable guilelessness when he was conferring information. And both he did largely. I am in a position to write the biographies of Mr. Rowley, Mr. Rowley's father and mother, his Aunt Eliza, and the miller's dog; and nothing but pity for the reader, and some misgivings as to the law of copyright, prevail on me to withhold them.

A general design to mould himself upon my example became early apparent, and I had not the heart to check it. He began to mimic my carriage; he acquired, with servile accuracy, a little manner I had of shrugging the shoulders; and I may say it was by observing it in him that I first discovered it in myself. One day it came out by chance that I was of the Catholic religion. He became plunged in thought, at which I was gently glad. Then suddenly—

"Odd-rabbit it! I'll be Catholic too!" he broke out. "You must teach me it, Mr. Anne—I mean, Ramornie."

I dissuaded him: alleging that he would find me very imperfectly informed as to the grounds and doctrines of the Church, and that, after all, in the matter of religions, it was a very poor idea to change. "Of course, my Church is the best," said I; "but that is not the reason why I belong to it: I belong to it because it was the faith of my house. I wish to take my chances with my own people, and so should you. If it is a question of going to hell, go to hell like a gentleman with your ancestors."

"Well, it wasn't that," he admitted. "I don't know that I was exactly thinking of hell. Then there's the inquisition, too. That's rather a cawker, you know."

"And I don't believe you were thinking of anything in the world," said I—which put a period to his respectable conversion.

He consoled himself by playing for awhile on a cheap flageolet, which was one of his diversions, and to which I owed many intervals of peace. When he first produced it, in the joints, from his pocket, he had the duplicity to ask me if I played upon it. I answered, no; and he put the instrument away with a sigh and the remark that he had thought I might. For some while he resisted the unspeakable temptation, his fingers visibly itching and twittering about his pocket, even his interest in the landscape and in sporadic anecdote entirely lost. Presently the pipe was in his hands again; he fitted, unfitted, refitted, and played upon it in dumb show for some time.

" I play it myself a little," says he.

" Do you? " said I, and yawned.

And then he broke down.

" Mr. Ramornie, if you please, would it disturb you, sir, if I was to play a chune? " he pleaded. And from that hour, the tooting of the flageolet cheered our way.

He was particularly keen on the details of battles, single combats, incidents of scouting parties, and the like. These he would make haste to cap with some of the exploits of Wallace, the only hero with whom he had the least acquaintance. His enthusiasm was genuine and pretty. When he learned we were going to Scotland, " Well, then," he broke out, " I'll see where Wallace lived! " And presently after, he fell to moralising. " It's a strange thing, sir," he began, " that I seem somehow to have always the wrong sow by the ear. I'm English after all, and I glory in it. My eye! don't I, though! Let some of your Frenchies come over here to invade, and you'll see whether or not! Oh yes, I'm English to the backbone, I am. And yet look at me! I got hold of this 'ere William Wallace and took to him right off; I never heard of such a man before! And then you came along, and I took to you. And both the two of you were my born enemies! I—I beg your pardon, Mr. Ramornie, but would you mind it very much if you didn't go for to do anything against England "—he brought the word out suddenly, like something hot—" when I was along of you? "

I was more affected than I can tell.

" Rowley," I said, " you need have no fear. By how much I love my own honour, by so much I will take care to protect yours. We are but fraternising at the outposts, as soldiers do. When the bugle calls, my boy, we must face each other, one for England, one for France, and may God defend the right! "

So I spoke at the moment; but for all my brave airs, the boy had wounded me in a vital quarter. His words continued to ring in my hearing. There was no remission all day of my

Character of Mr. Rowley

remorseful thoughts; and that night (which we lay at Lich-field, I believe) there was no sleep for me in my bed. I put out the candle and lay down with a good resolution; and in a moment all was light about me like a theatre, and I saw myself upon the stage of it playing ignoble parts. I remembered France and my Emperor, now depending on the arbitrament of war, bent down, fighting on their knees and with their teeth against so many and such various assailants. And I burned with shame to be here in England, cherishing an English fortune, pursuing an English mistress, and not there, to handle a musket in my native fields, and to manure them with my body if I fell. I remembered that I belonged to France. All my fathers had fought for her, and some had died; the voice in my throat, the sight of my eyes, the tears that now sprang there, the whole man of me, was fashioned of French earth and born of a French mother; I had been tended and caressed by a succession of the daughters of France, the fairest, the most ill-starred; and I had fought and conquered shoulder to shoulder with her sons. A soldier, a noble, of the proudest and bravest race in Europe, it had been left to the prattle of a hobbledehoy lackey in an English chaise to recall me to the consciousness of duty.

When I saw how it was I did not lose time in indecision. The old classical conflict of love and honour being once fairly before me, it did not cost me a thought. I was a Saint-Yves de Kéroual; and I decided to strike off on the morrow for Wakefield and Burchell Fenn, and embark, as soon as it should be morally possible, for the succour of my downtrodden fatherland and my beleaguered Emperor. Pursuant to this resolve, I leaped from bed, made a light, and as the watchman was crying half-past two in the dark streets of Lichfield, sat down to pen a letter of farewell to Flora. And then—whether it was the sudden chill of the night, whether it came by association of ideas from the remembrance of Swanston Cottage I know not, but there appeared before me—to the barking of sheep-dogs—a couple of snuffy and shambling figures, each wrapped in a plaid, each armed with a rude staff; and I was immediately bowed down to have forgotten them so long, and of late to have thought of them so cavalierly.

Sure enough there was my errand! As a private person I was neither French nor English; I was something else first: a loyal gentleman, an honest man. Sim and Candlish must not be left to pay the penalty of my unfortunate blow. They held my honour tacitly pledged to succour them; and it is a sort of stoical refinement entirely foreign to my nature to set the political obligation above the personal and private. If France fell in the interval for the lack of Anne de Saint-Yves, fall she must! But I was both surprised and humiliated to have had so plain a duty bound upon me for so long—and for so long to have neglected and forgotten it. I think any brave man will understand me when I say that I went to bed and to sleep with a conscience very much relieved and woke again in the morning with a light heart. The very danger of the enterprise reassured me: to save Sim and Candlish (suppose the worst to come to the worst) it would be necessary for me to declare myself in a court of justice, with consequences which I did not dare to dwell upon; it could never be said that I had chosen the cheap and the easy—only that in a very perplexing competition of duties I had risked my life for the most immediate.

We resumed the journey with more diligence: thenceforward posted day and night; did not halt beyond what was necessary for meals; and the postillions were excited by gratuities, after the habit of my cousin Alain. For twopence I could have gone farther and taken four horses; so extreme was my haste, running as I was before the terrors of an awakened conscience. But I feared to be conspicuous. Even as it was, we attracted only too much attention, with our pair and that white elephant, the seventy-pounds-worth of claret-coloured chaise.

Meanwhile I was ashamed to look Rowley in the face. The young shaver had contrived to put me wholly in the wrong; he had cost me a night's rest and a severe and healthful humiliation; and I was grateful and embarrassed in his society. This would never do; it was contrary to all my ideas of discipline; if the officer has to blush before the private, or the master before the servant, nothing is left to hope for but discharge or death. I hit upon the idea of teaching him French; and accordingly, from Lichfield, I became the distracted master, and he the scholar—how shall I say? indefatigable, but uninspired. His interest never flagged. He would hear the same word twenty times with profound refreshment, mispronounce it in several different ways, and forget it again with magical celerity. Say it happened to be *stirrup*.

" No, I don't seem to remember that word, Mr. Anne," he would say; " it don't seem to stick to me, that word don't." And then, when I had told it him again, " *Etrier !* " he would cry. " To be sure! I had it on the tip of my tongue. *Eterier !* " (going wrong already, as if by a fatal instinct). " What will I remember it by, now? Why, *interior*, to be sure! I'll remember it by its being something that ain't in the interior of a horse." And when next I had occasion to ask him the French for stirrup, it was a toss-up whether he had forgotten all about it, or gave me *exterior* for an answer. He was never a hair discouraged. He seemed to consider that he was covering the ground at a normal rate. He came up smiling day after day. " Now, sir, shall we do our French? " he would say; and I would put questions, and elicit copious commentary and explanation, but never the shadow of an answer. My hands fell to my sides; I could have wept to hear him. When I reflected that he had as yet learned nothing, and what a vast deal more there was for him to learn, the period of these lessons seemed to unroll before me vast as eternity, and I saw myself a teacher of a hundred, and Rowley a pupil of ninety, still hammering on the rudiments! The wretched boy, I should say, was quite unspoiled by the inevitable familiarities of the journey. He turned out at each stage the pink of serving-lads, deft, civil, prompt, attentive, touching his hat like an automaton, raising the status of Mr. Ramornie in the eyes of all the inn by his smiling service, and seeming capable of anything in the world but the one thing I had chosen—learning French!

CHAPTER XXIII

THE ADVENTURE OF THE RUNAWAY COUPLE

THE country had for some time back been changing in character. By a thousand indications I could judge that I was again drawing near to Scotland. I saw it written in the face of the hills, in the growth of the trees, and in the glint of the waterbrooks that kept the high-road company. It might have occurred to me, also, that I was, at the same time, approaching a place of some fame in Britain—Gretna Green. Over these same leagues of road—which Rowley and I now traversed in the claret-coloured chaise, to the note of the flageolet and the French lesson—how many pairs of lovers had gone bowling northwards to the music of sixteen scampering horseshoes; and how many irate persons, parents, uncles, guardians, evicted rivals, had come tearing after, clapping the frequent red face to the chaise-window, lavishly shedding their gold about the post-houses, sedulously loading and re-loading, as they went, their avenging pistols! But I doubt if I had thought of it at all, before a wayside hazard swept me into the thick of an adventure of this nature; and I found myself playing providence with other people's lives, to my own admiration at the moment—and subsequently to my own brief but passionate regret.

At rather an ugly corner of an uphill reach I came on the wreck of a chaise lying on one side of the ditch, a man and a woman in animated discourse in the middle of the road, and the two postillions, each with his pair of horses, looking on and laughing from the saddle.

" Morning breezes! here's a smash!" cried Rowley, pocketing his flageolet in the middle of the *Tight Little Island*.

I was perhaps more conscious of the moral smash than the physical—more alive to broken hearts than to broken chaises; for, as plain as the sun at morning, there was a screw loose in this runaway match. It is always a bad sign when the lower classes laugh: their taste in humour is both poor and sinister; and for a man, running the posts with four horses, presumably with open pockets, and in the company of the most entrancing little creature conceivable, to have come down so far as to be laughed at by his own postillions, was only to be explained on the double hypothesis, that he was a fool and no gentleman.

I have said they were man and woman. I should have said man and child. She was certainly not more than seventeen, pretty as an angel, just plump enough to damn a saint, and dressed in various shades of blue from her stockings to her saucy cap, in a kind of taking gamut, the top note of which she flung me in a beam from her too appreciative eye. There was no doubt about the case. I saw it all. From a boarding-school, a blackboard, a piano, and Clementi's *Sonatinas*, the child had made a rash adventure upon life in the company of a half-bred hawbuck; and she was already not only regretting it, but expressing her regret with point and pungency.

Adventure of the Runaway Couple

As I alighted they both paused with that unmistakable air of being interrupted in a scene. I uncovered to the lady and placed my services at their disposal.

It was the man who answered. "There's no use in shamming, sir," said he. "This lady and I have run away, and her father's after us: road to Gretna, sir. And here have these nincompoops spilt us in the ditch and smashed the chaise!"

"Very provoking," said I.

"I don't know when I've been so provoked!" cried he, with a glance down the road, of mortal terror.

"The father is no doubt very much incensed?" I pursued civilly.

"O God!" cried the hawbuck. "In short, you see, we must get out of this. And I'll tell you what—it may seem cool, but necessity has no law—if you would lend us your chaise to the next post-house, it would be the very thing, sir."

"I confess it seems cool," I replied.

"What's that you say, sir?" he snapped.

"I was agreeing with you," said I. "Yes, it does seem cool; and what is more to the point, it seems unnecessary. This thing can be arranged in a more satisfactory manner otherwise, I think. You can doubtless ride?"

This opened a door on the matter of their previous dispute, and the fellow appeared life-sized in his true colours. "That's what I've been telling her: that, damn her! she must ride!" he broke out. "And if the gentleman's of the same mind, why, damme, you shall!"

As he said so, he made a snatch at her wrist, which she evaded with horror.

I stepped between them.

"No, sir," said I; "the lady shall not."

He turned on me raging. "And who are you to interfere?" he roared.

"There is here no question of who I am," I replied. "I may be the devil or the Archbishop of Canterbury for what you know, or need know. The point is that I can help you—it appears that nobody else can; and I will tell you how I propose to do it. I will give the lady a seat in my chaise, if you will return the compliment by allowing my servant to ride one of your horses."

I thought he would have sprung at my throat.

" You have always the alternative before you: to wait here for the arrival of papa," I added.

And that settled him. He cast another haggard look down the road, and capitulated.

" I am sure, sir, the lady is very much obliged to you," he said, with an ill grace.

I gave her my hand; she mounted like a bird into the chaise; Rowley, grinning from ear to ear, closed the door behind us; the two impudent rascals of post-boys cheered and laughed aloud as we drove off; and my own postillion urged his horses at once into a rattling trot. It was plain I was supposed by all to have done a very dashing act, and ravished the bride from the ravisher.

In the meantime I stole a look at the little lady. She was in a state of pitiable discomposure, and her arms shook on her lap in her black lace mittens.

" Madam——" I began.

And she, in the same moment, finding her voice: " Oh, what you must think of me! "

" Madam," says I, " what must any gentleman think when he sees youth, beauty and innocence in distress? I wish I could tell you that I was old enough to be your father; I think we must give that up," I continued, with a smile. " But I will tell you something about myself which ought to do as well, and to set that little heart at rest in my society. I am a lover. May I say it of myself—for I am not quite used to all the niceties of English—that I am a true lover? There is one whom I admire, adore, obey; she is no less good than she is beautiful; if she were here, she would take you to her arms: conceive that she has sent me—that she has said to me, ' Go, be her knight! ' "

" Oh, I know she must be sweet, I know she must be worthy of you! " cried the little lady. " She would never forget female decorum—nor make the terrible *erratum* I've done! "

And at this she lifted up her voice and wept.

This did not forward matters: it was in vain that I begged her to be more composed and to tell me a plain, consecutive tale of her misadventures; but she continued instead to pour forth the most extraordinary mixture of the correct school miss and the poor untutored little piece of womanhood in a false position—of engrafted pedantry and incoherent nature.

Adventure of the Runaway Couple

"I am certain it must have been judicial blindness," she sobbed. "I can't think how I didn't see it, but I didn't; and he isn't, is he? And then a curtain rose.... Oh, what a moment was that! But I knew at once that *you were;* you had but to appear from your carriage, and I knew it. Oh, she must be a fortunate young lady! And I have no fear with you, none—a perfect confidence."

"Madam," said I, "a gentleman."

"That's what I mean—a gentleman," she exclaimed. "And he—and that—*he* isn't. Oh, how shall I dare meet father!" And disclosing to me her tear-stained face, and opening her arms with a tragic gesture: "And I am quite disgraced before all the young ladies, my school-companions!" she added.

"Oh, not so bad as that!" I cried. "Come, come, you exaggerate, my dear Miss ——? Excuse me if I am too familiar: I have not yet heard your name."

"My name is Dorothy Greensleeves, sir: why should I conceal it? I fear it will only serve to point an adage to future generations, and I had meant so differently! There was no young female in the country more emulous to be thought well of than I. And what a fall was there! Oh, dear me, what a wicked, piggish donkey of a girl I have made of myself, to be sure! And there is no hope! Oh, Mr. ——"

And at that she paused and asked my name.

I am not writing my eulogium for the Academy; I will admit it was unpardonably imbecile, but I told it her. If you had been there—and seen her, ravishingly pretty and little, a baby in years and mind—and heard her talking like a book, with so much of schoolroom propriety in her manner, with such an innocent despair in the matter—you would probably have told her yours. She repeated it after me.

"I shall pray for you all my life," she said. "Every night, when I retire to rest, the last thing I shall do is to remember you by name."

Presently I succeeded in winning from her her tale, which was much what I had anticipated: a tale of a schoolhouse, a walled garden, a fruit-tree that concealed a bench, an impudent raff posturing in church, an exchange of flowers and vows over the garden wall, a silly schoolmate for a confidante, a chaise and four, and the most immediate and perfect disenchantment on the part of the little lady. "And there is nothing to be done!" she wailed in conclusion. "My error is irretrievable, I am quite forced to that conclusion. Oh, Monsieur de Saint-Yves! who would have thought that I could have been such a blind, wicked donkey!"

I should have said it before—only that I really do not know when it came in—that we had been overtaken by the two post-boys, Rowley and Mr. Bellamy, which was the haw-buck's name, bestriding the four post-horses; and that these formed a sort of cavalry escort, riding now before, now behind the chaise, and Bellamy occasionally posturing at the window and obliging us with some of his conversation. He was so ill-received that I declare I was tempted to pity him, remembering from what a height he had fallen, and how few hours ago it was since the lady had herself fled to his arms, all blushes and ardour. Well, these great strokes of fortune usually befall the unworthy, and Bellamy was now the legitimate object of my commiseration and the ridicule of his own post-boys!

"Miss Dorothy," said I, "you wish to be delivered from this man?"

"Oh, if it were possible!" she cried. "But not by violence."

"Not in the least, ma'am," I replied. "The simplest thing in life. We are in a civilised country; the man's a malefactor——"

"Oh, never!" she cried. "Do not even dream it! With all his faults, I know he is not *that*."

"Anyway, he's in the wrong in this affair—on the wrong side of the law, call it what you please," said I; and with that, our four horsemen having for the moment headed us by a considerable interval, I hailed my post-boy and inquired who was the nearest magistrate and where he lived. Arch-deacon Clitheroe, he told me, a prodigious dignitary, and one who lived but a lane or two back, and at the distance of only a mile or two out of the direct road. I showed him the king's medallion.

"Take the lady there, and at full gallop," I cried.

"Right, sir! Mind yourself," says the postillion.

And before I could have thought it possible, he had turned the carriage to the rightabout and we were galloping south.

Our outriders were quick to remark and imitate the

Adventure of the Runaway Couple

manœuvre, and came flying after us with a vast deal of indiscriminate shouting; so that the fine, sober picture of a carriage and escort, that we had presented but a moment back, was transformed in the twinkling of an eye into the image of a noisy fox-chase. The two postillions and my own saucy rogue were, of course, disinterested actors in the comedy; they rode for the mere sport, keeping in a body, their mouths full of laughter, waving their hats as they came on, and crying (as the fancy struck them) " Tally-ho! " " Stop, thief! " " A highwayman! A highwayman! " It was other guess-work with Bellamy. That gentleman no sooner observed our change of direction than he turned his horse with so much violence that the poor animal was almost cast upon its side, and launched her in immediate and desperate pursuit. As he approached I saw that his face was deadly white and that he carried a drawn pistol in his hand. I turned at once to the poor little bride that was to have been, and now was not to be; she, upon her side, deserting the other window, turned as if to meet me.

" Oh, oh, don't let him kill me! " she screamed.

" Never fear," I replied.

Her face was distorted with terror. Her hands took hold upon me with the instinctive clutch of an infant. The chaise gave a flying lurch, which took the feet from under me and tumbled us anyhow upon the seat. And almost in the same moment the head of Bellamy appeared in the window which Missy had left free for him.

Conceive the situation! The little lady and I were falling— or had just fallen—backward on the seat, and offered to the eye a somewhat ambiguous picture. The chaise was speeding at a furious pace, and with the most violent leaps and lurches, along the highway. Into this bounding receptacle Bellamy interjected his head, his pistol arm, and his pistol; and since his own horse was travelling still faster than the chaise, he must withdraw all of them again in the inside of the fraction of a minute. He did so, but he left the charge of the pistol behind him—whether by design or accident I shall never know, and I dare say he has forgotten! Probably he had only meant to threaten, in hopes of causing us to arrest our flight. In the same moment came the explosion and a pitiful cry from Missy; and my gentleman, making certain he had struck her, went down the road pursued by the furies, turned at the first corner, took a flying leap over the thorn hedge, and disappeared across country in the least possible time.

Rowley was ready and eager to pursue; but I withheld him, thinking we were excellently quit of Mr. Bellamy, at no more cost than a scratch on the forearm and a bullet-hole in the left-hand claret-coloured panel. And accordingly, but now at a more decent pace, we proceeded on our way to Archdeacon Clitheroe's. Missy's gratitude and admiration were aroused to a high pitch by this dramatic scene, and what she was pleased to call my wound. She must dress it for me with her handkerchief, a service which she rendered me even with tears. I could well have spared them, not loving on the whole to be made ridiculous, and the injury being in the nature of a cat's scratch. Indeed, I would have suggested for her kind care rather the cure of my coat-sleeve, which had suffered worse in the encounter; but I was too wise to risk the anti-climax. That she had been rescued by a hero, that the hero should have been wounded in the affray, and his wound bandaged with her handkerchief (which it could not even bloody), ministered incredibly to the recovery of her self-respect; and I could hear her relate the incident to " the young ladies, my school companions," in the most approved manner of Mrs. Radcliffe! To have insisted on the torn coat-sleeve would have been unmannerly, if not inhuman.

Presently the residence of the archdeacon began to heave in sight. A chaise and four smoking horses stood by the steps, and made way for us on our approach; and even as we alighted there appeared from the interior of the house a tall ecclesiastic, and beside him a little, headstrong, ruddy man, in a towering passion, and brandishing over his head a roll of paper. At sight of him Miss Dorothy flung herself on her knees with the most moving adjurations, calling him father, assuring him she was wholly cured and entirely repentant of her disobedience, and entreating forgiveness; and I soon saw that she need fear no great severity from Mr. Greensleeves, who showed himself extraordinarily fond, loud, greedy of caresses and prodigal of tears.

To give myself a countenance, as well as to have all ready for the road when I should find occasion, I turned to quit scores with Bellamy's two postillions. They had not the least claim on me, but one of which they were quite ignorant— that I was a fugitive. It is the worst feature of that false

Adventure of the Runaway Couple

position that every gratuity becomes a case of conscience. You must not leave behind you any one discontented nor any one grateful. But the whole business had been such a "hurrah-boys" from the beginning, and had gone off in the fifth act so like a melodrama, in explosions, reconciliations, and the rape of a post-horse, that it was plainly impossible to keep it covered. It was plain it would have to be talked over in all the inn-kitchens for thirty miles about, and likely for six months to come. It only remained for me, therefore, to settle on that gratuity which should be least conspicuous— so large that nobody could grumble, so small that nobody would be tempted to boast. My decision was hastily and not wisely taken. The one fellow spat on his tip (so he called it) for luck; the other, developing a sudden streak of piety, prayed God bless me with fervour. It seemed a demonstration was brewing, and I determined to be off at once. Bidding my own post-boy and Rowley be in readiness for an immediate start, I reascended the terrace and presented myself, hat in hand, before Mr. Greensleeves and the archdeacon.

"You will excuse me, I trust," said I. "I think shame to interrupt this agreeable scene of family effusion, which I have been privileged in some small degree to bring about."

And at these words the storm broke.

"Small degree! small degree, sir!" cried the father; "that shall not pass, Mr. St. Eaves! If I've got my darling back, and none the worse for that vagabone rascal, I know whom I have to thank. Shake hands with me—up to the elbows, sir! A Frenchman you may be, but you're one of the right breed, by God! And, by God, sir, you may have anything you care to ask of me, down to Dolly's hand, by God!"

All this he roared out in a voice surprisingly powerful from so small a person. Every word was thus audible to the servants, who had followed them out of the house and now congregated about us on the terrace, as well as to Rowley and the five postillions on the gravel sweep below. The sentiments expressed were popular; some ass, whom the devil moved to be my enemy, proposed three cheers, and they were given with a will. To hear my own name resounding amid acclamations in the hills of Westmorland was flattering, perhaps; but it was inconvenient at a moment when (as I

189

was morally persuaded) police handbills were already speeding after me at the rate of a hundred miles a day.

Nor was that the end of it. The archdeacon must present his compliments, and pressed upon me some of his West India sherry, and I was carried into a vastly fine library, where I was presented to his lady wife. While we were at sherry in the library, ale was handed round upon the terrace. Speeches were made, hands were shaken, Miss (at her father's request) kissed me farewell, and the whole party reaccompanied me to the terrace, where they stood waving hats and handkerchiefs, and crying farewells to all the echoes of the mountains until the chaise had disappeared.

The echoes of the mountains were engaged in saying to me privately: "You fool, you have done it now!"

"They do seem to have got 'old of your name, Mr. Anne," said Rowley. "It weren't my fault this time."

"It was one of those accidents that can never be foreseen," said I, affecting a dignity that I was far from feeling. "Some one recognised me."

"Which on 'em, Mr. Anne?" said the rascal.

"That is a senseless question; it can make no difference who it was," I returned.

"No, nor that it can't!" cried Rowley. "I say, Mr. Anne, sir, it's what you would call a jolly mess, ain't it? looks like 'clean bowled out in the middle stump,' don't it?"

"I fail to understand you, Rowley."

"Well, what I mean is, what are we to do about this one?" pointing to the postillion in front of us, as he alternately hid and revealed his patched breeches to the trot of his horse. "He see you get in this morning under Mr. Ramornie—I was very piticular to *Mr. Ramornie* you, if you remember, sir—and he see you get in again under Mr. Saint Eaves, and whatever's he going to see you get out under? that's what worries me, sir. It don't seem to me like as if the position was what you call *strategic !*"

"*Parrrbleu !* will you let me be!" I cried. "I have to think; you cannot imagine how your constant idiotic prattle annoys me."

"Beg pardon, Mr. Anne," said he; and the next moment, "You wouldn't like for us to do our French now, would you, Mr. Anne?"

"Certainly not," said I. "Play upon your flageolet."

The which he did with what seemed to me to be irony.

Conscience doth make cowards of us all! I was so down-cast by my pitiful mismanagement of the morning's business that I shrank from the eye of my own hired infant, and read offensive meanings into his idle tootling.

I took off my coat, and set to mending it, soldier-fashion, with a needle and thread. There is nothing more conducive to thought, above all in arduous circumstances; and as I sewed, I gradually gained a clearness upon my affairs. I must be done with the claret-coloured chaise at once. It should be sold at the next stage for what it would bring. Rowley and I must take back to the road on our four feet, and after a decent interval of trudging, get places on some coach for Edinburgh again under new names! So much trouble and toil, so much extra risk and expense and loss of time, and all for a slip of the tongue to a little lady in blue!

CHAPTER XXIV

THE INN-KEEPER OF KIRKBY-LONSDALE

I HAD hitherto conceived and partly carried out an ideal that was dear to my heart. Rowley and I descended from our claret-coloured chaise, a couple of correctly-dressed, brisk, bright-eyed young fellows, like a pair of aristocratic mice; attending singly to our own affairs, communicating solely with each other, and that with the niceties and civilities of drill. We would pass through the little crowd before the door with high-bred preoccupation, inoffensively haughty, after the best English pattern; and disappear within, fol-lowed by the envy and admiration of the bystanders, a model master and servant, point-device in every part. It was a heavy thought to me, as we drew up before the inn at Kirkby-Lonsdale, that this scene was now to be enacted for the last time. Alas! and had I known it, it was to go off with so inferior a grace!

I had been injudiciously liberal to the post-boys of the chaise and four. My own post-boy, he of the patched breeches, now stood before me, his eyes glittering with greed, his hand advanced. It was plain he anticipated something extraordinary by way of a *pourboire* ; and considering the marches and countermarches by which I had extended the stage, the military character of our affairs with Mr. Bellamy, and the bad example I had set before him at the archdeacon's, something exceptional was certainly to be done. But these are always nice questions, to a foreigner above all: a shade too little will suggest niggardliness, a shilling too much smells of hush-money. Fresh from the scene at the archdeacon's, and flushed by the idea that I was now nearly done with the responsibilities of the claret-coloured chaise, I put into his hands five guineas; and the amount served only to waken his cupidity.

"Oh, come, sir, you ain't going to fob me off with this? Why, I seen fire at your side!" he cried.

It would never do to give him more; I felt I would become the fable of Kirkby-Lonsdale if I did; and I looked him in the face, sternly but still smiling, and addressed him with a voice of uncompromising firmness.

"If you do not like it, give it back," said I.

He pocketed the guineas with the quickness of a conjurer, and, like a base-born cockney as he was, fell instantly to casting dirt.

"'Ave your own way of it, Mr. Ramornie—leastways Mr. St. Eaves, or whatever your blessed name may be. Look 'ere "—turning for sympathy to the stable-boys—" this is a blessed business. Blessed 'ard, I calls it. 'Ere I takes up a blessed son of a pop-gun what calls hisself anything you care to mention, and turns out to be a blessed *mounseer* at the end of it! 'Ere 'ave I been drivin' of him up and down all day, a-carrying off of gals, a shootin' of pistyils, and a-drinkin' of sherry and hale; and wot does he up and give me but a blank, blank, blanketing blank!"

The fellow's language had become too powerful for reproduction, and I passed it by.

Meanwhile I observed Rowley fretting visibly at the bit; another moment, and he would have added a last touch of the ridiculous to our arrival by coming to his hands with the postillion.

"Rowley!" cried I reprovingly.

Strictly it should have been Gammon; but in the hurry of the moment my fault (I can only hope) passed unperceived. At the same time I caught the eye of the postmaster. He was long and lean, and brown and bilious; he had the droop-

The Inn-Keeper of Kirkby-Lonsdale

ing nose of the humorist, and the quick attention of a man of parts. He read my embarrassment in a glance, stepped instantly forward, sent the post-boy to the rightabout with half a word, and was back next moment at my side.

"Dinner in a private room, sir? Very well. John, No. 4! What wine would you care to mention? Very well, sir. Will you please to order fresh horses? Not, sir? Very well."

Each of these expressions was accompanied by something in the nature of a bow, and all were prefaced by something in the nature of a smile, which I could very well have done without. The man's politeness was from the teeth outwards; behind and within, I was conscious of a perpetual scrutiny; the scene at his doorstep, the random confidences of the post-boy, had not been thrown away on this observer; and it was under a strong fear of coming trouble that I was shown at last into my private room. I was in half a mind to have put off the whole business. But the truth is, now my name had got abroad, my fear of the mail that was coming, and the handbills it should contain, had waxed inordinately, and I felt I could never eat a meal in peace till I had severed my connection with the claret-coloured chaise.

Accordingly as soon as I had done with dinner, I sent my compliments to the landlord and requested he should take a glass of wine with me. He came; we exchanged the necessary civilities, and presently I approached my business.

"By-the-bye," said I, "we had a brush down the road to-day. I dare say you may have heard of it?"

He nodded.

"And I was so unlucky as to get a pistol ball in the panel of my chaise," I continued, "which makes it simply useless to me. Do you know any one likely to buy?"

"I can well understand that," said the landlord. "I was looking at it just now; it's as good as ruined, is that chaise. General rule, people don't like chaises with bullet-holes."

"Too much *Romance of the Forest*?" I suggested, recalling my little friend of the morning, and what I was sure had been her favourite reading—Mrs. Radcliffe's novels.

"Just so," said he. "They may be right, they may be wrong; I'm not the judge. But I suppose it's natural, after all, for respectable people to like things respectable about them; not bullet-holes, nor puddles of blood, nor men with aliases."

I took a glass of wine and held it up to the light to show that my hand was steady.

" Yes," said I, " I suppose so."

" You have papers, of course, showing you are the proper owner? " he inquired.

" There is the bill, stamped and receipted," said I, tossing it across to him.

He looked at it.

" This all you have? " he asked.

" It is enough, at least," said I. " It shows you where I bought and what I paid for it."

" Well, I don't know," he said. " You want some paper of identification."

" To identify the chaise? " I inquired.

" Not at all: to identify *you*," said he.

" My good sir, remember yourself," said I. " The title-deeds of my estate are in that despatch-box; but you do not seriously suppose that I should allow you to examine them? "

" Well, you see, this paper proves that some Mr. Ramornie paid seventy guineas for a chaise," said the fellow. " That's all well and good; but who's to prove to me that you are Mr. Ramornie? "

" Fellow! " cried I.

" Oh, fellow as much as you please! " said he. " Fellow, with all my heart! That changes nothing. I am fellow, of course—obtrusive fellow, impudent fellow, if you like—but who are you? I hear of you with two names; I hear of you running away with young ladies, and getting cheered for a Frenchman, which seems odd; and one thing I will go bail for, that you were in a blue fright when the post-boy began to tell tales at my door. In short, sir, you may be a very good gentleman; but I don't know enough about you, and I'll trouble you for your papers, or to go before a magistrate. Take your choice; if I'm not fine enough, I hope the magistrates are."

" My good man," I stammered, for though I had found my voice, I could scarce be said to have recovered my wits, " this is most unusual, most rude. Is it the custom in Westmorland that gentlemen should be insulted? "

" That depends," said he. " When it's suspected that gentlemen are spies it *is* the custom; and a good custom, too.

No, no," he broke out, perceiving me to make a movement. " Both hands upon the table, my gentleman! I want no pistol balls in my chaise panels."

"Surely, sir, you do me strange injustice!" said I, now master of myself. " You see me sitting here, a monument of tranquillity; pray may I help myself to wine without umbraging you?"

I took this attitude in sheer despair. I had no plan, no hope. The best I could imagine was to spin the business out some minutes longer, then capitulate. At least, I would not capitulate one moment too soon.

" Am I to take that for *no* ?" he asked.

" Referring to your former obliging proposal?" said I. " My good sir, you are to take it, as you say, for ' No!' Certainly I will not show you my deeds; certainly I will not rise from table and trundle out to see your magistrates. I have too much respect for my digestion, and too little curiosity in justices of the peace."

He leaned forward, looked me nearly in the face, and reached out one hand to the bell-rope. " See here, my fine fellow!" said he. " Do you see that bell-rope? Let me tell you, there's a boy waiting below: one jingle, and he goes to fetch the constable."

" Do you tell me so?" said I. " Well, there's no accounting for tastes! I have a prejudice against the society of constables, but if it is your fancy to have one in for the dessert——" I shrugged my shoulders lightly. " Really, you know," I added, "this is vastly entertaining. I assure you, I am looking on, with all the interest of a man of the world, at the development of your highly original character."

He continued to study my face without speech, his hand still on the button of the bell-rope, his eyes in mine; this was the decisive heat. My face seemed to myself to dislimn under his gaze, my expression to change, the smile (with which I had begun) to degenerate into the grin of the man upon the rack. I was besides harassed with doubts. An innocent man, I argued, would have resented the fellow's impudence an hour ago; and by my continued endurance of the ordeal, I was simply signing and sealing my confession; in short, I had reached the end of my powers.

" Have you any objection to my putting my hands in my breeches pockets?" I inquired. " Excuse me mentioning it, but you showed yourself so extremely nervous a moment back."

My voice was not all I could have wished, but it sufficed. I could hear it tremble, but the landlord apparently could not. He turned away and drew a long breath, and you may be sure I was quick to follow his example.

"You're a cool hand at least, and that's the sort I like," said he. "Be you what you please, I'll deal square. I'll take the chaise for a hundred pound down, and throw the dinner in."

"I beg your pardon," I cried, wholly mystified by this form of words.

"You pay me a hundred down," he repeated, "and I'll take the chaise. It's very little more than it cost," he added, with a grin, "and you know you must get it off your hands somehow."

I do not know when I have been better entertained than by this impudent proposal. It was broadly funny, and I suppose the least tempting offer in the world. For all that it came very welcome, for it gave me the occasion to laugh. This I did with the most complete abandonment, till the tears ran down my cheeks; and ever and again, as the fit abated, I would get another view of the landlord's face, and go off into another paroxysm.

"You droll creature, you will be the death of me yet!" I cried, drying my eyes.

My friend was now wholly disconcerted; he knew not where to look, nor yet what to say; and began for the first time to conceive it possible he was mistaken.

"You seem rather to enjoy a laugh, sir," said he.

"Oh yes! I am quite an original," I replied, and laughed again.

Presently, in a changed voice, he offered me twenty pounds for the chaise; I ran him up to twenty-five, and closed with the offer: indeed, I was glad to get anything; and if I haggled it was not in the desire of gain, but with the view at any price of securing a safe retreat. For, although hostilities were suspended, he was yet far from satisfied; and I could read his continued suspicions in the cloudy eye, that still hovered about my face. At last they took shape in words.

"This is all very well," says he: "you carry it off well; but for all that, I must do my duty."

The Inn-Keeper of Kirkby-Lonsdale

I had my strong effect in reserve; it was to burn my ships with a vengeance! I rose. "Leave the room," said I. "This is insufferable. Is the man mad?" And then, as if already half-ashamed of my passion: "I can take a joke as well as any one," I added; "but this passes measure. Send my servant and the bill."

When he had left me alone, I considered my own valour with amazement. I had insulted him; I had sent him away alone; now, if ever, he would take what was the only sensible resource, and fetch the constable. But there was something instinctively treacherous about the man which shrank from plain courses. And, with all his cleverness, he missed the occasion of fame. Rowley and I were suffered to walk out of his door, with all our baggage, on foot, with no destination named, except in the vague statement that we were come "to view the lakes"; and my friend only watched our departure with his chin in his hand, still moodily irresolute.

I think this one of my great successes. I was exposed, unmasked, summoned to do a perfectly natural act, which must prove my doom, and which I had not the slightest pretext for refusing. I kept my head, stuck to my guns, and, against all likelihood, here I was once more at liberty and in the king's highway. This was a strong lesson never to despair; and, at the same time, how many hints to be cautious! and what a perplexed and dubious business the whole question of my escape now appeared! That I should have risked perishing upon a trumpery question of a *pourboire*, depicted in lively colours the perils that perpetually surrounded us. Though, to be sure, the initial mistake had been committed before that; and if I had not suffered myself to be drawn a little deep in confidences to the innocent Dolly, there need have been no tumble at the inn of Kirkby-Lonsdale. I took the lesson to heart, and promised myself in the future to be more reserved. It was none of my business to attend to broken chaises or shipwrecked travellers. I had my hands full of my own affairs; and my best defence would be a little more natural selfishness and a trifle less imbecile good-nature.

St. Ives

CHAPTER XXV

I MEET A CHEERFUL EXTRAVAGANT

I PASS over the next fifty or sixty leagues of our journey without comment. The reader must be growing weary of scenes of travel; and for my own part I have no cause to recall these particular miles with any pleasure. We were mainly occupied with attempts to obliterate our trail, which (as the result showed) were far from successful; for, on my cousin following, he was able to run me home with the least possible loss of time, following the claret-coloured chaise to Kirkby-Lonsdale, where I think the landlord must have wept to learn what he had missed, and tracing us thereafter to the doors of the coach-office in Edinburgh without a single check. Fortune did not favour me, and why should I recapitulate the details of futile precautions which deceived nobody, and wearisome arts which proved to be artless?

The day was drawing to an end when Mr. Rowley and I bowled into Edinburgh to the stirring sound of the guard's bugle and the clattering team. I was here upon my field of battle; on the scene of my former captivity, escape and exploits; and in the same city with my love. My heart expanded; I have rarely felt more of a hero. All down the Bridges I sat by the driver with my arms folded and my face set, unflinchingly meeting every eye, and prepared every moment for a cry of recognition. Hundreds of the population were in the habit of visiting the Castle, where it was my practice (before the days of Flora) to make myself conspicuous among the prisoners; and I think it an extraordinary thing that I should have encountered so few to recognise me. But doubtless a clean chin is a disguise in itself; and the change is great from a suit of sulphur-yellow to fine linen, a well-fitting mouse-coloured greatcoat furred in black, a pair of tight trousers of fashionable cut, and a hat of inimitable curl. After all, it was more likely that I should have recognised our visitors, than that they should have identified the modish gentleman with the miserable prisoner in the Castle.

I was glad to set foot on the flagstones, and to escape from the crowd that had assembled to receive the mail. Here we were, with but little daylight before us, and that on Saturday

I Meet a Cheerful Extravagant

afternoon, the eve of the famous Scottish Sabbath, adrift in the New Town of Edinburgh, and overladen with baggage. We carried it ourselves. I would not take a cab, nor so much as hire a porter, who might afterwards serve as a link between my lodgings and the mail, and connect me again with the claret-coloured chaise and Aylesbury. For I was resolved to break the chain of evidence for good, and to begin life afresh (so far as regards caution) with a new character. The first step was to find lodgings, and to find them quickly. This was the more needful as Mr. Rowley and I, in our smart clothes and with our cumbrous burthen, made a noticeable appearance in the streets at that time of the day and in that quarter of the town, which was largely given up to fine folk, bucks and dandies and young ladies, or respectable professional men on their way home to dinner.

On the north side of St. James' Square I was so happy as to spy a bill in a third-floor window. I was equally indifferent to cost and convenience in my choice of a lodging—" any port in a storm " was the principle on which I was prepared to act; and Rowley and I made at once for the common entrance and scaled the stair.

We were admitted by a very sour-looking female in bombazine. I gathered she had all her life been depressed by a series of bereavements, the last of which might very well have befallen her the day before; and I instinctively lowered my voice when I addressed her. She admitted she had rooms to let—even showed them to us—a sitting-room and bedroom in a *suite*, commanding a fine prospect to the Firth and Fifeshire, and in themselves well proportioned and comfortably furnished, with pictures on the wall, shells on the mantelpiece, and several books upon the table, which I found afterwards to be all of a devotional character, and all presentation copies, " to my Christian friend," or " to my devout acquaintance in the Lord, Bethiah McRankine." Beyond this my " Christian friend " could not be made to advance: no, not even to do that which seemed the most natural and pleasing thing in the world—I mean to name her price—but stood before us shaking her head, and at times mourning like the dove, the picture of depression and defence. She had a voice the most querulous I have ever heard, and with this she produced a whole regiment of difficulties and criticisms.

She could not promise an attendance.

" Well, madam," said I, " and what is my servant for? "

" Him? " she asked. " Be gude to us! Is *he* your servant?"

" I am sorry, ma'am, he meets with your disapproval."

" Na, I never said that. But he's young. He'll be a great breaker, I'm thinkin'. Ay! he'll be a great responsi-beelity to ye, like. Does he attend to his releegion? "

" Yes, m'm," returned Rowley, with admirable promp-titude, and, immediately closing his eyes, as if from habit, repeated the following distich with more celerity than fervour:—

> " Matthew, Mark, Luke and John,
> Bless the bed that I lie on! "

" Nhm! " said the lady, and maintained an awful silence.

" Well, ma'am," said I, " it seems we are never to hear the beginning of your terms, let alone the end of them. Come— a good movement! and let us be either off or on."

She opened her lips slowly. " Ony raferences? " she inquired, in a voice like a bell.

I opened my pocket-book and showed her a handful of bank-bills. " I think, madam, that these are unexception-able," said I.

" Ye'll be wantin' breakfast late? " was her reply.

" Madam, we want breakfast at whatever hour it suits you to give it, from four in the morning till four in the afternoon! " I cried. " Only tell us your figure, if your mouth be large enough to let it out! "

" I couldnae give ye supper the nicht," came the echo.

" We shall go out to supper, you incorrigible female! " I vowed, between laughter and tears. " Here—this is going to end! I want you for a landlady—let me tell you that!— and I am going to have my way. You won't tell me what you charge? Very well; I will do without! I can trust you! You don't seem to know when you have a good lodger; but I know perfectly when I have an honest landlady! Rowley, unstrap the valises! "

Will it be credited? The monomaniac fell to rating me for my indiscretion! But the battle was over; these were her last guns, and more in the nature of a salute than of renewed hostilities. And presently she condescended on very moder-ate terms, and Rowley and I were able to escape in quest of supper. Much time had, however, been lost; the sun was long down, the lamps glimmered along the streets, and the

I Meet a Cheerful Extravagant

voice of a watchman already resounded in the neighbouring Leith Road. On our first arrival I had observed a place of entertainment not far off, in a street behind the Register House. Thither we found our way, and sat down to a late dinner alone. But we had scarce given our orders before the door opened, and a tall young fellow entered with something of a lurch, looked about him, and approached the same table.

"Give you good evening, most grave and reverend seniors!" said he. "Will you permit a wanderer, a pilgrim —the pilgrim of love, in short—to come to temporary anchor under your lee? I care not who knows it, but I have a passionate aversion from the bestial practice of solitary feeding!"

"You are welcome, sir," said I, "if I may take upon me so far to play the host in a public place."

He looked startled, and fixed a hazy eye on me, as he sat down.

"Sir," said he, "you are a man not without some tincture of letters, I perceive! What shall we drink, sir?"

I mentioned I had already called for a pot of porter.

"A modest pot—the seasonable quencher?" said he. "Well, I do not know but what I could look at a modest pot myself! I am, for the moment, in precarious health. Much study hath heated my brain, much walking wearied my well, it seems to be more my eyes!"

"You have walked far, I dare say?" I suggested.

"Not so much far as often," he replied. "There is in this city—to which, I think, you are a stranger? Sir, to your very good health and our better acquaintance!—there is, in this city of Dunedin, a certain implication of streets which reflects the utmost credit on the designer and the publicans—at every hundred yards is seated the Judicious Tavern, so that persons of contemplative mind are secure, at moderate distances, of refreshment. I have been doing a trot in that favoured quarter, favoured by art and nature. A few chosen comrades—enemies of publicity and friends to wit and wine— obliged me with their society. 'Along the cool sequestered vale of Register Street we kept the uneven tenor of our way,' sir."

"It struck me, as you came in——" I began.

"Oh, don't make any bones about it!" he interrupted.

St. Ives

" Of course it struck you! and let me tell you I was devilish lucky not to strike myself. When I entered this apartment I shone ' with all the pomp and prodigality of brandy and water,' as the poet Gray has in another place expressed it. Powerful bard, Gray! but a niminy-piminy creature, afraid of a petticoat and a bottle—not a man, sir, not a man! Excuse me for being so troublesome, but what the devil have I done with my fork? Thank you, I am sure. *Temulentia, quoad me ipsum, brevis colligo est.* I sit and eat, sir, in a London fog. I should bring a link-boy to table with me; and I would too, if the little brutes were only washed! I intend to found a Philanthropical Society for Washing the Deserving Poor and Shaving Soldiers. I am pleased to observe that, although not of an unmilitary bearing, you are apparently shaved. In my calendar of the virtues shaving comes next to drinking. A gentleman may be a low-minded ruffian without sixpence, but he will always be close shaved. See me, with the eye of fancy, in the chill hours of the morning, say about a quarter to twelve, noon—see me awake! First thing of all, without one thought of the plausible but unsatisfactory small beer, or the healthful though insipid soda-water, I take the deadly razor in my vacillating grasp; I proceed to skate upon the margin of eternity. Stimulating thought! I bleed, perhaps, but with medicable wounds. The stubble reaped, I pass out of my chamber, calm but triumphant. To employ a hackneyed phrase, I would not call Lord Wellington my uncle! I, too, have dared, perhaps bled, before the imminent deadly shaving-table."

In this manner the bombastic fellow continued to entertain me all through dinner, and by a common error of drunkards, because he had been extremely talkative himself, leaped to the conclusion that he had chanced on very genial company. He told me his name, his address; he begged we should meet again; finally he proposed that I should dine with him in the country at an early date.

" The dinner is official," he explained. " The office-bearers and Senatus of the University of Cramond—an educational institution in which I have the honour to be Professor of Nonsense—meet to do honour to our friend Icarus, at the old-established *howff*, Cramond Bridge. One place is vacant, fascinating stranger,—I offer it to you! "

" And who is your friend Icarus? " I asked.

The Cottage at Night

" The aspiring son of Dædalus ! " said he. " Is it possible that you have never heard the name of Byfield? "

" Possible and true," said I.

" And is fame so small a thing? " cried he. " Byfield, sir, is an aëronaut. He apes the fame of a Lunardi, and is on the point of offering to the inhabitants—I beg your pardon, to the nobility and gentry of our neighbourhood—the spectacle of an ascension. As one of the gentry concerned I may be permitted to remark that I am unmoved. I care not a Tinker's Damn for his ascension. No more—I breathe it in your ear—does anybody else. The business is stale, sir, stale. Lunardi did it, and overdid it. A whimsical, fiddling, vain fellow, by all accounts—for I was at that time rocking in my cradle. But once was enough. If Lunardi went up and came down, there was the matter settled. We prefer to grant the point. We do not want to see the experiment repeated *ad nauseam* by Byfield, and Brown, and Butler, and Brodie, and Bottomley. Ah! if they would go up and *not* come down again! But this is by the question. The University of Cramond delights to honour merit in the man, sir, rather than utility in the profession; and Byfield, though an ignorant dog, is a sound reliable drinker, and really not amiss over his cups. Under the radiance of the kindly jar partiality might even credit him with wit."

It will be seen afterwards that this was more my business than I thought it at the time. Indeed, I was impatient to be gone. Even as my friend maundered ahead a squall burst, the jaws of the rain were opened against the coffee-house windows, and at that inclement signal I remembered I was due elsewhere.

CHAPTER XXVI

THE COTTAGE AT NIGHT

AT the door I was nearly blown back by the unbridled violence of the squall, and Rowley and I must shout our parting words. All the way along Princes Street (whither my way led) the wind hunted me behind and screamed in my ears. The city was flushed with bucketfuls of rain that tasted salt from the neighbouring ocean. It seemed to darken and lighten again in the vicissitudes of the gusts. Now you would say the lamps had been blown out from end to end of the long thoroughfare; now, in a lull, they would revive, re-multiply, shine again on the wet pavements, and make darkness sparingly visible.

By the time I had got to the corner of the Lothian Road there was a distinct improvement. For one thing, I had now my shoulder to the wind; for a second, I came in the lee of my old prison-house, the Castle; and, at any rate, the excessive fury of the blast was itself moderating. The thought of what errand I was on re-awoke within me, and I seemed to breast the rough weather with increasing ease. With such a destination, what mattered a little buffeting of wind or a sprinkle of cold water? I recalled Flora's image, I took her in fancy to my arms, and my heart throbbed. And the next moment I had recognised the inanity of that fool's paradise. If I could spy her taper as she went to bed, I might count myself lucky.

I had about two leagues before me of a road mostly uphill, and now deep in mire. So soon as I was clear of the last street lamp, darkness received me—a darkness only pointed by the lights of occasional rustic farms, where the dogs howled with uplifted heads as I went by. The wind continued to decline: it had been but a squall, not a tempest. The rain, on the other hand, settled into a steady deluge, which had soon drenched me thoroughly. I continued to tramp forward in the night, contending with gloomy thoughts and accompanied by the dismal ululation of the dogs. What ailed them that they should have thus been wakeful, and perceived the small sound of my steps amid the general reverberation of the rain, was more than I could fancy. I remembered tales with which I had been entertained in childhood. I told myself some murderer was going by, and the brutes perceived upon him the faint smell of blood; and the next moment, with a physical shock, I had applied the words to my own case!

Here was a dismal disposition for a lover. "Was ever lady in this humour wooed?" I asked myself, and came near turning back. It is never wise to risk a critical interview when your spirits are depressed, your clothes muddy, and your hands wet! But the boisterous night was in itself favourable to my enterprise: now, or perhaps never, I might find some way to have an interview with Flora; and if I had

The Cottage at Night

one interview (wet clothes, low spirits and all), I told myself there would certainly be another.

Arrived in the cottage-garden I found the circumstances mighty inclement. From the round holes in the shutters of the parlour, shafts of candle-light streamed forth; elsewhere the darkness was complete. The trees, the thickets, were saturated; the lower parts of the garden turned into a morass. At intervals, when the wind broke forth again, there passed overhead a wild coil of clashing branches; and between whiles the whole enclosure continuously and stridently resounded with the rain. I advanced close to the window and contrived to read the face of my watch. It was half-past seven; they would not retire before ten, they might not before midnight, and the prospect was unpleasant. In a lull of the wind I could hear from the inside the voice of Flora reading aloud; the words of course inaudible—only a flow of undecipherable speech, quiet, cordial, colourless, more intimate and winning, more eloquent of her personality, but not less beautiful than song. And the next moment the clamour of a fresh squall broke out about the cottage; the voice was drowned in its bellowing, and I was glad to retreat from my dangerous post.

For three egregious hours I must now suffer the elements to do their worst upon me, and continue to hold my ground in patience. I recalled the least fortunate of my services in the field: being out-sentry of the pickets in weather no less vile, sometimes unsuppered, and with nothing to look forward to by way of breakfast but musket-balls; and they seemed light in comparison. So strangely are we built: so much more strong is the love of woman than the mere love of life.

At last my patience was rewarded. The light disappeared from the parlour and reappeared a moment after in the room above. I was pretty well informed for the enterprise that lay before me. I knew the lair of the dragon—that which was just illuminated. I knew the bower of my Rosamond, and how excellently it was placed on the ground-level, round the flank of the cottage and out of earshot of her formidable aunt. Nothing was left but to apply my knowledge. I was then at the bottom of the garden, whither I had gone (Heaven save the mark!) for warmth, that I might walk to and fro unheard and keep myself from perishing. The night had fallen still, the wind ceased; the noise of the rain had much lightened, if it had not stopped, and was succeeded by the dripping of the garden trees. In the midst of this lull, and as I was already drawing near to the cottage, I was startled by the sound of a window-sash screaming in its channels; and a step or two beyond I became aware of a gush of light upon the darkness. It fell from Flora's window, which she had flung open on the night, and where she now sat, roseate and pensive, in the shine of two candles falling from behind, her tresses deeply embowering and shading her; the suspended comb still in one hand, the other idly clinging to the iron stanchions with which the window was barred.

Keeping to the turf, and favoured by the darkness of the night and the patter of the rain which was now returning, though without wind, I approached until I could almost have touched her. It seemed a grossness of which I was incapable to break up her reverie by speech. I stood and drank her in with my eyes; how the light made a glory in her hair, and (what I have always thought the most ravishing thing in nature) how the planes ran into each other, and were distinguished, and how the hues blended and varied, and were shaded off, between the cheek and neck. At first I was abashed: she wore her beauty like an immediate halo of refinement; she discouraged me like an angel, or what I suspect to be the next most discouraging, a modern lady. But as I continued to gaze, hope and life returned to me; I forgot my timidity, I forgot the sickening pack of wet clothes with which I stood burdened, I tingled with new blood.

Still unconscious of my presence, still gazing before her upon the illuminated image of the window, the straight shadows of the bars, the glinting of pebbles on the path, and the impenetrable night on the garden and the hills beyond it, she heaved a deep breath that struck upon my heart like an appeal.

"Why does Miss Gilchrist sigh?" I whispered. "Does she recall absent friends?"

She turned her head swiftly in my direction; it was the only sign of surprise she deigned to make. At the same time I stepped into the light and bowed profoundly.

"You!" she said. "Here?"

"Yes, I am here," I replied. "I have come very far, it may be a hundred and fifty leagues, to see you. I have

The Cottage at Night

waited all this night in your garden. Will Miss Gilchrist not offer her hand—to a friend in trouble?"

She extended it between the bars, and I dropped upon one knee on the wet path and kissed it twice. At the second it was withdrawn suddenly, methought with more of a start than she had hitherto displayed. I regained my former attitude, and we were both silent awhile. My timidity returned on me tenfold. I looked in her face for any signals of anger, and seeing her eyes to waver and fall aside from mine, augured that all was well.

"You must have been mad to come here!" she broke out. "Of all places under heaven this is no place for you to come. And I was just thinking you were safe in France!"

"You were thinking of me!" I cried.

"Mr. St. Ives, you cannot understand your danger," she replied. "I am sure of it, and yet I cannot find it in my heart to tell you. Oh, be persuaded, and go!"

"I believe I know the worst. But I was never one to set an undue value on life, the life that we share with beasts. My university has been in the wars—not a famous place of education, but one where a man learns to carry his life in his hand as lightly as a glove, and for his lady or his honour to lay it as lightly down. You appeal to my fears, and you do wrong. I have come to Scotland with my eyes quite open to see you and to speak with you—it may be for the last time. With my eyes quite open, I say; and if I did not hesitate at the beginning, do you think that I would draw back now?"

"You do not know!" she cried, with rising agitation. "This country, even this garden, is death to you. They all believe it; I am the only one that does not. If they hear you now, if they heard a whisper—I dread to think of it. Oh, go, go this instant. It is my prayer."

"Dear lady, do not refuse me what I have come so far to seek; and remember that out of all the millions in England there is no other but yourself in whom I can dare confide. I have all the world against me; you are my only ally; and as I have to speak, you have to listen. All is true that they say of me, and all of it false at the same time. I did kill this man Goguelat—it was that you meant?"

She mutely signed to me that it was; she had become deadly pale.

"But I killed him in fair fight. Till then, I had never

taken a life unless in battle, which is my trade. But I was grateful, I was on fire with gratitude, to one who had been good to me, who had been better to me than I could have dreamed of—an angel, who had come into the darkness of my prison like sunrise. The man Goguelat insulted her. Oh, he had insulted *me* often, it was his favourite pastime, and he might insult me as he pleased—for who was I? But with that lady it was different. I could never forgive myself if I had let it pass. And we fought, and he fell, and I have no remorse."

I waited anxiously for some reply. The worst was now out, and I knew that she had heard of it before; but it was impossible for me to go on with my narrative without some shadow of encouragement.

" You blame me? "

" No, not at all. It is a point I cannot speak on—I am only a girl. I am sure you were in the right: I have always said so—to Ronald. Not, of course, to my aunt. I am afraid I let her speak as she will. You must not think me a disloyal friend; and even with the Major—I did not tell you he had become quite a friend of ours—Major Chevenix, I mean—he has taken such a fancy to Ronald! It was he that brought the news to us of that hateful Clausel being captured, and all that he was saying. I was indignant with him. I said—I dare say I said too much—and I must say he was very good-natured. He said, ' You and I, who are his friends, *know* that Champdivers is innocent. But what is the use of saying it? ' All this was in the corner of the room, in what they call an aside. And then he said, ' Give me a chance to speak to you in private, I have much to tell you.' And he did. And told me just what you did—that it was an affair of honour, and no blame attached to you. Oh, I must say I like that Major Chevenix! "

At this I was seized with a great pang of jealousy. I remembered the first time that he had seen her; the interest that he seemed immediately to conceive; and I could not but admire the dog for the use he had been ingenious enough to make of our acquaintance in order to supplant me. All is fair in love and war. For all that, I was now no less anxious to do the speaking myself than I had been before to hear Flora. At least, I could keep clear of the hateful image of Major Chevenix. Accordingly I burst at once on the narrative of my adventures. It was the same as you have read,

The Cottage at Night

but briefer, and told with a very different purpose. Now every incident had a particular bearing, every by-way branched off to Rome—and that was Flora.

When I had begun to speak I had kneeled upon the gravel withoutside the low window, rested my arms upon the sill, and lowered my voice to the most confidential whisper. Flora herself must kneel upon the other side, and this brought our heads upon a level, with only the bars between us. So placed, so separated, it seemed that our proximity, and the continuous and low sounds of my pleading voice, worked progressively and powerfully on her heart, and perhaps not less so on my own. For these sp lls are double-edged. The silly birds may be charmed with the pipe of the fowler, which is but a tube of reeds. Not so with a bird of our own feather! As I went on, and my resolve strengthened, and my voice found new modulations, and our faces were drawn closer to the bars and to each other, not only she, but I, succumbed to the fascination, and were kindled by the charm. We make love, and thereby ourselves fall the deeper in it. It is with the heart only that one captures a heart.

" And now," I continued, " I will tell you what you can still do for me. I run a little risk just now, and you see for yourself how unavoidable it is for any man of honour. But if—but in case of the worst I do not choose to enrich either my enemies or the Prince Regent. I have here the bulk of what my uncle gave me. Eight thousand odd pounds. Will you take care of it for me? Do not think of it merely as money; take and keep it as a relic of your friend or some precious piece of him. I may have bitter need of it ere long. Do you know the old country story of the giant who gave his heart to his wife to keep for him, thinking it safer to repose on her loyalty than his own strength? Flora, I am the giant —a very little one: will you be the keeper of my life? It is my heart I offer you in this symbol. In the sight of God, if you will have it, I give you my name, I endow you with my money. If the worst come, if I may never hope to call you wife, let me at least think you will use my uncle's legacy as my widow."

" No, not that," she said. " Never that."

" What then? " I said. " What else, my angel? What are words to me? There is but one name that I care to know you by. Flora, my love! "

" Anne ! " she said.

What sound is so full of music as one's own name uttered for the first time in the voice of her we love !

" My darling ! " said I.

The jealous bars, set at the top and bottom in stone and lime, obstructed the rapture of the moment; but I took her to myself as wholly as they allowed. She did not shun my lips. My arms were wound round her body, which yielded itself generously to my embrace. As we so remained, entwined and yet severed, bruising our faces unconsciously on the cold bars, the irony of the universe—or as I prefer to say, envy of some of the gods—again stirred up the elements of that stormy night. The wind blew again in the tree-tops; a volley of cold sea-rain deluged the garden, and, as the deuce would have it, a gutter which had been hitherto choked up began suddenly to play upon my head and shoulders with the vivacity of a fountain. We parted with a shock; I sprang to my feet, and she to hers, as though we had been discovered. A moment after, but now both standing, we had again approached the window on either side.

" Flora," I said, " this is but a poor offer I can make you."

She took my hand in hers and clasped it to her bosom.

" Rich enough for a queen ! " she said, with a lift in her breathing that was more eloquent than words. " Anne, my brave Anne ! I would be glad to be your maidservant; I could envy that boy Rowley. But, no ! " she broke off, " I envy no one—I need not—I am yours."

" Mine," said I, " for ever ! By this and this, mine ! "

" All of me," she repeated. " Altogether, and for ever ! "

And if the god were envious he must have seen with mortification how little he could do to mar the happiness of mortals. I stood in a mere waterspout; she herself was wet, not from my embrace only, but from the splashing of the storm. The candles had guttered out; we were in darkness. I could scarce see anything but the shining of her eyes in the dark room. To her I must have appeared as a silhouette, haloed by rain and the spouting of the ancient Gothic gutter above my head.

Presently we became more calm and confidential; and when that squall, which proved to be the last of the storm, had blown by, fell into a talk of ways and means. It seemed she knew Mr. Robbie, to whom I had been so slenderly accredited by Romaine—was even invited to his house for the evening of Monday, and gave me a sketch of the old gentleman's character, which implied a great deal of penetration in herself, and proved of great use to me in the immediate sequel. It seemed he was an enthusiastic antiquary, and in particular a fanatic of heraldry. I heard it with delight, for I was myself, thanks to M. de Culemberg, fairly grounded in that science, and acquainted with the blazons of most families of note in Europe. And I had made up my mind— even as she spoke, it was my fixed determination, though I was a hundred miles from saying it—to meet Flora on Monday night as a fellow-guest in Mr. Robbie's house.

I gave her my money—it was, of course, only paper I had brought. I gave it her, to be her marriage portion, I declared.

"Not so bad a marriage-portion for a private soldier," I told her, laughing, as I passed it through the bars.

"O Anne, and where am I to keep it?" she cried. "If my aunt should find it! What would I say!"

"Next your heart," I suggested.

"Then you will always be near your treasure," she cried, "for you are always there!"

We were interrupted by a sudden clearness that fell upon the night. The clouds dispersed; the stars shone in every part of the heavens; and, consulting my watch, I was startled to find it already hard on five in the morning.

CHAPTER XXVII

THE SABBATH DAY

IT was indeed high time I should be gone from Swanston; but what I was to do in the meanwhile was another question. Rowley had received his orders last night: he was to say that I had met a friend, and Mrs. McRankine was not to expect me before morning. A good enough tale in itself; but the dreadful pickle I was in made it out of the question. I could not go home till I had found harbourage, a fire to dry my clothes at, and a bed where I might lie till they were ready.

Fortune favoured me again. I had scarce got to the top

of the first hill when I spied a light on my left, about a furlong away. It might be a case of sickness; what else it was likely to be—in so rustic a neighbourhood, and at such an ungodly time of the morning—was beyond my fancy. A faint sound of singing became audible, and gradually swelled as I drew near, until at last I could make out the words, which were singularly appropriate both to the hour and to the condition of the singers. "The cock may craw, the day may daw," they sang; and sang it with such laxity both in time and tune, and such sentimental complaisance in the expression, as assured me they had got far into the third bottle at least.

I found a plain rustic cottage by the wayside, of the sort called double, with a signboard over the door; and, the lights within streaming forth and somewhat mitigating the darkness of the morning, I was enabled to decipher the inscription: "The Hunters' Tryst, by Alexander Hendry. Porter, Ales, and British Spirits. Beds."

My first knock put a period to the music, and a voice challenged tipsily from within.

"Who goes there?" it said; and I replied, "A lawful traveller."

Immediately after, the door was unbarred by a company of the tallest lads my eyes had ever rested on, all astonishingly drunk and very decently dressed, and one (who was perhaps the drunkest of the lot) carrying a tallow candle, from which he impartially bedewed the clothes of the whole company. As soon as I saw them I could not help smiling to myself to remember the anxiety with which I had approached. They received me and my hastily-concocted story, that I had been walking from Peebles and had lost my way, with incoherent benignity; jostled me among them into the room where they had been sitting, a plain hedgerow alehouse parlour, with a roaring fire in the chimney and a prodigious number of empty bottles on the floor; and informed me that I was made, by this reception, a temporary member of the *Six-Feet-High Club*, an athletic society of young men in a good station, who made of the Hunters' Tryst a frequent resort. They told me I had intruded on an "all-night sitting," following upon an "all-day Saturday tramp" of forty miles; and that the members would all be up and "as right as ninepence" for the noon-day service at some neighbouring church—Collingwood, if memory serves me right. At this I could have

The Sabbath Day

laughed, but the moment seemed ill-chosen. For, though six feet was their standard, they all exceeded that measurement considerably; and I tasted again some of the sensations of childhood, as I looked up to all these lads from a lower plane, and wondered what they would do next. But the Six-Footers, if they were very drunk, proved no less kind. The landlord and servants of the Hunters' Tryst were in bed and asleep long ago. Whether by natural gift or acquired habit they could suffer pandemonium to reign all over the house, and yet lie ranked in the kitchen like Egyptian mummies, only that the sound of their snoring rose and fell ceaselessly like the drone of a bagpipe. Here the Six-Footers invaded them —in their citadel, so to speak; counted the bunks and the sleepers; proposed to put me in bed to one of the lasses, proposed to have one of the lasses out to make room for me, fell over chairs, and made noise enough to waken the dead: the whole illuminated by the same young torch-bearer, but now with two candles, and rapidly beginning to look like a man in a snowstorm. At last a bed was found for me, my clothes were hung out to dry before the parlour fire, and I was mercifully left to my repose.

I awoke about nine with the sun shining in my eyes. The landlord came at my summons, brought me my clothes dried and decently brushed, and gave me the good news that the Six-Feet-High Club were all abed and sleeping off their excesses. Where they were bestowed was a puzzle to me until (as I was strolling about the garden patch waiting for breakfast) I came on a barn door, and, looking in, saw all the red faces mixed in the straw like plums in a cake. Quoth the stalwart maid who brought me my porridge and bade me "eat them while they were hot," "Ay, they were a' on the ran-dan last nicht! Hoot! they're fine lads, and they'll be nane the waur of it. Forby Farbes's coat. I dinna see wha's to get the creish off that!" she added with a sigh; in which, identifying Forbes as the torch-bearer, I mentally joined.

It was a brave morning when I took the road; the sun shone, spring seemed in the air, it smelt like April or May, and some over-venturous birds sang in the coppices as I went by. I had plenty to think of, plenty to be grateful for, that gallant morning; and yet I had a twitter at my heart. To enter the city by daylight might be compared to marching on a battery; every face that I confronted would threaten me like the muzzle of a gun; and it came into my head suddenly with how much better a countenance I should be able to do it if I could but improvise a companion. Hard by Merchiston I was so fortunate as to observe a bulky gentleman in broadcloth and gaiters, stooping with his head almost between his knees, before a stone wall. Seizing occasion by the forelock, I drew up as I came alongside and inquired what he had found to interest him.

He turned upon me a countenance not much less broad than his back.

" Why, sir," he replied, " I was even marvelling at my own indefeasible stupeedity: that I should walk this way every week of my life, weather permitting, and should never before have *notticed* that stone," touching it at the same time with a goodly oak staff.

I followed the indication. The stone, which had been built sideways into the wall, offered traces of heraldic sculpture. At once there came a wild idea into my mind: his appearance tallied with Flora's description of Mr. Robbie; a knowledge of heraldry would go far to clinch the proof; and what could be more desirable than to scrape an informal acquaintance with the man whom I must approach next day with my tale of the drovers, and whom I yet wished to please? I stooped in turn.

" A chevron," I said; " on a chief three mullets? Looks like Douglas, does it not? "

" Yes, sir, it does; you are right," said he: " it *does* look like Douglas; though, without the tinctures, and the whole thing being so battered and broken up, who shall venture an opinion? But allow me to be more personal, sir. In these degenerate days I am astonished you should display so much proficiency."

" Oh, I was well grounded in my youth by an old gentleman, a friend of my family, and I may say my guardian," said I; " but I have forgotten it since. God forbid I should delude you into thinking me a herald, sir! I am only an ungrammatical amateur."

" And a little modesty does no harm even in a herald," says my new acquaintance graciously.

In short, we fell together on our onward way, and maintained very amicable discourse along what remained of the country road, past the suburbs, and on into the streets of the

The Sabbath Day

New Town, which was as deserted and silent as a city of the dead. The shops were closed, no vehicle ran, cats sported in the midst of the sunny causeway; and our steps and voices re-echoed from the quiet houses. It was the high-water, full and strange, of that weekly trance to which the city of Edinburgh is subjected: the apotheosis of the *Sawbath ;* and I confess the spectacle wanted not grandeur, however much it may have lacked cheerfulness. There are few religious ceremonies more imposing. As we thus walked and talked in a public seclusion the bells broke out ringing through all the bounds of the city, and the streets began immediately to be thronged with decent church-goers.

" Ah! " said my companion, " there are the bells! Now, sir, as you are a stranger I must offer you the hospitality of my pew. I do not know whether you are at all used with our Scottish form; but in case you are not I will find your places for you; and Dr. Henry Gray, of St. Mary's (under whom I sit), is as good a preacher as we have to show you."

This put me in a quandary. It was a degree of risk I was scarce prepared for. Dozens of people, who might pass me by in the street with no more than a second look, would go on from the second to the third, and from that to a final recognition, if I were set before them, immobilised in a pew, during the whole time of service. An unlucky turn of the head would suffice to arrest their attention. " Who is that? " they would think: " surely I should know him! " and, a church being the place in all the world where one has least to think of, it was ten to one they would end by remembering me before the benediction. However, my mind was made up: I thanked my obliging friend, and placed myself at his disposal.

Our way now led us into the north-east quarter of the town, among pleasant new faubourgs, to a decent new church of a good size, where I was soon seated by the side of my good Samaritan, and looked upon by a whole congregation of menacing faces. At first the possibility of danger kept me awake; but by the time I had assured myself there was none to be apprehended, and the service was not in the least likely to be enlivened by the arrest of a French spy, I had to resign myself to the task of listening to Dr. Henry Gray.

As we moved out, after this ordeal was over, my friend was at once surrounded and claimed by his acquaintances of the congregation; and I was rejoiced to hear him addressed by the expected name of Robbie.

So soon as we were clear of the crowd—" Mr. Robbie? " said I, bowing.

" The very same, sir," said he.

" If I mistake not, a lawyer? "

" A writer to His Majesty's Signet, at your service."

" It seems we were predestined to be acquaintances! " I exclaimed. " I have here a card in my pocket intended for you. It is from my family lawyer. It was his last word, as I was leaving, to ask to be remembered kindly, and to trust you would pass over so informal an introduction."

And I offered him the card.

" Ay, ay, my old friend Daniel! " says he, looking on the card. " And how does my old friend Daniel? "

I gave a favourable view of Mr. Romaine's health.

" Well, this is certainly a whimsical incident," he continued. " And since we are thus met already—and so much to my advantage!— the simplest thing will be to prosecute the acquaintance instantly. Let me propose a snack between sermons, a bottle of my particular green seal—and when nobody is looking we can talk blazons, Mr. Ducie! "—which was the name I then used and had already incidentally mentioned, in the vain hope of provoking a return in kind.

" I beg your pardon, sir: do I understand you to invite me to your house? " said I.

" That was the idea I was trying to convey," said he. " We have the name of hospitable people up here, and I would like you to try mine."

" Mr. Robbie, I shall hope to try it some day, but not yet," I replied. " I hope you will not misunderstand me. My business, which brings me to your city, is of a peculiar kind. Till you shall have heard it, and, indeed, till its issue is known, I should feel as if I had stolen your invitation."

" Well, well," said he, a little sobered, " it must be as you wish, though you would hardly speak otherwise if you had committed homicide! Mine is the loss. I must eat alone; a very pernicious thing for a person of my habit of body, content myself with a pint of skinking claret, and meditate the discourse. But about this business of yours: if it is so particular as all that, it will doubtless admit of no delay."

" I must confess, sir, it presses," I acknowledged.

The Sabbath Day

" Then, let us say to-morrow at half-past eight in the morning," said he; " and I hope, when your mind is at rest (and it does you much honour to take it as you do), that you will sit down with me to the postponed meal, not forgetting the bottle. You have my address? " he added, and gave it me—which was the only thing I wanted.

At last, at the level of York Place, we parted with mutual civilities, and I was free to pursue my way, through the mobs of people returning from church, to my lodgings in St. James' Square.

Almost at the house door whom should I overtake but my landlady in a dress of gorgeous severity, and dragging a prize in her wake; no less than Rowley, with the cockade in his hat, and a smart pair of tops to his boots! When I said he was in the lady's wake I spoke but in metaphor. As a matter of fact he was squiring her, with the utmost dignity, on his arm; and I followed them up the stairs, smiling to myself.

Both were quick to salute me as soon as I was perceived, and Mrs. McRankine inquired where I had been. I told her boastfully, giving her the name of the church and the divine, and ignorantly supposed I should have gained caste. But she soon opened my eyes. In the roots of the Scottish character there are knots and contortions that not only no stranger can understand, but no stranger can follow; he walks among explosives; and his best course is to throw himself upon their mercy—" Just as I am, without one plea," a citation from one of the lady's favourite hymns.

The sound she made was unmistakable in meaning, though it was impossible to be written down; and I at once executed the manœuvre I have recommended.

" You must remember I am a perfect stranger in your city," said I. " If I have done wrong, it was in mere ignorance, my dear lady; and this afternoon, if you will be so good as to take me, I shall accompany *you*."

But she was not to be pacified at the moment, and departed to her own quarters murmuring.

" Well, Rowley," said I; " and have you been to church? "

" If you please, sir," he said.

" Well, you have not been any less unlucky than I have," I returned. " And how did you get on with the Scottish form? "

" Well, sir, it was pretty 'ard, the form was, and reether

narrow," he replied. "I don't know w'y it is, but it seems
to me like as if things were a good bit changed since William
Wallace! That was a main queer church she took me to,
Mr. Anne! I don't know as I could have sat it out,
if she 'adn't 'a' give me peppermints. She ain't a bad one
at bottom, the old girl; she do pounce a bit, and she do worry,
but, law bless you, Mr. Anne, it ain't nothink really—she
don't *mean* it. W'y, she was down on me like a 'undred-
weight of bricks this morning. You see, last night she 'ad me
in to supper, and, I beg your pardon, sir, but I took the freedom of playing her a chune or two. She didn't mind a bit;
so this morning I began to play to myself, and she flounced
in, and flew up, and carried on no end about Sunday!"

"You see, Rowley," said I, "they're all mad up here, and
you have to humour them. See and don't quarrel with Mrs.
McRankine; and, above all, don't argue with her, or you'll
get the worst of it. Whatever she says, touch your forelock
and say, 'If you please!' or 'I beg pardon, ma'am.' And
let me tell you one thing: I am sorry, but you have to go to
church with her again this afternoon. That's duty, my boy!"

As I had foreseen, the bells had scarce begun before Mrs.
McRankine presented herself to be our escort, upon which I
sprang up with readiness and offered her my arm. Rowley
followed behind. I was beginning to grow accustomed to
the risks of my stay in Edinburgh, and it even amused me to
confront a new churchful. I confess the amusement did not
last until the end; for if Dr. Gray were long, Mr. McCraw was
not only longer but more incoherent, and the matter of his
sermon (which was a direct attack, apparently, on all the
Churches of the world, my own among the number), where it
had not the tonic quality of personal insult, rather inclined
me to slumber. But I braced myself for my life, kept up
Rowley with the end of a pin, and came through it awake,
but no more.

Bethiah was quite conquered by this "mark of grace,"
though, I am afraid, she was also moved by more worldly
considerations. The first is, the lady had not the least objection to go to church on the arm of an elegantly dressed young
gentleman, and be followed by a spruce servant with a
cockade in his hat. I could see it by the way she took possession of us, found us the places in the Bible, whispered to me
the name of the minister, passed us lozenges, which I (for my

The Sabbath Day

part) handed on to Rowley, and at each fresh attention stole a little glance about the church to make sure she was observed. Rowley was a pretty boy; you will pardon me if I also remembered that I was a favourable-looking young man. When we grow elderly, how the room brightens, and begins to look as it ought to look, on the entrance of youth, grace, health and comeliness! You do not want them for yourself, perhaps not even for your son, but you look on smiling; and when you recall their images—again, it is with a smile. I defy you to see or think of them and not smile with an infinite and intimate, but quite impersonal, pleasure. Well, either I know nothing of women, or that was the case with Bethiah McRankine. She had been to church with a cockade behind her, on the one hand; on the other, her house was brightened by the presence of a pair of good-looking young fellows of the other sex, who were always pleased and deferential in her society, and accepted her views as final.

These were sentiments to be encouraged; and, on the way home from church—if church it could be called—I adopted a most insidious device to magnify her interest. I took her into the confidence, that is, of my love affair, and I had no sooner mentioned a young lady with whom my affections were engaged than she turned upon me a face of awful gravity.

" Is she bonny? " she inquired.

I gave her full assurances upon that.

" To what denoamination does she beloang? " came next, and was so unexpected as almost to deprive me of breath.

" Upon my word, ma'am, I have never inquired," cried I; " I only know that she is a heartfelt Christian, and that is enough."

" Ah! " she sighed, " if she has the root of the maitter! There's a remnant practically in most of the denoaminations. There's some in the McGlashanites, and some in the Glassites, and mony in the McMillanites, and there's a leeven even in the Estayblishment."

" I have known some very good Papists even, if you go to that," said I.

" Mr. Ducie, think shame to yoursel'! " she cried.

" Why, my dear madam! I only——" I began.

" You shouldnae jest in sairious maitters," she interrupted.

On the whole, she entered into what I chose to tell her of our idyll with avidity, like a cat licking her whiskers over a

219

dish of cream; and, strange to say—and so expansive a passion is that of love!—that I derived a perhaps equal satisfaction from confiding in that breast of iron. It made an immediate bond: from that hour we seemed to be welded into a family-party; and I had little difficulty in persuading her to join us and to preside over our tea-table. Surely there was never so ill-matched a trio as Rowley, Mrs. McRankine, and the Viscount Anne! But I am of the Apostle's way, with a difference: all things to all women! When I cannot please a woman, hang me in my cravat!

CHAPTER XXVIII

EVENTS OF MONDAY: THE LAWYER'S PARTY

By half-past eight o'clock on the next morning, I was ringing the bell of the lawyer's office in Castle Street, where I found him ensconced at a business table, in a room surrounded by several tiers of green tin cases. He greeted me like an old friend.

" Come away, sir, come away! " said he. " Here is the dentist ready for you, and I think I can promise you that the operation will be practically painless."

" I am not so sure of that, Mr. Robbie," I replied, as I shook hands with him. " But at least there shall be no time lost with me."

I had to confess to having gone a-roving with a pair of drovers and their cattle, to having used a false name, to having murdered or half-murdered a fellow-creature in a scuffle on the moors, and to having suffered a couple of quite innocent men to lie some time in prison on a charge from which I could have immediately freed them. All this I gave him first of all, to be done with the worst of it; and all this he took with gravity, but without the least appearance of surpris .

" Now, sir," I continued, " I expect to have to pay for my unhappy frolic, but I would like very well if it could be managed without my personal appearance or even the mention of my real name. I had so much wisdom as to sail under false colours in this foolish jaunt of mine; my family would be extremely concerned if they had wind of it; but at the

The Lawyer's Party

same time, if the case of this Faa has terminated fatally, and there are proceedings against Todd and Candlish, I am not going to stand by and see them vexed, far less punished; and I authorise you to give me up for trial if you think that best —or, if you think it unnecessary, in the meanwhile to make preparations for their defence. I hope, sir, that I am as little anxious to be Quixotic, as I am determined to be just."

" Very fairly spoken," said Mr. Robbie. " It is not much in my line, as doubtless your friend, Mr. Romaine, will have told you. I rarely mix myself up with anything on the criminal side, or approaching it. However, for a young gentleman like you, I may stretch a point, and I dare say I may be able to accomplish more than perhaps another. I will go at once to the Procurator Fiscal's office and inquire."

" Wait a moment, Mr. Robbie," said I. " You forget the chapter of expenses. I had thought, for a beginning, of placing a thousand pounds in your hands."

" My dear sir, you will kindly wait until I render you my bill," said Mr. Robbie severely.

" It seemed to me," I protested, " that coming to you almost as a stranger, and placing in your hands a piece of business so contrary to your habits, some substantial guarantee of my good faith——"

" Not the way that we do business in Scotland, sir," he interrupted, with an air of closing the dispute.

" And yet, Mr. Robbie," I continued, " I must ask you to allow me to proceed. I do not merely refer to the expenses of the case. I have my eye besides on Todd and Candlish. They are thoroughly deserving fellows; they have been subjected through me to a considerable term of imprisonment; and I suggest, sir, that you should not spare money for their indemnification. This will explain," I added, smiling, " my offer of the thousand pounds. It was in the nature of a measure by which you should judge the scale on which I can afford to have this business carried through."

" I take you perfectly, Mr. Ducie," said he. " But the sooner I am off, the better this affair is like to be guided. My clerk will show you into the waiting-room and give you the day's *Caledonian Mercury* and the last *Register* to amuse yourself with in the interval."

I believe Mr. Robbie was at least three hours gone. I saw him descend from a cab at the door, and almost immediately after I was shown again into his study, where the solemnity of his manner led me to augur the worst. For some time he had the inhumanity to read me a lecture as to the incredible silliness, "not to say immorality," of my behaviour. "I have the satisfaction in telling you my opinion, because it appears that you are going to get off scot-free," he continued, where, indeed, I thought he might have begun.

"The man, Faa, has been dischairged cured; and the two men, Todd and Candlish, would have been leeberated long ago, if it had not been for their extraordinary loyalty to yourself, Mr. Ducie—or Mr. St. Ivey, as I believe I should now call you. Never a word would either of the two old fools volunteer that in any manner pointed at the existence of such a person; and when they were confronted with Faa's version of the affair, they gave accounts so entirely discrepant with their own former declarations, as well as with each other, that the Fiscal was quite nonplussed, and imaigined there was something behind it. You may believe I soon laughed him out of that! And I had the satisfaction of seeing your two friends set free, and very glad to be on the causeway again."

"Oh, sir," I cried, "you should have brought them here."

"No instructions, Mr. Ducie!" said he. "How did I know you wished to renew an acquaintance which you had just terminated so fortunately? And, indeed, to be frank with you, I should have set my face against it, if you had! Let them go! They are paid and contented, and have the highest possible opinion of Mr. St. Ivey! When I gave them fifty pounds apiece—which was rather more than enough, Mr. Ducie, whatever you may think—the man Todd, who has the only tongue of the party, struck his staff on the ground. 'Weel,' says he, 'I aye said he was a gentleman!' 'Man, Todd,' said I, 'that was just what Mr. St. Ivey said of yourself.'"

"So it was a case of 'Compliments fly when gentlefolk meet.'"

"No, no, Mr. Ducie, man Todd and man Candlish are gone out of your life, and a good riddance! They are fine fellows in their way, but no proper associates for the like of yourself; and do you finally agree to be done with all eccentricity—take up with no more drovers, or rovers, or tinkers, but enjoy the naitural pleesures for which your age, your wealth, your intelligence, and (if I may be allowed to say it) your appear-

The Lawyer's Party

ance so completely fit you. And the first of these," quoth he, looking at his watch, "will be to step through to my dining-room and share a bachelor's luncheon."

Over the meal, which was good, Mr. Robbie continued to develop the same theme. "You're, no doubt, what they call a dancing-man?" said he. "Well, on Thursday night there is the Assembly Ball. You must certainly go there, and you must permit me besides to do the honours of the ceety and send you a ticket. I am a thorough believer in a young man being a young man—but no more drovers or rovers, if you love me! Talking of which puts me in mind that you may be short of partners at the Assembly—oh, I have been young myself!—and if ye care to come to anything so portentiously tedious as a tea-party at the house of a bachelor lawyer, consisting mainly of his nieces and nephews, and his grand-nieces and grand-nephews, and his wards, and generally the whole clan of the descendants of his clients, you might drop in to-night towards seven o'clock. I think I can show you one or two that are worth looking at, and you can dance with them later on at the Assembly."

He proceeded to give me a sketch of one or two eligible young ladies whom I might expect to meet. "And then there's my parteecular friend, Miss Flora," said he. "But I'll make no attempt of a description. You shall see her for yourself."

It will be readily supposed that I accepted his invitation; and returned home to make a toilette worthy of her I was to meet and the good news of which I was the bearer. The toilette, I have reason to believe, was a success. Mr. Rowley dismissed me with a farewell: "Crikey! Mr. Anne, but you do look prime!" Even the stony Bethiah was—how shall I say?—dazzled, but scandalised, by my appearance; and while, of course, she deplored the vanity that led to it, she could not wholly prevent herself from admiring the result.

"Ay, Mr. Ducie, this is a poor employment for a wayfaring Christian man!" she said. "Wi' Christ despised and rejectit in all pairts of the world, and the flag of the Covenant flung doon, you will be muckle better on your knees! However, I'll have to confess that it sets you weel. And if it's the lassie ye're gaun to see the nicht, I suppose I'll just have to excuse ye! Bairns maun be bairns!" she said, with a sigh. "I mind when Mr. McRankine came courtin', and that's lang by-gane—I mind I had a green gown, passementit, that was thocht to become me to admiration. I was nae just exactly what ye would ca' bonny; but I was pale, penetratin', and interestin'." And she leaned over the stair-rail with a candle to watch my descent as long as it should be possible.

It was but a little party at Mr. Robbie's—by which, I do not so much mean that there were few people, for the rooms were crowded, as that there was very little attempted to entertain them. In one apartment there were tables set out where the elders were solemnly engaged upon whist; in the other and larger one, a great number of youth of both sexes entertained themselves languidly, the ladies sitting upon chairs to be courted, the gentlemen standing about in various attitudes of insinuation or indifference. Conversation appeared the sole resource, except in so far as it was modified by a number of keepsakes and annuals which lay dispersed upon the tables, and of which the young beaux displayed the illustrations to the ladies. Mr. Robbie himself was customarily in the card-room; only now and again, when he cut out, he made an incursion among the young folks, and rolled about jovially from one to another, the very picture of the general uncle.

It chanced that Flora had met Mr. Robbie in the course of the afternoon. "Now, Miss Flora," he had said, "come early, for I have a Phœnix to show you—one Mr. Ducie, a new client of mine that, I vow, I have fallen in love with"; and he was so good as to add a word or two on my appearance, from which Flora conceived a suspicion of the truth. She had come to the party, in consequence, on the knife-edge of anticipation and alarm; had chosen a place by the door, where I found her, on my arrival, surrounded by a posse of vapid youths; and, when I drew near, sprang up to meet me in the most natural manner in the world, and, obviously, with a prepared form of words.

"How do you do, Mr. Ducie?" she said. "It is quite an age since I have seen you!"

"I have much to tell you, Miss Gilchrist," I replied. "May I sit down?"

For the artful girl, by sitting near the door, and the judicious use of her shawl, had contrived to keep a chair empty by her side.

The Lawyer's Party

She made room for me, as a matter of course, and the youths had the discretion to melt before us. As soon as I was once seated her fan flew out, and she whispered behind it:

" Are you mad? "

" Madly in love," I replied; " but in no other sense."

" I have no patience! You cannot understand what I am suffering! " she said. " What are you to say to Ronald, to Major Chevenix, to my aunt? "

" Your aunt? " I cried, with a start. " *Peccavi!* is she here? "

" She is in the card-room at whist," said Flora.

" Where she will probably stay all the evening? " I suggested.

" She may," she admitted; " she generally does! "

" Well, then, I must avoid the card-room," said I, " which is very much what I had counted upon doing. I did not come here to play cards, but to contemplate a certain young lady to my heart's content—if it can ever be contented!—and to tell her some good news."

" But there are still Ronald and the Major! " she persisted. " They are not card-room fixtures! Ronald will be coming and going. And as for Mr. Chevenix, he——"

" Always sits with Miss Flora? " I interrupted. " And they talk of poor St. Ives? I had gathered as much, my dear; and Mr. Ducie has come to prevent it! But pray dismiss these fears! I mind no one but your aunt."

" Why my aunt? "

" Because your aunt is a lady, my dear, and a very clever lady, and, like all clever ladies, a very rash lady," said I. " You can never count upon them, unless you are sure of getting them in a corner, as I have got you, and talking them over rationally, as I am just engaged on with yourself! It would be quite the same to your aunt to make the worst kind of a scandal, with an equal indifference to my danger and to the feelings of our good host! "

" Well," she said, "and what of Ronald, then? Do you think *he* is above making a scandal? You must know him very little! "

" On the other hand, it is my pretension that I know him very well! " I replied. " I must speak to Ronald first—not Ronald to me—that is all! "

" Then, please, go and speak to him at once! " she pleaded.

" He is there—do you see?—at the upper end of the room, talking to that girl in pink."

" And so lose this seat before I have told you my good news? " I exclaimed. " Catch me! And, besides, my dear one, think a little of me and my good news! I thought the bearer of good news was always welcome! I hoped he might be a little welcome for himself! Consider! I have but one friend; and let me stay by her! And there is only one thing I care to hear; and let me hear it! "

" O Anne," she sighed, " if I did not love you why should I be so uneasy? I am turned into a coward, dear! Think, if it were the other way round—if you were quite safe and I was in, oh, such danger! "

She had no sooner said it than I was convicted of being a dullard. " God forgive me, dear! " I made haste to reply, " I never saw before that there were two sides to this! " And I told her my tale as briefly as I could, and rose to seek Ronald. " You see, my dear, you are obeyed," I said.

She gave me a look that was a reward in itself; and as I turned away from her, with a strong sense of turning away from the sun, I carried that look in my bosom like a caress. The girl in pink was an arch, ogling person, with a good deal of eyes and teeth, and a great play of shoulders and rattle of conversation. There could be no doubt, from Mr. Ronald's attitude, that he worshipped the very chair she sat on. But I was quite ruthless. I laid my hand on his shoulder, as he was stooping over her like a hen over a chicken.

" Excuse me for one moment, Mr. Gilchrist! " said I.

He started and span about in answer to my touch, and exhibited a face of inarticulate wonder.

" Yes! " I continued, " it is even myself! Pardon me for interrupting so agreeable a *tête-à-tête*, but you know, my good fellow, we owe a first duty to Mr. Robbie. It would never do to risk making a scene in the man's drawing-room; so the first thing I had to attend to was to have you warned. The name I go by is Ducie, too, in case of accidents."

" I—I say, you know! " cried Ronald. " Deuce take it, what are you doing here? "

" Hush, hush! " said I. " Not the place, my dear fellow— not the place. Come to my rooms, if you like, to-night after the party, or to-morrow in the morning, and we can talk it out over a segar. But here, you know, it really won't do at all."

The Lawyer's Party

Before he could collect his mind for an answer, I had given him my address in St. James' Square, and had again mingled with the crowd. Alas! I was not fated to get back to Flora so easily! Mr. Robbie was in the path: he was insatiably loquacious; and as he continued to palaver I watched the insipid youths gather again about my idol, and cursed my fate and my host. He remembered suddenly that I was to attend the Assembly Ball on Thursday, and had only attended to-night by way of a preparative. This put it into his head to present me to another young lady; but I managed this interview with so much art that, while I was scrupulously polite and even cordial to the fair one, I contrived to keep Robbie beside me all the time and to leave along with him when the ordeal was over. We were just walking away arm in arm, when I spied my friend the Major approaching, stiff as a ramrod and, as usual, obtrusively clean.

"Oh! there's a man I want to know," said I, taking the bull by the horns. "Won't you introduce me to Major Chevenix?"

"At a word, my dear fellow," said Robbie; and "Major!" he cried, "come here and let me present to you my friend Mr. Ducie, who desires the honour of your acquaintance."

The Major flushed visibly, but otherwise preserved his composure. He bowed very low. "I'm not very sure," he said: "I have an idea we have met before?"

"Informally," I said, returning his bow; "and I have long looked forward to the pleasure of regularising our acquaintance."

"You are very good, Mr. Ducie," he returned. "Perhaps you could aid my memory a little? Where was it that I had the pleasure?"

"Oh, that would be telling tales out of school," said I, with a laugh, "and before my lawyer, too!"

"I'll wager," broke in Mr. Robbie, "that, when you knew my client, Chevenix—the past of our friend Mr. Ducie is an obscure chapter full of horrid secrets—I'll wager, now, you knew him as St. Ivey," says he, nudging me violently.

"I think not, sir," said the Major, with pinched lips.

"Well, I wish he may prove all right!" continued the lawyer, with certainly the worst-inspired jocularity in the world. "I know nothing by him! He may be a swell mobsman for me with his aliases. You must put your memory on the rack, Major, and when ye've remembered when and where ye met him, be sure ye tell me."

" I will not fail, sir," said Chevenix.

" Seek to him!" cried Robbie, waving his hand as he departed.

The Major, as soon as we were alone, turned upon me his impassive countenance.

" Well," he said, " you have courage."

" It is undoubted as your honour, sir," I returned, bowing.

" Did you expect to meet me, may I ask? " said he.

" You saw, at least, that I courted the presentation," said I.

" And you were not afraid? " said Chevenix.

" I was perfectly at ease. I knew I was dealing with a gentleman. Be that your epitaph."

" Well, there are some other people looking for you," he said, " who will make no bones about the point of honour. The police, my dear sir, are simply agog about you."

" And I think that that was coarse," said I.

" You have seen Miss Gilchrist? " he inquired, changing the subject.

" With whom, I am led to understand, we are on a footing of rivalry? " I asked. " Yes, I have seen her."

" And I was just seeking her," he replied.

I was conscious of a certain thrill of temper; so, I suppose, was he. We looked each other up and down.

" The situation is original," he resumed.

" Quite," said I. " But let me tell you frankly you are blowing a cold coal. I owe you so much for your kindness to the prisoner Champdivers."

" Meaning that the lady's affections are more advantageously disposed of? " he asked, with a sneer. " Thank you, I am sure. And, since you have given me a lead, just hear a word of good advice in your turn. Is it fair, is it delicate, is it like a gentleman, to compromise the young lady by attentions which (as you know very well) can come to nothing? "

I was utterly unable to find words in answer.

" Excuse me if I cut this interview short," he went on. " It seems to me doomed to come to nothing, and there is more attractive metal."

" Yes," I replied, " as you say, it cannot amount to much.

The Lawyer's Party

You are impotent, bound hand and foot in honour. You know me to be a man falsely accused, and even if you did not know it, from your position as my rival you have only the choice to stand quite still or to be infamous."

" I would not say that," he returned, with another change of colour. " I may hear it once too often."

With which he moved off straight for where Flora was sitting amidst her court of vapid youths, and I had no choice but to follow him, a bad second, and reading myself, as I went, a sharp lesson on the command of temper.

It is a strange thing how young men in their teens go down at the mere wind of the coming of men of twenty-five and upwards! The vapid ones fled without thought of resistance before the Major and me; a few dallied awhile in the neighbourhood—so to speak, with their fingers in their mouths—but presently these also followed the rout, and we remained face to face before Flora. There was a draught in that corner by the door; she had thrown her pelisse over her bare arms and neck, and the dark fur of the trimming set them off. She shone by contrast; the light played on her smooth skin to admiration, and the colour changed in her excited face. For the least fraction of a second she looked from one to the other of her pair of rival swains, and seemed to hesitate. Then she addressed Chevenix.

" You are coming to the Assembly, of course, Major Chevenix? " said she.

" I fear not; I fear I shall be otherwise engaged," he replied. " Even the pleasure of dancing with you, Miss Flora, must give way to duty."

For awhile the talk ran harmlessly on the weather, and then branched off towards the war. It seemed to be by no one's fault; it was in the air, and had to come.

" Good news from the scene of operations," said the Major.

" Good news while it lasts," I said. " But will Miss Gilchrist tell us her private thought upon the war? In her admiration for the victors, does not there mingle some pity for the vanquished? "

" Indeed, sir," she said, with animation, " only too much of it! War is a subject that I do not think should be talked of to a girl. I am, I have to be—what do you call it?—a non-combatant? And to remind me of what others have to do and suffer: no, it is not fair! "

"Miss Gilchrist has the tender female heart," said Chevenix.

"Do not be too sure of that!" she cried. "I would love to be allowed to fight myself!"

"On which side?" I asked.

"Can you ask?" she exclaimed. "I am a Scottish girl!"

"She is a Scottish girl!" repeated the Major, looking at me. "And no one grudges you her pity!"

"And I glory in every grain of it she has to spare," said I. "Pity is akin to love."

"Well, and let us put that question to Miss Gilchrist. It is for her to decide, and for us to bow to the decision. Is pity, Miss Flora, or is admiration, nearest love?"

"Oh, come," said I, "let us be more concrete. Lay before the lady a complete case: describe your man, then I'll describe *mine*, and Miss Flora shall decide."

"I think I see your meaning," said he, "and I'll try. You think that pity—and the kindred sentiments—have the greatest power upon the heart. I think more nobly of women. To my view, the man they love will first of all command their respect; he will be steadfast—proud, if you please; dry, possibly—but of all things steadfast. They will look at him in doubt; at last they will see that stern face which he presents to all the rest of the world soften to them alone. First, trust, I say. It is so that a woman loves who is worthy of heroes."

"Your man is very ambitious, sir," said I, "and very much of a hero! Mine is a humbler, and, I would fain think, a more human dog. He is one with no particular trust in himself, with no superior steadfastness to be admired for, who sees a lady's face, who hears her voice, and, without any phrase about the matter, falls in love. What does he ask for, then, but pity?—pity for his weakness, pity for his love, which is his life. You would make women always the inferiors, gaping up at your imaginary lover; he, like a marble statue, with his nose in the air! But God has been wiser than you; and the most steadfast of your heroes may prove human, after all. We appeal to the queen for judgment," I added, turning and bowing before Flora.

"And how shall the queen judge?" she asked. "I must give you an answer that is no answer at all. 'The wind bloweth where it listeth': she goes where her heart goes."

Her face flushed as she said it; mine also, for I read in it a declaration, and my heart swelled for joy. But Chevenix grew pale.

" You make of life a very dreadful kind of lottery, ma'am," said he. " But I will not despair. Honest and unornamental is still my choice."

And I must say he looked extremely handsome and very amusingly like the marble statue with its nose in the air to which I had compared him.

" I cannot imagine how we got upon this subject," said Flora.

" Madame, it was through the war," replied Chevenix.

" All roads lead to Rome," I commented. " What else would you expect Mr. Chevenix and myself to talk of? "

About this time I was conscious of a certain bustle and movement in the room behind me, but did not pay to it that degree of attention which perhaps would have been wise. There came a certain change in Flora's face; she signalled repeatedly with her fan; her eyes appealed to me obsequiously; there could be no doubt that she wanted something—as well as I could make out, that I should go away and leave the field clear for my rival, which I had not the least idea of doing. At last she rose from her chair with impatience.

" I think it time you were saying good-night, Mr. Ducie!" she said.

I could not in the least see why, and said so.

Whereupon she gave me this appalling answer, " My aunt is coming out of the card-room."

In less time than it takes to tell, I had made my bow and my escape. Looking back from the doorway, I was privileged to see, for a moment, the august profile and gold eye-glasses of Miss Gilchrist issuing from the card-room; and the sight lent me wings. I stood not on the order of my going; and a moment after, I was on the pavement of Castle Street, and the lighted windows shone down on me, and were crossed by ironical shadows of those who had remained behind.

St. Ives

CHAPTER XXIX
EVENTS OF TUESDAY: THE TOILS CLOSING

THIS day began with a surprise. I found a letter on my breakfast-table addressed to Edward Ducie, Esquire; and at first I was startled beyond measure. " Conscience doth make cowards of us all! " When I had opened it, it proved to be only a note from the lawyer, enclosing a card for the Assembly Ball on Thursday evening. Shortly after, as I was composing my mind with a segar at one of the windows of the sitting-room, and Rowley, having finished the light share of work that fell to him, sat not far off tooting with great spirit and a marked preference for the upper octave, Ronald was suddenly shown in. I got him a segar, drew in a chair to the side of the fire, and installed him there—I was going to say, at his ease, but no expression could be farther from the truth. He was plainly on pins and needles, did not know whether to take or to refuse the segar, and, after he had taken it, did not know whether to light or to return it. I saw he had something to say; I did not think it was his own something; and I was ready to offer a large bet it was really something of Major Chevenix's.

" Well, and so here you are! " I observed, with pointless cordiality, for I was bound I should do nothing to help him out. If he were, indeed, here running errands for my rival, he might have a fair field, but certainly no favour.

" The fact is," he began, " I would rather see you alone."

" Why, certainly," I replied. " Rowley, you can step into the bedroom. My dear fellow," I continued, " this sounds serious. Nothing wrong, I trust."

" Well, I'll be quite honest," said he. " I *am* a good deal bothered."

" And I bet I know why! " I exclaimed. " And I bet I can put you to rights, too! "

" What do you mean! " he asked.

" You must be hard up," said I, " and all I can say is, you've come to the right place. If you have the least use for a hundred pounds, or any such trifling sum as that, please mention it. It's here, quite at your service."

" I am sure it is most kind of you," said Ronald, " and the truth is, though I can't think how you guessed it, that I really *am* a little behind board. But I haven't come to talk about that."

"No, I dare say!" cried I. "Not worth talking about! But remember, Ronald, you and I are on different sides of the business. Remember that you did me one of those services that make men friends for ever. And since I have had the fortune to come into a fair share of money, just oblige me, and consider so much of it as your own."

"No," he said, "I couldn't take it; I couldn't, really. Besides, the fact is, I've come on a very different matter. It's about my sister, St. Ives," and he shook his head menacingly at me.

"You're quite sure?" I persisted. "It's here, at your service—up to five hundred pounds, if you like. Well, all right; only remember where it is, when you do want it."

"Oh, please let me alone!" cried Ronald: "I've come to say something unpleasant; and how on earth can I do it, if you don't give a fellow a chance? It's about my sister, as I said. You can see for yourself that it can't be allowed to go on. It's compromising; it don't lead to anything; and you're not the kind of man (you must feel it yourself) that I can allow my female relatives to have anything to do with. I hate saying this, St. Ives; it looks like hitting a man when he's down, you know; and I told the Major I very much disliked it from the first. However, it had to be said; and now it has been, and, between gentlemen, it shouldn't be necessary to refer to it again."

"It's compromising; it doesn't lead to anything; not the kind of man," I repeated thoughtfully. "Yes, I believe I understand, and shall make haste to put myself *en règle*." I stood up, and laid my segar down. "Mr. Gilchrist," said I, with a bow, "in answer to your very natural observations, I beg to offer myself as a suitor for your sister's hand. I am a man of title, of which we think lightly in France, but of ancient lineage, which is everywhere prized. I can display thirty-two quarterings without a blot. My expectations are certainly above the average: I believe my uncle's income averages about thirty thousand pounds, though I admit I was not careful to inform myself. Put it anywhere between fifteen and fifty thousand; it is certainly not less."

"All this is very easy to say," said Ronald, with a pitying smile. "Unfortunately, these things are in the air."

"Pardon me,—in Buckinghamshire," said I, smiling.

"Well, what I mean is, my dear St. Ives, that you *can't prove* them," he continued. "They might just as well not be: do you follow me? You can't bring us any third party to back you up."

"Oh, come!" cried I, springing up and hurrying to the table. "You must excuse me!" I wrote Romaine's address. "There is my reference, Mr. Gilchrist. Until you have written to him, and received his negative answer, I have a right to be treated, and I shall see that you treat me, as a gentleman."

He was brought up with a round turn at that.

"I beg your pardon, St. Ives," said he. "Believe me, I had no wish to be offensive. But there's the difficulty of this affair; I can't make any of my points without offence! You must excuse me, it's not my fault. But, at any rate, you must see for yourself this proposal of marriage is—is merely impossible, my dear fellow. It's nonsense! Our countries are at war; you are a prisoner."

"My ancestor of the time of the Ligue," I replied, "married a Huguenot lady out of the Saintonge, riding two hundred miles through an enemy's country to bring off his bride; and it was a happy marriage."

"Well!" he began; and then looked down into the fire, and became silent.

"Well?" I asked.

"Well, there's this business of—Goguelat," said he, still looking at the coals in the grate.

"What!" I exclaimed, starting in my chair. "What's that you say?"

"This business about Goguelat," he repeated.

"Ronald," said I, "this is not your doing. These are not your own words. I know where they come from: a coward put them in your mouth."

"St. Ives!" he cried, "why do you make it so hard for me? and where's the use of insulting other people? The plain English is, that I can't hear of any proposal of marriage from a man under a charge like that. You must see it for yourself, man! It's the most absurd thing I ever heard of! And you go on forcing me to argue with you, too!"

"Because I have had an affair of honour which terminated unhappily, you—a young soldier, or next-door to it—refuse my offer? Do I understand you aright?" said I.

The Toils Closing

" My dear fellow ! " he wailed, " of course you can twist my words, if you like. You *say* it was an affair of honour. Well, I can't, of course, tell you that—I can't——I mean, you must see that that's just the point! Was it? I don't know."

" I have the honour to inform you," said I.

" Well, other people say the reverse, you see ! "

" They lie, Ronald, and I will prove it in time."

" The short and the long of it is, that any man who is so unfortunate as to have such things said about him is not the man to be my brother-in-law ! " he cried.

" Do you know who will be my first witness at the court? Arthur Chevenix ! " said I.

'' I don't care ! " he cried, rising from his chair and beginning to pace outrageously about the room. " What do you mean, St. Ives? What is this about? It's like a dream, I declare ! You made an offer, and I have refused it. I don't like it, I don't want it; and whatever I did, or didn't, wouldn't matter—my aunt wouldn't hear of it anyway ! Can't you take your answer, man ? "

" You must remember, Ronald, that we are playing with edged tools," said I. " An offer of marriage is a delicate subject to handle. You have refused, and you have justified your refusal by several statements: first, that I was an impostor; second, that our countries were at war; and third—— No, I will speak," said I; " you can answer when I have done,—and third, that I had dishonourably killed—or was said to have done so—the man Goguelat. Now, my dear fellow, these are very awkward grounds to be taking. From any one else's lips I need scarce tell you how I should resent them; but my hands are tied. I have so much gratitude to you, without talking of the love I bear your sister, that you insult me, when you do so, under the cover of a complete impunity. I must feel the pain—and I do feel it acutely—I can do nothing to protect myself."

He had been anxious enough to interrupt me in the beginning; but now, and after I had ceased, he stood a long while silent.

" St. Ives," he said at last, " I think I had better go away. This has been very irritating. I never at all meant to say anything of the kind, and I apologise to you. I have all the esteem for you that one gentleman should have for another.

St. Ives

I only meant to tell you—to show you what had influenced my mind; and that, in short, the thing was impossible. One thing you may be quite sure of: *I* shall do nothing against you. Will you shake hands before I go away? " he blurted out.

" Yes," said I, " I agree with you—the interview has been irritating. Let bygones be bygones. Good-bye, Ronald."

" Good-bye, St. Ives," he returned. " I'm heartily sorry."

And with that he was gone.

The windows of my own sitting-room looked towards the north; but the entrance passage drew its light from the direction of the square. Hence I was able to observe Ronald's departure, his very disheartened gait, and the fact that he was joined, about half-way, by no less a man than Major Chevenix. At this, I could scarce keep from smiling; so unpalatable an interview must be before the pair of them, and I could hear their voices, clashing like crossed swords, in that eternal antiphony of " I told you," and " I told you not." Without doubt, they had gained very little by their visit; but then I had gained less than nothing, and had been bitterly dispirited into the bargain. Ronald had stuck to his guns and refused me to the last. It was no news; but, on the other hand, it could not be contorted into good news. I was now certain that during my temporary absence in France, all irons would be put into the fire, and the world turned upside down, to make Flora disown the obtrusive Frenchman and accept Chevenix. Without doubt she would resist these instances; but the thought of them did not please me, and I felt she should be warned and prepared for the battle.

It was no use to try and see her now, but I promised myself early that evening to return to Swanston. In the meantime I had to make all my preparations, and look the coming journey in the face. Here in Edinburgh I was within four miles of the sea, yet the business of approaching random fishermen with my hat in the one hand and a knife in the other, appeared so desperate, that I saw nothing for it but to retrace my steps over the northern counties, and knock a second time at the doors of Birchell Fenn. To do this, money would be necessary; and after leaving my paper in the hands of Flora I had still a balance of about fifteen hundred pounds. Or rather I may say I had them and I had them not; for after my luncheon with Mr. Robbie I had placed the amount all but thirty pounds of change, in a bank in George Street, on a

The Toils Closing

deposit receipt in the name of Mr. Rowley. This I had designed to be my gift to him, in case I must suddenly depart. But now, thinking better of the arrangement, I despatched my little man, cockade and all, to lift the fifteen hundred.

He was not long gone, and returned with a flushed face, and the deposit receipt still in his hand.

" No go, Mr. Anne," says he.

" How's that? " I inquired.

" Well, sir, I found the place all right, and no mistake," said he. " But I tell you what gave me a blue fright! There was a customer standing by the door, and I recognised him! Who do you think it was, Mr. Anne? W'y, that same Red-Breast—him I had breakfast with near Aylesbury."

" You are sure you are not mistaken? " I asked.

" Certain sure," he replied. " Not Mr. Lavender, I don't mean, sir; I mean the other party. ' Wot's he doing here? ' says I. ' It don't look right.' "

" Not by any means," I agreed.

I walked to and fro in the apartment reflecting. This particular Bow Street runner might be here by accident; but it was to imagine a singular play of coincidence that he, who had met Rowley and spoken with him in the " Green Dragon," hard by Aylesbury, should be now in Scotland, where he could have no legitimate business, and by the doors of the bank where Rowley kept his account.

" Rowley," said I, " he didn't see you, did he? "

" Never a fear," quoth Rowley. " W'y, Mr. Anne, sir, if he 'ad, you wouldn't have seen *me* any more! I ain't a hass, sir! "

" Well, my boy, you can put that receipt in your pocket. You'll have no more use for it till you're quite clear of me. Don't lose it, though; it's your share of the Christmas-box: fifteen hundred pounds all for yourself."

" Begging your pardon, Mr. Anne, sir, but wot for? " said Rowley.

" To set up a public-house upon," said I.

" If you'll excuse me, sir, I ain't got any call to set up a public-house, sir," he replied stoutly. " And I tell you wot, sir, it seems to me I'm reether young for the billet. I'm your body servant, Mr. Anne, or else I'm nothink."

" Well, Rowley," I said, " I'll tell you what it's for. It's for the good service you have done me, of which I don't care

—and don't dare—to speak. It's for your loyalty and cheerfulness, my dear boy. I had meant it for you; but to tell you the truth, it's past mending now—it has to be yours. Since that man is waiting by the bank, the money can't be touched until I'm gone."

"Until you're gone, sir?" re-echoed Rowley. "You don't go anywheres without me, I can tell you that, Mr. Anne, sir!"

"Yes, my boy," said I, "we are going to part very soon now; probably to-morrow. And it's for my sake, Rowley! Depend upon it, if there was any reason at all for that Bow Street man being at the bank, he was not there to look out for *you*. How they could have found out about the account so early is more than I can fathom; some strange coincidence must have played me false! But there the fact is; and Rowley, I'll not only have to say farewell to you presently, I'll have to ask you to stay indoors until I can say it. Remember, my boy, it's only so that you can serve me now."

"W'y, sir, you say the word, and of course I'll do it!" he cried. "'Nothink by 'alves,' is my motto! I'm your man, through thick and thin, live or die, I am!"

In the meantime there was nothing to be done till towards sunset. My only chance now was to come again as quickly as possible to speech of Flora, who was my only practicable banker; and not before evening was it worth while to think of that. I might compose myself as well as I was able over the *Caledonian Mercury*, with its ill news of the campaign of France and belated documents about the retreat from Russia; and, as I sat there by the fire, I was sometimes all awake with anger and mortification at what I was reading, and sometimes again I would be three parts asleep as I dozed over the barren items of home intelligence. "Lately arrived"—this is what I suddenly stumbled on—"at Dumbreck's Hotel, the Viscount of Saint-Yves."

"Rowley," said I.

"If you please, Mr. Anne, sir," answered the obsequious, lowering his pipe.

"Come and look at this, my boy," said I, holding out the paper.

"My crikey!" said he. "That's 'im, sir, sure enough!"

"Sure enough, Rowley," said I. "He's on the trail. He has fairly caught up with us. He and this Bow Street man have come together, I would swear. And now here is the

The Toils Closing

whole field, quarry, hounds and hunters, all together in this city of Edinburgh."

"And wot are you goin' to do now, sir? Tell you wot, let me take it in 'and, please! Gimme a minute, and I'll disguise myself, and go out to this Dum—to this hotel, leastways, sir—and see wot he's up to. You put your trust in me, Mr. Anne: I'm fly, don't you make no mistake about it. I'm all a-growing and a-blowing, I am."

"Not one foot of you," said I. "You are a prisoner, Rowley, and make up your mind to that. So am I, or next door to it. I showed it you for a caution; if you go on the streets, it spells death to me, Rowley."

"If you please, sir," says Rowley.

"Come to think of it," I continued, "you must take a cold or something. No good of awakening Mrs. McRankine's suspicions."

"A cold?" he cried, recovering immediately from his depression. "I can do it, Mr. Anne."

And he proceeded to sneeze and cough and blow his nose, till I could not restrain myself from smiling.

"Oh, I tell you, I know a lot of them dodges," he observed proudly.

"Well, they come in very handy," said I.

"I'd better go at once and show it to the old gal, 'adn't I?" he asked.

I told him, by all means; and he was gone upon the instant, gleeful, as though to a game of football.

I took up the paper and read carelessly on, my thoughts engaged with my immediate danger, till I struck on the next paragraph:—

"In connection with the recent horrid murder in the Castle, we are desired to make public the following intelligence. The soldier, Champdivers, is supposed to be in the neighbourhood of this city. He is about the middle height or rather under, of a pleasing appearance and highly genteel address. When last heard of he wore a fashionable suit of pearl-grey, and boots with fawn-coloured tops. He is accompanied by a servant about sixteen years of age, speaks English without any accent, and passed under the *alias* of Ramornie. A reward is offered for his apprehension."

In a moment I was in the next room, stripping from me the pearl-coloured suit!

I confess I was now a good deal agitated. It is difficult to watch the toils closing slowly and surely about you, and to retain your composure; and I was glad that Rowley was not present to spy on my confusion. I was flushed, my breath came thick; I cannot remember a time when I was more put out.

And yet I must wait and do nothing, and partake of my meals, and entertain the ever-garrulous Rowley, as though I were entirely my own man. And if I did not require to entertain Mrs. McRankine also, that was but another drop of bitterness in my cup! For what ailed my landlady, that she should hold herself so severely aloof, that she should refuse conversation, that her eyes should be reddened, that I should so continually hear the voice of her private supplications sounding through the house? I was much deceived, or she had read the insidious paragraph and recognised the comminated pearl-grey suit. I remember now a certain air with which she had laid the paper on my table, and a certain sniff, between sympathy and defiance, with which she had announced it: " There's your *Mercury* for ye! "

In this direction, at least, I saw no pressing danger; her tragic countenance betokened agitation; it was plain she was wrestling with her conscience, and the battle still hung dubious. The question of what to do troubled me extremely. I could not venture to touch such an intricate and mysterious piece of machinery as my landlady's spiritual nature; it might go off at a word, and in any direction, like a badly-made firework. And while I praised myself extremely for my wisdom in the past, that I had made so much a friend of her, I was all abroad as to my conduct in the present. There seemed an equal danger in pressing and in neglecting the accustomed marks of familiarity. The one extreme looked like impudence, and might annoy, the other was a practical confession of guilt. Altogether, it was a good hour for me when the dusk began to fall in earnest on the streets of Edinburgh, and the voice of an early watchman bade me set forth.

I reached the neighbourhood of the cottage before seven; and as I breasted the steep ascent which leads to the garden wall, I was struck with surprise to hear a dog. Dogs I had heard before, but only from the hamlet on the hillside above. Now, this dog was in the garden itself, where it roared aloud in

The Toils Closing

paroxysms of fury, and I could hear it leaping and straining on the chain. I waited some while, until the brute's fit of passion had roared itself out. Then, with the utmost precaution, I drew near again, and finally approached the garden wall. So soon as I had clapped my head above the level, however, the barking broke forth again with redoubled energy. Almost at the same time, the door of the cottage opened, and Ronald and the Major appeared upon the threshold with a lantern. As they so stood, they were almost immediately below me, strongly illuminated, and within easy earshot. The Major pacified the dog, who took instead to low, uneasy growling intermingled with occasional yelps.

"Good thing I brought Towzer!" said Chevenix.

"Damn him, I wonder where he is!" said Ronald; and he moved the lantern up and down, and turned the night into a shifting puzzle-work of gleam and shadow. "I think I'll make a sally."

"I don't think you will," replied Chevenix. "When I agreed to come out here and do sentry-go, it was on one condition, Master Ronald: don't you forget that! Military discipline, my boy! Our beat is this path close about the house. Down, Towzer! good boy, good boy—gently, then!" he went on, caressing his confounded monster.

"To think! The beggar may be hearing us this minute!" cried Ronald.

"Nothing more probable," said the Major. "You there, St. Ives?" he added, in a distinct but guarded voice. "I only want to tell you, you had better go home. Mr. Gilchrist and I take watch and watch."

The game was up. "*Beaucoup de plaisir !*" I replied, in the same tones. "*Il fait un peu froid pour veiller ; gardez-vous des engelures !*"

I suppose it was done in a moment of ungovernable rage; but in spite of the excellent advice he had given to Ronald the moment before, Chevenix slipped the chain, and the dog sprang, straight as an arrow, up the bank. I stepped back, picked up a stone of about twelve pounds weight, and stood ready. With a bound the beast landed on the cope-stone of the wall; and, almost in the same instant, my missile caught him fair in the face. He gave a stifled cry, went tumbling back where he had come from, and I could hear the twelve-pounder accompany him in his fall. Chevenix, at the same moment, broke out in a roaring voice: "The hell-hound! If he's killed my dog!" and I judged, upon all grounds, it was as well to be off.

CHAPTER XXX

EVENTS OF WEDNESDAY; THE UNIVERSITY OF CRAMOND

I AWOKE to much diffidence, even to a feeling that might be called the beginnings of panic, and lay for hours in my bed considering the situation. Seek where I pleased, there was nothing to encourage me and plenty to appal. They kept a close watch about the cottage; they had a beast of a watch-dog—at least, unless I had settled it; and if I had, I knew its bereaved master would only watch the more indefatigably for the loss. In the pardonable ostentation of love I had given all the money I could spare to Flora; I had thought it glorious that the hunted exile should come down, like Jupiter, in a shower of gold, and pour thousands in the lap of the beloved. Then I had in an hour of arrant folly buried what remained to me in a bank in George Street. And now I must get back the one or the other; and which? and how?

As I tossed in my bed, I could see three possible courses, all extremely perilous. First, Rowley might have been mistaken; the bank might not be watched; it might still be possible for him to draw the money on the deposit receipt. Second, I might apply again to Robbie. Or, third, I might dare everything, go to the Assembly Ball, and speak with Flora under the eyes of all Edinburgh. This last alternative, involving as it did the most horrid risks, and the delay of forty-eight hours, I did but glance at with an averted head, and turned again to the consideration of the others. It was the likeliest thing in the world that Robbie had been warned to have no more to do with me. The whole policy of the Gilchrists was in the hands of Chevenix; and I thought this was a precaution so elementary that he was certain to have taken it. If he had not, of course I was all right: Robbie would manage to communicate with Flora; and by four o'clock I might be on the south road and, I was going to say, a free man. Lastly, I must assure myself with my own eyes whether the bank in George Street were beleaguered.

The University of Cramond

I called to Rowley and questioned him tightly as to the appearance of the Bow Street officer.

" What sort of looking man is he, Rowley? " I asked, as I began to dress.

" Wot sort of a looking man he is? " repeated Rowley. " Well, I don't very well know wot you would say, Mr. Anne. He ain't a beauty, any'ow."

" Is he tall? "

" Tall? Well, no, I shouldn't say *tall*, Mr. Anne."

" Well, then, is he short? "

" Short? No, I don't think I would say he was what you would call *short*. No, not piticular short, sir."

" Then, I suppose, he must be about the middle height? "

" Well, you might say it, sir; but not remarkable so."

I smothered an oath.

" Is he clean-shaved? " I tried him again.

" Clean-shaved? " he repeated, with the same air of anxious candour.

" Good heavens, man, don't repeat my words like a parrot!" I cried. " Tell me what the man was like: it is of the first importance that I should be able to recognise him."

" I'm trying to, Mr. Anne. But *clean-shaved?* I don't seem to rightly get hold of that p'int. Sometimes it might appear to me like as if he was; and sometimes like as if he wasn't. No, it wouldn't surprise me now if you was to tell me he 'ad a bit o' whisker."

" Was the man red-faced? " I roared, dwelling on each syllable.

" I don't think you need go for to get cross about it, Mr. Anne! " said he. " I'm tellin' you every blessed thing I see! Red-faced? Well, no, not as you would remark upon."

A dreadful calm fell upon me.

" Was he anywise pale? " I asked.

" Well, it don't seem to me as though he were. But I tell you truly, I didn't take much heed to that."

" Did he look like a drinking man? "

" Well, no. If you please, sir, he looked more like an eating one."

" Oh, he was stout, was he? "

" No, sir. I couldn't go so far as that. No, he wasn't not to say *stout*. If anything, lean rather."

I need not go on with the infuriating interview. It ended

243

as it began, except that Rowley was in tears, and that I had acquired one fact. The man was drawn for me as being of any height you like to mention, and of any degree of corpulence or leanness; clean-shaved or not, as the case might be; the colour of his hair Rowley " could not take it upon himself to put a name on "; that of his eyes he thought to have been blue—nay, it was the one point on which he attained to a kind of tearful certainty. " I'll take my davy on it," he asseverated. They proved to have been as black as sloes, very little and very near together. So much for the evidence of the artless! And the fact, or rather the facts, acquired? Well, they had to do not with the person but with his clothing. The man wore knee-breeches and white stockings; his coat was "some kind of a lightish colour—or betwixt that and dark "; and he wore a " moleskin weskit." As if this were not enough, he presently haled me from my breakfast in a prodigious flutter, and showed me an honest and rather venerable citizen passing in the Square.

" That's *him*, sir," he cried, " the very moral of him! Well, this one is better dressed, and p'r'aps a trifler taller; and in the face he don't favour him noways at all, sir. No, not when I come to look again, 'e don't seem to favour him noways."

" Jackass! " said I, and I think the greatest stickler for manners will admit the epithet to have been justified.

Meanwhile the appearance of my landlady added a great load of anxiety to what I already suffered. It was plain that she had not slept; equally plain that she had wept copiously. She sighed, she groaned, she drew in her breath, she shook her head, as she waited on table. In short, she seemed in so precarious a state, like a petard three times charged with hysteria, that I did not dare to address her; and stole out of the house on tiptoe, and actually ran downstairs, in the fear that she might call me back. It was plain that this degree of tension could not last long.

It was my first care to go to George Street, which I reached (by good luck) as a boy was taking down the bank shutters. A man was conversing with him; he had white stockings and a moleskin waistcoat, and was as ill-looking a rogue as you would want to see in a day's journey. This seemed to agree fairly well with Rowley's *signalement:* he had declared emphatically (if you remember), and had stuck to it besides, that the companion of the great Lavender was no beauty.

The University of Cramond

Thence I made my way to Mr. Robbie's, where I rang the bell. A servant answered the summons, and told me the lawyer was engaged, as I had half expected.

" Wha shall I say was callin'? " she pursued; and when I had told her " Mr. Ducie," " I think this'll be for you, then? " she added, and handed me a letter from the hall table. It ran:—

" DEAR MR. DUCIE,
  " My single advice to you is to leave *quam primum* for the South.—Yours,   T. ROBBIE."

That was short and sweet. It emphatically extinguished hope in one direction. No more was to be gotten of Robbie; and I wondered, from my heart, how much had been told him. Not too much, I hoped, for I liked the lawyer who had thus deserted me, and I placed a certain reliance on the discretion of Chevenix. He would not be merciful; on the other hand, I did not think he would be cruel without cause.

It was my next affair to go back along George Street, and assure myself whether the man in the moleskin vest was still on guard. There was no sign of him on the pavement. Spying the door of a common stair nearly opposite the bank, I took it in my head that this would be a good point of observation, crossed the street, entered with a businesslike air and fell immediately against the man in the moleskin vest. I stopped and apologised to him; he replied in an unmistakable English accent, thus putting the matter almost beyond doubt. After this encounter I must, of course, ascend to the top storey, ring the bell of a suite of apartments, inquire for Mr. Vavasour, learn (with no great surprise) that he did not live there, come down again and, again politely saluting the man from Bow Street, make my escape at last into the street.

I was now driven back upon the Assembly Ball. Robbie had failed me. The bank was watched; it would never do to risk Rowley in that neighbourhood. All I could do was to wait until the morrow evening, and present myself at the Assembly, let it end as it might. But I must say I came to this decision with a good deal of genuine fright; and here I came for the first time to one of those places where my courage stuck. I do not mean that my courage boggled and made a bit of a bother over it, as it did over the escape from the Castle; I mean, stuck, like a stopped watch or a dead man.

Certainly I would go to the ball; certainly I must see this morning about my clothes. That was all decided. But the most of the shops were on the other side of the valley, in the Old Town; and it was now my strange discovery that I was physically unable to cross the North Bridge! It was as though a precipice had stood between us, or the deep sea had intervened. Nearer to the Castle my legs refused to bear me.

I told myself this was mere superstition; I made wagers with myself—and gained them; I went down on the esplanade of Princes Street, walked and stood there, alone and conspicuous, looking across the garden at the old grey bastions of the fortress, where all these troubles had begun. I cocked my hat, set my hand on my hip, and swaggered on the pavement, confronting detection. And I found I could do all this with a sense of exhilaration that was not unpleasing, and with a certain *crânerie* of manner that raised me in my own esteem. And yet there was one thing I could not bring my mind to face up to, or my limbs to execute; and that was to cross the valley into the Old Town. It seemed to me I must be arrested immediately if I had done so; I must go straight into the twilight of a prison cell, and pass straight thence to the gross and final embraces of the nightcap and the halter. And yet it was from no reasoned fear of the consequences that I could not go. I was unable. My horse baulked, and there was an end!

My nerve was gone: here was a discovery for a man in such imminent peril, set down to so desperate a game, which I could only hope to win by continual luck and unflagging effrontery! The strain had been too long continued, and my nerve was gone. I fell into what they call panic fear, as I have seen soldiers do on the alarm of a night attack, and turned out of Princes Street at random as though the devil were at my heels. In St. Andrew Square, I remember vaguely hearing some one call out. I paid no heed, but pressed on blindly. A moment after, a hand fell heavily on my shoulder, and I thought I had fainted. Certainly the world went black about me for some seconds; and when that spasm passed I found myself standing face to face with the "cheerful extravagant," in what sort of disarray I really dare not imagine, dead white at least, shaking like an aspen, and mowing at the man with speechless lips. And this was the

The University of Cramond

soldier of Napoleon, and the gentleman who intended going next night to an Assembly Ball! I am the more particular in telling of my breakdown, because it was my only experience of the sort; and it is a good tale for officers. I will allow no man to call me coward; I have made my proofs; few men more. And yet I (come of the best blood in France and inured to danger from a child) did, for some ten or twenty minutes, make this hideous exhibition of myself on the streets of the New Town of Edinburgh.

With my first available breath I begged his pardon. I was of an extremely nervous disposition, recently increased by late hours; I could not bear the slightest start.

He seemed much concerned. " You must be in a devil of a state!" said he; "though of course it was my fault— damnably silly, vulgar sort of thing to do! A thousand apologies! But you really must be run down; you should consult a medico. My dear sir, a hair of the dog that bit you is clearly indicated. A touch of Blue Ruin, now? Or, come: it's early, but is man the slave of hours? what do you say to a chop and a bottle in Dumbreck's Hotel? "

I refused all false comfort; but when he went on to remind me that this was the day when the University of Cramond met; and to propose a five-mile walk into the country and a dinner in the company of young asses like himself, I began to think otherwise. I had to wait until to-morrow evening, at any rate; this might serve as well as anything else to bridge the dreary hours. The country was the very place for me: and walking is an excellent sedative for the nerves. Remembering poor Rowley, feigning a cold in our lodgings and immediately under the guns of the formidable and now doubtful Bethiah, I asked if I might bring my servant. " Poor devil! it is dull for him," I explained.

" The merciful man is merciful to his ass," observed my sententious friend. " Bring him by all means!

' The harp, his sole remaining joy,
    Was carried by an orphan boy;'

and I have no doubt the orphan boy can get some cold victuals in the kitchen, while the Senatus dines."

Accordingly, being now quite recovered from my unmanly condition, except that nothing could yet induce me to cross the North Bridge, I arranged for my ball dress at a shop in Leith Street, where I was not served ill, cut out Rowley from his seclusion, and was ready along with him at the trysting-place, the corner of Duke Street and York Place, by a little after two. The University was represented in force: eleven persons, including ourselves, Byfield the aëronaut, and the tall lad, Forbes, whom I had met on the Sunday morning, bedewed with tallow, at the " Hunters' Rest." I was introduced; and we set off by way of Newhaven and the sea beach; at first through pleasant country roads, and afterwards along a succession of bays of a fairylike prettiness, to our destination—Cramond on the Almond—a little hamlet on a little river, embowered in woods, and looking forth over a great flat of quicksand to where a little islet stood planted in the sea. It was miniature scenery, but charming of its kind. The air of this good February afternoon was bracing, but not cold. All the way my companions were skylarking, jesting and making puns, and I felt as if a load had been taken off my lungs and spirits, and skylarked with the best of them.

Byfield I observed, because I had heard of him before, and seen his advertisements, not at all because I was disposed to feel interest in the man. He was dark and bilious and very silent; frigid in his manners, but burning internally with a great fire of excitement; and he was so good as to bestow a good deal of his company and conversation (such as it was) upon myself, who was not in the least grateful. If I had known how I was to be connected with him in the immediate future, I might have taken more pains.

In the hamlet of Cramond there is a hostelry of no very promising appearance, and here a room had been prepared for us, and we sat down to table.

" Here you will find no guttling or gormandising, no turtle or nightingales' tongues," said the extravagant, whose name, by the way, was Dalmahoy. " The device, sir, of the University of Cramond is⸴Plain Living and High Drinking."

Grace was said by the Professor of Divinity, in a macaronic Latin, which I could by no means follow, only I could hear it rhymed, and I guessed it to be more witty than reverent. After which the *Senatus Academicus* sat down to rough plenty in the shape of rizzar'd haddocks and mustard, a sheep's head, a haggis, and other delicacies of Scotland. The dinner was washed down with brown stout in bottle, and as soon as the cloth was removed, glasses, boiling water, sugar, and whisky were set out for the manufacture of toddy. I played a good

The University of Cramond

knife and fork, did not shun the bowl, and took part, so far as I was able, in the continual fire of pleasantry with which the meal was seasoned. Greatly daring, I ventured, before all these Scotsmen, to tell Sim's Tale of Tweedie's dog; and I was held to have done such extraordinary justice to the dialect, " for a Southron," that I was immediately voted into the Chair of Scots, and became, from that moment, a full member of the University of Cramond. A little after, I found myself entertaining them with a song; and a little after—perhaps a little in consequence—it occurred to me that I had had enough, and would be very well inspired to take French leave. It was not difficult to manage, for it was nobody's business to observe my movements, and conviviality had banished suspicion.

I got easily forth of the chamber, which reverberated with the voices of these merry and learned gentlemen, and breathed a long breath. I had passed an agreeable afternoon and evening, and I had apparently escaped scot-free. Alas! when I looked into the kitchen, there was my monkey, drunk as a lord, toppling on the edge of the dresser, and performing on the flageolet to an audience of the house lassies and some neighbouring ploughmen.

I routed him promptly from his perch, stuck his hat on, put his instrument in his pocket, and set off with him for Edinburgh.

His limbs were of paper, his mind quite in abeyance; I must uphold and guide him, prevent his frantic dives and set him continually on his legs again. At first he sang wildly, with occasional outbursts of causeless laughter. Gradually an inarticulate melancholy succeeded; he wept gently at times; would stop in the middle of the road, say firmly, " No, no, no," and then fall on his back: or else address me solemnly as " M'lord " and fall on his face by way of variety. I am afraid I was not always so gentle with the little pig as I might have been, but really the position was unbearable. We made no headway at all, and I suppose we were scarce gotten a mile away from Cramond, when the whole *Senatus Academicus* was heard hailing, and doubling the pace to overtake us.

Some of them were fairly presentable; and they were all Christian martyrs compared to Rowley; but they were in a frolicsome and rollicking humour that promised danger as we approached the town. They sang songs, they ran races, they fenced with their walking-sticks and umbrellas; and, in spite of this violent exercise, the fun grew only the more extravagant with the miles they traversed. Their drunkenness was deep-seated and permanent, like fire in a peat; or rather—to be quite just to them—it was not so much to be called drunkenness at all, as the effect of youth and high spirits—a fine night, and the night young, a good road under foot, and the world before you!

I had left them once somewhat unceremoniously; I could not attempt it a second time; and, burthened as I was with Mr. Rowley, I was really glad of assistance. But I saw the lamps of Edinburgh draw near on their hill-top with a good deal of uneasiness, which increased after we had entered the lighted streets, to positive alarm. All the passers-by were addressed, some of them by name. A worthy man was stopped by Forbes. "Sir," said he, "in the name of the Senatus of the University of Cramond, I confer upon you the degree of LL.D.," and with the words he bonneted him. Conceive the predicament of St. Ives, committed to the society of these outrageous youths, in a town where the police and his cousin were both looking for him! So far, we had pursued our way unmolested, although raising a clamour fit to wake the dead; but at last, in Abercromby Place, I believe —at least it was a crescent of highly respectable houses fronting on a garden—Byfield and I, having fallen somewhat in the rear with Rowley, came to a simultaneous halt. Our ruffians were beginning to wrench off bells and door-plates!

"Oh, I say!" says Byfield, "this is too much of a good thing! Confound it, I'm a respectable man — a public character, by George! I can't afford to get taken up by the police."

"My own case exactly," said I.

"Here, let's bilk them," said he.

And we turned back and took our way down hill again.

It was none too soon: voices and alarm bells sounded; watchmen here and there began to spring their rattles; it was plain the University of Cramond would soon be at blows with the police of Edinburgh! Byfield and I, running the semi-inanimate Rowley before us, made good despatch, and did not stop till we were several streets away, and the hubbub was already softened by distance.

The Assembly Ball

" Well, sir," said he, " we are well out of that! Did ever any one see such a pack of young barbarians? "

" We are properly punished, Mr. Byfield; we had no business there," I replied.

" No, indeed, sir, you may well say that! Outrageous! And my ascension announced for Friday, you know! " cried the aëronaut. " A pretty scandal! Byfield the aëronaut at the police-court! Tut-tut! Will you be able to get your rascal home, sir? Allow me to offer you my card. I am staying at Walker and Poole's Hotel, sir, where I should be pleased to see you."

" The pleasure would be mutual, sir," said I; but I must say my heart was not in my words, and as I watched Mr. By-field departing I desired nothing less than to pursue the acquaintance.

One more ordeal remained for me to pass. I carried my senseless load upstairs to our lodging, and was admitted by the landlady in a tall white nightcap and with an expression singularly grim. She lighted us into the sitting-room; where, when I had seated Rowley in a chair, she dropped me a cast-iron courtesy. I smelt gunpowder on the woman. Her voice tottered with emotion.

" I give ye nottice, Mr. Ducie," said she. " Dacent folks' houses . . ."

And at that apparently temper cut off her utterance, and she took herself off without more words.

I looked about me at the room, the goggling Rowley, the extinguished fire; my mind reviewed the laughable incidents of the day and night; and I laughed out loud to myself— lonely and cheerless laughter! . . .

[At this point the Author's MS. breaks off: what follows is the work of Mr. A. T. Quiller-Couch.]

CHAPTER XXXI

EVENTS OF THURSDAY: THE ASSEMBLY BALL

But I awoke to the chill reminder of dawn, and found myself no master even of cheerless mirth. I had supped with the *Senatus Academicus* of Cramond: so much my head informed me. It was Thursday, the day of the Assembly Ball. But the ball was fixed by the card for 8 P.M., and I had, therefore, twelve mortal hours to wear through as best I could. Doubtless it was this reflection which prompted me to leap out of bed instanter and ring for Mr. Rowley and my shaving water.

Mr. Rowley, it appeared, was in no such hurry. I tugged a second time at the bell-rope. A groan answered me: and there in the doorway stood, or rather titubated, my paragon of body-servants. He was collarless, unkempt; his face a tinted map of shame and bodily disorder. His hand shook on the hot-water can, and spilled its contents into his shoes. I opened on him with a tirade, but had no heart to continue. The fault, after all, was mine: and it argued something like heroism in the lad that he had fought his nausea down and come up to time.

" But not smiling," I assured him.

" Oh, please, Mr. Anne. Go on, sir; I deserve it. But I'll never do it again, strike me sky-blue scarlet! "

" In so far as that differed from your present colouring, I believe," said I, " it would be an improvement."

" Never again, Mr. Anne."

"Certainly not, Rowley. Even to good men this may happen once: beyond that, carelessness shades off into depravity."

" Yessir."

" You gave a good deal of trouble last night. I have yet to meet Mrs. McRankine."

" As for that, Mr. Anne," said he, with an incongruous twinkle in his bloodshot eye, " she've been up with a tray: dry toast and a pot of tea. The old gal's bark is worse than her bite, sir, begging your pardon, and meaning as she's a decent one, she is."

" I was fearing that might be just the trouble," I answered.

One thing was certain. Rowley, that morning, should not be entrusted with a razor and the handling of my chin. I sent him back to his bed, with orders not to rise from it without permission; and went about my toilette deliberately. In spite of the lad, I did not enjoy the prospect of Mrs. McRankine.

I enjoyed it so little, indeed, that I fell to poking the sitting-room fire when she entered with the *Mercury ;* and read the *Mercury* assiduously while she brought in breakfast. She set down the tray with a slam and stood beside it, her hands on her hips, her whole attitude breathing challenge.

The Assembly Ball

" Well, Mrs. McRankine? " I began, upturning a hypo-
critical eye from the newspaper.

" ' Well,' is it? Nhm! "

I lifted the breakfast cover, and saw before me a damnatory
red herring.

" Rowley was very foolish last night," I remarked, with
a discriminating stress on the name.

" ' The ass knoweth his master's crib.' " She pointed to the
herring. " It's all ye'll get, Mr.—Ducie, if that's your name."

" Madam,"—I held out the fish at the end of my fork—
" you drag it across the track of an apology." I set it back
on the dish and replaced the cover. " It is clear that you
wish us gone. Well and good : grant Rowley a day for
recovery, and to-morrow you shall be quit of us." I reached
for my hat.

" Whaur are ye gaun? "

" To seek other lodgings."

" I'll no say—Man, man! have a care! And me beat to
close an eye the nicht! " She dropped into a chair. " Nay,
Mr. Ducie, ye daurna! Think o' that innocent lamb! "

" That little pig."

" He's ower young to die," sobbed my landlady.

" In the abstract I agree with you: but I am not aware
that Rowley's death is required. Say rather that he is ower
young to turn King's evidence." I stepped back from the
door. " Mrs. McRankine," I said, " I believe you to be soft-
hearted. I know you to be curious. You will be pleased to
sit perfectly still and listen to me."

And, resuming my seat, I leaned across the corner of the
table and put my case before her without suppression or
extenuation. Her breathing tightened over my sketch of
the duel with Goguelat; and again more sharply as I told
of my descent of the rock. Of Alain she said, " I ken his
sort," and of Flora twice, " I'm wonderin' will I have seen
her? " For the rest, she heard me out in silence, and rose
and walked to the door without a word. Then she turned.
" It's a verra queer tale. If McRankine had told me the like
I'd have gien him the lie to his face."

Two minutes later I heard the vials of her speech unsealed
above stairs, with detonations that shook the house. I had
touched off my rocket, and the stick descended—on the
prostrate Rowley.

St. Ives

And now I must face the inert hours. I sat down, and read my way through the *Mercury*. "The escaped French soldier, Champdivers, who is wanted in connection with the recent horrid murder at the Castle, remains at large——" the rest but repeated the advertisement of Tuesday. "At large!" I set down the paper, and turned to my landlady's library. It consisted of Derham's *Physico- and Astro-Theology*, *The Scripture Doctrine of Original Sin*, by one Taylor, D.D., *The Ready Reckoner or Tradesman's Sure Guide*, and *The Path to the Pit delineated, with Twelve Engravings on Copper-plate*. For distraction I fell to pacing the room, and rehearsing those remembered tags of Latin verse concerning which M. de Culemberg had long ago assured me, "My son, we know not when, but some day they will come back to you with solace if not with charm." Good man! My feet trod the carpet to Horace's Alcaics. *Virtus recludens immeritis mori Coelum*—h'm, h'm—*raro*—

> *raro antecedentem scelestum*
> *deseruit pede Pœna claudo.*

I paused by the window. In this there was no indiscretion; for a cold drizzle washed the panes, and the warmth of the apartment dimmed their inner surface.

"*Pede Pœna claudo*," my finger traced the words on the damp glass.

A sudden clamour of the street-door bell sent me skipping back to the fire-place with my heart in my mouth. Interminable minutes followed, and at length Mrs. McRankine entered with my ball suit from the tailor's. I carried it into the next room, and disposed it on the bed—olive-green coat with gilt buttons and facings of watered silk, olive-green pantaloons, white waistcoat sprigged with blue and green forget-me-nots. The survey carried me on to midday and the midday meal.

The ministry of meal-time is twice blest: for prisoners and men without appetite it punctuates and makes time of eternity. I dawdled over my chop and pint of brown stout until Mrs. McRankine, after twice entering to clear away, with the face of a Cumæan sibyl, so far relaxed the tension of unnatural calm as to inquire if I meant to be all night about it.

The afternoon wore into dusk; and with dusk she reappeared with a tea-tray. At six I retired to dress.

The Assembly Ball

Behold me now issuing from my chamber, conscious of a well-fitting coat and a shapely pair of legs : the dignified simplicity of my *tournure* (simplicity so proper to the scion of an exiled house) relieved by a dandiacal hint of shirt-frill, and corrected into tenderness by the virgin waistcoat sprigged with forget-me-nots (for constancy), and buttoned with pink coral (for hope). Satisfied of the effect, I sought the apartment of Mr. Rowley of the Rueful Countenance, and found him less yellow, but still contrite, and listening to Mrs. McRankine, who sat with open book by his bedside, and plied him with pertinent dehortations from the Book of Proverbs.

He brightened.

" My heye, Mr. Hann, if that ain't up to the knocker ! "

Mrs. McRankine closed the book, and conned me with austerer approval.

" Ye carry it well, I will say."

" It fits, I think."

I turned myself complacently about.

" The drink, I am meaning. I kenned McRankine."

" Shall we talk of business, madam ? In the first place, the quittance for our board and lodging."

" I mak' it out on Saturdays."

" Do so; and deduct it out of this." I handed twenty-five of my guineas into her keeping : this left me with five and a crown piece in my pocket. " The balance, while it lasts, will serve for Rowley's keep and current expenses. Before long I hope he may lift the money which lies in the bank at his service, as he knows."

" But you'll come back, Mr. Anne ? " cried the lad.

" I'm afraid it's a toss up, my boy. Discipline, remember ! "
—for he was preparing to leap out of bed there and then—
" You can serve me better in Edinburgh. All you have to do is to wait for a clear coast, and seek and present yourself in private before Mr. T. Robbie of Castle Street, or Miss Flora Gilchrist of Swanston Cottage. From either or both of these you will take your instructions. Here are the addresses."

" If that's a' your need for the lad," said Mrs. McRankine, " he'll be eating his head off : no to say drinking." Rowley winced. " I'll tak' him on mysel'."

" My dear woman——"

" He'll be a brand frae the burnin' : and he'll do to clean the knives."

She would hear no denial. I committed the lad to her in this double capacity; and equipped with a pair of goloshes from the wardrobe of the late McRankine, sallied forth upon the rain-swept street.

The card of admission directed me to Buccleuch Place, a little off George Square; and here I found a wet rag of a crowd gathered about a couple of lanterns and a striped awning. Beneath the awning a panel of light fell on the plashy pavement. Already the guests were arriving. I whipped in briskly, presented my card, and passed up a staircase decorated with flags, evergreens, and national emblems. A venerable flunkey waited for me at the summit. " Cloak lobby to the left, sir." I obeyed, and exchanged my overcoat and goloshes for a circular metal ticket. " What name, sir? " he purred over my card, as I lingered in the vestibule for a moment to scan the ballroom and my field of action: then, having cleared his throat, bawled suddenly, " Mr. Ducie! "

It might have been a stage direction. " *A tucket sounds. Enter the Vicomte, disguised.*" To tell the truth, this entry was a daunting business. A dance had just come to an end; and the musicians in the gallery had fallen to tuning their violins. The chairs arrayed along the walls were thinly occupied, and as yet the social temperature scarce rose to thawing-point. In fact, the second-rate people had arrived, and from the far end of the room were nervously watching the door for notables. Consequently my entrance drew a disquieting fire of observation. The mirrors, reflectors, and girandoles had eyes for me; and as I advanced up the perspective of waxed floor, the very boards winked detection. A little Master of Ceremonies, as round as the rosette on his lapel, detached himself from the nearest group, and approached with something of a skater's motion and an insinuating smile.

" Mr.-a-Ducie, if I heard aright? A stranger, I believe, to our northern capital, and I hope a dancer? " I bowed. " Grant me the pleasure, Mr. Ducie, of finding you a partner."

" If," said I, " you would present me to the young lady yonder, beneath the musician's gallery——" For I recognised Master Ronald's flame, the girl in pink of Mr. Robbie's party, to-night gowned in apple-green.

" Miss McBean—Miss Camilla McBean? With pleasure.

The Assembly Ball

Great discrimination you show, sir. Be so good as to follow me."

I was led forward and presented. Miss McBean responded to my bow with great play of shoulders; and in turn presented me to her mother, a moustachioed lady in stiff black silk, surmounted with a black cap and coquelicot trimmings.

" *Any* friend of Mr. Robbie's, I'm sure," murmured Mrs. McBean, affably inclining. " Look, Camilla dear—Sir William and Lady Frazer—in laylock sarsnet—how well that diamond bandeau becomes her! They are early to-night. As I was saying, Mr.——"

" Ducie."

" *To* be sure. As I was saying, *any* friend of Mr. Robbie— one of my oldest acquaintance. If you can manage now to break him of his bachelor habits? You are making a long stay in Edinburgh? "

" I fear, madam, that I must leave it to-morrow."

" You have seen all our lions, I suppose? The Castle, now? Ah, the attractions of London!—now don't shake your head, Mr. Ducie. I hope I know a Londoner when I see one. And yet 'twould surprise you how fast we are advancing in Edinburgh. Camilla dear, that Miss Scrymgeour has edged her China crape with the very ribbon trimmings—black satin with pearl edge—we saw in that new shop in Princes Street yesterday; sixpenny width at the bottom, and three-three-farthings round the bodice. Perhaps you can tell me, Mr. Ducie, if it's really true that ribbon trimmings are *the height* in London and Bath this year? "

But the band struck up, and I swept the unresisting Camilla towards the set. After the dance, the ladies (who were kind enough to compliment me on my performance) suffered themselves to be led to the tea-room. By this time the arrivals were following each other thick and fast; and, standing by the tea-table, I heard name after name vociferated at the ball-room door, but never the name my nerves were on the strain to echo. Surely Flora would come: surely none of her guardians, natural or officious, would expect to find me at the ball. But the minutes passed, and I must convey Mrs. and Miss McBean back to their seats beneath the gallery.

" Miss Gilchrist—Miss Flora Gilchrist—Mr. Ronald Gilchrist! Mr. Robbie! Major Arthur Chevenix! "

The first name plumped like a shot across my bows, and

brought me up standing—for a second only. Before the catalogue was out, I had dropped the McBeans at their moorings, and was heading down on my enemies' line of battle. Their faces were a picture. Flora's cheek flushed, and her lips parted in the prettiest cry of wonder. Mr. Robbie took snuff. Ronald went red in the face, and Major Chevenix white. The intrepid Miss Gilchrist turned not a hair.

" What will be the meaning of this? " she demanded, drawing to a stand, and surveying me through her gold-rimmed eye-glasses.

" Madam," said I, with a glance at Chevenix, " you may call it a cutting-out expedition."

" Miss Gilchrist," he began, " you will surely not——"

But I was too quick for him.

" Madam, since when has the gallant Major superseded Mr. Robbie as your family adviser? "

" H'mph! " said Miss Gilchrist; which in itself was not reassuring. But she turned to the lawyer.

" My dear lady," he answered her look, " this very imprudent young man seems to have burnt his boats, and no doubt recks very little if, in that heroical conflagration, he burns our fingers. Speaking, however, as your family adviser "—and he laid enough stress on it to convince me that there was no love lost between him and the interloping Chevenix—" I suggest that we gain nothing by protracting this scene in the face of a crowded assembly. Are you for the card-room, madam? "

She took his proffered arm, and they swept from us, leaving Master Ronald red and glum, and the Major pale but nonplussed.

" Four from six leaves two," said I; and promptly engaged Flora's arm, and towed her away from the silenced batteries.

" And now, my dear," I added, as we found two isolated chairs, " you will kindly demean yourself as if we were met for the first or second time in our lives. Open your fan—so. Now listen; my cousin, Alain, is in Edinburgh, at Dumbreck's Hotel. No, don't lower it."

She held up the fan, though her small wrist trembled.

" There is worse to come. He has brought Bow Street with him, and likely enough at this moment the runners are ransacking the city hot-foot for my lodgings."

" And you linger and show yourself here!—here of all places! Oh, it is mad! Anne, why will you be so rash? "

The Assembly Ball

" For the simple reason that I have been a fool, my dear. I banked the balance of my money in George Street, and the bank is watched. I must have money to win my way south. Therefore I must find you and reclaim the notes you were kind enough to keep for me. I go to Swanston and find you under surveillance of Chevenix, supported by an animal called Towzer. I may have killed Towzer, by the way. If so, transported to an equal sky, he may shortly have the faithful Chevenix to bear him company. I grow tired of Chevenix."

But the fan dropped: her arms lay limp in her lap; and she was staring up at me piteously, with a world of self-reproach in her beautiful eyes.

" And I locked up the notes at home to-night—when I dressed for the ball—the first time they have left my heart! Oh, false!—false of trust that I am! "

" Why, dearest, that is not fatal, I hope. You reach home to-night—you slip them into some hiding—say in the corner of the wall below the garden——"

" Stop: let me think." She picked up her fan again, and behind it her eyes darkened while I watched, and she considered. " You know the hill we pass before we reach Swanston?—it has no name, I believe, but Ronald and I have called it the Fish-back since we were children: it has a clump of firs above it, like a fin. There is a quarry on the east slope. If you will be there at eight—I can manage it, I think, and bring the money."

" But why should you run the risk? "

" Please, Anne—oh, please let me *do* something! If you knew what it is to sit at home while your—your dearest——"

' THE VISCOUNT OF SAINT-YVES! "

The name, shouted from the doorway, rang down her faltering sentence as with the clash of an alarm bell. I saw Ronald—in talk with Miss McBean but a few yards away—spin round on his heel and turn slowly back on it with a face of sheer bewilderment. There was no time to conceal myself. To reach either the tea-room or the card-room, I must traverse twelve feet of open floor. We sat in clear view of the main entrance; and there already, with eyeglass lifted, raffish, flamboyant, exuding pomades and bad style, stood my detestable cousin. He saw us at once; wheeled right-about-face and spoke to some one in the vestibule; wheeled round again, and bore straight down, a full swagger varnishing his malign triumph. Flora caught her breath as I stood up to accost him.

"Good evening, my cousin! The newspaper told me you were favouring this city with a stay."

"At Dumbreck's Hotel: where, my dear Anne, you have not yet done me the pleasure to seek me out."

"I gathered," said I, "that you were forestalling the compliment. Our meeting, then, is unexpected?"

"Why, no; for, to tell you the truth, the secretary of the Ball Committee, this afternoon, allowed me a glance over his list of *invités*. I am apt to be nice about my company, cousin."

Ass that I was! I had never given this obvious danger so much as a thought.

"I fancy I have seen one of your latest intimates about the street."

He eyed me, and answered, with a bluff laugh, "Ah! You gave us the very devil of a chase. You appear, my dear Anne, to have a hare's propensity for running in your tracks. And begad, I don't wonder at it!" he wound up, ogling Flora with an insolent stare.

Him one might have hunted by scent alone. He reeked of essences.

"Present me, *mon brave*."

"I'll be shot if I do."

"I believe they reserve that privilege for soldiers," he mused.

"At any rate they don't extend it to——" I pulled up on the word. He had the upper hand, but I could at least play the game out with decency. "Come," said I, "a *contre-danse* will begin presently. Find yourself a partner, and I promise you shall be our *vis-à-vis*."

"You have blood in you, my cousin."

He bowed, and went in search of the Master of Ceremonies. I gave an arm to Flora. "Well, and how does Alain strike you?" I asked.

"He is a handsome man," she allowed. "If your uncle had treated him differently, I believe——"

"And I believe that no woman alive can distinguish between a gentleman and a dancing-master! A posture or two, and you interpret worth. My dear girl—that fellow!"

She was silent. I have since learnt why. It seems, if you

The Assembly Ball

please, that the very same remark had been made to her by that idiot Chevenix, upon me!

We were close to the door: we passed it, and I flung a glance into the vestibule. There, sure enough, at the head of the stairs, was posted my friend of the moleskin waistcoat, in talk with a confederate by some shades uglier than himself, a red-headed, loose-legged scoundrel in cinder-grey.

I was fairly in the trap. I turned, and between the moving crowd caught Alain's eye and his evil smile. He had found a partner: no less a personage than Lady Frazer of the lilac sarsnet and diamond bandeau.

For some unaccountable reason, in this infernal *impasse* my spirits began to rise, to soar. I declare it: I led Flora forward to the set with a gaiety which may have been unnatural, but was certainly not factitious. A Scotsman would have called me fey. As the song goes—and it matters not if I had it then, or read it later in my wife's library—

> " Sae rantingly, sae wantonly,
>   Sae dauntingly gaed he;
> He played a spring and danced it round
>   Beneath——"

never mind what. The band played the spring, and I danced it round, while my cousin eyed me with extorted approval. The quadrille includes an absurd figure—called, I think, *La Pastourelle*. You take a lady with either hand, and jig them to and fro, for all the world like an Englishman of legend parading a couple of wives for sale at Smithfield; while the other male, like a timid purchaser, backs and advances with his arms dangling.

> " I've lived a life of sturt and strife,
>   I die by treacherie——"

I challenged Alain with an open smile as he backed before us; and no sooner was the dance over, than I saw him desert Lady Frazer on a hurried excuse, and seek the door to satisfy himself that his men were on guard.

I dropped laughing into a chair beside Flora. " Anne," she whispered; " who is on the stairs? "

" Two Bow Street runners."

If you have seen a dove—a dove caught in a gin! " The back stairs! " she urged.

" They will be watched too. But let us make sure." I crossed to the tea-room, and, encountering a waiter, drew him aside. Was there a man watching the back entrance? He could not tell me. For a guinea would he find out? He went, and returned in less than a minute. Yes, there was a constable below. " It's just a young gentleman to be put to the Law for debt," I explained, recalling the barbarous and, to me, still unmeaning phrase. " I'm no speiring," replied the waiter.

I made my way back, and was not a little disgusted to find my chair occupied by the unconscionable Chevenix.

" My dear Miss Flora, you are unwell! " Indeed, she was pale enough, poor child, and trembling. " Major, she will be swooning in another minute. Get her to the tea-room, quick! while I fetch Miss Gilchrist. She must be taken home."

" It is nothing," she faltered, " it will pass. Pray do not ——-" As she glanced up, she caught my meaning. " Yes, yes: I will go home."

She took the Major's arm, while I hurried to the card-room. As luck would have it, the old lady was in the act of rising from the green table, having just cut out from a rubber. Mr. Robbie was her partner; and I saw (and blessed my star for the first time that night) the little heap of silver, which told that she had been winning.

" Miss Gilchrist," I whispered, " Miss Flora is faint: the heat of the room——"

" I've not observed it. The ventilation is considered pair-fect."

" She wishes to be taken home."

With fine composure she counted back her money, piece by piece, into a velvet reticule.

" Twelve and sixpence," she proclaimed. " Ye held good cards, Mr. Robbie. Well, Mosha the Viscount, we'll go and see about it."

I led her to the tea-room: Mr. Robbie followed. Flora rested on a sofa in a truly dismal state of collapse, while the Major fussed about her with a cup of tea. " I have sent Ronald for the carriage," he announced.

" H'm," said Miss Gilchrist, eyeing him oddly. " Well, it's your risk. Ye'd best hand me the teacup, and get our shawls from the lobby. You have the tickets. Be ready for us at the top of the stairs."

No sooner was the Major gone than, keeping an eye on her

The Assembly Ball

niece, this imperturbable lady stirred the tea and drank it down herself. As she drained the cup—her back for the moment being turned on Mr. Robbie—I was aware of a facial contortion. Was the tea (as children say) going the wrong way?

No: I believe—aid me Apollo and the Nine! I believe—though I have never dared, and shall never dare to ask—that Miss Gilchrist was doing her best to wink!

On the instant entered Master Ronald with word that the carriage was ready. I slipped to the door and reconnoitred. The crowd was thick in the ball-room; a dance in full swing; my cousin gambolling vivaciously, and, for the moment, with his back to us. Flora leaned on Ronald, and, skirting the wall, our party gained the great door and the vestibule, where Chevenix stood with an armful of cloaks.

" You and Ronald can return and enjoy yourselves," said the old lady, " as soon as ye've packed us off. Ye'll find a hackney coach, no doubt, to bring ye home." Her eye rested on the two runners, who were putting their heads together behind the Major. She turned on me with a stiff courtesy. " Good-night, sir, and I am obliged for your services. Or stay—you may see us to the carriage, if ye'll be so kind. Major, hand Mr. What-d'ye-call some of your wraps."

My eyes did not dare to bless her. We moved down the stairs—Miss Gilchrist leading, Flora supported by her brother and Mr. Robbie, the Major and I behind. As I descended the first step, the red-headed runner made a move forward. Though my gaze was glued upon the pattern of Miss Gilchrist's Paisley shawl, I saw his finger touch my arm! Yes, and I felt it like a touch of hot iron. The other man—Moleskin—plucked him by the arm: they whispered. They saw me bareheaded, without my overcoat. They argued, no doubt, that I was unaware; was seeing the ladies to their carriage; would of course return. They let me pass.

Once in the boisterous street, I darted round to the dark side of the carriage. Ronald ran forward to the coachman (whom I recognised for the gardener, Robie). " Miss Flora is faint. Home, as fast as you can! " He skipped back under the awning. " A guinea to make it faster! " I called up from the other side of the box-seat; and out of the darkness and rain I held up the coin and pressed it into Robie's damp palm. " What in the name——! " He peered round, but I was back and close against the step. The door was slammed. " Right away! "

It may have been fancy; but with the shout I seemed to hear the voice of Alain lifted in imprecation on the Assembly Room stairs. As Robie touched up the grey, I whipped open the door on my side and tumbled in—upon Miss Gilchrist's lap.

Flora choked down a cry. I recovered myself, dropped into a heap of rugs on the seat facing the ladies, and pulled-to the door by its strap.

Dead silence from Miss Gilchrist!

I had to apologise, of course. The wheels rumbled and jolted over the cobbles of Edinburgh; the windows rattled and shook under the uncertain gusts of the city. When we passed a street lamp it shed no light into the vehicle, but the awful profile of my protectress loomed out for a second against the yellow haze of the pane, and sank back into impenetrable shade.

" Madam, some explanation—enough at least to mitigate your resentment—natural, I allow."—Jolt, jolt! And still a mortuary silence within the coach! It was disconcerting. Robie for a certainty was driving his best, and already we were beyond the last rare outposts of light on the Lothian Road.

" I believe, madam, the inside of five minutes—if you will allow——"

I stretched out a protesting hand. In the darkness it encountered Flora's. Our fingers closed upon the thrill. For five, ten beatific seconds our pulses sang together, " I love you! I love you! " in the stuffy silence.

" Mosha Saint Yvey! " spoke up a deliberate voice (Flora caught her hand away), " as far as I can make head and tail of your business—supposing it to have a modicum of head, which I doubt—it appears to me that I have just done you a service; and that makes twice."

" A service, madam, I shall ever remember."

" I'll chance that, sir; if ye'll kindly not forget *yoursel'*."

In resumed silence we must have travelled a mile and a half, or two miles, when Miss Gilchrist let down the sash with a clatter, and thrust her head and mamelone cap forth into the night.

" Robie! "

Robie pulled up.

" The gentleman will alight."

The Cutting of the Gordian Knot

It was only wisdom, for we were nearing Swanston. I rose. " Miss Gilchrist, you are a good woman; and I think the cleverest I have met." " Umph," replied she. In the act of stepping forth I turned for a final handshake with Flora, and my foot caught in something and dragged it out upon the road. I stooped to pick it up, and heard the door bang by my ear.

" Madam—your shawl! "

But the coach lurched forward; the wheels splashed me; and I was left standing alone on the inclement highway.

While yet I watched the little red eyes of the vehicle, and almost as they vanished, I heard more rumbling of wheels, and descried two pairs of yellow eyes upon the road towards Edinburgh. There was just time enough to plunge aside, to leap a fence into a rain-soaked pasture; and there I crouched, the water squishing over my dancing-shoes, while with a flare, a slant of rain, and a glimpse of flogging drivers, two hackney carriages pelted by at a gallop.

CHAPTER XXXII

EVENTS OF FRIDAY MORNING: THE CUTTING OF THE GORDIAN KNOT

I PULLED out my watch. A fickle ray—the merest filtration of moonlight—glimmered on the dial. Fourteen minutes past one! " Past yin o'clock, and a dark, haary moarnin'." I recalled the bull voice of the watchman as he had called it on the night of our escape from the Castle—its very tones: and this echo of memory seemed to strike and reverberate the hour closing a long day of fate. Truly, since that night the hands had run full circle, and were back at the old starting-point. I had seen dawn, day: I had basked in the sunshine of men's respect; I was back in Stygian night—back in the shadow of that infernal Castle—still hunted by the law—with possibly a smaller chance than ever of escape—the cockshy of the elements—with no shelter for my head but a Paisley shawl of violent pattern. It occurred to me that I had travelled much in the interval, and run many risks, to exchange a suit of mustard-yellow for a Paisley shawl and a ball dress that matched neither it nor the climate of the Pentlands. The exhilaration of the ball, the fighting spirit, the last communicated thrill of Flora's hand, died out of me. In the thickening envelope of sea fog I felt like a squirrel in a rotatory cage. That was a lugubrious hour.

To speak precisely, those were seven lugubrious hours; since Flora would not be due before eight o'clock, if, indeed, I might count on her eluding her double cordon of spies. The question was, whither to turn in the meantime? Certainly not back to the town. In the near neighbourhood I knew of no roof but The Hunter's Tryst, by Alexander Hendry. Suppose that I found it (and the chances in that fog were perhaps against me), would Alexander Hendry, aroused from his bed, be likely to extend his hospitality to a traveller with no more luggage than a Paisley shawl? He might think I had stolen it. I had borne it down the staircase under the eyes of the runners, and the pattern was bitten upon my brain. It was doubtless unique in the district and familiar: an oriflamme of battle over the barter of dairy produce and malt liquors. Alexander Hendry *must* recognise it, and with an instinct of antagonism. Patently it formed no part of my proper wardrobe: hardly could it be explained as a *gage d'amour*. Eccentric hunters trysted under Hendry's roof; the Six Foot Club, for instance. But a hunter in a frilled shirt and waistcoat sprigged with forget-me-nots! And the house would be watched, perhaps. Every house around would be watched.

The end was that I wore through the remaining hours of darkness upon the sodden hillside. Superlative Miss Gilchrist! Folded in the mantle of that Spartan dame; huddled upon a boulder, while the rain descended upon my bare head, and coursed down my nose, and filled my shoes, and insinuated a playful trickle down the ridge of my spine; I hugged the lacerating fox of self-reproach, and hugged it again, and set my teeth as it bit upon my vitals. Once, indeed, I lifted an accusing arm to heaven. It was as if I had pulled the string of a douche-bath. Heaven flooded the fool with gratuitous tears; and the fool sat in the puddle of them and knew his folly. But heaven at the same time mercifully veiled that figure of abasement; and I will lift but a corner of the sheet.

Wind in hidden gullies, and the talk of lapsing waters on the hillside, filled all the spaces of the night. The high-road lay at my feet, fifty yards or so below my boulder. Soon after two o'clock (as I made it) lamps appeared in the direction of Swanston, and drew nearer; and two hackney coaches passed me at a jog-trot, towards the opaline haze into which

The Cutting of the Gordian Knot

the weather had subdued the lights of Edinburgh. I heard one of the drivers curse as he went by, and inferred that my open-handed cousin had shirked the weather and gone comfortably from the Assembly Rooms to Dumbreck's Hotel and bed, leaving the chase to his mercenaries.

After this you are to believe that I dozed and woke by snatches. I watched the moon descend in her foggy circle; but I saw also the mulberry face and minatory forefinger of Mr. Romaine, and caught myself explaining to him and Mr. Robbie that their joint proposal to mortgage my inheritance for a flying broomstick took no account of the working-model of the whole Rock and Castle of Edinburgh, which I dragged about by an ankle chain. Anon I was pelting with Rowley in a claret-coloured chaise through a cloud of robin-redbreasts; and with that I awoke to the veritable chatter of birds and the white light of dawn upon the hills.

The truth is, I had come very near to the end of my endurance. Cold and rain together, supervening in that hour of the spirit's default, may well have made me light-headed; nor was it easy to distinguish the tooth of self-reproach from that of genuine hunger. Stiff, qualmish, vacant of body, heart, and brain, I left my penitential boulder and crawled down to the road. Glancing along it for sight or warning of the runners, I spied, at two gunshots' distance or less, a milestone with a splash of white upon it—a draggled placard. Abhorrent thought! Did it announce the price upon the head of Champdivers? " At least I will see how they describe him " —this I told myself; but that which tugged at my feet was the baser fascination of fright. I had thought my spine inured by the night's experiences to anything in the way of cold shivers. I discovered my mistake while approaching that scrap of paper.

"AERIAL ASCENSION EXTRAORDINARY ! ! !

IN

THE MONSTRE BALLOON
' LUNARDI '

PROFESSOR BYFIELD (BY DIPLOMA), THE WORLD-
RENOWNED EXPONENT OF AEROSTATICS
AND AERONAUTICS,

Has the honour to inform the Nobility and Gentry of Edinburgh and the neighbourhood——"

St. Ives

The shock of it—the sudden descent upon sublimity, according to Byfield—took me in the face. I put up my hands. I broke into elfish laughter, and ended with a sob. Sobs and laughter together shook my fasting body like a leaf; and I zigzagged across the fields, buffeted this side and that by a mirth as uncontrollable as it was idiotic. Once I pulled up in the middle of a spasm to marvel irresponsibly at the sound of my own voice. You may wonder that I had will and wit to be drifted towards Flora's trysting place. But in truth there was no missing it—the low chine looming through the weather, the line of firs topping it, and, towards the west, diminishing like a fish's dorsal fin. I had conned it often enough from the other side; had looked right across it on the day when she stood beside me on the bastion and pointed out the smoke of Swanston Cottage. Only on this side the fish-tail (so to speak) had a nick in it; and through that nick ran the path to the old quarry.

I reached it a little before eight. The quarry lay to the left of the path, which passed on and out upon the hill's northern slope. Upon that slope there was no need to show myself. I measured out some fifty yards of the path, and paced it to and fro, idly counting my steps; for the chill crept back into my bones if I halted for a minute. Once or twice I turned aside into the quarry, and stood there tracing the veins in the hewn rock: then back to my quarterdeck tramp and the study of my watch. Ten minutes past eight! Fool—to expect her to cheat so many spies. This hunger of mine was becoming serious. . . .

A stone dislodged—a light footfall on the path—and my heart leapt. It was she! She came, and earth flowered again, as beneath the feet of the goddess, her namesake. I declare it for a fact that from the moment of her coming the weather began to mend.

" Flora! "

" My poor Anne! "

" The shawl has been useful," said I.

" You are starving."

" That is unpleasantly near the truth."

" I knew it. See, dear." A shawl of hodden grey covered her head and shoulders and from beneath it she produced a small basket and held it up. " The scones will be hot yet, for they went straight from the hearth into the napkin."

The Cutting of the Gordian Knot

She led the way to the quarry. I praised her forethought; having in those days still to learn that woman's first instinct, when a man is dear to her and in trouble, is to feed him.

We spread the napkin on a big stone of the quarry, and set out the feast: scones, oat-cake, hard-boiled eggs, a bottle of milk, and a small flask of usquebaugh. Our hands met as we prepared the table. This was our first housekeeping; the first breakfast of our honeymoon I called it, rallying her. " Starving I may be; but starve I will in sight of food, unless you share it," and, " It escapes me for the moment, madam, if you take sugar." We leaned to each other across the rock, and our faces touched. Her cold cheek with the rain upon it, and one small damp curl—for many days I had to feed upon the memory of that kiss, and I feed upon it yet.

" But it beats me how you escaped them," said I.

She laid down the bannock she had been making pretence to nibble. " Janet—that is our dairy girl—lent me her frock and shawl: her shoes too. She goes out to the milking at six, and I took her place. The fog helped me. They are hateful."

" They are, my dear. Chevenix——"

" I mean these clothes. And I am thinking, too, of the poor cows."

" The instinct of animals——" I lifted my glass. " Let us trust it to find means to attract the notice of two paid detectives and two volunteers."

" I had rather count on Aunt," said Flora, with one of her rare and adorable smiles, which fleeted as it came. " But, Anne, we must not waste time. They are so many against you, and so near. Oh, be serious ! "

" Now you are talking like Mr. Romaine."

" For my sake, dear ! " She clasped her hands. I took them in mine across the table, and, unclasping them, kissed the palms.

" Sweetheart," I said, " before this weather clears——"

" It is clearing."

" We will give it time. Before this weather clears, I must be across the valley and fetching a circuit for the drovers' road, if you can teach me when to hit it."

She withdrew one of her hands. It went up to the throat of her bodice, and came forth with my packet of notes.

" Good Lord ! " said I: " if I hadn't forgotten the money ! "

" I think nothing teaches you," sighed she.

She had sewn them tightly in a little bag of yellow oiled silk; and as I held it, warm from her young bosom, and turned it over in my hand, I saw that it was embroidered in scarlet thread with the one word " Anne " beneath the Lion Rampant of Scotland, in imitation of the poor toy I had carved for her—it seemed so long ago!

" I wear the original," she murmured.

I crushed the parcel into my breast-pocket, and, taking both hands again, fell on my knees before her on the stones.

" Flora—my angel! my heart's bride! "

" Hush! " She sprang away. Heavy footsteps were coming up the path. I had just time enough to fling Miss Gilchrist's shawl over my head and resume my seat, when a couple of buxom country wives bustled past the mouth of the quarry. They saw us, beyond a doubt: indeed, they stared hard at us, and muttered some comment as they went by, and left us gazing at each other.

" They took us for a picnic," I whispered.

" The queer thing," said Flora, " is that they were not surprised. The sight of you——"

" Seen sideways in this shawl, and with my legs hidden by the stone here, I might pass for an elderly female junketer."

" This is scarcely the hour for a picnic," answered my wise girl, " and decidedly not the weather."

The sound of another footstep prevented my reply. This time the wayfarer was an old farmer-looking fellow in a shepherd's plaid and bonnet powdered with mist. He halted before us and nodded, leaning rheumatically on his staff.

" A coarse moarnin'. Ye'll be from Leadburn, I'm thinkin'? "

" Put it at Peebles," said I, making shift to pull the shawl close about my damning finery.

" Peebles! " he said reflectively. " I've ne'er ventured so far as Peebles. I've contemplated it! But I was none sure whether I would like it when I got there. See here: I recommend ye no to be lazin' ower the meat, gin ye'd drap in for the fun. A'm full late, mysel'! "

He passed on. What could it mean? We hearkened after his tread. Before it died away, I sprang and caught Flora by the hand.

" Listen! Heavens above us, what is *that* ? "

" It sounds to me like Gow's version of *The Caledonian Hunt's Delight*, on a brass band."

The Cutting of the Gordian Knot

Jealous powers! Had Olympus conspired to ridicule our love, that we must exchange our parting vows to the public strains of *The Caledonian Hunt's Delight,* in Gow's version and a semitone flat? For three seconds Flora and I (in the words of a later British bard) looked at each other with a wild surmise, silent. Then she darted to the path and gazed along it down the hill.

" We must run, Anne. There are more coming! "

We left the scattered relics of breakfast, and, taking hands, scurried along the path northwards. A few yards, and with a sharp turn it led us out of the cutting and upon the hillside. And here we pulled up together with a gasp.

Right beneath us lay a green meadow, dotted with a crowd of two or three hundred people; and over the nucleus of this gathering, where it condensed into a black swarm, as of bees, there floated, not only the dispiriting music of *The Caledonian Hunt's Delight,* but an object of size and shape suggesting the Genie escaped from the Fisherman's Bottle, as described in M. Galland's ingenious *Thousand and One Nights.* It was Byfield's balloon—the monster *Lunardi*—in process of inflation.

" Confound Byfield! " I ejaculated in my haste.

" Who is Byfield? "

" An aeronaut, my dear, of bilious humour; which no doubt accounts for his owning a balloon striped alternately with liver-colour and pale blue, and for his arranging it and a brass band in the very line of my escape. That man dogs me like fate." I broke off sharply. " And after all, why not? " I mused.

The next instant I swung round, as Flora uttered a piteous little cry; and there, behind us, in the outlet of the cutting, stood Major Chevenix and Ronald.

The boy stepped forward, and, ignoring my bow, laid a hand on Flora's arm.

" You will come home at once."

I touched his shoulder. " Surely not," I said, " seeing that the spectacle apparently wants but ten minutes of its climax."

He swung on me in a passion. " For God's sake, St. Yves, don't force a quarrel now, of all moments! Man, haven't you compromised my sister enough? "

" It seems to me that, having set a watch on your sister at the suggestion, and with the help of a casual Major of Foot,

271

you might in decency reserve the word 'compromise' for home consumption; and further, that against adversaries so poorly sensitive to her feelings, your sister may be pardoned for putting her resentment into action."

"Major Chevenix is a friend of the family." But the lad blushed as he said it.

"The family?" I echoed. "So? Pray did your aunt invite his help? No, no, my dear Ronald! you cannot answer that. And while you play the game of insult to your sister, sir, I will see that you eat the discredit of it."

"Excuse me," interposed the Major, stepping forward. "As Ronald said, this is not the moment for quarrelling; and, as you observed, sir, the climax is not so far off. The runner and his men are even now coming round the hill. We saw them mounting the slope, and (I may add) your cousin's carriage drawn up on the road below. The fact is, Miss Gilchrist has been traced to the hill: and as it secretly occurred to us that the quarry might be her objective, we arranged to take the ascent on this side. See there!" he cried, and flung out a hand.

I looked up. Sure enough, at that instant, a grey-coated figure appeared on the summit of the hill, not five hundred yards away to the left. He was followed closely by my friend of the moleskin waistcoat; and the pair came sidling down the slope towards us.

"Gentlemen," said I, "it appears that I owe you my thanks. Your stratagem in any case was kindly meant."

"There was Miss Gilchrist to consider," said the Major stiffly. But Ronald cried, "Quick, St. Ives! Make a dash back by the quarry path. I warrant we don't hinder."

"Thank you, my friend: I have another notion. Flora," I said, and took her hand, "here is our parting. The next five minutes will decide much. Be brave, dearest; and your thoughts go with me till I come again."

"Wherever you go, I'll think of you. Whatever happens, I'll love you. Go, and God defend you, Anne!" Her breast heaved, as she faced the Major, red and shamefast indeed, but gloriously defiant.

"Quick!" cried she and her brother together. I kissed her hand and sprang down the hill.

I heard a shout behind me; and, glancing back, saw my pursuers—three now, with my full-bodied cousin for whipper-

The Cutting of the Gordian Knot

in—change their course as I leapt a brook and headed for the crowded inclosure. A somnolent fat man, bulging, like a feather-bed, on a three-legged stool, dozed at the receipt of custom, with a deal table and a bowl of sixpences before him. I dashed on him with a crown-piece.

" No change given," he objected, waking up and fumbling with a bundle of pink tickets.

" None required." I snatched the ticket and ran through the gateway.

I gave myself time for another look before mingling with the crowd. The moleskin waistcoat was leading now, and had reached the brook; with red-head a yard or two behind, and my cousin a very bad third, panting—it pleased me to imagine how sorely—across the lower slopes to the eastward. The janitor leaned against his toll-bar and still followed me with a stare. Doubtless by my uncovered head and gala dress he judged me an all-night reveller—a strayed Bacchanal fooling in the morrow's eye.

Prompt upon the inference came inspiration. I must win to the centre of the crowd, and a crowd is invariably indulgent to a drunkard. I hung out the glaring signboard of crapulous glee. Lurching, hiccoughing, jostling, apologising to all and sundry with spacious incoherence, I plunged my way through the sightseers, and they gave me passage with all the good-humour in life.

I believe that I descended upon that crowd as a godsend, a dancing rivulet of laughter. They needed entertainment. A damper, less enthusiastic company never gathered to a public show. Though the rain had ceased, and the sun shone, those who possessed umbrellas were not to be coaxed, but held them aloft with a settled air of gloom which defied the lenitives of nature and the spasmodic cajolery of the worst band in Edinburgh. " It'll be near full, Jock? " " It wull." " He'll be startin' in a meenit? " " Aiblins he wull." " Wull this be the sixt time ye've seen him? " " I shudna wonder." It occurred to me that, had we come to bury Byfield, not to praise him, we might have displayed a blither interest.

Byfield himself, bending from the car beneath his gently swaying canopy of liver-colour and pale blue, directed the proceedings with a mien of saturnine preoccupation. He may have been calculating the receipts. As I squeezed to the front, his underlings were shifting the pipe which conveyed the

273

hydrogen gas, and the *Lunardi* strained gently at its ropes. Somebody with a playful thrust sent me staggering into the clear space beneath.

And here a voice hailed and fetched me up with a round turn.

" Ducie, by all that's friendly! Playmate of my youth and prop of my declining years, how goes it? "

It was the egregious Dalmahoy. He clung and steadied himself by one of the dozen ropes binding the car to earth; and with an air of doing it all by his unaided cleverness—an air so indescribably, so majestically drunken, that I could have blushed for the poor expedients which had carried me through the throng.

" You'll excuse me if I don't let go. Fact is, we've been keeping it up a bit all night. Byfield leaves us—to expatiate in realms untrodden by the foot of man—

> ' The feathered tribes on pinions cleave the air;
> Not so the mackerel, and, still less, the bear.'

But Byfield does it—Byfield in his Monster Foolardi. One stroke of this knife (always supposing I miss my own hand), and the rope is severed: our common friend scales the empyrean. But he'll come back—oh, never doubt he'll come back!—and begin the dam business over again. Tha's the law 'gravity 'cording to Byfield."

Mr. Dalmahoy concluded inconsequently with a vocal imitation of a post-horn; and, looking up, I saw the head and shoulders of Byfield projected over the rim of the car.

He drew the natural inference from my dress and demeanour, and groaned aloud.

" Oh, go away—get out of it, Ducie! Isn't one natural born ass enough for me to deal with? You fellows are guying the whole show! "

" Byfield! " I called up eagerly, " I'm not drunk. Reach me down a ladder, quick! A hundred guineas if you'll take me with you! " I saw over the crowd, not ten deep behind me, the red head of the man in grey.

" That proves it," said Byfield. " Go away; or at least keep quiet. I'm going to make a speech." He cleared his throat. " Ladies and gentlemen——"

I held up my packet of notes, " Here's the money—for pity's sake, man! There are bailiffs after me, in the crowd! "

" ——the spectacle which you have honoured with your en-

The Cutting of the Gordian Knot

lightened patronage—I tell you I can't." He cast a glance behind him into the car—"with your enlightened patronage, needs but few words of introduction or commendation."

" Hear, hear! " from Dalmahoy.

" Your attendance proves the sincerity of your interest——"

I spread out the notes under his eyes. He blinked, but resolutely lifted his voice.

" The spectacle of a solitary voyager——"

" Two hundred! " I called up.

" The spectacle of two hundred solitary voyagers—cradled in the brain of a Montgolfier and a Charles—Oh, stop it! I'm no public speaker! How the deuce——? "

There was a lurch and a heave in the crowd. " Pitch oot the drunken loon! " cried a voice. The next moment I heard my cousin bawling for a clear passage. With the tail of my eye I caught a glimpse of his plethoric perspiring face as he came charging past the barrels of the hydrogen-apparatus; and, with that, Byfield had shaken down a rope-ladder and fixed it, and I was scrambling up like a cat.

" Cut the ropes! "

" Stop him! " my cousin bawled. " Stop the balloon! It's Champdivers, the murderer! "

" Cut the ropes! " vociferated Byfield; and to my infinite relief I saw that Dalmahoy was doing his best. A hand clutched at my heel. I let out viciously, amid a roar of the crowd, felt the kick reach and rattle home on somebody's teeth; and, as the crowd made a rush and the balloon swayed and shot upwards, heaved myself over the rim into the car.

Recovering myself on the instant, I bent over. I had on my tongue a neat farewell for Alain, but the sight of a hundred upturned and contorted faces silenced me as a blow might. There had lain my real peril, in the sudden wild-beast rage now suddenly baffled. I read it, as clear as print, and sickened. Nor was Alain in a posture to listen. My kick had sent Moleskin flying on top of him; and borne to earth, prone beneath the superincumbent bulk of his retainer, he lay with hands outspread like a swimmer's and nose buried in the plashy soil.

St. Ives

CHAPTER XXXIII

THE INCOMPLETE AERONAUTS

ALL this I took in at a glance: I dare say in three seconds or less. The hubbub beneath us dropped to a low, rumbling bass. Suddenly a woman's scream divided it—one high-pitched, penetrating scream, followed by silence. And then, as a pack of hounds will start into cry, voice after voice caught up the scream and reduplicated it until the whole enclosure rang with alarm.

"Hullo!" Byfield called to me: "what the deuce is happening now?" and ran to his side of the car. "Good Lord, it's Dalmahoy!"

It was. Beneath us, at the tail of a depending rope, that unhappy lunatic dangled between earth and sky. He had been the first to cut the tether; and, having severed it below his grasp, had held on while the others cut loose, taking even the asinine precaution to loop the end twice round his wrist. Of course the upward surge of the balloon had heaved him off his feet, and his muddled instinct did the rest. Clutching now with both hands, he was borne aloft like a lamb from the flock.

So we reasoned afterwards. "The grapnel!" gasped Byfield: for Dalmahoy's rope was fastened beneath the floor of the car, and not to be reached by us. We fumbled to cast the grapnel loose, and shouted down together—

"For God's sake hold on! Catch the anchor when it comes! You'll break your neck if you drop!"

He swung into sight again beyond the edge of the floor, and uplifted a strained, white face.

We cast loose the grapnel, lowered it and jerked it towards him. He swung past it like a pendulum, caught at it with one hand, and missed: came flying back on the receding curve and missed again. At the third attempt he blundered right against it, and flung an arm over one of the flukes, next a leg, and in a trice we were hauling up, hand over hand.

We dragged him inboard. He was pale, but undefeatedly voluble.

"Must apologise to you fellows, really. Dam silly, clumsy kind of thing to do; might have been awkward too. Thank

The Incomplete Aeronauts

you, Byfield, my boy, I will: two fingers only—a harmless steadier."

He took the flask and was lifting it. But his jaw dropped and his hand hung arrested.

" He's going to faint," I cried. " The strain——"

" Strain on your grandmother, Ducie! What's *that* ? "

He was staring past my shoulder, and on the instant I was aware of a voice—not the aeronaut's—speaking behind me, and, as it were, out of the clouds—

" I tak' ye to witness, Mister Byfield——"

Consider, if you please. For six days I had been oscillating within a pretty complete circumference of alarms. It is small blame to me, I hope, that with my nerve on so nice a pivot, I quivered and swung to this new apprehension like a needle in a compass-box.

On the floor of the car, at my feet, lay a heap of plaid rugs and overcoats, from which, successively and painfully disinvolved, there emerged first a hand clutching a rusty beaver hat, next a mildly indignant face, in spectacles, and finally the rearward of a very small man in a seedy suit of black. He rose on his knees, his finger-tips resting on the floor, and contemplated the aeronaut over his glasses with a world of reproach.

" I tak' ye to witness, Mr. Byfield! "

Byfield mopped a perspiring brow.

" My dear sir," he stammered, " all a mistake—no fault of mine—explain presently," then, as one catching at an inspiration, " Allow me to introduce you. Mr. Dalmahoy, Mr.——"

" My name is Sheepshanks," said the little man stiffly. " But you'll excuse me——"

Mr. Dalmahoy interrupted with a playful cat-call.

" Hear, hear! *Silence !* ' His name is Sheepshanks. On the Grampian Hills his father kept his flocks—a thousand sheep,' and, I make no doubt, shanks in proportion. Excuse you, Sheepshanks? My *dear* sir! At this altitude one shank was more than we had a right to expect: the plural multiplies the obligation." Keeping a tight hold on his hysteria, Dalmahoy steadied himself by a rope and bowed.

" And I, sir "—as Mr. Sheepshanks' thoroughly bewildered gaze travelled around and met mine—" I, sir, am the Vicomte Anne de Kéroual de St. Yves, at your service. I haven't a notion how or why you come to be here: but you seem likely to be an acquisition. On my part," I continued, as there leapt into my mind the stanza I had vainly tried to recover in Mrs. McRankine's sitting-room, " I have the honour to refer you to the inimitable Roman, Flaccus—

> ' Virtus, recludens immeritis mori
> Coelum negata temptat iter via,
> Coetusque vulgares et udam
>   Spernit humum fugiente penna.'

—you have the Latin, sir? "

" Not a word." He subsided upon the pile of rugs and spread out his hands in protest. " I tak' ye to witness, Mr. Byfield! "

" Then in a minute or so I will do myself the pleasure of construing," said I, and turned to scan the earth we were leaving—I had not guessed how rapidly.

We contemplated it from the height of six hundred feet —or so Byfield asserted after consulting his barometer. He added that this was a mere nothing: the wonder was the balloon had risen at all with one-half of the total folly of Edinburgh clinging to the car. I passed the possible inaccuracy and certain ill-temper of this calculation. He had (he explained) made jettison of at least a hundredweight of sand ballast. I could only hope it had fallen on my cousin. To me, six hundred feet appeared a very respectable eminence. And the view was ravishing.

The *Lunardi* mounting through a stagnant calm in a line almost vertical, had pierced the morning mists, and now swam emancipated in a heaven of exquisite blue. Below us, by some trick of eyesight, the country had grown concave, its horizons curving up like the rim of a shallow bowl—a bowl heaped, in point of fact, with sea-fog, but to our eyes with a froth delicate and dazzling as a whipped syllabub of snow. Upon it the travelling shadow of the balloon became no shadow but a stain: an amethyst (you might call it) purged of all grosser properties than colour and lucency. At times thrilled by no perceptible wind, rather by the pulse of the sun's rays, the froth shook and parted: and then behold, deep in the *crevasses*, vignetted and shining, an acre or two of the earth of man's business and fret—tilled slopes of the Lothians, ships dotted on the Forth, the capital like a hive that some child had smoked—the ear of fancy could almost hear it buzzing.

The Incomplete Aeronauts

I snatched the glass from Byfield, and brought it to focus upon one of these peepshow rifts: and lo! at the foot of the shaft, imaged, as it were far down in a luminous well, a green hillside and three figures standing. A white speck fluttered and fluttered until the rift closed again. Flora's handkerchief! Blessings on the brave hand that waved it!—at a moment when (as I have since heard and knew without need of hearing) her heart was down in her shoes, or, to speak accurately, in the milkmaid Janet's. Singular in many things, she was at one with the rest of her sex in its native and incurable distrust of man's inventions.

I am bound to say that my own faith in aërostatics was a plant—a sensitive plant—of extremely tender growth. Either I failed, a while back, in painting the emotions of my descent of the *Devil's Elbow*, or the reader knows that I am a chicken-hearted fellow about a height. I make him a present of the admission. Set me on a plane superficies, and I will jog with all the *insouciance* of a rolling stone: toss me in air, and, with the stone in the child's adage, I am in the hands of the devil. Even to the qualified instability of a sea-going ship I have ever committed myself with resignation rather than confidence.

But to my unspeakable relief the *Lunardi* floated upwards, and continued to float, almost without a tremor. Only by reading the barometer, or by casting scraps of paper overboard, could we tell that the machine moved at all. Now and again we revolved slowly: so Byfield's compass informed us, but for ourselves we had never guessed it. Of dizziness I felt no longer a symptom, for the sufficient reason that the provocatives were nowhere at hand. We were the only point in space, without possibility of comparison with another. We were made one with the clean silences receiving us; and speaking only for the Vicomte Anne de St. Yves, I dare assert that for five minutes a newly bathed infant had not been less conscious of original sin.

" But look here, you know "—it was Byfield at my elbow—" I'm a public character, by George; and this puts me in a devilish awkward position."

"So it does," I agreed. " You proclaimed yourself a solitary voyager: and here, to the naked eye, are four of us."

" And pray how can I help that? If, at the last moment, a couple of lunatics come rushing in——"

St. Ives

"They still leave Sheepshanks to be accounted for." Byfield began to irritate me. I turned to the stowaway. "Perhaps," said I, "Mr. Sheepshanks will explain."

"I paid in advance," Mr. Sheepshanks began, eager to seize the opening presented. "The fact is, I'm a married man."

"Already at two points you have the advantage of us. Proceed, sir."

"You were good enough, just now, to give me your name, Mr.——"

"The Vicomte Anne de Kéroual de St. Yves."

"It is a somewhat difficult name to remember."

"If that be all, sir, within two minutes you shall have a *memoria technica* prepared for use during the voyage."

Mr. Sheepshanks harked back. "I am a married man, and—d'ye see?—Mrs. Sheepshanks, as you might say, has no sympathy with ballooning. She was a Guthrie of Dumfries."

"Which accounts for it, to be sure," said I.

"To me, sir, on the contrary, aërostatics have long been an alluring study. I might even, Mr.——, I might even, I say, term it the passion of my life." His mild eyes shone behind their glasses. "I remember Vincent Lunardi, sir. I was present in Heriot's Gardens when he made an ascension there in October '85. He came down at Cupar. The Society of Gentlemen Golfers at Cupar presented him with an address; and at Edinburgh he was admitted Knight Companion of the Beggar's Benison, a social company, or (as I may say) crew, since defunct. A thin-faced man, sir. He wore a peculiar bonnet, if I may use the expression, very much cocked up behind. The shape became fashionable. He once pawned his watch with me, sir; that being my profession. I regret to say he redeemed it subsequently: otherwise I might have the pleasure of showing it to you. Oh yes, the theory of ballooning has long been a passion with me. But in deference to Mrs. Sheepshanks I have abstained from the actual practice—until to-day. To tell you the truth, my wife believes me to be brushing off the cobwebs in the Kyles of Bute."

"*Are* there any cobwebs in the Kyles of Bute?" asked Dalmahoy, in a tone unnaturally calm.

"A figure of speech, sir—as one might say, holiday-keeping there. I paid Mr. Byfield five pounds in advance. I have

The Incomplete Aeronauts

his receipt. And the stipulation was that I should be concealed in the car and make the ascension with him alone."

" Are we then to take it, sir, that our company offends you? " I demanded.

He made haste to disclaim. " Not at all: decidedly not in the least. But the chances were for less agreeable associates." I bowed. " And a bargain's a bargain," he wound up.

" So it is," said I. " Byfield, hand Mr. Sheepshanks back his five pounds."

" Oh, come now! " the aeronaut objected. " And who may you be, to be ordering a man about? "

" I believe I have already answered that question twice in your hearing."

" Mosha the Viscount Thingamy de Something-or-other? I dare say! "

" Have you any objection? "

" Not the smallest. For all I care, you are Robert Burns, or Napoleon Buonaparte, or anything, from the Mother of the Gracchi to Balaam's Ass. But I knew you first as Mr. Ducie; and you may take it that I'm Mr. Don't see." He reached up a hand towards the valve-string.

" What are you proposing to do? "

" To descend."

" What?—back to the enclosure? "

" Scarcely that, seeing that we have struck a northerly current, and are travelling at the rate of thirty miles an hour, perhaps. That's Broad Law to the south of us, as I make it out."

" But why descend at all? "

" Because it sticks in my head that some one in the crowd called you by a name that wasn't Ducie; and by a title, for that matter, which didn't sound like ' Viscount.' I took it at the time for a constable's trick; but I begin to have my strong doubts."

The fellow was dangerous. I stooped nonchalantly, on pretence of picking up a plaid; for the air had turned bitterly cold, of a sudden.

" Mr. Byfield, a word in your private ear, if you will."

" As you please," said he, dropping the valve-string.

We leaned together over the breastwork of the car. " If I mistake not," I said, speaking low, " the name was Champdivers."

He nodded.

" The gentleman who raised that foolish but infernally risky cry was my own cousin, the Viscount de St. Yves. I give you my word of honour to that." Observing that this staggered him, I added, mighty slyly, " I suppose it doesn't occur to you now that the whole affair was a game, for a friendly wager? "

" No," he answered brutally, " it doesn't. And what's more, it won't go down."

" In that respect," said I, with a sudden change of key, " it resembles your balloon. But I admire the obstinacy of your suspicions; since, as a matter of fact, I am Champdivers."

" The mur——"

" Certainly not. I killed the man in fair duel."

" Ha! " he eyed me with sour distrust. " That is what you have to prove."

" Man alive, you don't expect me to demonstrate it up here, by the simple apparatus of ballooning! "

" There is no talk of ' up here,' " said he, and reached for the valve-string.

" Say ' down there,' then. Down there it is no business of the accused to prove his innocence. By what I have heard of the law, English or Scotch, the boot is on the other leg. But I'll tell you what I *can* prove. I can prove, sir, that I have been a deal in your company of late; that I supped with you and Mr. Dalmahoy no longer ago than Wednesday. You may put it that we three are here together again by accident; that you never suspected me; that my invasion of your machine was a complete surprise to you, and, so far as you were concerned, wholly fortuitous. But ask yourself what any intelligent jury is likely to make of that cock-and-bull story." Mr. Byfield was visibly shaken. " Add to this," I proceeded, " that you have to explain Sheepshanks; to confess that you gulled the public by advertising a lonely ascension, and haranguing a befooled multitude to the same intent, when, all the time, you had a companion concealed in the car. ' A public character! ' you call yourself! My word, sir! there'll be no mistake about it this time."

I paused, took breath, and shook a finger at him:—

" Now just you listen to me, Mr. Byfield. Pull that string, and a sadly discredited aeronaut descends upon the least

The Incomplete Aeronauts

charitable of worlds. Why, sir, in any case your game in Edinburgh is up. The public is dog-tired of you and your ascensions, as any observant child in to-day's crowd could have told you. The truth was there staring you in the face; and next time even your purblind vanity must recognise it. Consider; I offered you two hundred guineas for the convenience of your balloon. I now double that offer on condition that I become its owner during this trip, and that you manipulate it as I wish. Here are the notes; and out of the total you will refund five pounds to Mr. Sheepshanks."

Byfield's complexion had grown streaky as his balloon; and with colours not so very dissimilar. I had stabbed upon his vital self-conceit, and the man was really hurt.

" You must give me time," he stammered.

" By all means." I knew he was beaten. But only the poorness of my case excused me, and I had no affection for the weapons used. I turned with relief to the others. Dalmahoy was seated on the floor of the car, and helping Mr. Sheepshanks to unpack a carpet bag.

" This will be whisky," the little pawnbroker announced: " three bottles. My wife said, ' Surely, Elshander, ye'll find whisky where ye're gaun.' ' No doubt I will,' said I, ' but I'm not very confident of its quality; and it's a far step.' My itinerary, Mr. Dalmahoy, was planned from Greenock to the Kyles of Bute and back, and thence coastwise to Saltcoats and the land of Burns. I told her, if she had anything to communicate, to address her letter to the care of the postmaster, Ayr—ha, ha!" He broke off and gazed reproachfully into Dalmahoy's impassive face. " Ayr — air," he explained: " a little play upon words."

" Skye would have been better," suggested Dalmahoy, without moving an eyelid.

" Skye? Dear me—capital, capital! Only you see," he urged, " she wouldn't expect me to be in Skye."

A minute later he drew me aside. " Excellent company your friend is, sir: most gentlemanly manners; but at times, if I may so say, not very gleg."

My hands by this time were numb with cold. We had been ascending steadily, and Byfield's English thermometer stood at thirteen degrees. I borrowed from the heap a thicker overcoat, in the pocket of which I was lucky enough to find a pair of furred gloves; and leaned over for another look below, still with a corner of my eye for the aeronaut, who stood biting his nails, as far from me as the car allowed.

The sea-fog had vanished, and the south of Scotland lay spread beneath us from sea to sea, like a map in monotint. Nay, yonder was England, with the Solway cleaving the coast —a broad, bright spearhead, slightly bent at the tip—and the fells of Cumberland beyond, mere hummocks on the horizon; all else flat as a board or as the bottom of a saucer. White threads of high-road connected town to town: the intervening hills had fallen down, and the towns, as if in fright, had shrunk into themselves, contracting their suburbs as a snail his horns. The old poet was right who said that the Olympians had a delicate view. The lace-makers of Valenciennes might have had the tracing of those towns and high-roads; those knots of *guipure* and ligatures of finest *réseau*-work. And when I considered that what I looked down on—this, with its arteries and nodules of public traffic— was a nation; that each silent nodule held some thousands of men, each man moderately ready to die in defence of his shopboard and hen-roost; it came into my mind that my Emperor's emblem was the bee, and this Britain the spider's web, sure enough.

Byfield came across and stood at my elbow.

" Mr. Ducie, I have considered your offer, and accept it. It's a curst position——"

" For a public character," I put in affably.

" Don't, sir! I beg that you don't. Your words just now made me suffer a good deal: the more, that I perceive a part of them to be true. An aeronaut, sir, has ambition—how can he help it? The public, the newspapers, feed it for a while; they *fête*, and flatter, and applaud him. But in its heart the public ranks him with the mountebank, and re- serves the right to drop him when tired of his tricks. Is it wonderful that he forgets this sometimes? For in his own thoughts he is not a mountebank—no, by God, he is not! "

The man spoke with genuine passion. I held out my hand.

" Mr. Byfield, my words were brutal. I beg you will allow me to take them back."

He shook his head. " They were true, sir; partly true, that is."

" I am not so sure. A balloon, as you hint and I begin to discover, may alter the perspective of man's ambitions.

The Incomplete Aeronauts

Here are the notes; and on the top of them I give you my word that you are not abetting a criminal. How long should the *Lunardi* be able to maintain itself in the air? "

" I have never tried it; but I calculate on twenty hours—say twenty-four at a pinch."

" We will test it. The current, I see, is still north-east, or from that to north-by-east. And our height? "

He consulted the barometer. " Something under three miles."

Dalmahoy heard, and whooped. " Hi! you fellows, come to lunch! Sandwiches, shortbread, and cleanest Glenlivet—Elshander's Feast:—

> ' Let old Timotheus yield the prize,
> Or both divide the crown;
> He raised a mortal to the skies——'

Sheepshanks provided the whisky. Rise, Elshander: observe that you have no worlds left to conquer, and having shed the perfunctory tear, pass the corkscrew. Come along, Ducie: come, my Dædalian boy; if you are not hungry, I am, and so is—Sheepshanks—what the dickens do you mean by consorting with a singular verb? *Verbum cum nominativo*— I should say, so *are* sheepshanks."

Byfield produced from one of the lockers a pork pie and a bottle of sherry (the *viaticum* in choice and assortment almost explained the man) and we sat down to the repast. Dalmahoy's tongue ran like a brook. He addressed Mr. Sheepshanks with light-hearted impartiality as Philip's royal son, as the Man of Ross, as the divine Clarinda. He elected him Professor of Marital Diplomacy to the University of Cramond. He passed the bottle and called on him for a toast, a song—" Oblige me, Sheepshanks, by making the welkin ring." Mr. Sheepshanks beamed, and gave us a sentiment instead. The little man was enjoying himself amazingly. " Fund of spirits your friend has, to be sure, sir —quite a fund."

Either my own spirits were running low or the bitter cold had congealed them. I was conscious of my thin ball-suit, and moreover of a masterful desire of sleep. I felt no inclination for food, but drained half a tumblerful of the Sheepshanks whisky, and crawled beneath the pile of plaids. Byfield considerately helped to arrange them. He may or may not have caught some accent of uncertainty in my thanks: at any rate he thought fit to add the assurance, " You may trust me, Mr. Ducie." I saw that I could, and began almost to like the fellow.

In this posture I dozed through the afternoon. In dreams I heard Dalmahoy and Sheepshanks lifting their voices in amœbæan song, and became languidly aware that they were growing uproarious. I heard Byfield expostulating, apparently in vain: for I awoke next to find that Sheepshanks had stumbled over me while illustrating, with an empty bottle, the motions of tossing the caber. " Old Hieland sports," explained Dalmahoy, wiping tears of vain laughter: " his mother's uncle was out in the Forty-five. Sorry to wake you, Ducie: balow, my babe!" It did not occur to me to smoke danger in this tomfoolery. I turned over and dozed again.

It seemed but a minute later that a buzzing in my ears awoke me; with a stab of pain as though my temples were being split with a wedge. On the instant I heard my name cried aloud, and sat up; to find myself blinking in a broad flood of moonlight over against the agitated face of Dalmahoy.

" Byfield——" I began.

Dalmahoy pointed. The aeronaut lay at my feet, collapsed like some monstrous marionette, with legs and arms a-splay. Across his legs, with head propped against a locker, reclined Sheepshanks, and gazed upwards with an approving smile. " Awkward business," explained Dalmahoy, between gasps. " Sheepshanks 'nmanageable; can't carry his liquor like a gentleman; thought it funny 'pitch out ballast. Byfield lost his temper: worst thing in the world. One thing I pride myself, 'menable to reason. No holding Sheepshanks: Byfield got him down; too late; faint both of us. Sheepshanks wants ring for 'shistance: pulls string: breaks. When string breaks *Lunardi* won't fall—tha's the devil of it."

" *With* my tol-de-rol," Mr. Sheepshanks murmured. " Pretty—very pretty."

I cast a look aloft. The *Lunardi* was transformed: every inch of it frosted as with silver. All the ropes and cords ran with silver too, or liquid mercury. And in the midst of this sparkling cage, a little below the hoop, and five feet at least above reach, dangled the broken valve-string.

" Well," I said, " you have made a handsome mess of it! Pass me the broken end, and be good enough not to lose your head."

The Incomplete Aeronauts

"I wish I could," he groaned, pressing it between his palms. "My dear sir, I'm not frightened, if that is your meaning."

I was, and horribly. But the thing had to be done. The reader will perhaps forgive me for touching shyly on the next two or three minutes, which still recur on the smallest provocation and play bogey with my dreams. To balance on the edge of night, quaking, gripping a frozen rope; to climb and feel the pit of one's stomach slipping like a bucket in a fathomless well—I suppose the intolerable pains in my head spurred me to the attempt—these and the urgent shortness of my breathing—much as toothache will drive a man up to the dentist's chair. I knotted the broken ends of the valve-string and slid back into the car: then tugged the valve open, while with my disengaged arm I wiped the sweat from my forehead. It froze upon the coat-cuff.

In a minute or so the drumming in my ears grew less violent. Dalmahoy bent over the aeronaut, who was bleeding at the nose and now began to breathe stertorously. Sheepshanks had fallen into placid slumber. I kept the valve open until we descended into a stratum of fog—from which, no doubt, the *Lunardi* had lately risen: the moisture collected here would account for its congelated coat of silver. By-and-by, still without rising, we were quit of the fog, and the moon swept the hollow beneath us, rescuing solitary scraps and sheets of water and letting them slip again like imprehensible ghosts. Small fiery eyes opened and shut on us; cressets of flame on factory chimneys, more and more frequent. I studied the compass. Our course lay south by west. But our whereabouts? Dalmahoy, being appealed to, suggested Glasgow: and thenceforward I let him alone. Byfield snored on.

I pulled out my watch, which I had forgotten to wind; and found it run down. The hands stood at twenty minutes past four. Daylight, then, could not be far off. Eighteen hours —say twenty: and Byfield had guessed our rate at one time to be thirty miles an hour. Five hundred miles——

A line of silver ahead: a ribbon drawn taut across the night, clean-edged, broadening—the sea! In a minute or two I caught the murmur of the coast. "Five hundred miles," I began to reckon again, and a holy calm dawned on me as the *Lunardi* swept high over the fringing surf, and its voice faded back with the glimmer of a whitewashed fishing-haven.

I roused Dalmahoy and pointed. " The sea! "

" Looks like it. Which, I wonder? "

" The English Channel, man."

" I say—are you sure? "

" Eh? " exclaimed Byfield, waking up and coming forward with a stagger.

" The English Channel."

" The French fiddlestick," said he with equal promptness.

" Oh, have it as you please! " I retorted. It was not worth arguing with the man.

" What is the hour? "

I told him that my watch had run down. His had done the same. Dalmahoy did not carry one. We searched the still prostrate Sheepshanks: his had stopped at ten minutes to four. Byfield replaced it and underlined his disgust with a kick.

" A nice lot! " he ejaculated. " I owe you my thanks, Mr. Ducie, all the same. It was touch and go with us, and my head's none the better for it."

" But I say," expostulated Dalmahoy. " France! This is getting past a joke."

" So you are really beginning to discover that, are you? "

Byfield stood, holding by a rope, and studied the darkness ahead. Beside him I hugged my conviction — hour after hour, it seemed: and still the dawn did not come.

He turned at length.

" I see a coast line to the south of us. This will be the Bristol Channel: and the balloon is sinking. Pitch out some ballast if these idiots have left any."

I found a couple of sand bags and emptied them overboard. The coast, as a matter of fact, was close at hand. But the *Lunardi* rose in time to clear the cliff barrier by some hundreds of feet. A wild sea ran on it: of its surf, as of a grey and agonising face, we caught one glimpse as we hurled high and clear over the roar: and, a minute later, to our infinite dismay were actually skimming the surface of a black hillside. " Hold on! " screamed Byfield, and I had barely time to tighten my grip when crash! the car struck the turf and pitched us together in a heap on the floor. Bump! the next blow shook us like peas in a bladder. I drew my legs up and waited for the third.

None came. The car gyrated madly and swung slowly

The Incomplete Aeronauts

back to equilibrium. We picked ourselves up, tossed rugs, coats, instruments, promiscuously overboard, and mounted again. The chine of the tall hill, our stumbling-block, fell back and was lost, and we swept forward into formless shadow.

"Confound it!" said Byfield, "the land can't be uninhabited!"

It was, for aught we could see. Not a light showed anywhere; and to make things worse the moon had abandoned us. For one good hour we swept through chaos to the tuneless lamentations of Sheepshanks, who declared that his collar-bone was broken.

Then Dalmahoy flung a hand upwards. Night lay like a sack around and below us: but right aloft, at the zenith, day was trembling. Slowly established, it spread and descended upon us until it touched a distant verge of hills, and there, cut by the rim of the rising sun, flowed suddenly with streams of crimson.

"Over with the grapnel!" Byfield sprang to the valve-string and pulled; and the featureless earth rushed up towards us.

The sunlight through which we were falling had not touched it yet. It leaped on us, drenched in shadow, like some incalculable beast from its covert: a land shaggy with woods and coppices. Between the woods a desolate river glimmered. A colony of herons rose from the tree-tops beneath us and flew squawking for the farther shore.

"This won't do," said Byfield, and shut the escape. "We must win clear of these woods. Hullo!" Ahead of us the river widened abruptly into a shining estuary, populous with anchored shipping. Tall hills flanked it, and in the curve of the westernmost hill a grey town rose from the waterside: its terraces climbing, tier upon tier, like seats in an amphitheatre; its chimneys lifting their smoke over against the dawn. The tiers curved away southward to a round castle and a spit of rock, off which a brig under white canvas stood out for the line of the open sea.

We swept across the roadstead towards the town, trailing our grapnel as it were a hooked fish, a bare hundred feet above the water. Faces stared up at us from the ships' decks. The crew of one lowered a boat to pursue; we were half a mile away before it touched the water. Should we clear the town? At Byfield's orders we stripped off our overcoats and stood ready to lighten ship: but seeing that the deflected wind in the estuary was carrying us towards the suburbs and the harbour's mouth, he changed his mind.

"It is devil or deep sea," he announced. "We will try the grapnel. Look to it, Ducie, while I take the valve!" He pressed a clasp-knife into my hand. "Cut, if I give the word."

We descended a few feet. We were skimming the ridge. The grapnel touched, and, in the time it takes you to wink, had ploughed through a kitchen garden, uprooting a regiment of currant bushes; had leaped clear, and was caught in the eaves of a wooden outhouse, fetching us up with a dislocating shock. I heard a rending noise, and picked myself up in time to see the building collapse like a house of cards and a pair of demented pigs emerge from the ruins and plunge across the garden-beds. And with that I was pitched off my feet again as the hook caught in an iron *chevaux-de-frise*, and held fast.

"Hold tight!" shouted Byfield, as the car lurched and struggled, careening desperately. "Don't cut, man! What the devil!"

Our rope had tautened over the coping of a high stone wall; and the straining *Lunardi* — a very large and handsome blossom, bending on a very thin stalk—overhung a gravelled yard; and lo! from the centre of it stared up at us, rigid with amazement, the faces of a squad of British red-coats!

I believe that the first glimpse of that abhorred uniform brought my knife down upon the rope. In two seconds I had slashed through the strands, and the flaccid machine lifted and bore us from their ken. But I see their faces yet, as in *basso relievo :* round-eyed, open-mouthed; honest country faces, and boyish, every one; an awkward squad of recruits at drill, fronting a red-headed sergeant; the sergeant with cane held horizontally across and behind his thighs, his face upturned with the rest, and "Irishman" on every feature of it. And so the vision fleeted, and Byfield's language claimed attention. The man took the whole vocabulary of British profanity at a rush, and swore himself to a standstill. As he paused for second wind I struck in:

"Mr. Byfield, you open the wrong valve. We drift, as you say, towards—nay, over the open sea. As master of this balloon, I suggest that we descend within reasonable distance of the brig yonder; which, as I make out, is backing her sails;

which, again, can only mean that she observes us and is preparing to lower a boat."

He saw the sense of this, and turned to business, though with a snarl. As a gull from the cliff, the *Lunardi* slanted downwards, and passing the brig by less than a cable's length to leeward, soused into the sea.

I say "soused"; for I confess that the shock belied the promise of our easy descent. The *Lunardi* floated: but it also drove before the wind. And as it dragged the car after it like a tilted pail, the four drenched and blinded aeronauts struggled through the spray and gripped the hoop, the netting —nay, dug their nails into the oiled silk. In its new element the machine became inspired with a sudden infernal malice. It sank like a pillow if we tried to climb it: it rolled us over in the brine; it allowed us no moment for a backward glance. I spied a small cutter-rigged craft tacking towards us, a mile and more to leeward, and wondered if the captain of the brig had left our rescue to it. He had not. I heard a shout behind us; a rattle of oars as the bowmen shipped them; and a hand gripped my collar. So one by one we were plucked— uncommon specimens!—from the deep; rescued from what Mr. Sheepshanks a minute later, as he sat on a thwart and wiped his spectacles, justly termed "a predicament, sir, as disconcerting as any my experience supplies."

CHAPTER XXXIV

CAPTAIN COLENSO

" But what be us to do with the balloon, sir? " the coxswain demanded.

Had it been my affair I believe I should have obeyed a ridiculous impulse and begged them to keep it for their trouble; so weary was I of the machine. Byfield, however, directed them to slit a seam of the oiled silk and cut away the car, which was by this time wholly submerged and not to be lifted. At once the *Lunardi* collapsed and became manageable; and having roped it to a ring-bolt astern, the crew fell to their oars.

My teeth were chattering. These operations of salvage had taken time, and it took us a further unconscionable time to cover the distance between us and the brig as she lay hove-to, her maintopsail aback and her head-sails drawing.

" Feels like towing a whale, sir," the oarsman behind me panted.

I whipped round. The voice—yes, and the face—were the voice and face of the seaman who sat and steered us: the voice English, of a sort; the face of no pattern that I recognised for English. The fellows were as like as two peas: as like as the two drovers Sim and Candlish had been: you might put them both at forty; grizzled men, pursed about the eyes with seafaring. And now that I came to look, the three rowers forward, though mere lads, repeated their elders' features and build; the gaunt frame, the long, serious face, the swarthy complexion and meditative eye—in short, Don Quixote of la Mancha at various stages of growth. Men and lads, I remarked, wore silver earrings.

I was speculating on this likeness when we shipped oars and fell alongside the brig's ladder. At the head of it my hand was taken, and I was helped on deck with ceremony by a tall man in loose blue jacket and duck trousers: an old man, bent and frail; by his air of dignity, the master of the vessel, and by his features as clearly the patriarch of the family. He lifted his cap and addressed us with a fine but (as I now recall it) somewhat tired courtesy.

" An awkward adventure, gentlemen."

We thanked him in proper form.

" I am pleased to have been of service. The pilot-cutter yonder could hardly have fetched you in less than twenty minutes. I have signalled her alongside, and she will convey you back to Falmouth; none the worse, I hope, for your wetting."

" A convenience," said I, " of which my friends will gladly avail themselves. For my part, I do not propose to return."

He paused, weighing my words; obviously puzzled, but politely anxious to understand. His eyes were grey and honest, even childishly honest, but dulled about the rim of the iris and a trifle vacant, as though the world with its train of affairs had passed beyond his active concern. I keep my own eyes about me when I travel, and have surprised just such a look, before now, behind the spectacles of very old men who sit by the roadside and break stones for a living.

" I fear, sir, that I do not take you precisely."

Captain Colenso

"Why," said I, "if I may guess, this is one of the famous Falmouth packets?"

"As to that, sir, you are right, and yet wrong. She *was* a Packet, and (if I may say it) a famous one." His gaze travelled aloft, and descending rested on mine with a sort of gentle resignation. "But the old pennon is down, as you see. At present she sails on a private adventure, and under private commission."

"A privateer?"

"You may call it that."

"The adventure hits my humour even more nicely. Accept me, Captain——"

"Colenso."

"Accept me, Captain Colenso, for your passenger: I will not say comrade-in-arms—naval warfare being so far beyond my knowledge, which it would perhaps be more descriptive to call ignorance. But I can pay——" I thrust a hand nervously into my breast pocket, and blessed Flora for her waterproof bag. "Excuse me, Captain, if I speak with my friend here in private for a moment."

I drew Byfield aside. "Your notes? The salt water——"

"You see," said he, "I am a martyr to acidity of the stomach."

"Man! do I invite the confidence of your stomach?"

"Consequently I never make an ascension unaccompanied by a small bottle of Epsom salts, tightly corked."

"And you threw away the salts and substituted the notes? —that was clever of you, Byfield."

I lifted my voice. "And Mr. Dalmahoy, I presume, returns to his sorrowing folk?"

The extravagant cheerfully corrected me. "They will not sorrow: but I shall return to them. Of their grudged pension I have eighteenpence in my pocket. But I propose to travel with Sheepshanks, and raise the wind by showing his tricks. He shall toss the caber from Land's End to Forthside, cheered by the plaudits of the intervening taverns and furthered by their bounty."

"A progress which we must try to expedite, if only out of regard for Mrs. Sheepshanks." I turned to Captain Colenso again. "Well, sir, will you accept me for your passenger?"

"I doubt that you are joking, sir."

" And I swear to you that I am not."

He hesitated; tottered to the companion, and called down, " Susannah! Susannah! A moment on deck, if you please. One of these gentlemen wishes to ship as passenger."

A dark-browed woman of middle age thrust her head above the ladder and eyed me. Even so might a ruminating cow gaze over her hedge upon some posting wayfarer.

" What's he dressed in? " she demanded abruptly.

" Madam, it was intended for a ball-suit."

" You will do no dancing here, young man."

" My dear lady, I accept that and every condition you may impose. Whatever the discipline of the ship——"

She cut me short. " Have you told him, father? "

" Why, no. You see, sir, I ought to tell you that this is not an ordinary voyage."

" Nor, for that matter, is mine."

" You will be exposed to risks."

" In a privateer that goes without saying."

" The risk of capture."

" Naturally: though a brave captain will not dwell on it." And I bowed.

" But I do dwell on it," he answered earnestly, a red spot showing on either cheek. " I must tell you, sir, that we are very likely indeed to fall into an enemy's hands."

" Say certain," chimed in Susannah.

" Yes, I will say we are certain. I cannot in conscience do less." He sought his daughter's eyes. She nodded.

" Oh, damn your conscience! " thought I, my stomach rising in contempt for this noble-looking but extremely faint-hearted privateersman. " Come," I said, rallying him, " we fall in with a Frenchman, or—let us suppose—an American: that is our object, eh? "

" Yes, with an American. That is our object, to be sure."

" Then I warrant we give a good account of ourselves. Tut, tut, man—an ex-packet captain! "

I pulled up in sheer wonder at the lunacy of our dispute and the side he was forcing me to take. Here was I haranguing a grey-headed veteran on his own quarter-deck and exhorting him to valour! In a flash I saw myself befooled, tricked into playing the patronising amateur, complacently posturing for the derision of gods and men. And Captain Colenso, who aimed but to be rid of me, was laughing in his

Captain Colenso

sleeve, no doubt. In a minute even Sheepshanks would catch the jest. Now, I do mortally hate to be laughed at: it may be disciplinary for most men, but it turns me obstinate.

Captain Colenso, at any rate, dissembled his mirth to perfection. The look which he shifted from me to Susannah and back was eloquent of senile indecision.

"I cannot explain to you, sir. The consequences — I might mitigate them for you—still you must risk them." He broke off and appealed to me. "I would rather you did not insist: I would indeed! I must beg of you, sir, not to press it."

"But I do press it," I answered, stubborn as a mule. "I tell you that I am ready to accept all risks. But if you want me to return with my friends in the cutter, you must summon your crew to pitch me down the ladder. And there's the end on't."

"Dear, dear! Tell me at least, sir, that you are an unmarried man."

"Up to now I have that misfortune." I aimed a bow at Mistress Susannah; but that lady had turned her broad shoulders, and it missed fire. "Which reminds me," I continued, "to ask for the favour of pen, ink, and paper. I wish to send a letter ashore, to the mail."

She invited me to follow her; and I descended to the main cabin, a spick-and-span apartment, where we surprised two passably good-looking damsels at their housework, the one polishing a mahogany swing-table, the other a brass door-handle. They picked up their cloths, dropped me a curtsey apiece, and disappeared at a word from Susannah, who bade me be seated at the swing-table and set writing materials before me. The room was lit by a broad stern-window, and lined along two of its sides with mahogany doors leading, as I supposed, to sleeping cabins: the panels—not to speak of the brass handles and finger-plates—shining so that a man might have seen his face in them, to shave by. "But why all these women, on board a privateer?" thought I, as I tried a quill on my thumb-nail, and embarked upon my first love-letter.

"DEAREST,—This line with my devotion to tell you that the balloon has descended safely, and your Anne finds himself on board . . ."

"By the way, Miss Susannah, what is the name of this ship?"

"She is called the *Lady Nepean;* and I am a married woman and the mother of six."

"I felicitate you, madam." I bowed, and resumed my writing:—

"... the *Lady Nepean* packet, outward bound from Falmouth to ..."

—"Excuse me, but where the dickens are we bound for?"

"For the coast of Massachusetts, I believe."

"You believe?"

She nodded. "Young man, if you'll take my advice, you'll go back."

"Madam," I answered, on the sudden impulse, "I am an escaped French prisoner." And with that, having tossed my cap over the mills (as they say), I leaned back in the settee, and we regarded each other.

"——escaped," I continued, still my eyes on hers, "with a trifle of money, but minus my heart. I write this to the fair daughter of Britain who has it in her keeping. And now what have you to say?"

"Ah, well," she mused, "the Lord's ways be past finding out. It may be the easier for you."

Apparently it was the habit of this ship's company to speak in enigmas. I caught up my pen again:—

"... The coast of Massachusetts, in the United States of America, whence I hope to make my way in good time to France. Though you have news, dearest, I fear none can reach me for a while. Yet, and though you have no more to write than 'I love you, Anne,' write it, and commit it to Mr. Robbie, who will forward it to Mr. Romaine, who in turn may find a means to get it smuggled through to Paris, Rue du Fouarre, 16. It should be consigned to the widow Jupille, 'to be called for by the corporal who praised her *vin blanc.*' She will remember; and in truth a man who had the courage to praise it deserves remembrance as singular among the levies of France. Should a youth of the name of Rowley present himself before you, you may trust his fidelity absolutely, his sagacity not at all. And so (since the boat waits to take this) I kiss the name of Flora, and subscribe myself—

Captain Colenso

until I come to claim her, and afterwards to eternity—her *prisoner*.   ANNE."

I had, in fact, a second reason for abbreviating this letter and sealing it in a hurry. The movements of the brig, though slight, were perceptible, and in the close air of the main cabin my head already began to swim. I hastened on deck in time to shake hands with my companions and confide the letter to Byfield with instructions for posting it. "And if your share in our adventure should come into public question," said I, "you must apply to a Major Chevenix, now quartered in Edinburgh Castle, who has a fair inkling of the facts, and as a man of honour will not decline to assist you. You have Dalmahoy, too, to back your assertion that you knew me only as Mr. Ducie." Upon Dalmahoy I pressed a note for his and Mr. Sheepshanks's travelling expenses. "My dear fellow," he protested, "I couldn't *dream* . . . if you are sure it won't inconvenience . . . merely as a loan . . . and deuced handsome of you, I will say." He kept the cutter waiting while he drew an I.O.U., in which I figured as Bursar and Almoner (*honoris causâ*) to the Senatus Academicus of Cramond-on-Almond. Mr. Sheepshanks meanwhile shook hands with me impressively. "It has been a memorable experience, sir. I shall have much to tell my wife on my return."

It occurred to me as probable that the lady would have even more to say to him. He stepped into the cutter, and, as they pushed off, was hilariously bonneted by Mr. Dalmahoy, by way of parting salute. "Starboard after braces!" Captain Colenso called to his crew. The yards were trimmed and the *Lady Nepean* slowly gathered way, while I stood by the bulwarks gazing after my friends and attempting to persuade myself that the fresh air was doing me good.

Captain Colenso perceived my queasiness, and advised me to seek my berth and lie down; and on my replying with haggard defiance, took my arm gently, as if I had been a wilful child, and led me below. I passed beyond one of the mahogany doors leading from the main cabin; and in that seclusion I ask you to leave me face to face with the next forty-eight hours. It was a dreadful time.

Nor at the end of it did gaiety wait on a partially recovered appetite. The ladies of the ship nursed me, and tickled my

palate with the lightest of sea diet. The men strowed seats for me on deck, and touched their caps with respectful sympathy. One and all were indefatigably kind, but taciturn to a degree beyond belief. A fog of mystery hung and deepened about them and the *Lady Nepean*, and I crept about the deck in a continuous evil dream, entangling myself in impossible theories. To begin with, there were eight women on board; a number not to be reconciled with serious privateering; all daughters or sons' wives or granddaughters of Captain Colenso. Of the men—twenty-three in all— those who were not called Colenso were called Pengelly; and most of them convicted landsmen by their bilious countenances and unhandy movements; men fresh from the plough-tail by their gait, yet with no ruddy impress of field-work and the open-air.

Twice every day, and thrice on Sundays, this extraordinary company gathered bare-headed to the poop for a religious service which it would be colourless to call frantic. It began decorously enough with a quavering exposition of some portion of Holy Writ by Captain Colenso. But by-and-by (and especially at the evening office) his listeners kindled and opened on him with a skirmishing fire of " Amens." Then, worked by degrees to an ecstasy, they broke into cries of thanksgiving and mutual encouragement; they jostled for the rostrum (a long nine-pounder swivel); and then speaker after speaker declaimed his soul's experiences until his voice cracked, while the others sobbed, exhorted, even leapt in the air. " Stronger, brother! " " 'Tis working, 'tis working! " " O deliverance! " " O streams of redemption! " For ten minutes, or a quarter of an hour maybe, the ship was a Babel, a Bedlam. And then the tumult would die down as suddenly as it had arisen, and dismissed by the old man, the crew, with faces once more inscrutable, but twitching with spent emotion, scattered to their usual tasks.

Five minutes after these singular outbreaks it was difficult to believe in them. Captain Colenso paced the quarter-deck once more with his customary shuffle, his hands beneath his coat-tails, his eyes conning the ship with their usual air of mild abstraction. Now and again he paused to instruct one of his incapables in the trimming of a brace, or to correct the tie of a knot. He never scolded; seldom lifted his voice. By his manner of speech, and the ease of his authority, he

and his family might have belonged to separate ranks of life. Yet I seemed to detect method in their obedience. The veriest fumbler went about his work with a concentrated gravity of bearing, as if he fulfilled a remoter purpose, and understood it while he tied his knots into " grannies," and generally mismanaged the job in hand.

Towards the middle of our second week out, we fell in with a storm—a rotatory affair, and soon over by reason that we struck the outer fringe of it; but to a landsman sufficiently daunting while it lasted. Late in the afternoon I thrust my head up for a look around. We were weltering along in horrible forty-foot seas, over which our bulwarks tilted at times until from the companion hatchway I stared plumb into the grey sliding chasms, and felt like a fly on the wall. The *Lady Nepean* hurled her old timbers along under close-reefed main-topsail, and a rag of a foresail only. The captain had housed topgallant masts and lashed his guns inboard; yet she rolled so that you would not have trusted a cat on her storm-washed decks. They were desolate but for the captain and helmsman on the poop; the helmsman, a mere lad—the one, in fact, who had pulled the bow-oar to our rescue—lashed and gripping the spokes pluckily, but with a white face which told that, though his eyes were strained on the binnacle, his mind ran on the infernal seas astern. Over him, in sea-boots and oilskins, towered Captain Colenso—rejuvenated, transfigured; his body swaying easily to every lurch and plunge of the brig, his face entirely composed and cheerful, his salt-rimmed eyes contracted a little, but alert and even boyishly bright. An heroical figure of a man!

My heart warmed to Captain Colenso; and next morning, as we bowled forward with a temperate breeze on our quarter, I took occasion to compliment him on the *Lady Nepean's* behaviour.

" Ay," said he abstractedly; " the old girl made pretty good weather of it."

" I suppose we were never in what you would call real danger? "

He faced me with sudden earnestness. " Mr. Ducie, I have served the Lord all my days, and He will not sink the ship that carries my honour." Giving me no time to puzzle over this, he changed his tone. " You'll scarce believe it, but in her young days she had a very fair turn of speed."

" Her business surely demands it still," said I. Only an arrant landsman could have reconciled the lumbering old craft with any idea of privateering; but this was only my theory, and I clung to it.

" We shall not need to test her."

" You rely on your guns, then? " I had observed the care lavished on these. They were of brass, and shone like the door-plates in the main cabin.

" Why, as to that," he answered evasively, " I've had to before now. The last voyage I commanded her—it was just after the war broke out with America—we fell in with a schooner off the Banks; we were outward bound for Halifax. She carried twelve nine-pounder carronades and two long nines, beside a big fellow on a traverse; and we had the guns you see—eight nine-pounders and one chaser of the same calibre—post-office guns, we call them. But we beat her off after two hours of it."

" And saved the mails? "

He rose abruptly (we had seated ourselves on a couple of hen-coops under the break of the poop). " You will excuse me. I have an order to give "; and he hurried up the steps to the quarter-deck.

It must have been ten days after this that he stopped me in one of my eternal listless promenades and invited me to sit beside him again.

" I wish to take your opinion, Mr. Ducie. You have not, I believe, found salvation? You are not one of us, as I may say? "

" Meaning by ' us '? "

" I and mine, sir, are unworthy followers of the Word, as preached by John Wesley."

" Why, no; that is not my religion."

" But you are a gentleman." I bowed. " And on a point of honour—do you think, sir, that as a servant of the King one should obey his earthly master even to doing what conscience forbids? "

" That might depend——"

" But on a point of honour, sir? Suppose that you had pledged your private word, in a just, nay, a generous bargain, and were commanded to break it. Is there anything could override that? "

I thought of my poor old French colonel and his broken

Captain Colenso

parole ; and was silent. " Can you not tell me the circumstances? " I suggested at length.

He had been watching me eagerly. But he shook his head now, sighed, and drew a small Bible from his pocket. " I am not a gentleman, sir. I laid it before the Lord: but," he continued naïvely, " I wanted to learn how a gentleman would look at it." He searched for a text, turning the pages with long, nervous fingers; but desisted with another sigh, and, a moment later, was summoned away to solve some difficulty with the ship's reckoning.

My respect for the captain had been steadily growing. He was so amiable, too, so untiringly courteous; he bore his sorrow—whatever the cause might be—with so gentle a resignation; that I caught myself pitying even while I cursed him and his crew for their inhuman reticence.

But my respect vanished pretty quickly next day. We were seated at dinner in the main cabin—the captain at the head of the table, and, as usual, crumbling his biscuit in a sort of waking trance—when Mr. Reuben Colenso, his eldest son and acting mate, put his solemn face in at the door with news of a sail about four miles distant on the lee bow. I followed the captain on deck. The stranger, a schooner, had been lying-to when first descried in the hazy weather; but was standing now to intercept us. At two miles' distance—it being then about two o'clock—I saw that she hoisted British colours.

" But that flag was never sewn in England," Captain Colenso observed, studying her through his glass. His cheeks, usually of that pallid ivory colour proper to old age, were flushed with a faint carmine, and I observed a suppressed excitement in all his crew. For my part, I expected no better than to play target in the coming engagement: but it surprised me that he served out no cutlasses, ordered up no powder from the hold, and, in short, took no single step to clear the *Lady Nepean* for action or put his men in fighting trim. The most of them were gathered about the fore-hatch, to the total neglect of their guns, which they had been cleaning assiduously all the morning. On we stood without shifting our course by a point, and were almost within range when the schooner ran up the stars-and-stripes and plumped a round shot ahead of us by way of hint.

I stared at Captain Colenso. Could he mean to surrender

without one blow? He had exchanged his glass for a speaking trumpet, and waited, fumbling with it, his face twitching painfully. A cold dishonouring suspicion gripped me. The man was here to betray his flag. I glanced aloft: the British ensign flew at the peak. And as I turned my head, I felt rather than saw the flash, heard the shattering din as the puzzled American luffed up and let fly across our bows with a raking broadside. Doubtless she, too, took note of our defiant ensign, and leaped at the nearest guess, that we meant to run her aboard.

Now, whether my glance awoke Captain Colenso, or this was left to the all but simultaneous voice of the guns, I know not. But as their smoke rolled between us I saw him drop his trumpet and run with a crazed face to the taffrail, where the halliards led. The traitor had forgotten to haul down his flag!

It was too late. While he fumbled with the halliards, a storm of musketry burst and swept the quarter-deck. He flung up both hands, spun round upon his heel, and pitched backwards at the helmsman's feet, and the loosened ensign dropped slowly and fell across him, as if to cover his shame.

Instantly the firing ceased. I stood there between compassion and disgust, willing yet loathing to touch the pitiful corpse, when a woman—Susannah—ran screaming by me and fell on her knees beside it. I saw a trickle of blood ooze beneath the scarlet folds of the flag. It crawled along the plank, hesitated at a seam, and grew there to an oddly shaped pool. I watched it. In shape I thought it remarkably like the map of Ireland. And I became aware that some one was speaking to me, and looked up to find a lean and lantern-jawed American come aboard and standing at my shoulder.

" Are you anywise hard of hearing, stranger? Or must I repeat to you that this licks cockfighting? "

" I, at any rate, am not disputing it, sir."

" The *Lady Nepean*, too! Is that the Cap'n yonder? I thought as much. Dead, hey? Well, he'd better *stay* dead; though I'd have enjoyed the inside o' five minutes' talk, just to find out what he did it for."

" Did what? "

" Why, brought the *Lady Nepean* into these waters, and Commodore Rodgers no farther away than Rhode Island, by all accounts. He must have had a nerve. And what post might *you* be holding on this all-fired packet? Darn *me*, but you have females enough on board!" For indeed there were three poor creatures kneeling now and crooning over the dead captain. The men had surrendered—they had no arms to fling down—and were collected in the waist, under guard of a cordon of Yankees. One lay senseless on deck, and two or three were bleeding from splinter wounds; for the enemy, her freeboard being lower by a foot or two than the wall sides of the *Lady Nepean*, had done little execution on deck, whatever the wounds in our hull might be.

" I beg your pardon, Captain——"

" Seccombe, sir, is my name. Alpheus Q. Seccombe, of the *Manhattan* schooner."

" Well, then, Captain Seccombe, I am a passenger on board this ship, and know neither her business here nor why she has behaved in a fashion that makes me blush for her flag—which, by the way, I have every reason to abominate."

" Oh, come now! You're trying it on. It's a yard-arm matter, and I don't blame you, to be sure. Cap'n sank the mails?"

" There were none to sink, I believe."

He conned me curiously.

" You don't look like a Britisher, either!"

" I trust not. I am the Viscount Anne de Kéroual de St. Yves, escaped from a British war-prison."

" Lucky for you if you prove it. We'll get to the bottom of this." He faced about and called, " Who's the first officer of this brig?"

Reuben Colenso was allowed to step forward. Blood from a scalp-wound had run and caked on his right cheek, but he stepped squarely enough.

" Bring him below," Captain Seccombe commanded. " And you, Mr. What's-your-name, lead the way. It's one or the other of us will get the hang of this affair."

He seated himself at the head of the table in the main cabin, and spat ceremoniously on the floor.

" Now, sir: you are, or were, first officer of this brig?"

The prisoner, standing between his two guards, gripped his stocking cap nervously. " Will you please to tell me, sir, if my father is killed?"

" Seth, my lad, I want room." One of the guards, a strapping youngster, stepped and flung open a pane of the stern window. Captain Seccombe spat out of it with nonchalant dexterity before answering:

"I guess he is. Brig's name?"

"The *Lady Nepean*."

"Mail packet?"

"Yes, sir; leastways——"

"Now see here, Mister First Officer Colenso junior, it's a shortish trip between this and the yard-arm, and it may save you some su-perfluous lying if I tell you that in August, last year, the *Lady Nepean* packet, Captain Colenso, outward bound for Halifax, met the *Hitchcock* privateer off the Great Bank of Newfoundland, and beat her off after two hours' fighting. You were on board of her?"

"I tended the stern gun."

"*Very* good. The next day, being still off the Banks, she fell in with Commodore Rodgers, of the United States frigate *President*, and surrendered to him right away."

"We sank the mails."

"You did, my man. Notwithstanding which, that lion-hearted hero treated you with the forbearance of a true-born son of freedom." Captain Seccombe's voice took an oratori-cal roll. "He saw that you were bleeding from your fray. He fed you at his hospitable board; he would not suffer you to be de-nuded of the least trifle. Nay, what did he promise? —but to send your father and his crew and passengers back to England in their own ship, on their swearing, upon their sacred honour, that she should return to Boston harbour with an equal number of American prisoners from England. Your father swore to that upon the Old and New Testaments, severally and conjointly; and the *Lady Nepean* sailed home for all the world like a lamb from the wolf's jaws, with a single American officer inside of her. And how did your dog-damned Government respect this noble confidence? In a way, sir, that would have brought a blush to the cheek of a low-down attorney's clerk. They re-pudiated. Under shelter of a notification that no exchange of prisoners on the high seas would count as valid, this perjured tyrant and his myr-midons went back on their captain's oath, and kept the brig; and the American officer came home empty-handed. Your father was told to resume his duties, immortal souls being cheap in a country where they press seamen's bodies. And now, Mister First Officer Colenso, perhaps you'll explain how he had the impudence to come within two hundred miles of a coast where his name smelt worse than vermin."

" He was coming back, sir."

" Hey? "

" Back to Boston, sir. You see, Cap'n, father wasn't a rich man, but he had saved a trifle. He didn't go back to the service, though told that he might. It preyed on his mind. We was all very fond of father; being all one family, as you might say, though some of us had wives and families, and some were over to Redruth, to the mines."

" Stick to the point."

" But this *is* the point, Cap'n. He was coming back, you see. The *Lady Nepean* wasn't fit for much after the handling she'd had. She was going for twelve hundred pounds: the Post Office didn't look for more. We got her for eleven hundred, with the guns, and the repairs may have cost a hundred and fifty; but you'll find the account books in the cupboard there. Father had a matter of five hundred laid by, and a little over."

Captain Seccombe removed his legs from the cabin-table, tilted his chair forward and half rose in his seat.

" You *bought* her? "

" That's what I'm telling you, sir: though father'd have put it much clearer. You see, he laid it before the Lord; and then he laid it before all of us. It preyed on his mind. My sister Susannah stood up and she said, ' I reckon I'm the most respectably married of all of you, having a farm of my own; but we can sell up, and all the world's a home to them that fears the Lord. We can't stock up with American prisoners, but we can go ourselves instead; and judging by the prisoners I've a-seen brought in, Commodore Rodgers 'll be glad to take us. What he does to us is the Lord's affair.' That's what she said, sir. Of course we kept it quiet: we put it about that the *Lady Nepean* was for Canada, and the whole family going out for emigrants. This here gentleman we picked up outside Falmouth; perhaps he've told you."

Captain Seccombe stared at me, and I at Captain Seccombe. Reuben Colenso stood wringing his cap.

At length the American found breath enough to whistle. " I'll have to put back to Boston about this, though it's money out of pocket. This here's a matter for Commodore Bainbridge. Take a seat, Mr. Colenso."

" I was going to ask," said the prisoner simply, " if before you put me in irons, I might go on deck and look at father. It'll be only a moment, sir."

" Yes, sir, you may. And if you can get the ladies to excuse me, I will follow in a few minutes. I wish to pay him my respects. It's my opinion," he added pensively, as the prisoner left the cabin—" it's my opinion that the man's story is genu-wine."

He repeated the word, five minutes later, as we stood on the quarter-deck beside the body. " A genu-wine man, sir, unless I am mistaken."

Well, the question is one for casuists. In my travels I have learnt this, that men are greater than governments; wiser sometimes, honester always. Heaven deliver me from any such problem as killed this old packet-captain! Between loyalty to his king and loyalty to his conscience he had to choose, and it is likely enough that he erred. But I believe that he fought it out, and found on his country's side a limit of shame to which he could not stoop. A man so placed, perhaps, may even betray his country to her honour. In this hope at least the flag which he had hauled down covered his body still as we committed it to the sea, its service or disservice done.

Two days later we anchored in the great harbour at Boston, where Captain Seccombe went with his story and his prisoners to Commodore Bainbridge, who kept them pending news of Commodore Rodgers. They were sent, a few weeks later, to Newport, Rhode Island, to be interrogated by that commander; and, to the honour of the republic, were released on a liberal *parole ;* but whether, when the war ended, they returned to England or took oath as American citizens, I have not learnt. I was luckier. The Commodore allowed Captain Seccombe to detain me while the French consul made inquiry into my story; and during the two months which the consul thought fit to take over it, I was a guest in the captain's house. And here I made my bow to Miss Amelia Seccombe, an accomplished young lady, " who," said her doating father, " has acquired a considerable proficiency in French, and will be glad to swap ideas with you in that language." Miss Seccombe and I did not hold our communications in French; and observing her disposition to substitute the warmer language of the glances, I took the bull by the horns, told her my secret, and rhapsodised on Flora. Consequently no Nausicaa figures

Alain Plays His Last Card

in this Odyssey of mine. Nay, the excellent girl flung herself into my cause, and bombarded her father and the consular office with such effect that on 2nd February 1814, I waved farewell to her from the deck of the barque *Shawmut*, bound from Boston to Bordeaux.

CHAPTER XXXV

IN PARIS—ALAIN PLAYS HIS LAST CARD

ON the 10th of March at sunset the *Shawmut* passed the Pointe de Grave fort and entered the mouth of the Gironde, and at eleven o'clock next morning dropped anchor a little below Blaye, under the guns of the *Regulus*, 74. We were just in time, a British fleet being daily expected there to co-operate with the Duc d'Angoulême and Count Lynch, who was then preparing to pull the tricolour from his shoulder and betray Bordeaux to Beresford, or, if you prefer it, to the Bourbon. News of his purpose had already travelled down to Blaye, and therefore no sooner were my feet once more on the soil of my beloved France, than I turned them towards Libourne, or rather Fronsac, and the morning after my arrival there, started for the capital.

But so desperately were the joints of travel dislocated (the war having deplenished the country alike of cattle and able-bodied drivers), and so frequent were the breakdowns by the way, that I might as expeditiously have trudged it. It cost me fifteen good days to reach Orleans, and at Étampes (which I reached on the morning of the 30th) the driver of the tottering diligence flatly declined to proceed. The Cossacks and Prussians were at the gates of Paris. "Last night we could see the fires of their bivouacs. If Monsieur listens he can hear the firing." The Empress had fled from the Tuileries. "Whither?" The driver, the aubergiste, the disinterested crowd, shrugged their shoulders. "To Rambouillet, probably. God knew what was happening or what would happen." The Emperor was at Troyes, or at Sens, or else as near as Fontainebleau; nobody knew for certain which. But the fugitives from Paris had been pouring in for days, and not a cart or four-footed beast was to be hired for love or money, though I hunted Étampes for hours.

At length, and at nightfall, I ran against a bow-kneed grey

mare, and a *cabriolet de place*, which, by its label, belonged
to Paris; the pair wandering the street under what it would
be flattery to call the guidance of an eminently drunken
driver. I boarded him; he dissolved at once into maudlin
tears and prolixity. It appeared that on the 29th he had
brought over a bourgeois family from the capital, and had
spent the last three days in perambulating Etampes, and the
past three nights in crapulous slumber within his vehicle.
Here was my chance, and I demanded to know if for a price
he would drive me back with him to Paris. He declared, still
weeping, that he was fit for anything. " For my part, I am
ready to die, and Monsieur knows that we shall never reach."

" Still anything is better than Etampes."

For some inscrutable reason this struck him as excessively
comic. He assured me that I was a brave fellow, and bade
me jump up at once. Within five minutes we were jolting
towards Paris. Our progress was all but inappreciable, for
the grey mare had come to the end of her powers, and her
master's monologue kept pace with her. His anecdotes were
all of the past three days. The iron of Etampes apparently
had entered his soul and effaced all memory of his antecedent
career. Of the war, of any recent public events, he could tell
me nothing.

I had half expected—supposing the Emperor to be near
Fontainebleau—to happen on his vedettes, but we had the
road to ourselves, and reached Longjumeau a little before
daybreak without having encountered a living creature.
Here we knocked up the proprietor of a cabaret, who assured
us between yawns that we were going to our doom, and after
baiting the grey and dosing ourselves with execrable brandy,
pushed forward again. As the sky grew pale about us, I had
my ears alert for the sound of artillery. But Paris kept
silence. We passed Sceaux, and arrived at length at Mont-
rouge and the barrier. It was open—abandoned—not a
sentry, not a douanier visible.

" Where will Monsieur be pleased to descend? " my driver
inquired, and added, with an effort of memory, that he had a
wife and two adorable children on a top floor in the Rue du
Mont Parnasse, and stabled his mare handy by. I paid and
watched him from the deserted pavement as he drove away.
A small child came running from a doorway behind me, and
blundered against my legs. I caught him by the collar and
demanded what had happened to Paris. " That I do not

Alain Plays His Last Card

know," said the child, "but mamma is dressing herself to take me to the review. Tenez!" he pointed, and at the head of the long street I saw advancing the front rank of a blue-coated regiment of Prussians, marching across Paris to take up position on the Orleans road.

That was my answer. Paris had surrendered! And I had entered it from the south just in time, if I wished, to witness the entry of His Majesty the Emperor Alexander from the north. Soon I found myself one of a crowd converging towards the bridges, to scatter northward along the line of His Majesty's progress, from the Barrière de Pantin to the Champs Elysées, where the grand review was to be held. I chose this for my objective, and making my way along the Quays, found myself shortly before ten o'clock in the Place de la Concorde, where a singular little scene brought me to a halt.

About a score of young men—aristocrats by their dress and carriage—were gathered about the centre of the square. Each wore a white scarf and the Bourbon cockade in his hat; and their leader, a weedy youth with hay-coloured hair, had drawn a paper from his pocket, and was declaiming its contents at the top of a voice by several sizes too big for him —

"For Paris is reserved the privilege, under circumstances now existing, to accelerate the dawn of Universal Peace. Her suffrage is awaited with the interest which so immense a result naturally inspires,"

et cetera. Later on, I possessed myself of a copy of the Prince of Schwartzenberg's proclamation, and identified the wooden rhetoric at once.

"Parisians! you have the example of Bordeaux before you" . . . Ay, by the Lord, they had—right under their eyes! The hay-coloured youth wound up his reading with a "Vive le Roi!" and his band of walking gentlemen took up the shout. The crowd looked on impassive; one or two edged away; and a grey-haired, soldierly horseman (whom I recognised for the Duc de Choiseul-Praslin) passing in full tenue of Colonel of the National Guard, reined up, and addressed the young men in a few words of grave rebuke. Two or three answered by snapping their fingers, and repeating their "Vive le Roi" with a kind of embarrassed defiance. But their performance, before so chilling an audience, was falling sadly flat when a dozen or more of young royalist bloods came riding up to reanimate it—among them, M. Louis de Chateaubriand, M. Talleyrand's brother, Archambaut de Périgord, the scoundrelly Marquis de Maubreuil—yes, and my cousin, the Vicomte de Saint Yves!

The indecency, the cynical and naked impudence of it, took me like a buffet. There, in a group of strangers, my cheek reddened under it, and for the moment I had a mind to run. I had done better to run. By a chance his eye missed mine as he swaggered past at a canter, for all the world like a tenore robusto on horseback, with the rouge on his face, and his air of expansive Olympian blackguardism. He carried a lace white handkerchief at the end of his riding switch, and this was bad enough. But as he wheeled his bay thoroughbred, I saw that he had followed the *déclassé* Maubreuil's example and decorated the brute's tail with a Cross of the Legion of Honour. That brought my teeth together, and I stood my ground.

" Vive le Roi! " " Vivent les Bourbons! " " A bas le sabot corse! " Maubreuil had brought a basketful of white brassards and cockades, and the gallant horsemen began to ride about and press them upon the unresponsive crowd. Alain held one of the badges at arm's length as he pushed into the little group about me, and our eyes met.

" *Merci,*" said I, " *retenez-le jusqu'à ce que nous nous rencontrons—Rue Grégoire de Tours !* "

His arm with the riding switch and laced handkerchief went up as though he had been stung. Before it could descend, I darted aside deep into the crowd which hustled around him, understanding nothing, but none the less sullenly hostile. " A bas les cocardes blanches! " cried one or two. " Who was the cur? " I heard Maubreuil's question as he pressed in to the rescue, and Alain's reply, " Peste! A young relative of mine who is in a hurry to lose his head; whereas I prefer to choose the time for that."

I took this for a splutter of hatred, and even found it laughable as I made my escape good. At the same time, our encounter had put me out of humour for gaping at the review, and I turned back and recrossed the river to seek the Rue du Fouarre and the Widow Jupille.

Now the Rue du Fouarre, though once a very famous thoroughfare, is to-day perhaps as squalid as any that drains its refuse by a single gutter into the Seine, and the widow had been no beauty even in the days when she followed the 106th of the line as vivandière and before she wedded Sergeant Jupille of

Alain Plays His Last Card

that regiment. But she and I had struck up a friendship over a flesh wound which I received in an affair of outposts on the Algueda, and thenceforward I taught myself to soften the edge of her white wine by the remembered virtues of her ointment, so that when Sergeant Jupille was cut off by a grapeshot in front of Salamanca, and his Philomène retired to take charge of his mother's wine shop in the Rue du Fouarre, she had enrolled my name high on the list of her prospective patrons. I felt myself, so to speak, a part of the goodwill of her house, and "Heaven knows," thought I, as I threaded the insalubrious street, "it is something for a soldier of the Empire to count even on this much in Paris to-day. *Est aliquid, quocunque loco, quocunque sacello. . . .*"

Madame Jupille knew me at once, and we fell (figuratively speaking) upon each other's neck. Her shop was empty, the whole quarter had trooped off to the review. After mingling our tears (again figuratively) over the fickleness of the capital, I inquired if she had any letters for me.

"Why, no, comrade."

"None?" I exclaimed with a very blank face.

"Not one;" Madame Jupille eyed me archly, and relented. "The reason being that Mademoiselle is too discreet."

"Ah!" I heaved a big sigh of relief. "You provoking woman, tell me what you mean by that?"

"Well, now, it may have been ten days ago that a stranger called in and asked if I had any news of the corporal who praised my white wine. 'Have I any news,' said I, 'of a needle in a bundle of hay? They all praise it.'" (Oh, Madame Jupille!)

"'The corporal I'm speaking of,' said he, 'is or was called Champdivers.' '*Was!*' I cried, 'you are not going to tell me he is dead?' and I declare to you, comrade, the tears came into my eyes. 'No, he is not,' said the stranger, 'and the best proof is that he will be here inquiring for letters before long. You are to tell him that if he expects one from'—see, I took the name down on a scrap of paper, and stuck it in the wine glass here—'from Miss Flora Gilchrist, he will do well to wait in Paris until a friend finds means to deliver it by hand. And if he asks more about me, say that I am from—tenez, I wrote the second name underneath—yes, that is it—'Mr. Romaine.'"

"Confound his caution!" said I. "What sort of man was this messenger?"

" Oh, a staid-looking man, dark and civil spoken. You might call him an upper servant, or perhaps a notary's clerk; very plainly dressed, in black."

" He spoke French? "

" *Parfaitement.* What else? "

" And he has not called again? "

" To be sure, yes, and the day before yesterday, and seemed quite disappointed. ' Is there anything Monsieur would like to add to his message? ' I asked. ' No,' said he, ' or stay, tell him that all goes well in the north, but he must not leave Paris until I see him.' "

You may guess how I cursed Mr. Romaine for this beating about the bush. If all went well in the north, what possible excuse of caution could the man have for holding back Flora's letter? And how, in any case, could it compromise me here in Paris? I had half a mind to take the bit in my teeth and post off at once for Calais. Still, there was the plain injunction, and the lawyer doubtless had a reason for it hidden somewhere behind his tiresome circumambulatory approaches. And his messenger might be back at any hour.

Therefore, though it went against the grain, I thought it prudent to take lodgings with Madame Jupille and possess my soul in patience. You will say that it should not have been difficult to kill time in Paris between the 31st of March and the 5th of April 1814. The entry of the Allies, Marmont's supreme betrayal, the Emperor's abdication, the Cossacks in the streets, the newspaper offices at work like hives under their new editors, and buzzing contradictory news from morning to night; a new rumour at every café, a scuffle, or the makings of one, at every street corner, and hour by hour a steady stream of manifestoes, placards, handbills, caricatures, and broadsheets of opprobrious verse—the din of it all went by me like the vain noises of a dream as I trod the pavements, intent upon my own hopes and perplexities. I cannot think that this was mere selfishness; rather, a deep disgust was weaning me from my country. If this Paris indeed were the reality, then was I the phantasm, the *revenant ;* then was France—the France for which I had fought and my parents gone to the scaffold—a land that had never been, and our patriotism the shadow of a shade. Judge me not too hardly if in the restless, aimless perambulations of those five days, I crossed the bridge between the country that held neither kin nor friends for me, but only my ineffectual past,

Alain Plays His Last Card

and the country wherein one human creature, if only one, had use for my devotion.

On the sixth day—that is, April 5th—my patience broke down. I took my resolution over lunch and a bottle of Beaujolais, and walked straight back from the restaurant to my lodgings, where I asked Madame Jupille for pen, ink, and paper, and sat down to advertise Mr. Romaine that, for good or ill, he might expect me in London within twenty-four hours of the receipt of this letter.

I had scarce composed the first sentence, when there came a knock at the door and Madame Jupille announced that two gentlemen desired to see me. "Show them up," said I, laying down my pen with a leaping heart; and in the doorway a moment later stood—my cousin Alain!

He was alone. He glanced with a grin of comprehension from me to the letter, advanced, set his hat on the table beside it, and his gloves (after blowing into them) beside his hat.

"My cousin," said he, "you show astonishing agility from time to time; but on the whole you are damned easy to hunt."

I had risen. "I take it you have pressing business to speak of, since amid your latest political occupations you have been at pains to seek me out. If so, I will ask you to be brief."

"No pains at all," he corrected affably. "I have known all the time that you were here. In fact, I expected you some while before you arrived, and sent my man, Paul, with a message."

"A message?"

"Certainly—touching a letter from *la belle Flora*. You received it? The message, I mean."

"Then it was not——"

"No, decidedly it was not Mr. Romaine, to whom"—with another glance at the letter—"I perceive you are writing for explanations. And since you are preparing to ask how on earth I traced you to this rather unsavoury den, permit me to inform you that a—b spells 'ab,' and that Bow Street, when on the track of a criminal, does not neglect to open his correspondence."

I felt my hand tremble as it gripped the top rail of my chair, but I managed to command the voice to answer, coldly enough—

"One moment, Monsieur le Vicomte, before I do myself the pleasure of pitching you out of window. You have detained me these five days in Paris, and have done so, you give me to understand, by the simple expedient of a lie. So far, so good; will you do me the favour to complete the interesting self-exposure, and inform me of your reasons?"

"With all the pleasure in life. My plans were not ready, a little detail wanting, that is all. It is now supplied." He took a chair, seated himself at the table, and drew a folded paper from his breast-pocket. "It will be news to you perhaps, that our uncle—our lamented uncle, if you choose—is dead these three weeks."

"Rest his soul!"

"Forgive me if I stop short of that pious hope." Alain hesitated, let his venom get the better of him, and spat out on his uncle's memory an obscene curse which only betrayed the essential weakness of the man. Recovering himself he went on: "I need not recall to you a certain scene (I confess too theatrical for my taste) arranged by the lawyer at his bedside; nor need I help you to an inkling of the contents of his last will. But possibly it may have slipped your memory that I gave Romaine fair warning. I promised him that I would raise the question of undue influence, and that I had my witnesses ready. I have added to them since; but I own to you that my case will be the stronger when you have obligingly signed the paper which I have the honour to submit to you." And he tossed it, unopened, across the table.

I picked it up and unfolded it:—"*I, the Viscount Anne de Kéroual de Saint Yves, formerly serving under the name of Champdivers in the Buonapartist army, and later under that name a prisoner of war in the Castle of Edinburgh, hereby state that I had neither knowledge of my uncle the Count de Kéroual de Saint Yves, nor expectations from him, nor was owned by him, until sought out by Mr. Daniel Romaine, in the Castle of Edinburgh, by him supplied with money to expedite my escape, and by him clandestinely smuggled at nightfall into Amersham Place; Further, that until that evening I had never set eyes on my uncle, nor have set eyes on him since; that he was bedridden when I saw him, and apparently in the last stage of senile decay. And I have reason to believe that Mr. Romaine did not fully inform him of the circumstances of my escape, and particularly of my concern in the death of a fellow prisoner named Goguelat, formerly a maréchal des logis in the 22nd Regiment of the Line. . . .*"

Of the contents of this precious document let a sample suffice. From end to end it was a tissue of distorted statements implicated with dishonouring suggestions. I read it through, and let it drop on the table.

" I beg your pardon," said I, " but what do you wish me to do with it? "

" Sign it," said he.

I laughed. " Once more I beg your pardon, but though you have apparently dressed for it, this is not comic opera."

" Nevertheless you will sign."

" Oh, you weary me." I seated myself, and flung a leg over the arm of my chair. " Shall we come to the alternative? For I assume you have one."

" The alternative, to be sure," he answered cheerfully. " I have a companion below, one Clausel, and at the Tête d'Or, a little way up the street, an escort of police."

Here was a pleasing predicament. But if Alain had started with a chance of daunting me (which I do not admit), he had spoilt it long since by working on the raw of my temper. I kept a steady eye on him, and considered: and the longer I considered the better assured was I that his game must have a disastrously weak point somewhere, which it was my business to find.

" You have reminded me of your warning to Mr. Romaine. The subject is an ugly one for two of our family to touch upon; but do you happen to recall Mr. Romaine's counter-threat? "

" Bluff! my young sir. It served his purpose for the moment, I grant you. I was unhinged. The indignity, the very monstrosity of it, the baselessness, staggered reason."

" It was baseless then? "

" The best proof is that in spite of his threat, and my open contempt and disregard of it, Mr. Romaine has not stirred a hand."

" You mean that my uncle destroyed the evidence? "

" I mean nothing of the kind," he retorted hotly, " for I deny that any such evidence at any time existed."

I kept my eye on him. " Alain," I said quietly, " you are a liar."

A flush darkened his face beneath its cosmetics, and with an oath he dipped finger and thumb into his waistcoat pocket and pulled out a dog whistle. " No more of that," said he, " or I whistle up the police this minute."

" Well, well, let us resume the discussion. You say this man Clausel has denounced me? "

He nodded.

" Soldiers of the Empire are cheap in Paris just now."

" So cheap that public opinion would be content if all the messieurs Champdivers were to kill all the messieurs Goguelat and be shot or guillotined for it. I forget which your case demands, and doubt if public opinion would inquire."

" And yet," I mused, " there must be preliminaries; some form of trial for instance, with witnesses. It is even possible that I might be found innocent."

" I have allowed for that unlikely chance, and I look beyond it. To be frank, it does not strike me as probable that a British jury will hand over the estates of the Comte de Kéroual de Saint Yves to an escaped Buonapartist prisoner who has stood his trial for the murder of a comrade, and received the benefit of the doubt."

" Allow me," said I, " to open the window an inch or two. No; put back your whistle. I do not propose to fling you out, at least not just yet; nor will I try to escape. To tell you the truth, you suggest the need of a little fresh air. And now, Monsieur, you assure me you hold the knave in your hand. Well then, play him. Before I tear your foolish paper up, let me have a look at your confederate." I stepped to the door and called down the stairs, " Madame Jupille, be so good as to ask my other visitor to ascend."

With that I turned to the window again and stood there looking out upon the foul gutter along which the refuse of some dye works at the head of the street found its way down to the Seine. And standing so, I heard the expected footsteps mounting the stairs.

" I must ask your pardon, Monsieur, for this intrusion——"

" Hey! " If the words had been a charge of shot fired into my back, I could not have spun round on them more suddenly. " Mr. Romaine! "

For indeed it was he, and not Clausel, who stood in the doorway. And to this day I do not know if Alain or I stared at him with the blanker bewilderment; though I believe there was a significant difference in our complexions.

" M. le Vicomte," said Romaine, advancing, " recently effected an exchange. I have taken the liberty to effect another, and have left Mr. Clausel below listening to some arguments which are being addressed to him by Mr. Dudgeon, my confidential clerk. I think I may promise "—with a chuckle, " they will prove effectual. By your faces, gentlemen, I see that you regard my appearance as something in

Alain Plays His Last Card

the nature of a miracle. Yet, M. le Viscount at least should be guessing by this time that it is the simplest, most natural affair in the world. I engaged my word, sir, to have you watched. Will it be set down to more than ordinary astuteness that finding you in negotiations for the exchange of the prisoner Clausel, we kept an eye upon him also?—that we followed him to Dover, and though unfortunate in missing the boat, reached Paris in time to watch the pair of you leave your lodgings this morning—nay, that knowing whither you were bound, we reached the Rue du Fouarre in time to watch you making your dispositions? But I run on too fast. Mr. Anne, I am entrusted with a letter for you. When, with Mr. Alain's permission, you have read it, we will resume our little conversation."

He handed me the letter and walked to the fireplace, where he took snuff copiously, while Alain eyed him like a mastiff about to spring. I broke open my letter and stooped to pick up a small enclosure which fell from it.

" MY DEAREST ANNE,—When your letter came and put life into me again, I sat down in my happiness and wrote you one that I shall never allow you to see; for it makes me wonder at myself. But when I took it to Mr. Robbie, he asked to see your letter, and when I showed him the *wrapper*, declared that it had been tampered with, and if I wrote and told you what we were doing for you, it might only make your enemies the wiser. For we have done something, and this (which is purely a business letter) is to tell you that the credit does not belong to Mr. Robbie, or to your Mr. Romaine (who by Mr. Robbie's account must be quite a tiresome old gentleman, though well-meaning no doubt). But on the Tuesday after you left us I had a talk with Major Chevenix, and when I really felt quite sorry for him (though it was no use and I told him so), he turned round in a way I could not but admire and said he wished me well and would prove it. He said the charge against you was really one for the military authorities alone; that he had reasons for feeling sure that you had been drawn into this affair on *a point of honour*, which was quite a different thing from *what they said ;* and that he could not only make an affidavit or something of the kind on his own account, but knew enough of that man Clausel to make him confess the truth. Which he did the very next day, and made Clausel sign it, and Mr. Robbie has a copy of the man's statement which he is sending with this to Mr. Romaine in London; and that is the reason why Rowley (who is a *dear*) has come over, and is waiting in the kitchen while I write these hurried lines. He says, too, that Major Chevenix was only just in time, since Clausel's friends are managing an exchange for him, and he is going back to France. And so in haste I write myself,—Your sincere friend,   FLORA.

"*P.S.*—My aunt is well; Ronald is expecting his commission.

"*P.P.S.*—You told me to write it, and so I must, ' I love you, Anne.' "

The enclosure was a note in a large and unformed hand, and ran:—

"DEAR MR. ANNE, RESPECTED SIR,—This comes hopeing to find you well as it leaves me at present, all is well as Miss Flora will tell you that double-died Clausel has confest. This is to tell you Mrs. Mac R. is going on nicely, bar the religion which is only put on to anoy people and being a widow who blames her, not me. Miss Flora says she will put this in with hers, and there is something else but it is a dead secret, so no more at present from, sir,—Yours Respectfully,

"JAS. ROWLEY."

Having read these letters through, I placed them in my breast-pocket, stepped to the table and handed Alain's document gravely back to him; then turned to Mr. Romaine, who shut his snuff-box with a snap.

"It only remains, I think," said the lawyer, "to discuss the terms which (merely as a matter of generosity, or say, for the credit of your house) can be granted to your—to Mr. Alain."

"You forget Clausel, I think," snarled my cousin.

"True, I had forgotten Clausel." Mr. Romaine stepped to the head of the stairs and called down, " Dudgeon! "

Mr. Dudgeon appeared, and endeavoured to throw into the stiffness of his salutation a denial that he had ever waltzed with me in the moonlight.

"Where is the man Clausel? "

"I hardly know, sir, if you would place the wine-shop of the Tête d'Or at the top or the bottom of this street; I presume the top, since the sewer runs in the opposite direction. At all events Mr. Clausel disappeared about two minutes ago in the same direction as the sewer."

Alain Plays His Last Card

Alain sprang up, whistle in hand.

" Put it down," said Mr. Romaine. " The man was cheating you. I can only hope," he added with a sour smile, " that you paid him on account with an I.O.U."

But Alain turned at bay. " One trivial point seems to have escaped you, Master Attorney, or your courage is more than I give you credit for. The English are none too popular in Paris as yet, and this is not the most scrupulous quarter. One blast of this whistle, a cry of *Espion Anglais !* and two Englishmen——"

" Say three," Mr. Romaine interrupted, and strode to the door. " Will Mr. Burchell Fenn be good enough to step upstairs? "

And here let me cry " Halt." There are things in this world, or that is my belief—too pitiful to be set down in writing, and of these, Alain's collapse was one. It may be, too, that Mr. Romaine's British righteousness accorded rather ill with the weapon he used so unsparingly. Of Fenn I need only say, that the luscious rogue shouldered through the doorway as though he had a public duty to discharge, and only the contrariness of circumstances had prevented his discharging it before. He cringed to Mr. Romaine, who held him and the whole nexus of his villainies in the hollow of his hand. He was even obsequiously eager to denounce his fellow-traitor. Under a like compulsion, he would (I feel sure) have denounced his own mother. I saw the sturdy Dudgeon's mouth working like a bull terrier's over a shrewmouse. And between them, Alain had never a chance. Not for the first time in this history, I found myself all but taking sides with him in sheer repulsion from the barbarity of the attack. It seemed that it was through Fenn that Mr. Romaine had first happened on the scent; and the greater rogue had held back a part of the evidence, and would trade it now—" having been led astray—to any gentleman that would let bygones be bygones." And it was I, at length, who interposed when my cousin was beaten to his knees, and having dismissed Mr. Burchell Fenn, restored the discussion to a business-like footing. The end of it was, that Alain renounced all his claims, and accepted a yearly pension of six thousand francs. Mr. Romaine made it a condition that he should never set foot again in England; but seeing that he would certainly be arrested for debt within twenty-four hours of his landing at Dover, I thought this unnecessary.

" A good day's work," said the lawyer, as we stood together in the street outside.

But I was silent.

" And now, Mr. Anne, if I may have the honour of your company at dinner—shall we say Tortoni's?—we will on our way step round to my hotel, the Quatre Saisons, behind the Hôtel de Ville, and order a *calèche* and four to be in readiness."

CHAPTER XXXVI

I GO TO CLAIM FLORA

BEHOLD me now speeding northwards on the wings of love, ballasted by Mr. Romaine. But, indeed, that worthy man climbed into the *calèche* with something less than his habitual gravity. He was obviously and pardonably flushed with triumph. I observed that now and again he smiled to himself in the twilight, or drew in his breath and emitted it with a martial *pouf!* And when he began to talk—which he did as soon as we were clear of the Saint Denis barrier—the points of the family lawyer were untrussed. He leaned back in the *calèche* with the air of a man who had subscribed to the Peace of Europe, and dined well on top of it. He criticised the fortifications with a wave of his tooth-pick, and discoursed derisively and at large on the Emperor's abdication, on the treachery of the Duke of Ragusa, on the prospects of the Bourbons, and on the character of M. Talleyrand, with anecdotes which made up in raciness for what they lacked in authenticity.

We were bowling through La Chapelle, when he pulled out his snuff-box and proffered it.

" You are silent, Mr. Anne."

" I was waiting for the chorus," said I. " Rule Britannia! Britannia rules the waves: and Britons never, never, never—Come, out with it!"

" Well," he retorted; " and I hope the tune will come natural to you before long."

" Oh, give me time, my dear sir! I have seen the Cossacks enter Paris, and the Parisians decorate their poodles with the Cross of the Legion of Honour. I have seen them hoist a wretch on the Vendôme column, to smite the bronze face of the man of Austerlitz. I have seen the *salle* of the Opera rise to applaud a blatant fat fellow singing the praises of the

I Go to Claim Flora

Prussian—and to the tune of *Vive Henri Quatre!* I have seen, in my cousin Alain, of what the best blood in France is capable. Also, I have seen peasant boys—unripe crops of the later levies—mown down by grape-shot—raise themselves on their elbows, to cheer for France and the little man in grey. In time, Mr. Romaine, no doubt my memory will confuse these lads with their betters, and their mothers with the ladies of the *salle de l'Opéra :* just as in time, no doubt, I shall find myself Justice of the Peace, and Deputy Lieutenant of the shire of Buckingham. I am changing my country, as you remind me: and, on my faith, she has no place for me. But, for the sake of her, I have explored and found the best of her—in my new country's prisons. And I repeat, you must give me time."

" Tut, tut! " was his comment, as I searched for tinder box and sulphur match to relight my segar. " We must get you into Parliament, Mr. Anne. You have the gift."

As we approached Saint Denis, the flow of his discourse sensibly slackened: and, a little beyond, he pulled his travelling cap over his ears, and settled down to slumber. I sat wide awake beside him. The spring night had a touch of chill in it, and the breath of our horses, steaming back upon the lamps of the *calèche*, kept a constant nimbus between me and the postillions. Above it, and over the black spires of the poplar avenues, the regiments of stars moved in parade. My gaze went up to the ensign of their noiseless evolutions, to the pole-star, and to Cassiopeia swinging beneath it, low in the north, over my Flora's pillow—*my* pole-star and journey's end.

Under this soothing reflection I composed myself to slumber; and awoke, to my surprise and annoyance, in a miserable flutter of the nerves. And this fretfulness increased with the hours, so that from Amiens to the coast, Mr. Romaine must have had the devil of a time with me. I bolted my meals at the way-houses, chafing all the while at the business of the relays. I popped up and down in the *calèche* like a shot on a hot shovel. I cursed our pace. I girded at the lawyer's snuff-box, and could have called him out upon Calais sands, when we reached them, to justify his vile methodical use of it. By good fortune we arrived to find the packet ready with her warps, and bundled ourselves on board in a hurry. We sought separate cabins for the night, and in mine, as in a sort of moral bath, the drastic cross seas of the Channel cleansed me of my irritable humour, and left me like a rag, beaten and hung on a clothes-line to the winds of heaven.

In the grey of the morning we disembarked at Dover, and here Mr. Romaine had prepared a surprise for me. For, as we drew to the shore, and the throng of porters and waterside loafers, on what should my gaze alight but the beaming countenance of Mr. Rowley! I declare it communicated a roseate flush to the pallid cliffs of Albion. I could have fallen on his neck. On his side the honest lad kept touching his hat and grinning in a speechless ecstasy. As he confessed to me later, " It was either hold my tongue, sir, or call for three cheers." He snatched my valise and ushered us through the crowd, to our hotel-breakfast. And, it seemed he must have filled up his time at Dover with trumpetings of our importance: for the landlord welcomed us on the *perron*, obsequiously cringing; we entered in a respectful hush that might have flattered his Grace of Wellington himself; and the waiters, I believe, would have gone on all fours, but for the difficulty of reconciling that posture with efficient service. I knew myself at last for a Personage: a great English land-owner: and did my best to command the mien proper to that tremendous class when, the meal despatched, we passed out between the bowing ranks to the door where our chaise stood ready.

" But hullo! " said I at sight of it; and my eye sought Rowley's.

" Begging your pardon, sir, but I took it on myself to order the colour, and hoping it wasn't a liberty."

" Claret and invisible green—a duplicate, but for a bullet-hole wanting."

" Which I didn't like to go so far on my own hook, Mr. Anne."

" We fight under the old colours, my lad."

" And walk in and win this time, sir, strike me lucky! "

While we bowled along the first stage towards London— Mr. Romaine and I within the chaise and Rowley perched upon the dickey—I told the lawyer of our progress from Aylesbury to Kirkby-Lonsdale. He took snuff.

" *Forsitan et hæc olim*—that Rowley of yours seems a good-hearted lad, and less of a fool than he looks. The next time I have to travel post with an impatient lover, I'll take a leaf out of his book and buy me a flageolet."

I Go to Claim Flora

" Sir, it was ungrateful of me——"

" Tut, tut, Mr. Anne. I was fresh from my little triumph, that is all; and perhaps would have felt the better for a word of approbation—a little pat on the back, as I may say. It is not often that I have felt the need of it—twice or thrice in my life, perhaps: not often enough to justify my anticipating your example and seeking a wife betimes: for that is a man's one chance if he wants another to taste his success."

" And yet I dare swear you rejoice in mine unselfishly enough."

" Why, no, sir: your cousin would have sent me to the right-about within a week of his succession. Still, I own to you that he offended something at least as deep as self-interest: the sight and scent of him habitually turned my gorge: whereas "—and he inclined to me with a dry smile—" your unwisdom at least was amiable, and—in short, sir, though you can be infernally provoking, it has been a pleasure to serve you."

You may be sure that this did not lessen my contrition. We reached London late that night; and here Mr. Romaine took leave of us. Business waited for him at Amersham Place. After a few hours' sleep, Rowley woke me to choose between two post-boys in blue jackets and white hats, and two in buff jackets and black hats, who were competing for the honour of conveying us as far as Barnet: and having decided in favour of the blue and white, and solaced the buff and black with a *pourboire*, we pushed forward once more.

We were now upon the Great North Road, along which the York mail rolled its steady ten miles an hour to the wafted music of the guard's bugle; a rate of speed which, to the more Dorian mood of Mr. Rowley's flageolet, I proposed to better by one-fifth. But first, having restored the lad to his old seat beside me, I must cross-question him upon his adventures in Edinburgh, and the latest news of Flora and her aunt, Mr. Robbie, Mrs. McRankine, and the rest of my friends. It came out that Mr. Rowley's surrender to my dear girl had been both instantaneous and complete. " She *is* a floorer, Mr. Anne. I suppose now, sir, you'll be standing up for that knock-me-down kind of thing? "

" Explain yourself, my lad."

" Beg your pardon, sir, what they call love at first sight." He wore an ingenuous blush and an expression at once shy and insinuating.

" The poets, Rowley, are on my side."

" Mrs. McRankine, sir——"

" The Queen of Navarre, Mr. Rowley——"

But he so far forgot himself as to interrupt. " It took Mrs. Rankine years, sir, to get used to her first husband. She told me so."

" It took us some days, if I remember, to get used to Mrs. McRankine. To be sure, her cooking——"

" That's what I say, Mr. Anne: it's more than skin-deep; and you'll hardly believe me, sir—that is, if you didn't take note of it—but she hev got an ankle."

He had produced the pieces of his flageolet, and was adjusting them nervously, with a face red as a turkey-cock's wattles. I regarded him with a new and incredulous amusement. That I served Mr. Rowley for a glass of fashion and a mould of form was of course no new discovery: and the traditions of body-service allow, nay enjoin, that when the gentleman goes a-wooing, the valet shall take a sympathetic wound. What could be more natural than that a gentleman of sixteen should select a lady of fifty for his first essay in the tender passion. Still—Bethiah McRankine!

I kept my countenance with an effort. " Mr. Rowley," said I, " if music be the food of love, play on." And Mr. Rowley gave " The Girl I left Behind Me," shyly at first, but anon with terrific expression. He broke off with a sigh: " Heigho ! " in fact, said Rowley: and started off again while I tapped out the time, and hummed:

> " But now I'm bound for Brighton camp,
> Kind heaven then pray guide me,
> And send me safely back again
> To the girl I left behind me ! "

Thenceforward that not uninspiriting air became the *motif* of our progress. We never tired of it. Whenever our conversation flagged, by tacit consent Mr. Rowley pieced his flageolet together and started it. The horses lilted it out in their gallop: the harness jingled, the postillions tittupped to it. And the *presto* with which it wound up as we came to a post-house and a fresh relay of horses had to be heard to be believed.

So with the chaise windows open to the vigorous airs of spring, and my own breast like a window flung wide to youth and health and happy expectations, I rattled homewards; impatient as a lover should be, yet not too impatient to taste

I Go to Claim Flora

the humour of spinning like a lord, with a pocketful of money, along the road which the *ci-devant* M. Champdivers had so fearfully dodged and skirted in Burchell Fenn's covered cart.

And yet so impatient that when we galloped over the Calton Hill and down into Edinburgh by the new London road, with the wind in our faces, and a sense of April in it, brisk and jolly, I must pack off Rowley to our lodgings with the valises, and stay only for a wash and breakfast at Dumbreck's before posting on to Swanston alone.

> " Whene'er my steps return that way,
>   Still faithful shall she find me,
> And never more again I'll stray
>   From the Girl I left behind me."

When the gables of the cottage rose into view over the hill's shoulder I dismissed my driver and walked forward, whistling the tune; but fell silent as I came under the lee of the garden wall, and sought for the exact spot of my old escalade. I found it by the wide beechen branches over the road, and hoisted myself noiselessly up to the coping where, as before, they screened me—or would have screened me had I cared to wait.

But I did not care to wait; and why? Because, not fifteen yards from me, she stood!—she, my Flora, my goddess, bare-headed, swept by chequers of morning sunshine and green shadows, with the dew on her sandal shoes and the lap of her morning gown appropriately heaped with flowers— with tulips, scarlet, yellow, and striped. And confronting her, with his back towards me and a remembered patch between the armholes of his stable-waistcoat, Robie the gardener rested both hands on his spade and expostulated.

" But I like to pick my tulips leaves and all, Robie! "

" Aweel, miss; it's clear ruinin' the bulbs, that's all I say to you."

And that was all I waited to hear. As he bent over and resumed his digging I shook a branch of the beech with both hands and set it swaying. She heard the rustle and glanced up, and, spying me, uttered a gasping little cry.

" What ails ye, miss? " Robie straightened himself instanter; but she had whipped right-about face and was gazing towards the kitchen garden:

" Isn't that a child among the arti—the strawberry beds, I mean? "

He cast down his spade and ran. She turned, let the

tulips fall at her feet, and, ah! her second cry of gladness, and her heavenly blush as she stretched out both arms to me! It was all happening over again—with the difference that now my arms too were stretched out.

> " Journeys end in lovers meeting,
> Every wise man's son doth know. . . ."

Robie had run a dozen yards perhaps, when either the noise I made in scrambling off the wall, or some recollection of having been served in this way before, brought him to a halt. At any rate he turned round, and just in time to witness our embrace.

" The good Lord behear! " he exclaimed, stood stock-still for a moment, and waddled off at top speed towards the back-door.

" We must tell Aunt at once! She will—why, Anne, where are you going? " She caught my sleeve.

" To the hen-house to be sure," said I.

A moment later, with peals of happy laughter we had taken hands and were running along the garden alleys towards the house. And I remember, as we ran, finding it somewhat singular that this should be the first time I had ever invaded Swanston Cottage by way of the front door.

We came upon Miss Gilchrist in the breakfast room. A pile of linen lay on the horse-hair sofa; and the good lady, with a measuring tape in one hand and a pair of scissors in the other, was walking around Ronald, who stood on the hearthrug in a very manly attitude. She regarded me over her gold-rimmed spectacles, and, shifting the scissors into her left hand, held out her right.

" H'm," said she; " I give ye good morning, Mosha. And what might you be wanting of us this time? "

" Madam," I answered, " that, I hope, is fairly evident."

Ronald came forward. " I congratulate you, Saint-Ives, with all my heart. And you may congratulate me: I have my commission."

" Nay, then," said I, " let me rather congratulate France that the war is over. Seriously, my dear fellow, I wish you joy. What's the regiment? "

" The 4–th."

" Chevenix's! "

" Chevenix is a decent fellow. He has behaved very well, indeed he has."

I Go to Claim Flora

" Very well indeed," said Flora, nodding her head.

" He has the knack. But if you expect me to like him any the better for it——"

" Major Chevenix," put in Miss Gilchrist in her most Rhadamanthine voice, " always sets me in mind of a pair of scissors." She opened and shut the pair in her hand, and I had to confess that the stiff and sawing action was admirably illustrative. " But I wish to heaven, madame," thought I, " you could have chosen another simile!"

In the evening of that beatific day I walked back to Edinburgh by some aerial and rose-clouded path not indicated on the maps. It led somehow to my lodgings, and my feet touched earth when the door was opened to me by Bethiah McRankine.

" But where is Rowley?" I asked a moment later, looking round my sitting room.

Mrs. McRankine smiled sardonically. " Him? He came back rolling his eyes so that I guessed him to be troubled in the wind. And he's in bed this hour past with a spoonful of peppermint in his little wame."

.   .   .   .

And here I may ring down the curtain upon the adventures of Anne de Saint-Yves.

Flora and I were married early in June, and had been settled for little over six months, amid the splendours of Amersham Place, when news came of the Emperor's escape from Elba. Throughout the consequent alarums and excursions of the Hundred Days (as M. de Chambord named them for us) I have to confess that the Vicomte Anne sat still and warmed his hands at the domestic hearth. To be sure, Napoleon had been my master, and I had no love for the *cocarde blanche*. But here was I, an Englishman, already, in legal but inaccurate phrase, a " naturalised " one, having, as Mr. Romaine put it, a stake in the country, not to speak of a nascent interest in its game-laws and the local administration of justice. In short, here was a situation to tickle a casuist. It did not, I may say, tickle me in the least, but played the mischief with my peace. If you, my friends, having weighed the *pro* and *contra*, would have counselled inaction, possibly, allowing for the *hébétude de foyer* and the fact that Flora was soon to become a mother, you might have predicted it. At any rate I sat still and read the newspapers: and on the top of them came a letter from Ronald, announcing that the 4–th had their marching, or rather their sailing, orders, and that within a week his boat would rock by the pier of Leith to convey him and his comrades to join the Duke of Wellington's forces in the Low Countries. Forthwith nothing would suit my dear girl but we must post to Edinburgh to bid him fare-well—in a chariot, this time, with a box seat for her maid and Mr. Rowley. We reached Swanston in time for Ronald to spend the eve of his departure with us at the Cottage, and very gallant the boy looked in his scarlet uniform, which he wore for the ladies' benefit, and which (God forgive us men!) they properly bedewed with their tears.

Early next morning we drove over to the city and drew up in the thick of the crowd gathered at the foot of the Castle Hill to see the 4-th march out. We had waited half-an-hour, perhaps, when we heard two thumps of a drum and the first notes of the regimental quick-step sounded within the walls; the sentry at the outer gate stepped back and presented arms, and the ponderous archway grew bright with the red coats and brazen instruments of the band. The farewells on their side had been said; and the inexorable *tramp—tramp* upon the drawbridge was the burthen of their answer to the waving handkerchiefs, the huzzas of the citizens, the cries of the women. On they came, and in the first rank, behind the band, rose Major Chevenix. He saw us, flushed a little and gravely saluted. I never liked the man; but will admit he made a fine figure there. And I pitied him a little; for while his eyes rested on Flora, hers wandered to the rear of the third company, where Ensign Ronald Gilchrist marched beside the tattered colours with chin held up and a high colour on his young cheeks and a lip that quivered as he passed us.

" God bless you, Ronald! "

" Left wheel! " The band and the Major riding behind it swung round the corner into North Bridge Street; the rear-rank and the adjutant behind it passed up the Lawnmarket. Our driver was touching up his horses to follow, when Flora's hand stole into mine. And I turned from my own conflicting thoughts to comfort her.

MIDLOTHIAN
COUNTY LIBRARY